Sholem Aleichem

The Letters of Menakhem-Mendl & Sheyne-Sheyndl

and

Motl, the Cantor's Son

Sholem Aleichem

The Letters of Menakhem-Mendl & Sheyne-Sheyndl

and

Motl, the Cantor's Son

Translated
and with an introduction by
Hillel Halkin

The Letters of Menakhem-Mendl and Sheyne-Sheyndl and *Motl, the Cantor's Son*
By Sholem Aleichem
Translated by Hillel Halkin

White Goat Press, the Yiddish Book Center's imprint
Yiddish Book Center
Amherst, MA 01002
whitegoatpress.org

Printed in the United States of America at The Studley Press, Dalton, MA
10 9 8 7 6 5 4 3 2 1

Paperback ISBN 979-8-9987798-8-6
Library of Congress Control Number: 2026940922

Cover design by Kandy Littrell

Stack of envelopes on front cover from Adobe Stock
Image of young boy on front cover: Jewish children, Sixth and Lyndale, Minneapolis, 1908. Photo credit: Minnesota Historical Society / Getty Images

Previously published in 2002 by Yale University Press / New Yiddish Library

This book has been made possible with the generous support of an anonymous donor in memory of their Yiddish-speaking Zadie and Bubbie.

While you tried your best, we weren't able to learn the language well enough to read in the original, but with the publication of this translation which we dedicate to you, we can now read Sholem Aleichem.

♦♦♦ Contents

Introduction by Hillel Halkin, vii

The Letters of Menakhem-Mendl and Sheyne-Sheyndl

Londons: The Odessa Exchange, 3

Stocks & Bonds: The Yehupetz Exchange, 19

Millions: Traders, Agents, and Speculators, 38

An Honorable Profession: Menakhem-Mendl Becomes a Writer, 72

It's No Go: Menakhem-Mendl the Matchmaker, 83

Always a Loser: Menakhem-Mendl the Insurance Agent, 96

Motl, the Cantor's Son

Part One, 105

Part Two, 237

Notes, 319

◆◆◆ Introduction

Taken together, Sholem Aleichem's three great semicomic works, *Tevye the Dairyman, The Letters of Menakhem-Mendl and Sheyne-Sheyndl,* and *Motl, the Cantor's Son,* might be said to compose a right triangle. The sides of the right angle are formed by *Tevye* and *Menakhem-Mendl,* which meet each other squarely. *Motl* joins the two obliquely. The trio bounds Sholem Aleichem's fictional world.

Each moves along a geographical line. Tevye shuttles back and forth from his native village of "Boiberik" to the nearby Ukrainian capital of Kiev, called "Yehupetz" by Sholem Aleichem. Boiberik is even closer to "Kasrilevke," the town in which Motl grows up and the wife and children of Menakhem-Mendl live. We encounter Menakhem-Mendl, however, mainly in Yehupetz before he heads for America, which is also the destination of Motl and his family. And it is in Yehupetz that Tevye and Menakhem-Mendl—quite literally in a chapter of *Tevye the Dairyman* —run into each other, while it is from Boiberik-Kasrilevke that Tevye and Motl set out and in New York City that Motl and Menakhem-Mendl (although only in one version of his story) end up. These three points are the physical coordinates of Sholem Aleichem's fiction, and nearly everything he wrote takes place in them or the intermediate space between.

Thematically, too, these three works, all of which share an episodic structure resulting from their irregular serialization in the Yiddish press, enclose a common world. In it we find the typical components of a Sholem Aleichem family: the roaming, harried, mentally curious husband; the conservative, querulous, stay-at-home wife; the strained but loyal relations between them; the independent child that goes its own way. We find the economic fight for survival, a preoccupation in most of Sholem Aleichem's writing as it was of the Russian Jewry he wrote about. We find the disintegration of traditional eastern European Jewish life beneath the hammer blows of modernization, emigration, and assimilation. And we find the recurrent sequence of dream, disappointment, and new dream, that repetitive pattern of nadir, rise, fall, and recovery that is the psychological matrix of Sholem Aleichem's most memorable characters and has been compared by the critic Dan Miron to the great life-death-resurrection cycles of religious myth.[1]

A cursory look at Sholem Aleichem's biography reveals this to have been the pattern of his own life. Born Sholem Rabinovich in 1859 in the Ukrainian town of Pereyaslav, he passed a happy childhood in the rural community of Voronko, where his father, Nachum, was a well-to-do and respected figure, a master of many trades who, as Sholem Aleichem's daughter Marie Waife-Goldberg wrote years later, "acted as agent for land-lease properties, supplied sugar mills with beets, ran the rural post office, traded in wheat, handled freight on barges on the Dnieper River, cut lumber, fattened oxen for the market," and managed at the same time to run a dry-goods store that also sold groceries, hay, oats, home remedies, and hardware.[2]

These years ended suddenly for Sholem, who was twelve, when his father was swindled and ruined by a business partner. The family moved back to Pereyaslav, where Nachum opened an inn in the hope of reestablishing himself. The venture failed, Nachum's wife died of cholera, and the new wife he took had all the attributes of the wicked stepmother of a fairy tale. One of the most vivid memories described in Sholem Aleichem's autobiography *From the Fair* is of being stationed in front of the inn to attract customers, daydreaming of the riches that would come his way if he succeeded, only to suffer his stepmother's curses when night fell on its empty rooms.[3]

Just as suddenly, however, this emotionally depressing adolescence underwent a miraculous reversal. Sent into the world by his father to seek work as a Hebrew tutor, the eighteen-year-old Sholem landed, by sheer luck, the ideal job: a position with a wealthy landowner named Elimelech Loyeff, one of the few Jews of the times to possess a country estate in the manner of a Russian aristocrat. Not only that, the child Loyeff sought a tutor for was his charming teenage daughter Olga. Tutor and pupil fell in love, and Sholem spent the next three years in a pastoral idyll as an honored member of the household.

Then disaster struck. The young couple made the mistake of showing their affections too openly, and Olga's father banished the tutor from his paradise. For the next four years the lovelorn Sholem drudged away as a small-town "certified rabbi"—little more than a government registry clerk for Jewish births, deaths, marriages, and divorces—until his luck changed again. Having stayed secretly in touch all along, he and Olga eloped, and Elimelech Loyeff unexpectedly made his peace with the match. Supported by his new father-in-law, Sholem now began to devote himself full time to his writing, using the pen name of Sholem Aleichem for the first time. When Loyeff died of a heart attack in 1884 the Rabinoviches inherited most of his property, which they sold for enough money to live comfortably for the rest of their lives.

The poor son of the wicked stepmother was now an independent author-prince. Between 1887 and 1890 he wrote his first three mature novels, *Sender Blank, Stempenyu,* and *Yosele Solovey,* and founded the Yiddishe Folks Bibliotek, or Jewish Folk Library, an ambitious project that made him Yiddish literature's foremost publisher. But the wheel of fortune was still spinning. In 1888 Sholem Aleichem moved with Olga to Kiev, where he took to speculating on the stock exchange. For a while he did well. Then, in 1890, the market crashed and he lost everything.

Elimelech Loyeff's inheritance had gone up in smoke, and the Rabinoviches were left bankrupt with four small children. (Two more were still to come.) They fled Kiev to escape their creditors, traveled homelessly for a while, and finally settled in Odessa, where Sholem Aleichem borrowed money from Olga's family and reinvested in the market, determined to recoup his losses. Once again he succeeded initially; once again his shares ultimately plunged, wiping him out. Forced to start over from scratch, the family returned to Kiev, where Olga studied dentistry and opened a practice while her husband found work as a broker and continued to write.

They remained in Kiev until 1905. This was the longest period of economic security that Sholem Aleichem was to know, and in it he wrote the serialized chapters of *Tevye the Dairyman,* his novel *The Bloody Hoax,* several volumes' worth of subsequently collected short stories, and a number of plays for the Yiddish stage. Life, so it seemed, had settled down at last—until, following the abortive 1905 revolution, a wave of pogroms swept over Russia and through Kiev, killing hundreds of Jews and coming dangerously close to the hotel in which the Rabinoviches were hiding. Badly shaken, they decided to leave Russia and join the mass westward flight of its Jews.

Sholem Aleichem's last years were marked by wandering (mostly in Switzerland, Germany, and Italy), illness, and financial worry. Although he was the world's most famous Jewish writer, read by a vast audience in the numerous Yiddish newspapers and periodicals in which he appeared, this rarely translated into economic success. Time and again he pinned his hopes on some new literary venture; time and again he fell victim to unscrupulous publishers, badly drawn contracts, feuding editors, papers forced to cut their budgets; time and again he had to resort to exhausting reading tours or hurried writing that did not reflect his full talents. In 1906 he traveled by himself to New York, hoping to capitalize on the vigorous cultural life of the Jewish immigrant community there. At first he was exhilarated by his reception, which included an annual five-thousand-dollar contract—an unprecedented sum in those days—with the new Hearst-published *Jewish American* and the commissioning of two plays for the Second Avenue Yiddish theater. But the *Jewish American* soon folded, the plays were box-office failures, and he returned to Europe with his hopes dashed.

In late 1914, more as a refugee from the world war that had broken out than as an immigrant counting on a better future, he sailed for New York again, this time with his family. He died there in May 1916, still struggling to make ends meet and writing practically to his last day. Despite failing health, he published in these months a large part of *From the Fair* and the unfinished American half of *Motl.* His funeral procession, said to have been the largest in New York City's history, included more than one hundred thousand participants. Most were devoted readers. All over the Jewish world—in Warsaw, in Odessa, in London, in Jerusalem, in Vilna, in Berlin, in Buenos Aires—he was mourned by many times that number.

♦♦♦

Menakhem-Mendl and his wife Sheyne-Sheyndl made their debut in 1892, when "Londons," the first of the six chapters that compose the second, 1910 edition of their letters, from which the present translation is made, was published in a volume of the Jewish Folk Library. Chapter 2, "Stocks & Bonds," appeared in 1896 in the periodical *Der Hoyz-fraynd,* and Chapter 3, "Millions," was serialized in the newspaper *Der Yid* in 1899–1900.

Although based on Sholem Aleichem's experience with the Kiev and Odessa stock markets, these letters are hardly autobiographical. Not only is the scolding Sheyne-Sheyndl purely fictional, Menakhem-Mendl himself is too fatuous a figure to be considered a full-bodied imaginative projection of the author. Sholem Aleichem took apparent pains to emphasize this when he wrote in a preface to the 1910 edition that Menakhem-Mendl was not imaginary but a real person, with whom

> the author is personally and intimately acquainted, having lived through a great deal with him for nearly twenty years. Since our first meeting in 1892 on the "Little Exchange" of Odessa, we have gone through all the circles of hell together. I was with him in the market in Kiev, all the way to St. Petersburg and Warsaw; went through crisis after crisis with him; threw myself with him into one livelihood after another; and—alas!—having had no luck, was forced to do what all Jews do and emigrate to America.[4]

And yet quite apart from the fact that Sholem Aleichem had not emigrated to America at this point and was reversing the order of the Kiev and Odessa crashes, this entire claim was fictional, since unlike Tevye, who was modeled on a real-life individual, no single prototype for Menakhem-Mendl existed. Or rather, the only such prototype with whom Sholem Aleichem went through "all the circles of hell" for "twenty years" was Sholem Aleichem himself, who, in inventing Menakhem-Mendl, isolated an element of his own character and exaggerated it wildly for comic purposes. Omitted in this translation, the 1910 preface is an ironically tongue-in-cheek document, designed to point the finger away from and toward the author at one and the same time.

Of course, the character of Menakhem-Mendl was also based on many of the small-time Jewish speculators and traders the author encountered in his years on and around the Exchange. Such types are described at length in the letters to Sheyne-Sheyndl and immediately identified by her, with her instinctive practicality, as *luftmentshn,* or "air people," a Yiddish term denoting those would-be alchemists of profit who seek to make a living out of nothing—an enterprise that, as Sheyne-Sheyndl repeatedly warns, more often turns to nothing even the little that exists. And Menakhem-Mendl is the *luftmentsh* par excellence, so much so that in Yiddish his name has become a synonym for the term. *Azoy a Menakhem-Mendl!*—"What a Menakhem-Mendl!"—is both a way of calling someone an inept spinner of financial fantasies and a tribute to Sholem Aleichem's powers of characterization.

But if Menakhem-Mendl is a superbly drawn caricature, he is one not only of the deluded believer in his own luck who compulsively gambles and loses each time, but also of a harsh economic reality in which the Jews of his time were trapped. Confined by tsarist regulations to the Pale of Settlement, the area of western and southwestern Russia whose largest metropolis, Kiev, was declared out of bounds to them (hence Menakhem-Mendl's worries about being there); increasingly squeezed from their traditional occupations as small tradesmen and petty merchants by heightened competition and the growing availability of industrialized goods and services; and lacking access to entrepreneurial capital, Russia's largely rural Jews were progressively reduced to marginal pursuits. One result was emigration. Another was proletarianization. Another was Menakhem-Mendelization—the creation of a newly urbanized class of Jewish fixers, jobbers, riggers, go-betweens, hangers-on, operators, and carpetbaggers frantically looking for the temporary niches and opportunities that could be manipulated for a quick gain. Menakhem-Mendl's letters to Sheyne-Sheyndl are the classic portrait of this class.

It is the class aspect of Menakhem-Mendl that has particularly endeared his letters to Marxist literary critics, who have tended to consider them the high point of Sholem Aleichem's career. Whereas, wrote the noted Soviet critic Max Erik, in *Tevye* "Sholem Aleichem glorified the petty bourgeois[ie] and portrayed it as an ideal . . . [in] Menakhem-Mendl, Sholem Aleichem *unmasked* the petty bourgeoisie." Menakhem-Mendl "embodies the stubborn efforts of the lower middle class to make it into the bourgeoisie, to achieve the latter's unfulfilled capitalist dreams"; he is "a compressed, highly trenchant expression of the *illusoriness* of the petty bourgeois existence under capitalism; a terribly bitter and decisive exposé of his ostensible independence and self-determination."[5] Precisely because, in other words, he is naively apolitical and makes no connection between politics and economics, or indeed, between the world of economic success he yearns to belong to and the system that controls this world for its own benefit, Menakhem-Mendl's letters are revolutionary in their implications; for they tell us that nothing short of an upheaval in both his consciousness and society at large can emancipate him from the treadmill on which he must otherwise run until he drops.

Even leaving aside Sholem Aleichem's own political views, however, which were conventionally middle class, critics like Erik exaggerate *Menakhem-Mendl*'s "bitterness" and overlook how its hero, for all his pathetic denial of reality, is affectionately individuated in a way that is fatally flattened by reduction to a mere economic symbol. He has a zest for experience that, while it rarely understands what it is looking at, makes Kasrilevke several sizes too small for him; a refusal to stay down that causes us to laugh at him but never to pity him; and feelings, however primitive, for his wife and children, revealed when we hear his voice crack or change at key moments, that periodically break the spell of his self-absorption. Even his abandonment of his family to pursue his pipe dreams is an attempt to become the admired husband and father that, henpecked by a domineering wife, he cannot be at home, where his only future is to become either the storekeeper Sheyne-Sheyndl would like him to be or the teacher of children for which his unfinished studies qualify him. The never-explained dowry money that he absconds with in his first letter, and that is Sholem Aleichem's device for setting the story in motion, is, we come to realize, the chance of a lifetime that Menakhem-Mendl can hardly be blamed—that he must even be credited with courage—for seizing.

Sheyne-Sheyndl, too, her narrow provincialism notwithstanding, is a sympathetically drawn figure. (This is especially true in the 1910 edition, in which Sholem Aleichem tempered her shrewishness.) Laughably ignorant and no more aware of her inner motives than Menakhem-Mendl is of his, she is nevertheless the more discerning of the two, and her love for her husband, or, more accurately, her pride in his education and ingrained sense of wifely duty that serve her as substitutes for love, survive—at least for as long as she keeps writing him—her growing exasperation at his folly. Nor, despite her complaints about his absence, is it clear how much she wants him back; rather, the more the two of them protest their mutual longing, the more we suspect that their separation suits them both. As unchallenged queen of her domestic realm, Sheyne-Sheyndl, sufficiently aided by her parents to manage financially, hardly needs a bumbling consort to get in her way, and considering that Yehupetz is a short journey from Kasrilevke, it is remarkable that she never carries out her threat of going there. Although her gossipy news items from Kasrilevke, which start in Chapter 2, may appear calculated at first glance to entice her husband back, a considered reading of them suggests that they represent more her acceptance of his permanent absence and the consequent need to keep him informed.

Indeed this is more than just a suspicion. In a letter written by Menakhem-Mendl not to Sheyne-Sheyndl but to (in the guise of an acquaintance) Sholem Aleichem and published in *Der Yid* in April 1900, two months after the last exchange in "Millions," Menakhem-Mendl actually returns for a Passover seder to Kasrilevke—and to a wife less than overjoyed to see him. Arriving the day before the holiday when Sheyne-Sheyndl and her compulsively proverb-quoting mother are at the height of their preparations, he is greeted in the language of her epistolary tirades:

"Why, damn your eyes!" she said to me. "A fine time you've found to come home! For years you rot in that sickbed, you live in every hole there is, there's no revolting thing you don't do, and of all the times to come creeping home you choose the day before Passover, when we're busy with the cleaning and there's not a moment to talk."[6]

Menakhem-Mendl dashes off this letter to Sholem Aleichem the same day, so that there is no knowing how long he stays in Kasrilevke, but when next heard from in August 1900 he is in Yehupetz again, writing Sheyne-Sheyndl about his new life as a writer. Sholem Aleichem never returned him to Kasrilevke and left the Passover visit out of the 1910 edition.

It should be apparent by now that the textual history of *Menakhem-Mendl* is complex. As was the case with Tevye, Sholem Aleichem did not at first create Menakhem-Mendl and Sheyne-Sheyndl with the idea of a book in mind. "Londons," the first round of their correspondence, was originally conceived as a finished product in itself, an epistolary short story to which no sequel was planned. As was also the case with Tevye, however, husband and wife took on a life of their own. They were liked by their audience; and Sholem Aleichem, who was in the habit of keeping successful characters in the wings for further use, brought them back for repeat performances in "Stocks & Bonds" and "Millions." Meanwhile, he introduced Menakhem-Mendl into other situations as well, making him a character in two plays and in the second chapter of *Tevye the Dairyman,* where he talks Tevye into lending him money for a joint investment that goes down the drain. In addition, Sholem Aleichem began a new series of letters between Menakhem-Mendl and himself, of which that describing the Passover visit to Kasrilevke was the second. Among the last of these were three letters from America, written in 1903–1904.[7]

Menakhem-Mendl's American letters were a follow-up to "Always a Loser," the sixth and last chapter of the 1910 edition, at the end of which Menakhem-Mendl informs Sheyne-Sheyndl that he is setting out for the port of Hamburg and the New World. When it originally appeared in 1901, however, "Always a Loser" was written to Sholem Aleichem, as also were Chapters 4 and 5 of the 1910 edition, "A Respectable Profession" and "It's No Go," both published in 1900.[8] This was the reason that in 1903, when Sholem Aleichem issued his first edition of Menakhem-Mendl and Sheyne-Sheyndl's collected letters, Chapters 4–6 were not in it. They were added to the 1910 edition after being rewritten and readdressed to Sheyne-Sheyndl, for whom the author composed replies for Chapter 4 alone.

Finally, Menakhem-Mendl was given one more lease on life in 1913, when Sholem Aleichem started a new series for the Warsaw newspaper *Haynt* in which Sheyne-Sheyndl is written regularly by her husband, now working for a Warsaw paper himself, on the subject of Jewish, Russian, and international politics. These letters (which conclude with several from Vienna, to which Menakhem-Mendl goes to cover a Zionist congress) fill a book twice the size of the 1910 edition. Yet not only do they lack the latter's madcap verve and verbal sparkle, they are a contradiction in terms, since a Menakhem-Mendl who holds a paying job as a journalist is by definition no longer a Menakhem-Mendl. Neither *Haynt* not Sholem Aleichem were particularly happy with the series, and it was discontinued before the year was out and omitted by the author from all editions of his collected work.[9]

Against such a background of improvisation, revision, addition and deletion of material, and multiple versions of the same texts and characters, it can be asked who the real Menakhem-Mendl is. Is he the man who reaches New York and returns from there to Warsaw, or the one last heard from heading for Hamburg? Has he or has he not been back to Kasrilevke? Has he blown Tevye's money or is there no evidence that the two men even know each other?

Of course such questions, like all that confuse fiction with reality, have no answer. They would never arise had the episodes left out of the 1910 edition been mere manuscript drafts that Sholem Aleichem discarded, it being their previous publication that makes one feel that they have "really happened." And yet this does not make it any less meaningful to ask whether the 1910 edition reflects sound literary judgment. Numerous Yiddish critics have felt it does not. Some, like Y. Y. Trunk, have claimed that the 1903 edition is superior, since the three chapters added in 1910 are of a farcical quality that fails to sustain, as Trunk put it, "the tragic rhythm" of the earlier letters. Others, like Moyshe Mezhritsky, have gone further by contending that even the 1903 edition mistakenly sought to create a book out of independent parts that do not add up to a greater whole. "The chapters [of *Menakhem-Mendl*]," wrote Mezhritsky, "are not organically bound to one another. . . . You can change the order of *Menakhem-Mendl,* putting the last chapter first, without it being any the worse off, because at the end of it the characters are no different from what they were at the beginning."[10]

The same accusation of being narratively static has also been leveled against *Tevye* and *Motl,* the forward movement of which, too, seems at times to be obstructed by repetitive patterns of plot, language, and behavior. Nor, inasmuch as Sholem Aleichem could not have written as voluminously as he did without occasionally resorting to such stratagems, is the charge wholly without merit. Ultimately, though, it is unjustified. Menakhem-Mendl, certainly, does change in the course of his letters, which span several years. (We can gauge the passing of time in them by the age of his son Moyshe-Hirshele, who is barely speaking in Chapter 2 and already learning to read in Chapter 4.) Although he may struggle to sound as jaunty in the last paragraph of his last letter as he does in the first paragraph of his first, his desperation grows perceptibly greater all the time. The man who writes to his wife in Chapter 6, after being bamboozled by a transparent insurance scam, "But it's as your mother says: once a loser, always a loser," is not the same man who wrote in Chapter 2, following the dive taken by his stocks, "When all is said and done, you see, I know the market inside and out. . . . Brains, praise God, I have as much of as any investor." His self-confidence and self-respect (more precisely, the facade of them, since at bottom he has none to begin with) have been badly eroded.

As for Sheyne-Sheyndl, even if we do not interpret her silence in Chapters 5 and 6 as a decision to stop writing her husband (there is after all a more practical explanation: he is on the road and she has no address for him), we see her attitude toward him shift from semi-credulous hope to furious impatience and thence to open contempt. Like him, she still begins and ends her letters with the same rote formulas (real features of traditional Yiddish epistolary style that are comically contrasted by Sholem Aleichem with the actual content that they frame), but her belief in him, and in the prospect of his ever supporting their family, steadily shrinks.

The Israeli scholar Abraham Novershtern has written an essay pointing out, not only how rigorously Sholem Aleichem weighed the contents of the 1910 edition from a literary point of view, but how, in editing and arranging them, he gave them a dramatic structure that might be described (the image is mine) as funnel-shaped, since the more Menakhem-Mendl slides downward, the more his horizons close in on him.[11] Starting out in the cosmopolitan port city of Odessa, where he dreams of making millions in the futures market, he next unsuccessfully buys and sells shares in more provincial Kiev; then flops as a middleman working on commission; then fails as a writer, a "respectable profession," as he puts it, but one that pays paltry sums; then, returning to small-town Ukraine, is made a fool of in the once but no longer reputable occupation of matchmaker; and finally is hoodwinked while peddling insurance in Bessarabia, a rural boondocks near the Rumanian border that makes Kasrilevke seem the center of the world. He has ended up considerably behind his starting point, and the lower the bar is set each time, the more crushing is his failure to clear it. What is left to try but America?

Although it would have been possible for Sholem Aleichem to readress Menakhem-Mendl's 1903–1904 letters from New York to Sheyne-Sheyndl also, thus adding a seventh, American chapter to the 1910 edition, he had good reasons for not doing so. Between 1904 and 1910 he had been in America himself, and despite his personal disappointments there, he had seen what a land of opportunity for its Jewish immigrants it was. Even in 1903, he had had Menakhem-Mendl comment on the fundamental economic difference between the United States and Russia. On the one hand, writes Menakhem-Mendl, the immigrant to America takes any work, does things no one would dream of doing back home; why, he relates, he has just met a man, a respected Jew in the Old Country, who is proud to have found a job sorting dirty underwear in a laundry! Yet on the other hand, in America even a menial job like this pays well enough for a man to save—Menakhem-Mendl uses the Yiddishized English word *onseyvn*—and get ahead. *Ot vos heyst a gebentsht land,* "Now that's what I call a blessed land," he concludes in a tone midway between irony and amazement.[12]

Of course, one can be a Menakhem-Mendl in America, too, but with a difference, for here one's failures are purely personal and in no way reflect the general condition. Even were he less of a shlemiel, Menakhem-Mendl could get nowhere in Russia, because there is no such thing there as upward mobility; he is indeed the stymied symbol of his class that the Marxist critics make him out to be, and his fantasies are his only alternative to accepting this. But who is to say what is fantasy in America? Ordinary people *do* make money there on the stock market, since it is not just a game for suckers, and Menakhem-Mendl's harebrained scheme of a super-efficient chain of matchmaking bureaus with a centralized list of customers is harebrained only in Yehupetz. In America, with the help of an affordable bank loan, it just might work.

Menakhem-Mendl must therefore never make it to America, for whether he fails or succeeds there (and in his letters from New York he does succeed, launching the journalist's career that eluded him in Yehupetz and that he is later to pursue in Warsaw), he either goes on being himself and ceases to be an archetype or becomes a new archetype and ceases to be himself. To be both the archetypal Jewish immigrant to America *and* himself, Sholem Aleichem had to invent someone else: Motl, Peysi the cantor's son.

♦♦♦

The "sunniest" of Sholem Aleichem's major works, as it has been called, one in which the characteristically rambling, anxious voice of his protagonists yields to the direct speech of a high-spirited child, *Motl, the Cantor's Son* has a simpler publishing history than *Menakhem-Mendl;* it too, however, bears the author's typical stamp of multiple versions and interrupted composition. Part I, written under the influence of Sholem Aleichem's 1906 visit to America, was serialized in 1907–1908 in the New York Yiddish paper *Der Amerikaner.* Twenty of its chapters were reprinted in book form in 1911; two others, "I Land a Swell Job" and "With the Emigrants," omitted from the 1911 edition, have been restored in the present translation.[13] Part II, serialized in

1916 in the New York Yiddish paper *Di Varhayt* and in English translation in the *New York World,* was never finished. Sholem Aleichem was still writing it at the time of his death, and one can feel his health flagging as he wrote, the weekly installments growing shorter and more fragmentary, as if gasping for breath like Motl's dying father in the book's opening pages. Besides its seventeen completed chapters, several paragraphs were written of an eighteenth, tentatively titled *Mir moofn,* "We Moof [to a new apartment]."[14]

It is his father's death in Kasrilevke, ironically, that makes Motl the most carefree boy in Jewish literature, for with it he has inherited the best of both worlds: a mother and an elder brother who still provide him with love and security, and a life unburdened by a patriarchal religion and its demands of strict decorum, long hours of study, and scrupulous attention to ritual observance. From the little we know about Peysi, Motl's father, he would have enforced these demands rigorously, since as a synagogue cantor (and one, it would seem, of stern temperament) he is a foremost member of the religious establishment of the shtetl. Motl's comic refrain of "Lucky me, I'm an orphan" is thus truer than a boy his age can comprehend. Emancipated from a tradition he is not weighed down by like his brother Elye, he is ready for the freedom of America before he even knows what or where it is.

Just how old Motl is when his father dies is, like the wanderings of Menakhem-Mendl or the number of Tevye's daughters, a question of variant texts. In the present translation his age is mentioned in Chapter 1, where his brother calls him "almost nine," in Chapter 4, and in Chapter 19, in which he tells us he is the same age as his friend Bumpy, who is "nine going on ten." But although this is the wording of the posthumous 1920 edition of *Motl* edited by Sholem Aleichem's son-in-law Y. D. Berkovits, his Hebrew translator and a Hebrew author in his own right, it is not that of the 1911 edition edited by the author himself. There, Elye calls Motl a "five-year-old" and Bumpy is described as "seven going on eight." "Nine" was Berkovits' emendation, based on his, and possibly Sholem Aleichem's reconsidered, judgment that Motl, as revealed to us by his language and perceptions, is too mature to be only five or even seven. Sholem Aleichem himself was clearly aware of this problem, because elsewhere he wavered over Motl's age, making him six and eight in other passages in the serialized version of Part I that were deleted from the 1911 edition, and casting him as a boy of twelve or thirteen in a 1915 outline for a film script.[15]

It has been argued that these differences were deliberate and reflect the passage of time in the story, which some critics have viewed as either indeterminate or spanning a very long period.[16] A careful reading of the text, however, shows that it is neither and that approximately two and a half years elapse from beginning to end: some six months from the death of Motl's father on the holiday of Shavuos in late spring to his family's departure from Kasrilevke in autumn, soon after the High Holy Days; a year of traveling to New York, which is reached several days after Yom Kippur; and another year in New York, where summer has ended as the story breaks off. Moreover, even if we allow for Motl's growing older—a boy of five-plus in Chapter 1 could indeed have turned seven by Chapter 19—the fact remains that it is in the book's opening paragraphs, when Motl is youngest, that his language is most unlike a child's. Conceivably, this could be explained by reading his narrative, or parts of it, as an adult recollection of childhood—a construction that, while it does not harmonize well with most of the text, is supported by a number of passages. (Most notably the lines in the chapter "On Solid Ground" in which Motl speaks of his friend Mendl from the vantage point of many years later.) Alternately, Khone Shmeruk has proposed that Sholem Aleichem might have begun the first chapter of *Motl* as a third- rather than first-person narrative and neglected to simplify its language when he made the switch.[17] One way or another, too much should not be made of such inconsistencies. Under the pressure of newspaper deadlines and bills to be paid Sholem Aleichem often wrote hurriedly, and the internal discrepancies resulting from this were not always eliminated in subsequent revisions.

Nor is the question of Motl's age that crucial, because in the final analysis, it is not what he understands but what he sees and hears, often without understanding, that makes him our window on events. Although he is too young and buoyant to be worried about the things that trouble the adult world around him, he is also keenly curious, and our knowledge of this world and its complexities is the product of a partnership in which he observes and we interpret. It is only, for example, because Motl itches to "find out every secret in the world" that we overhear Pinye and Elye's conversation in Kasrilevke about emigrating to America; but it is left to us to formulate what lies at the heart of the two men's competitive relationship—namely, that while Elye prides himself on his enterprise and practicality, it is the absentminded Pinye who is the real innovator and initiator and Elye who gets dragged along behind him.

Motl and Pinye are natural allies. It is they, Motl tells us, who feel "made for America" and are sure they'll "make it to the top there," for they alone are sufficiently open to new experience to embrace it with both arms. Even before New York is reached, we know who in our party of travelers will Americanize the quickest, with the list headed by Motl, followed by Pinye, Elye, Brokheh, Taybl, and (although she will prove to have a resourcefulness of her own) Motl's mother. Sholem Aleichem, a writer adept at making his main characters both believable individuals and representative types, was well aware that this reflected general categories. Young Jewish males, sociologically, were more eager to emigrate from eastern Europe than females, and less tradition-minded males like Pinye were the most so; upon arrival in the United States, acculturation proceeded in the same order. Unlike Elye, who continues to think in Old World terms, Pinye has cast these aside even before reaching "Ella's Island." It is he who supports going to work in a sweatshop as a first step up the economic ladder when Elye feels this is beneath his dignity; who throws himself into the garment workers' strike that Elye holds back from; who first shaves off the beard that is a symbol of religious orthodoxy; who presses for going into business; who realizes that a corner stand is too small an operation; who grasps that aggressive advertising is the key to economic success in America. There may be something in him of Menakhem-Mendl, whose faith in the capitalist dream he shares, but Pinye understands the workings of capitalism as Menakhem-Mendl does not, and in him we see—although only in its earliest stages, since *Motl, the Cantor's Son* breaks off before he can rise very far—the dream coming true.

Beginning with the writing of its first chapters, Sholem Aleichem intended *Motl, the Cantor's Son* to be a saga of Russian-Jewish emigration to America in which Motl's story would be continued through adolescence and into adulthood. His initial plan was for his hero to be a successful musician taking after his father, and the opening of Part I abounds in references to Motl's musical talents. On his return trip from New York to Europe in 1907, however, Sholem Aleichem met aboard ship a young man, the son of Jewish immigrants to America, who was traveling to Europe to study art, and, much taken by him, converted Motl into a budding artist—a motif introduced for the first time in Chapter 17 of Part I, in which Motl tells us, "I've liked to draw since I was little." As Dan Miron perceptively points out, the reason for this change was probably the author's realization that, on a symbolic level, the character of Motl worked better if he did not follow in his father's footsteps but rather struck out on his own in a creative field that, unlike music, was not traditionally Jewish.[18]

It is entertaining to speculate what would have become of Motl had his creator lived to keep writing about him. A well-known painter? A syndicated cartoonist? Perhaps even an animated filmmaker in Hollywood? Any of these would have been in keeping with Sholem Aleichem's expansive sense of the prospects America held for its Jews, the historical acumen of which seems even greater in light of his own failure to do well there. (*Motl* itself was discontinued in 1908 because the editor of *Der Amerikaner* thought it boring!)

As for Pinye, who knows? "Prehzident," which in his ignorance of constitutional law he believes himself eligible for, he will never be, nor as rich as his triumvirate of heroes, "Kahnegi," "Rahknfelleh," and "Vendehbilt." But why not (if not a writer of lyrics for songs and Broadway musicals) president of his own large ad agency? He is still young, in his late teens or early twenties (Kasrilevke marriages take place at an early age—Elye's when he has barely begun to grow a beard), and with his drive and a few years of night school, there is no reason why Pinye cannot go far.

Elye should do well as a small-time businessman. Despite his comic entrepreneurial adventures in Kasrilevke, he is too hesitant and brooding to take larger risks and has Brokheh at his side to see that he doesn't. A nice "foinitsheh" store—after all, he already knows the business—seems a good bet, unless he ends up going into his father-in-law's knish business.

Elye and even Pinye will always remain immigrants; they are too old to learn to speak English without an accent and this alone will mark them as first-generation Americans. Not Motl, however, who in a year or two will be indistinguishable from native-born New Yorkers his age. Already he is shooting marbles in the street; before long it will be stickball, handball, and off-the-stoop. He will become a Yankee, Dodger, or Giant fan; will finish P.S. 75 or 147 and go to Seward or Stuyvesant High; will spend long summer days at Coney Island. If he was nine in 1907, he may be sent to fight in World War I. He will be a young man during Prohibition; he will still be young when the Depression comes along. Too old to serve in World War II, he will be in his mid-fifties when he hears his first rock 'n' roll and in his mid-sixties when John F. Kennedy is shot.

It is a bit of a shock to think of him this way. It is a shock to realize that his memories of Kasrilevke will become few and fuzzy; that although he will not forget his Yiddish, he will rarely or never speak it once his mother dies. In fact, had Sholem Aleichem lived to continue Motl's story, he would have been confronted by a dilemma, because Motl will soon stop thinking in Yiddish. Would it have been feasible, from a literary point of view, to have him continue narrating in it? What psychological sense would this have made?

The rapid encroachment of English on Yiddish is a central theme in Part II of *Motl*. Put to comic effect there, it is nevertheless a reliable gauge of the speed with which Americanization is taking place. By contrast, one of the salient things about the book's second half is how small a role Jewish tradition plays in it. Even in Part I, tradition fades increasingly into the background after Peysi the cantor's death; although Motl grudgingly goes to synagogue to say the mourner's prayer, it is not clear how long he keeps this up, and once the family is on the road, the only religious rituals we hear of are a single accidental prayer quorum in London and the Yom Kippur service aboard the *Prince Albert*. Yet in America there is not even that much. Though Elye, it would seem, still observes the basics of Judaism and says his morning prayers before going to work, only his mother attends synagogue services, and the cuffs Elye gives Motl for smoking on the Sabbath—an act strictly prohibited by Jewish law—are less noteworthy than Motl's reaction to them. "It seems that if Peysi the cantor's son is caught smawkink on the Sabbath, you're allowed to beat him to death," Motl declares, not with defiance or guilt (*that* we last see aboard the *Prince Albert,* when he hopes God doesn't know he is dreaming of food on Yom Kippur), but with the precocious amusement of one who no longer understands how such things could matter to anyone. If Motl—who once told us in Kasrilevke, in one of his few expressions of visceral Jewishness, of his hatred for pigs—has not already eaten his first New York ham sandwich, can we doubt that this is only a matter of time?

Will he one day marry out of his people—something that, to his family and even to himself, is still unimaginable in 1907? Perhaps not, since the years when he is most likely to marry will be ones of low intermarriage rates for American Jews. If he does raise Jewish children, however, this will be strictly sociologically determined. Internally, there is nothing we can detect in him—no inelasticity of self, no allegiance to his father's memory—to keep him within the Jewish fold.

This is why *Motl, the Cantor's Son* is not so cloudlessly sunny a work after all—or rather, why its sunshine is that of the summer that ends three times in the book: with the departure from Kasrilevke, with the embarkation from London, and with the final breaking off of the narrative. Though his two stays in New York barely added up to two years, Sholem Aleichem was quick to intuit the full enormity of the transformation that Jews in America were about to undergo. He was not oblivious to the sweatshops, the tenements, or the eastern European atmosphere of neighborhoods like the Jewish Lower East Side; these things are featured in *Motl,* too. But more than most Jewish writers and intellectuals of his time, with their view of America's immigrant Jewish community as either another chapter in the repetitive cycle of Jewish history or part of a worldwide struggle against an oppressive capitalist order, he understood that America was something radically new: a truly *gebentsht land* for its Jews, who in return for its blessings would gladly relinquish the rich ethnic particularity that all his writing was about.

Motl is the happy ending of the eastern European Jewish tragedy, the rise after which there is no longer any fall. But he is also the end of Sholem Aleichem's world, his face lifted to the kiss that will kill it benignly at the same time that it is being murdered brutally in Europe. Even had Sholem Aleichem kept writing about him, Motl would have outstripped his creator, venturing into realms that Sholem Aleichem did not know and could not have followed him in without holding him back. Sholem Aleichem died before he could lose him, just as Peysi the cantor did.

NOTES

1. See, for instance, Dan Miron, "Bouncing Back: Destruction and Recovery in Sholem-Aleykhem's 'Motl Peyse dem khazns,'" *Yivo Annual of Jewish Social Science* 17 (1978), p. 180.
2. Marie Waife-Goldberg, *My Father, Sholom Aleichem* (London, 1968), p. 31.
3. *From the Fair: The Autobiography of Sholem Aleichem,* translated by Curt Leviant (New York, 1985), chapter 45.
4. *Menakhem-Mendl, "Tsu der tsveyter oyflage,"* volume 10 of the Folksfond Edition (New York, 1917–1925), pp. i–ii.
5. Max Erik, "Menakhem-Mendl: A Marxist Critique," translated by David G. Roskies, *Prooftexts* 6 (1986), pp. 24–25.
6. This story, titled *Bekhipozn* ("In Haste"), was republished in Part I of Sholem Aleichem's collection of short stories *Lekoved yontef,* volume 22 of the Folksfond Edition, pp. 17–31.
7. The plays in which Menakhem-Mendl appears are *Yoknehaz* (1894) and *Agentn* (1905), in *Komedyes,* volume 24 of the Folksfond Edition, pp. 29–133 and 197–218. Chapter 2 of *Tevye* was first published in 1899.

   The first two of the letters from America were published in the August 1903 *Di tsukunft* under the title "Tsvey letste briv fun Menakhem-Mendl" ("Two Recent Letters from Menakhem-Mendl"). The third, cited by me here, appeared in the October 1903 *Der fraynd* as "Adieu: Der letster briv fun Menakhem-Mendl" ("Adieu: The Latest Letter from Menakhem-Mendl").
8. "It's No Go" was first published in *Der Yid* as "Es fidlt nisht: briv fun Menakhem-Mendlen tsu Sholem-Aleikhemen"; "A Respectable Profession" in *Der Yid* as "A bekovedike parnose: briv fun Menakhem-Mendlen

tsu Sholem Aleikhemen"; and "Always a Loser" in *Der Yid* as "Shlim-Shlimazl: briv fun Menakhem-Mendlen tsu Sholem-Aleikhemen."

9. The complete text of these letters can be found in *Menakhem-Mendl (New York–Varshe–Vin–Yehupets)* (Tel Aviv, Bet Shalom Aleikhem–Y. L. Peretz Faerlag, 1976).
10. Y. Y. Trunk, *Tevye un Menakhem-Mendl in yidishn velt-goyrl* (New York, 1944), p. 284. Moyshe Mezhritsky, "Menakhem-Mendl fun Sholem-Aleykhem," *Di royte velt,* May–June 1926, p. 141.
11. Avraham Novershtern, "Menahem-Mendl le-Shalom Aleikhem: beyn toldot ha-tekst le-mivneh ha-yetsirah," *Tarbiz* 54 (1985), pp. 105–146.
12. "Adieu: Der letster briv fun Menakhem-Mendlen," *Menakhem-Mendl (New York–Varshe–Vin–Yehupetz),* pp. 31–32.
13. The reason for the omission of these two chapters in the 1911 edition of *Motl,* issued by the Progres publishing house of Warsaw as the fifth volume of Sholem Aleichem's collected works, was the publisher's wish to promote *Motl* as a children's book, or at least as a book readable by children. Both "I Land a Swell Job," with its old Jew who threatens—comically from an adult's point of view but frighteningly from a child's—to eat Motl alive, and "With the Emigrants," with its brief but disturbing description of a pogrom, were deemed unsuitable for this purpose. In this Progres was following the precedent of Chaim Nachman Bialik and Yehoshua Ravnitzky's 1910 translation of *Motl* into Hebrew, published as part of a children's book series issued by Moriah in Odessa. Although Sholem Aleichem himself did not think of *Motl* as a children's book, he seems to have accepted the commercial logic behind the decision. See the discussions of this in Khone Shmeruk, "Sippurei Motl ben he-hazan le-Shalom Aleikhem: ha-situatsiya ha-epit ve-toldotav shel ha-sefer," *Siman Kri'ah* 12/13 (1981), pp. 310–326, and in Shmeruk's afterword to his variorum edition of *Motl, Peysi dem Khazns* (Jerusalem, 1997), pp. 320–322.

   The Yiddish text on which the present translation is based is that of Shmeruk's 1997 edition. "I Land a Swell Job" and "Emigrants" appear there in an appendix to Part I. In the appendix to Part II there is also a chapter called *Di vasrshtub,* "The House on Water." This chapter appeared in June 1914 in the periodical *Di yidishe velt* and represented Sholem Aleichem's first attempt to resume the adventures of Motl and his family that had been broken off in 1907. It was an isolated effort, however, and when, in 1916, Sholem Aleichem once again took up the task of bringing Motl and his family to America, he recycled most of "The House on Water" in the two chapters "Congratulations! We're in America" and "Crossing the Red Sea."

14. These paragraphs appear in Shmeruk's variorum edition, pp. 299–300, but have been omitted from the present translation. Although it is noteworthy that Sholem Aleichem planned to have Motl's family move to a new apartment, apparently as another indication of its economic progress, only the first two of the extant paragraphs of *Mir moofn* touch on this subject. In the first of these Motl tells us: "The Americans have a custom—they moof. That means you pack and go from one place to another. From one strit to another. From one biznis to another. Everyone has to moof. If you don't want to, someone makes you."

15. See Shmeruk, "Sippurei Motl ben he-hazan le-Shalom Aleikhem," p. 315n.24. Berkovits was extremely close to Sholem Aleichem and consulted him often when translating his work, so that it is quite possible that the subject of Motl's age came up between them. In any case, I have accepted his emendation in my translation. It makes good sense, since a five-year-old Motl is not credible.

    For a brief discussion of how many daughters Tevye has, see the introduction to my translation of *Tevye the Dairyman and The Railroad Stories* (New York, 1987), pp. xviii–xix.

16. Dan Miron, for instance ("Bouncing Back," pp. 130–133), calls the time frame in *Motl* "non-realistic" and "non-linear" and claims the book takes place during an "endless summer." But although Miron is right that the book's chronology is sometimes slapdash (as when, even though it supposedly takes place in 1907–1908, it refers to Woodrow Wilson as America's president), this does not mean that no chronology was intended.

    On the other hand, a critic like Sidra DeKoven Ezrahi (*Booking Passage: Exile and Homecoming in the Modern Jewish Imagination*, University of California Press, 2000, p. 123), does think that the passage of time in *Motl* is calculable—and that it adds up to nine years. How such a figure is arrived at is not clear, but its absurdity is only made possible by the accompanying assumption (one held by a number of *Motl*'s critics) that Motl "doesn't grow" psychologically in the course of the book and has no psychological age at all, so that, if he is five years old when the story begins and fourteen when it ends, this can be accepted as a literary given. But Motl *does* grow, his changing attitude toward religion being only one of several significant examples, and this growth is consistent with a boy who goes from being a little under nine to a little over eleven in the course of the book.

17. Shmeruk, "Sippurei Motl ben he-hazan," p. 324. Shmeruk credits the Yiddish critic M. Viner with being the first to broach this theory.
18. Miron, "Bouncing Back," p. 170.

The Letters of Menakhem-Mendl and Sheyne-Sheyndl

♦♦♦ *Londons: The Odessa Exchange*

FROM MENAKHEM-MENDL IN ODESSA TO HIS WIFE SHEYNE-SHEYNDL IN KASRILEVKE

To my wise, esteemed, & virtuous wife Sheyne-Sheyndl, may you have a long life!

Firstly, rest assured that I am, praise God, in the best of health. God grant that we hear from each other only good and pleasing news, amen!

Secondly, words fail me in describing the grandeur and beauty of the city of Odessa, the fine character of its inhabitants, and the wonderful opportunities that exist here. Just imagine: I take my walking stick and venture out on Greek Street, as the place where Jews do business is called, and there are twenty thousand different things to deal in. If I want wheat, there's wheat. If I feel like wool, there's wool. If I'm in the mood for bran, there's bran. Flour, salt, feathers, raisins, jute, herring —name it and you have it in Odessa. I sounded out several possibilities, none of which were my cup of tea, and shopped along Greek Street until I hit on just the right thing. In a word, I'm dealing in Londons and not doing badly! You can clear 25 or 50 rubles at a go, and sometimes, with a bit of luck, 100. On Londons you can make your fortune in a day. There was a fellow not long ago, a synagogue sexton, mind you, who walked away with 30,000 faster than you can say your bedtime prayers and now he cocks his snoot at the world. I tell you, my dearest, the streets of Odessa are paved with gold! I don't regret for a moment having come here. But what am I doing in Odessa, you ask, when I was on my way to Kishinev? It seems God wanted to deal me in. Listen to what He does for a man.

I arrived at Uncle Menashe's in Kishinev and asked for the dowry money. "How come you need it?" he asks. "I need it," I say, "because I wouldn't be here if I didn't." Well, he says, he can't give me cash but he can give me a letter of credit to Brodsky in Yehupetz. "Let it be Yehupetz," I say. "As long as it's cash." That's just it, he says. He's not sure there is cash in Yehupetz. He can give me a letter of credit to Bachrach in Warsaw. "Warsaw's fine, too," I say. "As long as it's cash." "But why go all the way to Warsaw?" he asks. "Suppose I give you a letter of credit to Barabash in Odessa?" "Make it Odessa," I say. "As long as it's cash." "So how come you need so much cash?" he asks. "If I didn't," I say, "I wouldn't be here."

To make a long story short, he went round and round—it helped like cupping helps a corpse. When I say cash, I mean cash. In the end he gave me two promissory notes for 500 rubles, due in five months, a letter of credit to Barabash for 300, and the rest in banknotes to help cover my expenses.

Because I'm in a hurry, I'll be brief. God willing, I'll write more in my next letter. Be well and give my fond greetings to your parents and the children, each and every one of them.

Your husband,
Menakhem-Mendl.

P.S. When I brought the letter of credit to Barabash, I was told it was nothing of the sort. What was it? A letter to the tooth-fairy! First, I was told, let Uncle Menashe's wagon of wheat arrive in Odessa and find a buyer—then I can see my money. Short, sweet, and to the point! Right away I sent a post card to Kishinev threatening to take action and send a telegram if the wheat wasn't shipped at once. In short, a post card here, a telegram there—I didn't have an easy time of it. But yesterday I received another 100 rubles from Kishinev and a promissory note for 200. Do you understand now why I've been out of touch? I had written off the 300 for lost. It just goes to show that a man should never give up! There's a God in heaven looking after things. I've put all the cash into Londons, a nice batch of them. Sometimes they're up and sometimes they're down, but so far, thank God, I'm ahead.

Yours, etc.

FROM SHEYNE-SHEYNDL IN KASRILEVKE TO HER HUSBAND MENAKHEM-MENDL IN ODESSA

To my dear, learned, & illustrious husband Menakhem-Mendl, may your light shine!

First, we're all well, thank God. I hope to hear no worse from you.

Second, I'm suffering from my old cramps again. I'd like to give them to your Uncle Menashe. You've made short shrift of the eighteen hundred rubles he owed us. Wouldn't that be just our luck! My mother would say you've sent the cat to the dairy with the cream. Why I'd sooner get the pox from Menashe than one of his promise notes! Five months of fever I'd give him! May I be proved a liar but you'll no more see those rubles than you'll see the back of the head your shoulders carried to Odessa. Be thankful my mother knows nothing about it, because she'd tan your hide if she did. And as for what you write, Mendl, about all the money you're making, you can be sure we're pleased. See here, though: the devil take it if the next time you don't write like a human being! Why can't you tell a body in plain words what you're dealing in? Does it sell by the yard or by the pound? For the life of me, I don't know if you eat, wear, or smoke it. And what are these quick profits you talk about? What merchandise shoots up just like that? Even mushrooms, my mother says, need a rain to sprout. But if it's gained so much value, you should sell. You're not hoping to corner the market, are you? And why don't you write where you're staying and eating? A person might think I was a stranger and not your wife of twenty years, some kind of parrymoor, God help us. "When the cow goes to pasture," says my mother, "it forgets to say good-bye." If you'll listen to me, you'll wind up your affairs and come home with a bit of money. You'll find better businesses here than those Lumdums of yours or whatever the deuce they're called. I am, from the bottom of my heart,

Your truly faithful wife,
Sheyne-Sheyndl

FROM MENAKHEM-MENDL IN ODESSA TO HIS WIFE SHEYNE-SHEYNDL IN KASRILEVKE

To my wise, esteemed, & virtuous wife Sheyne-Sheyndl, may you have a long life!

Firstly, rest assured that I am, praise God, in the best of health. God grant that we hear from each other only good and pleasing news, amen.

Secondly, I'm not surprised that you fail to grasp how Londons work. There are businessmen, serious Jews, who can't make head or tails of them either, let alone a woman like you. Allow me to explain. Londons, you should know, are highly perishable. You buy and sell them on a pledge without seeing them. Every minute you have to check if they're up or down—that is, if the ruble has risen or fallen in Berlin. It all depends on Berlin, you see; it's Berlin that has the last word. The rates soar and tumble like crazy, the telegrams fly back and forth, the Jews run around as though at a country fair, and so do I. There's such a racket you can't hear yourself think. Yesterday, for example, I played the market for 50 rubles and by noon today I'd lost them all. But I haven't told you what playing the market is. You can buy futures for 50 R's, or double that, or hedge until closing time. (That's the time between the afternoon and evening prayers in Kasrilevke.) Well, I bought short, the market was up, and there went my 50 smackeroos. That's how you play it—but don't you worry, my dear! Fifty smackers are nothing in Odessa. With God's help my lucky number will come up. And as for Uncle Menashe's promissory notes, you're mistaken. They're as good as gold, a solid investment. I could turn a nice profit on them even now, but I'd rather not. I can always make money from hedging. But I don't want to do that either. I prefer futures. There's nothing like a night spent sleeping on them. And because I'm in a hurry, I'll be brief.

God willing, I'll write more in my next letter. Meanwhile, may He grant you health and success.

Your husband,
Menakhem-Mendl

P.S. As for where I'm lodging and eating, I can't rightly tell you myself. Odessa is a monstrous big city and everything is very dear. The buildings are sky-high and you climb half-an-hour's worth of iron stairs to get to your room at the top of them. And the window is as tiny as a dungeon's! It's a relief to get out and head for Greek Street, where I take my meals—that is, where I grab what I can. Who has time to sit and eat when you have to keep your eyes on Berlin? But fruit costs next to nothing here. People eat grapes in the street, not just once a year for Rosh Hashanah like Kasrilevkans. They're not at all embarrassed to do it.

Yours, etc.

FROM SHEYNE-SHEYNDL IN KASRILEVKE TO HER HUSBAND MENAKHEM-MENDL IN ODESSA

To my dear, learned, & illustrious husband Menakhem-Mendl, may your light shine!

First, we're all well thank God. I hope to hear no worse from you.

Second, you write like a madman. Forgive me for saying so, but I hope to hear no more of your Odessa than I understand about your blasted shorts and hedgerows! You're throwing rubles away like last week's noodles. Money-shmoney, eh? I suppose it grows on trees over there. I'll be blamed, though, if one thing doesn't stump me: what kind of cat in a bag can you trade in but not see? Listen here, Mendl, I don't like it one bit! I wasn't raised in a home where we bought and sold air and God keep me from doing it now. From air you catch cold, my mother says. Who ever heard of a grown man playing in a market? You'd make more sense if you wrote in Turkish. And as for the profit you can turn on Menashe's notes, I hate to be a wet blanket, but the proof of the pudding, my mother says, is in the eating. You know what, Mendl? Listen to your wife, tell Odessa where it can go, and come home to Kasrilevke. We have a place to live in at my father's, you have five hundred rubles, opening a store is no problem—what more could you want? Why must I hear the world telling lies about your throwing me over for Odessa? Don't think you'll live to see the day! You can take your monster houses with their iron steps you climb like a lunatic and give me Kasrilevke any time. Because grapes are cheap there I should have a stomach ache here? Kasrilevke plums aren't sweet enough? There's such a glut this year that they're a kopeck a bucket. But a lot we matter to you! You don't even ask about the children. I suppose you've forgotten you have three of them, God bless them! Out of sight, out of mind, my mother says. I'll be blamed if she isn't right. I wish you all the best from the bottom of my heart.

Your truly faithful wife
Sheyne-Sheyndl.

FROM MENAKHEM-MENDL IN ODESSA TO HIS WIFE SHEYNE-SHEYNDL IN KASRILEVKE

To my wise, esteemed, & virtuous wife Sheyne-Sheyndl, may you have a long life!

Firstly, rest assured that I am, praise God, in the best of health. God grant that we hear from each other only good and pleasing news, amen.

Secondly, the market has been hitting fearsome lows. I've bought another batch of Londons and covered myself with 8 orders for 17 shorts. If I can shave a few points, I'll buy more. If only you understood, my dearest, how business is done on a man's word alone, you would know all there is to know about Odessa. A nod is as good as a signature. I walk down Greek Street, drop into a cafe, sit at a table, order tea or coffee, and wait for the brokers to come by. There's no need for a contract or written agreement. Each broker carries a pad in which he writes, say, that I've bought two shorts. I hand over the cash and that's it—it's a pleasure how easy it is! A few hours go by, the Berlin closings arrive, and back comes the broker with 25 smackers. The next morning the openings arrive and he has 50 more—and don't think God can't make it 100. 300 is no big deal either. Why should it be? We're talking about the market! It's a game, like roulette. . . . And as for your not believing in Uncle Menashe's promissory notes, I have news: I've made a tidy sum from them already. Where else would I get the money to buy so many futures on spot? The market is not, as you seem to think, a place that sells fruit and vegetables. You're only called on futures when they're due. That means, you're a free agent. If you want to buy, you buy, and if you want to sell, you sell. Now do you understand what playing the market is? If God is out to boost Londons, he starts a war scare in the papers, the ruble drops, and Londons shoot up faster than bean stalks. Just this week there were rumors that the Queen of England was ailing: the ruble plunged again, and whoever bought short made a killing. Now the papers say she's better, so the ruble has rallied and it's time to buy long. In short, my dearest, never fear! Everything will be "tip-top," as they say in Odessa. And because I'm in a hurry, I'll be brief. God willing, I'll write more in my next letter. Meanwhile, may He grant you health and success. Give my greetings to the children and my fondest wishes to everyone.

Your husband,

Menakhem-Mendl

P.S. We're all burning up from the heat. At night we go around like melting wax. The streets are deserted. All Odessa goes to the public fountains or the seashore. You can find anything you want there. You can even bathe in the sea or listen to free music—it doesn't cost a blessed kopeck.

Yours etc.

FROM SHEYNE-SHEYNDL IN KASRILEVKE TO HER HUSBAND MENAKHEM-MENDL IN ODESSA

To my dear, learned, & illustrious husband Menakhem-Mendl, may your light shine!

First, we're all well, thank God. I hope to hear no worse from you.

Second, I'm having trouble with my teeth. I wish Odessa and its market had my toothache! It's killing me. So are the children—and his lordship couldn't care less. He lives in Odessa like God, buys seventeen pairs of shorts, and bathes in the sea to music! What more could a body want? Well, you may go around in short pants and half-shaven, but my mother would say you've outgrown your britches. For heaven's sake, if you're dealing in Lumdums, keep your mind on them and not on the Queen of England! Better yet, think of your wife. She'll be around for a while, God willing. And you have three children, bless them. "Remember your own and you'll forget the next man's," my mother says. All your winnings make my head spin. Blow me down if I can believe that a man just sticks out his hand and watches the rubles fly into it. What kind of hocus-pocus is that? And you better not touch the dowry money, because my mother will make you rue the day you were born if a kopeck of it is missing. There are a few other things you might think about too. You know perfectly well I'm in desperate need of a silk shawl, some wool for a dress, and two bolts of Morazev calico. Though of course it's too much to expect you to think of such trifles, especially when you've taken leave of your senses. My mother says a man with more ribs than brains needs a poke in them.

I am, from the bottom of my heart,

Your truly faithful wife,
Sheyne-Sheyndl

FROM MENAKHEM-MENDL IN ODESSA TO HIS WIFE SHEYNE-SHEYNDL IN KASRILEVKE

To my wise, esteemed, & virtuous wife Sheyne-Sheyndl, may you have a long life!

Firstly, rest assured that I am, praise God, in the best of health. God grant that we hear from each other only good and pleasing news, amen.

Secondly, I'm holding shorts in a big way. I'm sitting on a pile of Londons. Each transaction is for 10 or 20,000 pounds in one shot. Of course, this means buying on margin. By now they know me in every brokerage. I take my seat in Fanconi's with all the dealers, pull up a chair at a marble table, and ask for a dish of iced cream. That's our Odessa custom: you sit yourself down and a waiter in a frock coat asks you to ask for iced cream. Well, you can't be a piker—and when you're finished, you're asked to ask for more. If you don't, you're out a table and in the street. That's no place for dealing, especially when there's an officer on the corner looking for loiterers. Not that our Jews don't hang out there anyway. They tease him with their wisecracks and scatter to see what he'll do. Just let him nab one! He latches on to him like a gemstone and it's off to the cooler with one more Jew . . .

Your doubts about the volatility of the market reveal a weak grasp of politics. There's a regular at Fanconi's, Gambetta is the name, who talks politics day and night. He has a thousand proofs that war is coming. In fact, he can already hear the cannon booming. Not here, he says, but in France. The French, he says, won't forgive Bismarck in a thousand years. It's a sure thing, he says—why, it's surer than sure—that war will break out any day. There are no two ways about it. If you go by Gambetta you'll sell everything, roll up your sleeves, and buy short, short, short all you can.

And as for buying you a coat, my dear wife, I've seen something better: a gold watch with a metalian, chain, and matching brooch, and a pair of bracelets in a window near Fanconi's—all the very best quality. But being in a hurry, I'll be brief. God willing, I'll write more in my next letter. Meanwhile, may He grant you health and success.

Your husband,

Menakhem-Mendl.

P.S. This town is so rich, and its Jews are so busy getting richer, that no one thinks about Sabbaths or Jewish holidays. I needn't tell you, though, that for me the Sabbath is still the Sabbath. I don't care if it's raining stones out, it's my day to go to synagogue. The Odessa synagogue is something to see. It's called the Choir Synagogue and everyone wears a top hat and sits on all sides of the cantor. His name is Pini and can he sing, even if he doesn't have a beard! And he knows Hebrew a sight better than that old dodo of a Moyshe-Dovid in Kasrilevke. You can pass out just from listening to him. I tell you, they could sell tickets! And the choir boys wear the cutest little prayer shawls. If Saturday came twice a week, I'd go both times just to hear Pini. Don't ask me why the local Jews stay away. Even those who come don't pray. They sit chewing their cud in their little prayer shawls and ritzy top hats and—shhhh, not a sound! Try praying loud enough for God to hear you and a beadle comes over and tells you to hush. I never saw such weird Jews in my life.

Yours etc.

FROM SHEYNE-SHEYNDL IN KASRILEVKE TO HER HUSBAND MENAKHEM-MENDL IN ODESSA

To my dear, learned, & illustrious husband Menakhem-Mendl, may your light shine!

First, we're all well, thank God. I hope to hear no worse from you.

Second, it's beyond me, dear husband, what's so special about your blamed Franconi's. I may never have eaten creamed ice on marble, but I know enough to ask: where's the money in it? And what kind of loon are you running around with who hears shooting in his dreams? He deserves to be shot dead himself! Is it wars that he wants? "One man's blood is another's water," my mother says. . . . You've seen gold watches and bracelets in a window? Well, bless my great-grandmother's soul! What are gifts in a window to me, Mendl? My mother says dumplings in a dream are a dream and not dumplings. You'd do better to step into a shop and buy new linen, cotton cloth for pillow cases, a couple of padded quilts, a few pieces of silver, and whatever else we could use around the house. Would you believe that Blume-Zlate has taken to preening herself each time she sees me? Let her preen till she bursts! So she has a pearl necklace, so what? For my part, let her choke on it. Is it my fault her husband gives her whatever she asks for? Some people have luck and mine was to be born on the wrong day. I have to remind his lordship of everything. All you think of is your longs and your shorts. I tell you to sell and what do you do? You rush right out and buy more! Are you afraid the world will run out of Lumdums? It's some business you're in and some city Odessa must be when a Sabbath is no Sabbath and a Jewish holiday is no holiday and a cantor has no beard. I wish he had my aches and pains! If I were you, I'd run from Odessa like the plague. But his lordship likes it there. Well, to quote my mother, a worm lies in horseradish and thinks there's nothing sweeter. I'm asking you, my husband, to think again and give up your merry life there. Let Odessa burn to the ground! I am, from the bottom of my heart,

Your truly faithful wife,
Sheyne-Sheyndl

And by the way, Mendl, who is this Franconi you're spending all your time with? Is it a he or a she?

FROM MENAKHEM-MENDL IN ODESSA TO HIS WIFE SHEYNE-SHEYNDL IN KASRILEVKE

To my dear, esteemed, & virtuous wife Sheyne-Sheyndl, may you have a long life!

Firstly, rest assured that I am, praise God, in the best of health. God grant that we hear from each other only good and pleasing news, amen.

Secondly, I'm now earning in the high thousands. If my position holds, I'll be a wealthy man. I'll cash in my spread, come back to Kasrilevke, and bring you with me, God willing, to Odessa. We'll rent a place on the boulevard, fill it with fine furniture, and live as only we Odessans know how to.

Meanwhile, I'm having stomach trouble. It shouldn't happen to you but all that iced cream has done me no good. Nowadays at Fanconi's I order a drink that's sipped through a straw: it has a bittersweet, licoricy taste and two or three glasses are my limit. After that I have to hang out in the street and worry about the officer, which is no fun at all because he has his eye on me. But by the grace of God, I've given him the slip so far. What a Jew mustn't do to earn a living! God grant the market goes my way and I'll buy you two of whatever Blume-Zlate has, more than you could ever imagine. . . . And as for Gambetta, he may be a hothead but he's no madman. God help the man who argues politics with him! He's quite capable of tearing him to shreds. He's sure war will break out any second—the calmer things are, the more certain it is. "It's the lull before the storm," he says. Yesterday I could have sold a few shorts on spot and come away with a nice little bundle, but Gambetta put his foot down. "I'll skin you alive," says he, "if you unload a single share now!" It won't be long, he says, before 50 rubles of shorts are worth 2 or 3 hundred, even 4. Why, they could even top 1,000! Let him be half-right and I'm sitting pretty. I'll take my profit, God willing, and switch to longs. I'll buy rubles and sell Londons like crazy and show the world a thing or two about the market. But as I'm in a hurry, I'll be brief. God willing, I'll write more in my next letter. Meanwhile, may He grant you health and success.

Your husband,
Menakhem-Mendl

P.S. Regarding Fanconi (and not "Franconi," as you write), it's neither a he nor a she but a cafe. That's a place where you drink coffee, eat iced cream, and deal in Londons. I wish I were worth half the daily volume there!

Yours etc.

FROM SHEYNE-SHEYNDL IN KASRILEVKE TO HER HUSBAND MENAKHEM-MENDL IN ODESSA

To my dear, learned, & illustrious husband Menakhem-Mendl, may your light shine!

First, we're all well, thank God. I hope to hear no worse from you.

Second, all three children have the measles and keep me up all night. And his lordship sits in Odessa drinking likrish-water! But why care about my worries in Kasrilevke when you're all in a sweat to carry me off from here? You think it's enough to say "Odessa" for me to sprout wings and fly away to you. Listen here, Mendl: take a deep breath and get it out of your head. My great-grandmother managed without Odessa and so will I. Don't think you can talk me into ditching my parents and good friends and moving to a wilderness. I'll see Odessa in flames first! Say what you will, the more I hear of it, the less I like it. Don't ask me why—I just don't. Something tells me you're pushing your luck. "The best dairy dish is a piece of meat," my mother says. Or are you afraid prices will keep rising and you'll look foolish for selling now? Everyone should only be such a fool!

And as for your Gambetta (forgive me for saying so, but he's stark, raving mad), I'd like to know what business of his or his grandmother's it is. You can tell him to his face that I said so. What kind of wars is he dragging you into? For heaven's sake, Mendl, listen to me: sell everything, and pull out now! You've made a few rubles? Quit while you're ahead. How much longer can you go on like this? It's a fine state of affairs when your Sheyne-Sheyndl's opinion means nothing to you. I wish I had a mouth like Blume-Zlate, who gives her husband the nine-year pox each time she opens it! For the love of God, Mendl, be a dear soul and get out while you can. Just don't forget to buy a dozen embroidered blouses and some satin for a dress for my mother—she deserves a souvenir from the days her son-in-law did business with madmen in Odessa. Get some calico, too, the latest prints, and as much glassware as fits into your suitcase, and whatever else you can think of and come home. I'm tired of taking it on the chin. My enemies should croak for every time you haven't listened to me, but please do it now. I am, from the bottom of my heart,

Your truly faithful wife,
Sheyne-Sheyndl

FROM MENAKHEM-MENDL IN ODESSA TO HIS WIFE SHEYNE-SHEYNDL IN KASRILEVKE

To my wise, esteemed, & virtuous wife, Sheyne-Sheyndl, may you have a long life!

Firstly, rest assured that I am, praise God, in the best of health. God grant that we hear from each other only good and pleasing news, amen.

Secondly, the market has crashed just as futures, God help us, were being called. I'll see the Messiah before I see my money again. Bismarck, they say, caught a bad cold and all politics went into a panic. No one knows what tomorrow will bring. Londons are worth more than gold, the ruble has hit rock bottom, and futures have fallen through the floor. But where, you ask, are the shorts I bought? That's just it: the shorts aren't short, the futures have no future, and call me a monkey's uncle! The small-time operators I entrusted my shares with have been wiped out. Odessa has been hit by a whirlwind, you wouldn't know the place. I should have made my move a day earlier. But go be a prophet! The dealers run around like chickens without their heads, you've never seen such pandemonium. They're all screaming at the top of their lungs—"Londons! Give us our Londons!"—but there are no Londons to be had. All the curses and brawls on the Exchange (everyone fights and so do I) can't produce a single one. In short, my dear wife, it's a dark and bitter day. I've lost all my earnings, plus the capital, plus the jewelry I bought you. I've even pawned my Sabbath gabardine, it's gone the way of all else . . .

You can imagine the wretched state I'm in. I'm so homesick I could weep. I curse my luck a hundred times a day. If only I had broken a leg instead of coming to Odessa, where a man is worth nothing. Why, you can drop dead in the street and no one will stop to look at you! When I think of the brokers who flocked around me, begged me to throw them a bone . . . and now they don't even know me! The man they called the Rothschild of Kasrilevke has become a big joke. I'm told I know nothing about futures. Not everyone understands Londons, they say. But where were all the big experts then? I'd get more sympathy if I were a corpse. In fact, I'd be better-off if I were one. And to make matters worse, that blasted Gambetta keeps blabbering about politics. "Ha!" he says. "Didn't I tell you to buy short?" "What good are your shorts," I say, "when there's not a London in sight?" But he only laughs and says: "Whose fault is that? You have to know futures. You can't buy and sell Londons likes potatoes . . . " I tell you, my dearest wife, I've had my fill of Odessa and its market and its Fanconi's and its petty thieves! All I want is to get out of here. And since I'm in a hurry, I'll be brief. God willing, I'll write more in my next letter. Meanwhile, may He grant you health and success. My fondest greetings to all the children and to your parents.

Your husband,
Menakhem-Mendl

P.S. It's not the custom in Odessa to go to a neighbor, friend, or relative when you need help as it is in Kasrilevke. That isn't because people are too proud to ask but because they know what the answer will be. Zilch! What, then, is a man to do? He goes to a pawnshop, where he can get all the money he wants as long as he has something to hock. It can be gold, silver, bronze, clothing, a samovar, a stool, even a cow—anything that's worth cash. The problem is that it's valued very low, at half its real worth. And the pawnbroker makes up for it by charging such high interest that you're left with nothing. Every two weeks the unredeemed items are auctioned off at bargain prices and he makes a nice pile. If I had money, I'd open a pawnshop myself and recoup my losses. I might even come out ahead—but that's easier said than done. There's no point being born poor in this world and if you are, you might as well not have been. Tell me about yourself, and what the children are doing, and give my fondest greetings to your parents.

Yours etc.

FROM SHEYNE-SHEYNDL IN KASRILEVKE TO HER HUSBAND MENAKHEM-MENDL IN ODESSA

To my dear, learned, & illustrious husband Menakhem-Mendl, may your light shine!

First, we're all well, thank God. I hope to hear no worse from you.

Second, just look at what you've done, you fool! What devil brought you to Odessa? What made your nose twitch so? Creamed ice his lordship craved! Lumdums! Likrish-water! Roast pheasant! If you knew you'd been Lumdummed, you big dummy, why didn't you settle for a percentage like a smart businessman? Where was everybody? Why didn't you run to the rabbi? What, in God's name, are futures-shmutures? You bought merchandise—where is it? You've made one holy mess of things, you have! I knew all along no good would come of your Odessa.

I'm telling you, Mendl, leave now. Hang Odessa and its Lumdums, a plague on them both! Run for your life, Mendl! "When the walls shake, don't wait for the quake," my mother says. . . . But of course nothing I say means a thing to his lordship. I'm only that nobody Sheyne-Sheyndl when I should be Blume-Zlate. Was my mother the smart one! She warned me never to let a husband go to town by himself. "Keep your thumb on his neck," she said. But what was I to do? I'm not a pushy one like Blume-Zlate. I can't rub a man's nose in the dirt, I simply can't! If only you had her for a wife instead of me, you'd know what the fear of God was . . .

And as for wanting to die, you big genius, you're even more of a moron than I thought. It's not up to us when to live and when to die. Since when does losing a dowry mean jumping off the roof? You're a dunce to think it's written in the stars that Menakhem-Mendl has to be rich. Is it a fight with God you want to pick? You can see He had other plans for you, so stop making such a fuss. Things could be worse. You might have been robbed in the forest or made to spend all your money on medicines for some blamed illness. Don't carry on like an old woman, Mendl. Put your trust in the Almighty and come on home! To the children you'll still be an honored guest.

I'm sending you a few rubles for your carfare. Don't go spending them on old junk or auctions. Stay away from all that. I beg you to say good-bye to your Odessa as soon as you get this letter with the money. May it catch fire the moment you leave and burn to ashes! I am, from the bottom of my heart,

Your truly faithful wife,
Sheyne-Sheyndl

◆◆◆ *Stocks & Bonds: The Yehupetz Exchange*

FROM MENAKHEM-MENDL IN YEHUPETZ TO HIS WIFE SHEYNE-SHEYNDL IN KASRILEVKE

To my wise, esteemed, & virtuous wife Sheyne-Sheyndl, may you have a long life!

Firstly, rest assured that I am, thank God, in the best of health. God grant that we hear from each other only good and pleasing news, amen.

Secondly, I have left Odessa for Yehupetz (a fine town, I declare) and am no longer dealing in perishables—that is, in Londons. I am at present, praise God, a bonified investor in stocks & bonds. But what brought me, you may ask, to Yehupetz? That, my dear wife, is a long story that I'll tell you once I ask your forgiveness for not writing. I simply had no news. And besides, I kept thinking I would soon be on my way home. But although God knows I hankered to be there, it seems I was fated for Yehupetz. I swear, my dearest, I was already in the coach for Kasrilevke when who sits next to me but a Yehupetz-bound Odessa investor. What takes him to Yehupetz, I ask. Stocks & bonds, he says. What kind of line is that, I ask. Well, he says, it's nothing like Londons. With Londons you're at the mercy of Berlin and Bismarck and the Queen of England. In stocks & bonds it's Warsaw and Petersburg. And not only that, Londons are as airy as a dream, while stocks & bonds are solid items.

You should have heard that Jew praise Yehupetz and its investors to the skies! Why, they're straight as an arrow, he says; they're the very soul of honor; he wouldn't swap one of them for ten Odessa slickers. The fellow made me so curious that I thought, seeing as I'm passing through Fastov, why not detour to Yehupetz and see the market? And wouldn't you know, the day I arrived it had sunk to such depths that stocks were going for a song with nary a kopeck up front. I decided to give it a try. What was there to lose? If the breaks went my way, I might earn some pocket money for the rest of my trip. And don't think I didn't! The market rose, I sold at a nice profit, reinvested my earnings, backed some more winners, and wound up with several hundred rubles in cash. At which point I thought: why pay someone a commission to sell me shares when I can be that someone myself? So off I went to an office in Petersburg and put together a portfoliage of every stock you can think of: Putivil, and Transport, and Volga, and Maltzev, and still more that's bound to go up. Praise God, I'm growing all the time. But since I'm in a hurry, I'll be brief. God willing, I'll write more in my next letter. Meanwhile, may He grant you health and success. My fondest greetings to the children and your parents,

Your husband,

Menakhem-Mendl

P.S. If you write, do it care of Boiberik, since Jews can't stay nights in Yehupetz. I spend my days in the Kreshchatik Square market and come back to Boiberik every evening. All the investors live there in dachas and sit around playing cards. (Men and women together—that's the custom.) The next morning they head for Yehupetz and so do I.

Yours, etc.

FROM SHEYNE-SHEYNDL IN KASRILEVKE TO HER HUSBAND MENAKHEM-MENDL IN YEHUPETZ

To my dear, learned, & illustrious husband Menakhem-Mendl, may your light shine!

First, we're all well, thank God. I hope to hear no worse from you.

Second, my dear husband, my enemies should have as much strength to go on living as I have to write you this short note. I can hardly get around on my legs and may need an operation. At least that's what the new doctor says. He should catch all ten of Pharaoh's plagues! The man thinks he'll get rich from me. Would you like to know what the trouble is? My blood has bad corpsicles from all the heartache you've given me. Who ever heard of such a thing? I send you money to come home to Kasrilevke and you run off with it to Yehupetz! A good-for-nothing like you deserves to be buried alive. You've blown your nose all over your face, that's what my mother would say. . . . A bonified business! Stockings & bands! And here I was thinking that, after his lordship's precious Lumdums had gone down the drain, he would give me the pleasure of coming home less dead than alive. But what does my angel of a breadwinner do? He dreams a new dream: Yehupetz. May a black desert swallow it! A Jew like you, selling stockings in the market square! You know what you can do with a business like that! I read your letter, dear husband, and I thought: God in heaven! Either you've gone clear out of your mind or else I have. You're speaking Chinese. Petersburg . . . Pottyboils . . . portfolderols . . . a haunt might be talking from your throat. By day it's Yehupetz and by night it's Boiberik, men and women together! What's going on there? Who do you think you are? Make up your mind! If you don't want me any more, come home to the rabbi and get a divorce, because if I'm going to be an abandoned wife with a house full of brats, I'd rather you vanished from the face of the earth in America like Yosl Leib-Arons and I never had to hear from you again. My enemies should be as sick as I am! It's my rotten luck that I'm laid up with my aches and pains and can't come after you, because I'd take the first coach from Kasrilevke and drag you home by the scruff of your neck. It's as my mother says, though: if you don't have a hand, don't expect to give anyone the finger. . . . But don't hold my harsh words against me. It's just my bad corpsicles. I'll get over them. A match, says my mother, flares up fast and goes out quickly. I am, from the bottom of my heart,

Your truly faithful wife,
Sheyne-Sheyndl

FROM MENAKHEM-MENDL IN YEHUPETZ TO HIS WIFE SHEYNE-SHEYNDL IN KASRILEVKE

To my dear, esteemed, & virtuous wife Sheyne-Sheyndl, may you have a long life!

Firstly, rest assured that I am, praise God, in the best of health. God grant that we hear from each other only good and pleasing news, amen.

Secondly, stocks & bonds are not what you think. They come from Petersburg. Putivil, Transport, Volga, Maltzev, etc., are manufacturers. They deal in rolling and floating stock—that is, railroads and 100-ruble shares that go for 300. That's because of the dividends. The more dividends, the more they're worth. But since nobody knows how many there'll be, you buy blind. That's called a bull market; all the Jews are cashing in on it and so am I. You would not believe, my dear wife, how small-time investors have become millionaires! They live in huge dachas, travel to Europinian spas, drape their women in silks and satins, speak French, play the piano, eat jam, and drink jewlips all day long. Their children have governors and ride icicles. A ruble means nothing to them. They live high and the sky is the limit. And it's all from stocks & bonds!

You should see Kreshchatik Square. It's mobbed with Jews. And why shouldn't it be? We're chased out of the brokerages and kept off the streets, and as we need to know the latest, it's sheer bedlam. But I mean bedlam! Today a new issue of Putivil 187's arrived from Petersburg. Well, who doesn't want new Putivils? And since Maltzevs, so they say, closed at 1,350, who can resist Maltzevs? Shares are up every day. On my Putivils alone, praise God, I could clear a few hundred rubles. But you can flog me before I'll sell them. In fact, I'm planning to buy 150 more, 5 Maltzevs, and a couple of Volgas—and some Transports too, if all goes well, because the word from Petersburg is, buy Transports for all you're worth! The whole world is holding them: Jews, housewives, doctors, teachers, servants, tradesmen—who doesn't have Transports? When two Jews meet, the first question is: "How are Transports today?" Walk into a restaurant and the owner's wife asks: "What's the latest on Transports?" Go buy a box of matches and the grocer has to know if Transports are up or down. In a word, there's money to be made here.

Everyone is investing, growing, getting rich, and so am I. But because I'm in a hurry, I'll be brief. God willing, I'll write more in my next letter. Meanwhile, may He grant you health and success. Give everyone my very fondest greetings.

Your husband,
Menakhem-Mendl

P.S. Regarding my nights in Boiberik, I've already explained that Yehupetz is off limits without a residence card. As soon as I balance my portfoliage, I'll see about getting one and becoming a Yehupetzer. Meanwhile it's best to lay low, for which there's no better place than Boiberik. It's full of dachas. The Jews who live in them commute to Yehupetz and so do I. Is everything clear now?

Yours etc.

FROM SHEYNE-SHEYNDL IN KASRILEVKE TO HER HUSBAND MENAKHEM-MENDL IN YEHUPETZ

To my dear, learned, & illustrious husband Menakhem-Mendl, may your light shine!

First, we're all well, thank God. I hope to hear no worse from you.

Second, we've had good and bad luck. Our Moyshe-Hirshele swallowed a kopeck! It was a Friday and I had just returned from the market with a Sabbath fish, a nice, fresh one, still flopping. I step into the house—the boy is crying his head off. He didn't even stop when I gave him a good smack and then another. Well, I began to scream myself: "You brainless little brat! What's the matter? You should only have my troubles! Here, here's a kopeck to play with. I wish it were a bellyache!" It got me down so I hardly could speak.

A few minutes later I remember the kopeck. "Moyshe-Hirshele," I say, "where's the kopeck?" "Topet go 'way," he says, pointing at his mouth. Oh my God, I think: don't tell me he's swallowed it! I look in his mouth—it's not there. I thought I would die. "Moyshe-Hershenyu! My darling! I'd give my life for you! What have you done with that kopeck?" I rocked him, I spanked him, I pinched him black-and-blue, but all he does is keep crying: "Go 'way!" To make a long story short, I took him to the doctor. The doctor told me to feed him potatoes. For two straight days I fed that poor child nothing but potatoes, potatoes, and more potatoes, without even a drop of milk or water. I didn't think he'd pull through. And then on the third day I pick up a pillow while cleaning and what do you think I find? The kopeck! Those doctors wouldn't know beans if they saw them.

But after the last straw, there's always more, as my mother says. Here I am, up to my ears with his lordship's children, with the doctors, with haunts and hobgoblins in my own home, and Mr. Goldfingers couldn't care less. He's off to Odessa, to Yehupetz, to Boiberik! How is that? He's made a great discovery: stockings & bands! Transports! Portfolderols! He only has to shut and open his eyes and he's a millionaire! The worst illness, says my mother, is gullibillness. You're a fool to think your big words impress me. Shares, shmares! I'd rather own a rotten egg. No one ever made money by counting on his fingers. You know what my mother says: invest a fever and you'll earn consumption. Mark my words, Mendl, all your overnight Yehupetz tycoons will soon by the grace of God be the same beggars they were before. I have as much faith in your Transports and your Shmaltzevs as I had in your Lumdums. Why, I'd sooner believe in black magic than in your portfolderols. I tell you, if a mad dog ate my heart it would go crazy! When I think there are wives in this world who are listened to by their husbands and will know the reason why if they aren't while I have to treat his lordship with kid gloves because God forbid he should hear a cross word from me! How I'd love once and for all to give you a piece of my mind instead of pretending to smile! "A pinch in the cheek," my mother says, "makes it rosy." But what's a poor woman to do? Burn quietly like a candle, I suppose. Or else be consumed by bad corpsicles. The worst enemies of the Jews should have them in my place! Or better yet, your Yehupetz hot shots. I am, from the bottom of my heart,

Your truly faithful wife,

Sheyne-Sheyndl.

Mum's the word but your uncle Menashe's son Berl is in hot water again. A week ago his house burned down and left him penniless, and now his enemies have ratted that it was insured at three times its value.

It looks like he lit the match himself. He was even called in for questioning. But Berl's no fool; he went and found witnesses to swear he was somewhere else that night. That's why he was arrested. His wife Zlatke had such a scare that she gave birth in her seventh month. Congratulations, the baby is doing well!

FROM MENAKHEM-MENDL IN YEHUPETZ TO HIS WIFE SHEYNE-SHEYNDL IN KASRILEVKE

To my wise, esteemed, & virtuous wife Sheyne-Sheyndl, may you live a long life!

Firstly, rest assured that I am, praise God, in the best of health. God grant that we hear from each other only good and pleasing news, amen.

Secondly, I'm soon off to Warsaw. I suppose you'll ask why, when I'm investing in Petersburg stocks, I need to go to Warsaw. But don't you fret. Warsaw is not a bad place. And does it have stocks & bonds! It's an investors' paradise, Warsaw is, not at all like Petersburg. 100-ruble notes are scrap paper there. Why, just this week Liliputs jumped in Warsaw from 1,200 to 2,000! I ask you: can a man twiddle his thumbs in Yehupetz at such a time? Or take Roads & Rails. A week ago it closed at 3 or 4 hundred and what do you think it's worth now? Five times as much! No one even asks for a stock certificate. It's a perfect crime, in my opinion, not to buy Roads & Rails in Warsaw while you can. Everything is on margin. You put down a few hundred smackers and pay the rest on the first of the month. (I mean the Christian month—they have them too.) And when the first arrives you have the option of taking your shares or not. But who lets you wait that long? Among God's creatures are speculators who stop you in the street and ask: "Maybe you have some Liliputs for me? How about Roads & Rails?" They make you think it's God's gift to find a buyer. Just yesterday two fellows from Odessa got hold of me and wouldn't take no for an answer. They thought they had come across a sucker. "Brothers," I said, "I'm all out. I should have as much on my conscience as I have Liliputs or Roads & Rails." They kept at it until I had parted with my last 5 shares of each. Don't think they got the best of me, though, because right away I bought those shares back from them at a slight mark-up. Lately, knock wood, whatever I've bought has gone up. They all say I have a gift for it. Let the first of the month come around and I'll pay off my portfoliage. Then I'll switch to another brokerage. The one I work in now has too many Jews for comfort. There's a new scene there every week. The last time it even came to blows. But because I'm in a hurry, I'll be brief. God willing, I'll write more in my next letter. Meanwhile, may He grant you health and success. My fondest regards to everyone,

Your husband,

Menakhem-Mendl

P.S. I can easily believe what you write about Berl. It's the only way for a Kasrilevke merchant to survive. Mind you, such things don't happen in Yehupetz. In the first place, we're all doing well. And secondly, if a fire breaks out here, God forbid, we have ways to deal with it. Before it can spread a battalion in brass helmets rushes up and sprays it with a rubber gut. A Yehupetz fire is a sight for sore eyes!

Yours, etc.

FROM SHEYNE-SHEYNDL IN KASRILEVKE TO HER HUSBAND MENAKHEM-MENDL IN WARSAW

To my dear, learned, & illustrious husband Menakhem-Mendl, may your light shine!

First, we're all well, thank God. I hope to hear no worse from you.

Second, my dear husband, I pronounce you a certified lunatic. You might as well run naked through the streets! As if it weren't enough for Odessa, Yehupetz, and Boiberik to know that M.M. stands for Market Maniac, you have to let Warsaw in on it too. First it was Lumdums and now it's stockings, Pottyboils, Lilyfoots, portfolderols, Rack & Ruin! For a box on the ear you have to go all the way to Warsaw? God in heaven, find me the wizard who can box the nonsense out of you! You who happen to have, should she still be alive when you read this, a wife who is up all day and all night with your children, because if it isn't one thing, it's another. Just yesterday one of them was almost burned to death by a colander of boiling water that barely missed it. There's good luck even in bad, my mother says—but what does that have to do with his lordship? He's too busy attending fires. He thinks Yehupetz is burning down just for him. It should burn and take Warsaw and Petersburg with it! I can't walk the streets without good, God-fearing folk washing their hands in my blood. They point and say, "There goes the Yehupetzer's Missus," and I could crawl into a hole in the ground. . . . My mother, bless her, wasn't joking when she said: "Never let a husband off the leash. Not even a carpenter knows where the chips will fly." She never doubted, she says, that my marriage would come to no good end. I should have married for money, she says. If I was going to marry a swine, I should have married a rich one. "I'd sooner send your husband a ten-foot tapeworm," she says, "than another letter!" She says a cane can accomplish more than a wink. I should bring you home on a broomstick, she says. No, on an oven poker!

I ask you: is she right or not? But what good does that do when a ninny like me believes all she's told and never stands up for herself! Anyone else—Blume-Zlate, say—would have been in Yehupetz long ago, lining up the rabbis. She would have waylaid you in the street and given you a hiding to make you forget you're Menakhem-Mendl the stocking dealer. . . . But what am I saying when all your fine gifts are proof of your wonderful business? The diamonds, the precious stones, the embroidered blouses, the goose-down mattresses—don't think I'm not grateful. . . . I tell you, my husband, I've put up with as much as I can. Either you get yourself home in a jiffy and act like a human being—or else! As I wish my enemies an early death, so I am from the bottom of my heart,

Your truly faithful wife,
Sheyne-Sheyndl

FROM MENAKHEM-MENDL IN YEHUPETZ TO HIS WIFE SHEYNE-SHEYNDL IN KASRILEVKE

To my wise, esteemed, & virtuous wife Sheyne-Sheyndl, may you have a long life!

Firstly, rest assured that I am, praise God, in the best of health. God grant that we hear from each other only good and pleasing things, amen.

Secondly, I'm going like a house afire. I'm growing all the time. The whole world is jealous that whatever I buy is worth more tomorrow. Roads & Rails are up 200 and my Liliputs, praise God, have broken 3,000. It doesn't pay to sell, though, because word is the market will keep rising. Rumor has it that Europinian money is flowing into it. A syndicate—that's a kind of high-class club—has been formed to buy us out down to the last share. If you're wondering why, it's quite simple. There's a glut of gold in the world; they're dumping gold in the streets. That's driven down interest rates and 4 or 5 percent is now considered a good return. Well, suppose I can get you 10 or 15 on the Yehupetz Exchange, wouldn't you call that a sound investment? . . . And as for what you incorrectly call "Lilyfoots," I've already told you it's a rolling stock that pays dividends. The factory is in Warsaw, the railroads are in Siberia, and the customers are in Yehupetz. Putivil, Roads & Rails, and Transport are the same. Don't imagine you actually get to see them. That's a common misconception I'll explain. Suppose you have a yen for Transports. You go to a broker, put down a few rubles, and get a letter saying you've purchased X number of shares at so much per share for so many rubles. If Transports drop you still pay the full price—but that never happens, so it's silly to worry about it. On the contrary, stocks keep rising. My position has never been so strong. If I can spare the time I'll scoot over to register in Vasilkov so that I can stop being a commuter. All the big investors do it. You should see how they live, what they eat! And the jewelry on their wives! I've asked around for the best places for diamonds and have my eyes on some stones that will, I promise you, knock them out in Yehupetz no less than in Kasrilevke. But as I'm a hurry, I'll be brief. God willing, I'll write more in my next letter. Meanwhile, may he grant you health and success. My fondest greetings to everyone,

Your husband,
Menakhem-Mendl

P.S. You may think, my dear wife, that I'm the biggest investor around. Let me tell you that Brodsky is bigger. The difference is that I buy what I can while he snaps up 1, 5, 10 thousand shares at a time. You can't take on Brodsky. The whole Kreshchatik trembles when he drives by.

All the Jews doff their hats and so do I. Imagine my being a Brodsky too one day! A foolish thought—but nothing is impossible with God . . .

FROM SHEYNE-SHEYNDL IN KASRILEVKE TO HER HUSBAND MENAKHEM-MENDL IN YEHUPETZ

To my dear, learned, & illustrious husband Menakhem-Mendl, may your light shine!

First, we're all well, thank God. I hope to hear no worse from you.

Second, my mother says you can't make a fur hat from a pig's tail. I'm referring to your charming sister-in-law Yentl. May she never live to see the day, but this week she spread the word around town that you'd run off to America and left me high and dry. What little bird told her that? She heard it from Soreh-Nekhameh, who had it from Leizi-Hirshke, who told her that Ben-Tsiyon's son Borukh saw a letter to Moyshe-Shmul from Meir-Motl in America. Straightaway I ran to Moyshe-Shmul. "Where's the letter?" I asked. "What letter?" he says. "The one Meir-Motl wrote you from America." "Who says he wrote me a letter?" "Ben-Tsiyon's son Borukh." "But how," he says, "could that lowdown sneak have told you that when I haven't spoken to him in a year?" I ran to Borukh's, half out of my mind. Wouldn't you know he'd left town three weeks ago! Off I go to give Leizi-Hirshke an earful for the crock he fed Soreh-Nekhameh about a letter from never-never land. "Who, *me?*" he says, staring as if I were mad. It turns out that your Yentl made it all up! She should roast in hell for her sins—and for ours while she's at it. Leave it to a tart like her!

But a lot you care when all you can think of is your fine Yehupetz ladies. They should gash themselves on their diamonds and bleed to death! Do you hear me, Mendl? I hate them so much I don't want to hear about them. And I'm sick of being told of all your presents. I've already written you, my dear husband, that if you're looking to buy me something, spare me your Yehupetz frippery. I don't need to doll myself up like a lot of women who aren't fit to tie my shoes. And I want to see you in person, not some piece of paper you've scribbled on. "Let's have more food and less talk," my mother would say. What are you waiting for? The business you're in will finish you if you don't finish with it first. Seeing is believing, say what you will. Not, God forbid, that I think you're lying, but those Yehupetz smoothies are selling you a bill of goods. Who are you to compare yourself to Brodsky? Did the two of you roll in the same mud when you were boys? If your shares are worth something, sell them and don't play hard to get. Some slick operators, you say, are out to get their hands on your treasure? Shake and call it a deal! Or as my mother would say: hold on to your hat and run!

But try talking to a madman! His lordship wants an address in Vasilkov, of all places. He's so rich he doesn't know where to live next. Why Vasilkov? But that's a silly question. If it's Yehupetz by day, and Boiberik by night, and Petersburg and Warsaw by the by, you might as well live in Vasilkov too—and why not in Hotzeplotz while you're at it? Just be careful, Mendl, that you don't turn into such a great success that I have to send you your carfare again. I am, from the bottom of my heart,

Your truly faithful wife,

Sheyne-Sheyndl

I have bad news for you, my dear husband. Your brother Berl-Binyomin has lost his wife. I had already sealed the envelope when word reached me. Yentl gave birth to twins. Both lived and she died. Now why couldn't it have been the other way around? But God loves to be contrary, as my mother says. I should only be spared such a fate! It's true that your sister-in-law and I, may she forgive my saying so, never got along, but at least she kept out of my hair. For my part she could have lived to be a hundred instead of leaving two little orphans, one tinier than the other. I even went to her funeral and cried so hard I could barely walk home. "Thinking of the dead," says my mother, "makes you wonder about the living . . ."

FROM MENAKHEM-MENDL IN YEHUPETZ TO HIS WIFE SHEYNE-SHEYNDL IN KASRILEVKE

To my wise, esteemed, & virtuous wife Sheyne-Sheyndl, may you have a long life!

Firstly, rest assured that I am, praise God, in the best of health. God grant that we hear from each other only good and pleasing news, amen.

Secondly, I've been laid up all week in Boiberik. It's more annoying than serious, thank God. I took a fall on my back and couldn't turn over onto my stomach. Now I'm feeling better. All week long I thought I would go out of my mind. Just imagine, eight whole days away from the Exchange, with no way of knowing the latest prices! From what I hear, though, things are hopping. God willing, I'll be back to work tomorrow or the day after. Meanwhile, I'm writing you this letter. It's a chance to chat and let you know what I'm worth. You mustn't think I'm raving if I tell you that I'm currently holding in my portfoliage 150 shares of Putivil, 100 of Transport, 5 Maltzevs, 5 Liliputs, and 5 Roads & Rails, quite apart from various premiums. The Putivils and Transports have been optioned for 3 rubles a share with the remainder due on delivery. If the deal goes through—and there's no reason why it shouldn't—I'll clear 4 to 5 grand after expenses. I've also bought long on a few dozen Putivils and Maltzevs, which should be good for another 1,800.

That's close to 7,000 rubles right there. My 5 Maltzevs are worth 4 G's at a dead minimum and it will be a scandal if I can't get 2 apiece for them despite their having dipped—that's just a sell-off by the Petersburg margin traders to cover their debts. And I'm still left with the two jewels in my crown, my Liliputs and Roads & Rails. They're as good as gold, both of them, with 18 whole days to go until the first! If Liliputs keep climbing at 100 a day, you have a surefire 1,800 x 5, which is 9,000 R's. And with Roads & Rails you're looking at 150 x 18 x 5, which comes, if I'm not mistaken, to 13,500. Mind you, I'm not even counting the Volgas, Dniepers, Dons, and other small change. In a word, once it's all in the bank I'll be worth roughly, in round numbers, give or take a bit, 40 to 50 grand! Let all go well until the first and I'll take my profits, switch to buying short, and work the other side of the street; then I'll go back to longs and rake it in again. If the good Lord wills it, my 50 G's will be worth 100, my 100, 200, my 200, 500, right up to a million! What, silly girl, will be the difference between me and Brodsky then? He's only human, Brodsky is: he eats, drinks, and sleeps just like the rest of us. Believe me, I've seen him with my own eyes and hope to see better.

In short, my dear, there's no need for concern. I've got the hang of the market and have become so good at it that I'm even asked for advice. Being urged by you to quit is nothing new. But just look at Khinkes. That's a big-time speculator who is also a fiend for gambling; he plays the market by day and the card tables by night. Just last week he dreamed a low card and ran off to Petersburg and Warsaw to sell off his entire portfoliage. Don't think he isn't tearing his hair out now. That will teach him to believe in dreams!

I can't wait for tomorrow's closings. As soon as I get to town, I'm going to a jeweler's to pick up a diamond brooch and earrings. If I have time, I'll also shop for linens, tablecloths, handkerchiefs, some smocks for the children, and a few other household items. You see how wrong you are to say I've forgotten you! And because I'm in a hurry, I'll be brief. God willing, I'll write more in my next letter. Meanwhile, God grant you health and success. Kiss the children for me and give regards to your parents and my fondest greetings to everyone. And tell Berl-Binyomin not to spend his nights playing klabberjass!

Your husband,

Menakhem-Mendl

P.S. About Vasilkov, you miss the point. A half-year's residence there is a must for a permit for Yehupetz. Once I'm established in Yehupetz, God willing, I'll buy an apartment in the best neighborhood and send for you and the children at once. You would be less critical if you knew it better; it's a lovely town, there's no comparing it to Odessa. You couldn't wish for nicer, more considerate people, men and women alike. Their only weakness is cards; they stay up calling "Deal!" until the wee hours. The older folk favor a game called Preference while the young ones play whist, rummy, and klabberjass.

Yours, etc.

FROM SHEYNE-SHEYNDL IN KASRILEVKE TO HER HUSBAND MENAKHEM-MENDL IN YEHUPETZ

To my dear, learned, & illustrious husband Menakhem-Mendl, may your light shine!

First, we're all well, thank God. I hope to hear no worse from you.

Second, my dear husband, in case you're fearing more bad news, mazel tov! Your baby brother Berl-Binyomin has remarried in record time. He didn't let two months go by before setting out for Berdichev, which is the world's biggest supplier of stepmothers, and coming back with one for his children. And she's all of nineteen, the lucky fellow! I tell you, it's disgusting. How right my mother, bless her, is to say: "Better to bury a husband than a mother." I suppose you might shed a few tears for me, Mendl, if God forbid I died before you, but I'll never give your Yehupetz ladies the satisfaction because they'd be all over you like flies. They wouldn't even wait for my unveiling. Well, the dirty pot deserves a dirty spoon, as my mother says. Think of the new life you can have in Yehupetz!

You say you're going like a house afire, Mendl? Why don't you jump into the flames! I wouldn't come see you in Boiberik if you were on your deathbed! And don't think your fifty thousand makes an impression. In the first place, you're the same husband with or without it. And in the second place, it isn't worth a pinch of snuff. "Money on paper is not even paper money," my mother says. . . . I'll tell you the truth, my dear husband: if you're not pocketing a few rubles now because you're waiting for them to turn into fifty thousand, you're either a madman or a heartless murderer with no pity for your children or wife, if you still have one when this letter reaches you. His lordship is a great one for tomorrows. Tomorrow he's going to the jeweler, tomorrow he's off to buy linen . . . any time but today. For heaven's sake, let God take care of tomorrow and do your shopping while you can! Strike while the iron is hot! You know what a clever woman my mother is. "What good," she says to me, "are all his promises of tablecloths and handkerchiefs when he should be sending you cash? The Angel of Death doesn't wait for a man to buy his shrouds . . ." Give me a few weeks to get my health back and I'm off to Boiberik, God willing—and I don't envy you when I get there. I'll dog your steps, I won't leave you alone for a minute—believe me, you won't wait for the morning to clear out! I am, from the bottom of my heart,

Your truly faithful wife,
Sheyne-Sheyndl

FROM MENAKHEM-MENDL IN YEHUPETZ TO HIS WIFE SHEYNE-SHEYNDL IN KASRILEVKE

To my wise, esteemed, & virtuous wife Sheyne-Sheyndl, may you have a long life!

Firstly, rest assured that I am, praise God, in the best of health. God grant that we hear from each other only good and pleasing news, amen.

Secondly, the sky has fallen in. The Petersburg closings have knocked us for a loop. It's like being struck by lightning or a bomb. Every broker is in mourning, the Kreshchatik looks hit by an earthquake. And once Petersburg lowered the boom, Warsaw followed suit. It's a disaster, a calamity, a catastrophe! All the investors are wiped out and so am I. The market is finished. The brokerages are deserted. The banks are desperate. It's as bad as the destruction of the Temple! Just imagine, my dear wife, that my Maltzevs, which I put at 2,000 come hell or high water, have gone and closed at 950! Or take Putivils: never in my darkest dreams did I imagine they would drop from 180 to 67. And don't even ask about Transports—Transports are in the pits, no one will touch them. It's the same with Volgas, with Dons, with every share on the board. And that's still nothing compared to Warsaw. Warsaw is a shambles, there hasn't been a slaughter like Warsaw in human history! In Warsaw your Liliputs nosedived from 2,450 to 620. And Roads & Rails! They were looking so good we were sure they would break 3,000. What do you think they're worth now? Would you believe 400 shmegaroos? How's that for a price? I tell you, it couldn't be worse. Who would have thought it of Warsaw? Up, up, up it all goes and suddenly, out of the blue—poof! Nobody knows where it came from. This person says one thing, that person says another. It's all a question of money—that is, of not having it. The Germans call it *Geltmangel,* but in plain Jewish it's known as going broke. . . . But how can that be, you ask, when just yesterday the streets were paved with gold? A good question. Still, everyone is ruined and so am I. To tell the truth, Petersburg is not as bad as Warsaw. The market is down there too, but at least it fell gradually, 20 or 30 points at a time, such things have been known to happen. But Warsaw—Warsaw shouldn't happen to a Jew! Sodom was nothing next to Warsaw. There isn't a day that Warsaw doesn't drop 100, 200,

300 points. We've taken one beating after another, we're too punch-drunk to know what's hit us. Millions have been lost in Warsaw, millions! Good lord, what were we thinking of? If only, my dear wife, I had listened to you, I'd have the world at my feet now. Not even Brodsky could have held a candle to me . . .

But it's the will of God. My time, it seems, has not yet come. The one comfort is that my banker, bless him, hasn't called in my debts. In fact, he's feeling so sorry for me that he's promised to help me make back a few rubles when things pick up. Right now, though, there's nothing to be done. There's not a rally in sight. The investors walk the floor like ghosts. The brokers are out of work. One man's story is more horrible than the next's. The market is dead and buried.

And yet if only I could, I would wait it out and hope for better times. Why take it to heart? It's not, as they say, the end of the world. God's in His heaven and Yehupetz is still on this earth; where there's a will, there's a way. . . . Only where is one to get the capital? Your mother is right about needing a hand to give the finger. I've tried talking a few fellows into a short-term loan, but they swear the whole city is cleaned out; the biggest operators are strapped for cash, everyone is flat on his back. It would take a miracle to save me. I tell you, my dear wife, I can't take any more of this. I'd rather be murdered by cutthroats than starve in the streets of Yehupetz. Why, it's beyond belief! There I was, riding high with everything going my way—and the next minute it's drop dead! But as I'm feeling low, I'll be brief. God willing, I'll write more in my next letter. Meanwhile, God grant you health and success. Write me about the children and how you are, and give my fond greetings to your parents and to everyone.

Your husband,
Menakhem-Mendl

P.S. There's a saying that wealth follows a fire. In fact, now is the time to buy, since everything is dirt cheap. The best stocks can be bought on full margin. I guarantee you that anyone investing in Warsaw or Petersburg today will be a happy man tomorrow. When all is said and done, you see, I know the market inside and out. Only three things are needed to succeed in it: brains, luck, and money. Brains, praise God, I have as much of as any investor in Yehupetz. Luck comes from God. And money? Go ask Brodsky!

Yours, etc.

FROM SHEYNE-SHEYNDL IN KASRILEVKE TO HER HUSBAND MENAKHEM-MENDL IN YEHUPETZ

To my dear, learned, & illustrious husband Menakhem-Mendl, may your light shine!

First, we're all well, thank God. I hope to hear no worse from you.

Second, although there is much that could be said, I've run out of words. What good would they do when all that's left is to stick you in the ground? I'm not like Blume-Zlate who eats men for breakfast. It isn't like me to be a scold. Just tell me one thing, though: as surely as I pray for all my enemies to croak, didn't I predict you would end up like this? Didn't I warn you to run for your life? What did you need all those stockings & bands for? "Stay at home," says my mother, "and you won't wear out your boots!"

But his lordship didn't want to listen. His lordship was sweet on Yehupetz. His lordship was in love with its fine ladies and gentlemen, who aren't worth my little finger. I hope to God I never need a favor from any of them, may He give them a year's worth of chilblains! Do you know what my mother would say? "Better late to synagogue than early to a rich man's house."

And there's something else that baffles me, Mendl. You know it says in the holy books that no one decides when to enter this world and no one decides when to leave it. How can you talk such nonsense? Everything comes from God. You can see for yourself that He wants you to stop dreaming of the easy life in Yehupetz. It's a Jew's job to work hard, sweat blood, and put bread on his family's table. Look at our neighbor Nekhemye. He's a fine young man with an education just like yours—I wish I had as much myself. And yet see how he works like a donkey, goes on foot to all the fairs, runs himself into the ground! I daresay he'd fancy strolling around Yehupetz with a walking stick himself. I daresay he'd cotton to taking hot baths, selling magic charms called shares, riding a sleigh around Boiberik, and watching the ladies play cabbage-glass. But he happens to have a wife called Blume-Zlate. A look from Blume-Zlate and Nekhemye bites his tongue! A nod and he's at her beck and call! Just let him go to Yarmilinetz without bringing her back a hat, a coat, a parasol, or whatever other weird thing she's set her heart on! And what do I get from you? Pie in the sky! Not that I'm waiting with bated breath for your presents. I need your diamond brooches and bracelets like last year's snow. All I want is to see you alive and well, which I'm beginning to doubt I ever will. Last night I dreamed of my Grandma Tsaytl, may she rest in peace, looking exactly as I remembered her. But I want to see you in more than just my dreams—the sooner the better! I am, from the bottom of my heart,

Your truly faithful wife,
Sheyne-Sheyndl

♦♦♦ *Millions: Traders, Agents, and Speculators*

FROM MENAKHEM-MENDL IN YEHUPETZ TO HIS WIFE SHEYNE-SHEYNDL IN KASRILEVKE

To my wise, esteemed, & virtuous wife, Sheyne-Sheyndl, may you have a long life!

Firstly, rest assured that I am, praise God, in the best of health. God grant that we hear from each other only good and pleasing news, amen.

Secondly, I'm through with investing. You can have it! It's no occupation for a Jew. It's made me old and gray before my time. I could write a book on all I've been through. Yehupetz is in ruins. The market has gone bust. There isn't a ray of hope. The carnage, I'm sorry to say, is worse than it was in Odessa. Everyone is in the soup. Everyone is bankrupt and so am I. Filing for bankruptcy is the latest fashion.

What more can I tell you? The biggest bankers have flown the coop. The first to take off was the fellow who underwrote our Warsaw and Petersburg shares. One fine morning I dropped by his office to see about some Maltzevs and Putivils I still owed him for. Where's the big cheese, I ask. It turns out he's taken a powder—all the way to America! To make a long story short, there was a near-riot. His strongbox was broken into and they found a bottle of ink, an old coin, and the sound of his laughter . . .

The next safe to be searched had a box of old Jewish calendars dating back to 1873; its owner was on his way to Palestine. And there was a third fellow, too, who didn't file in time, got clobbered for a few million, and lost everything in a week but his given name. Only Brodsky, by some miracle, came through unscathed. If it isn't in the cards, it seems there's nothing to be done.

Fortunately, I had the wits to look around and find another profession. In short, I'm now in commodities, a trader on the Yehupetz Exchange. They're as common, traders are, as stars in the sky and I asked myself: what do they have that I don't? If it's two hands, two feet, two eyes, and a nose, I have that too, and not a few of them come from families as good as mine. If it isn't beneath them to put on their walking shoes and peddle commodities, why not me also? It doesn't take any expertise. All that's called for is some cheek and a straight face—the straighter, the better. I swear, there are traders in Yehupetz who can barely sign their names and couldn't land a job as a wagon driver or a shop clerk in Kasrilevke. Your mother would say about them: "If God wills it, even a broomstick can shoot like a gun." You only have to put on a white shirt with a nice hat, circulate, make conversation, keep your ear to the ground, bow and scrape a bit, and—"My commission, please!"

A commission is the trader's percentage. A more painless way to make a kopeck has yet to be devised. Just yesterday I earned 50 rubles—so help the two of us if I know what it was for. I also sold 300 tons of sugar as easily as smoking a cigar. That is, the sugar wasn't mine, but I got into the act, which was good for 50 more. With God's help, I'll be back on my feet in half a year, because money is everything in Yehupetz. A man is trash without it. No one cares where you come from. You can be any joker in the deck as long as you have cash. But being in a hurry, I'll be brief. God willing, I'll write more in my next letter. Meanwhile, may He grant you health and success. Give my fond greetings to your parents and the children, each and every one of them.

Your husband,

Menakhem-Mendl

P.S. Please write me all the news, and if there's been rain, and how the beet crop is doing, and whether there are field pests. I need to know as soon as possible!

Yours, etc.

FROM SHEYNE-SHEYNDL IN KASRILEVKE TO HER HUSBAND MENAKHEM-MENDL IN YEHUPETZ

To my dear, learned, & illustrious husband Menakhem-Mendl, may your light shine!

First, we're all well, thank God. I hope to hear no worse from you.

Second, I'm writing you, my sweetheart, to wish a cruel death to all my enemies. You fiend, you murderer, you wicked man! As if you didn't know your wife was lying on her deathbed after being operated on by our wonderful doctor for her corpsicles, may they be poison in the blood of your Yehupetz ladies! I can hardly stand on my feet and your children have come down with every illness there is—their teeth, their throats, their stomachs, the whooping cough, diphtheria, all kinds of horrors I could wish on more deserving people. And you sit in Yehupetz without a word! There's no excuse. If you're dead, the least you could do is let me know, and if you're alive, all the more reason to write.

But go argue with an imbecile! "A drunk grows sober before a fool grows wise," says my mother, more health to her. Just imagine what we've come to when Boruch-Hirsh and Leah-Dvosi's Sheyne-Sheyndl has to have a trader for a husband! But I suppose it's worth being anything to live in Yehupetz—a bagel vendor, a dog trainer, even a trader. You write that you've made fifty rubles in your fine new business and hope to make as much each day. As if every day were payday! Have you forgotten your Odessa Lumdums, and your Pottyboils and your Lilyfoots, and all your golden opportunities that are ashes in my mouth? Your eyes, you dunce, will fall from your head fifty times before you see fifty rubles again! I don't believe one bit in your Yehupetz windfalls, which start with a bang and end with a lot of hot air.

And as for your having your wits about you, permit me my doubts. What are you asking about rain for? Did you expect it to snow in midsummer? And what does a man like you care about beets? Now is the time for sorrel borscht. There won't be beets before autumn. We have enough pests in the form of bedbugs without your becoming one too. Isn't there enough to occupy you in Yehupetz, with all the sugar and rubles coming your way?

But it's as my mother, bless her, says: When a madman breaks a window, it's never his own. . . . Listen to me, Mendl: put aside your foolishness, and if you still have those fifty rubles, come on home. If you don't, I'll send you carfare. Keep in mind that you have a wife and little children who await you every day. It's time I stopped being the talk of the town and my cheeks no longer burned with shame.

I am, from the bottom of my heart,

Your truly faithful wife,
Sheyne-Sheyndl

If people interested you half as much as beets, I suppose you'd ask about them. But what's it to you if my mother has broken off my little sister's engagement? I suppose you think it was over money. Well, money had nothing to do with it. It started when my sister's fiancé came for a Sabbath meal. He and my mother began to quarrel, and his father being a butcher, she said you can't expect veal from an ox. One thing led to another and the blamed fellow went home and tore up the engagement contract. It's the third time poor Nekhameh-Breindl hasn't made it to her own wedding.

FROM MENAKHEM-MENDL IN YEHUPETZ TO HIS WIFE SHEYNE-SHEYNDL IN KASRILEVKE

To my wise, esteemed, & virtuous wife Sheyne-Sheyndl, may you have a long life!

Firstly, rest assured that I am, praise God, in the best of health. May God grant that we hear from each other only good and pleasing news, amen.

Secondly, you misconstrued what I wrote. My having given up investing for commodities is no reason to worry, because it's all for the best. I'm not the only trader in Yehupetz. We have, I don't mind telling you, a whole slew of them. There are sugar traders, and bond traders, and wheat traders, and money traders, and property traders, and lumber traders, and diamond traders, and manufacturing traders, and freight traders, and whatever else your heart desires. Nothing gets done without a trader—in fact without two, since someone with a seller needs someone with a buyer. Moreover, it's not uncommon for a few more traders to come along for the ride. They split the commission, and if they can't agree on it, they either ask an outsider to decide or resort to the tried-and-true Odessa method of pugilistic arbitration.

Now you know what a trader is. And the biggest traders of all are the sugar traders, since all the sugar passes through their hands. They're rich as the devil, ride around in carriages, live in dachas in Boiberik, play cards all day long, and have courtasins and conquerbines. In a word, commodities are the best business because you needn't invest a cent. It's all off the top. If you and I strike a deal, the two of us make a pretty penny, and if we don't, it's off to bed for us both without our supper. Of course, you're quite right: 50 rubles don't come along every day. In fact, my first transaction was my last one and the 50 smackers didn't last long, since I have so many debts that I don't even own the hairs on my head. In the end I was left with a bit of change that I gave to charity and I'm now out of pocket again.

Never mind, though! With God's help I hope to have a business going soon, at which time I'll send you a money order. And regarding your question about rain, it's really quite simple. Sugar, as you know, is made from beets, and beets can't grow without rain. If God is good it will be a rainless summer and pests will eat all the beets. That means there'll be no sugar, or rather, sugar will be worth its weight in gold. The speculators will make a killing, the traders will get their commissions, and so will I. But as I'm busy and in a hurry, I'll be brief. God willing I'll write more in my next letter. Meanwhile, may He grant you health and success. Give the children my greetings, each and every one of them.

Your husband,

Menakhem-Mendl

P.S. As for your sister, if she isn't engaged again, I have just the man for her. He's a rare find, a Yehupetzer and still a bachelor, although not as young as all that. In fact he's a graybeard and getting on in years. I can't say he's rich, either. But he has a good job—that is, he's in sugar. It's the perfect match, in my opinion, because he's a very quiet fellow. If the notion takes your fancy, send me a telegram or post card and I'll come out with him.

Yours, etc.

FROM SHEYNE-SHEYNDL IN KASRILEVKE TO HER HUSBAND MENAKHEM-MENDL IN YEHUPETZ

To my dear, learned, & illustrious husband Menakhem-Mendl, may your light shine!

First, we're all well, thank God. I hope to hear no worse from you.

Second, may all the bad dreams I dreamed last night, and the night before that, and every night of the year before that, come true for my enemies. Happy times are here again! If it doesn't rain there won't be beets, and if there are no beets there won't be sugar, and if there is no sugar you may actually make some money. Talk about skinning the bear before it's shot! Suppose I tell you, Mendl, that it has been raining cats and dogs, and that beets are growing like nobody's business, and that there isn't a pest in sight besides bedbugs and cockroaches. What would you say to that? I swear to God, I knew all along that nothing would remain of those fifty blasted rubles. Why remember you have a wife who may live to see you again when you can give all you have to charity? A year's worth of heartburn I would have given! A fine lot of charity *you*'d get if ever you went knocking on Yehupetz's doors. "Families," says my mother, "have brothers. Pockets don't."

But I have only myself to blame. Not everyone would do for a husband what I've done. All that fancy living has gone to his lordship's head. He goes about Yehupetz like a count, has everything but rain and pests, and leaves me to lead a dog's life. Nothing goes right for me. I have a little boy, Moyshe-Hirshele, drat his soul? Leave it to him to fall and split his lip. I have a wedding ring with gold filigree? Naturally, the servant girl steals it. I catch it coming and going. I should have listened to my mother when she said, "Never throw your luck out with the dishwater . . . "

Was I right or not that fifty rubles can't be had for the asking? And as for the lovely match you have for Nekhameh-Breindl, your old graybeard can split his gut first. Yehupetz won't live to see the day we marry into it. Guess who my sister is being fixed up with now: her first fiancé, since married and divorced and ready for more! It seems the rogue is stuck on her for good. Well, better a thief you know than a rabbi you don't, says my mother. . . . As soon as they're engaged there'll be a wedding, and I'd like to see you not show up for it. I am, from the bottom of my heart,

Your truly faithful wife,
Sheyne-Sheyndl

Our Kopl has done it again. He's gone bankrupt for three hundred rubles and can now show his face without fearing the bailiff. And your Uncle Menashe's son Berl had another fire—a hundred rubles' worth of damage for which the insurance paid three-fifty. Something tells me it's our last one, because they say the company has stopped insuring Jews. And I almost forgot: Miriam-Beyle has stopped wearing a wig and goes around with her own hair in public! I suppose she thinks she's high society—pretty soon she'll be playing cards. But I don't like to gossip. "Mind your business," says my mother, "and no one else will mind it for you." . . . Just tell me about "courtasins" and "conquerbines." What are they and what do you do with them?

FROM MENAKHEM-MENDL IN YEHUPETZ TO HIS WIFE SHEYNE-SHEYNDL IN KASRILEVKE

To my wise, esteemed, & virtuous wife Sheyne-Sheyndl, may you have a long life!

Firstly, rest assured that I am, praise God, in the best of health. May we hear from each other only good and pleasing news, amen.

Secondly, you're absolutely right. The sugar business is not for me. There's no competing with the big traders. You can't close a deal without them muscling in—and go file a complaint against God. "It isn't fair" cuts no ice in Yehupetz. Fairness is not at a premium here; no one owes you an explanation or apology. That's for starters. And besides, I ask you: what kind of business is it in which you have to look at the sky every day and either pray for rain or against it? In a word, I'm not cut out for it. Not only do you have to be a bluffer, you have to work a seven-day week and jaw away at the speculators until they're so flummoxed they break into a cold sweat. I assure you, it isn't for me. And being as ready as the next man to earn an honest ruble, I now have, with God's help, a more suitable line of work. In a word, I'm in finance—that is,

I'm a factor—I mean I buy and sell loans at a modest discount. How does the saying go? "Earning less and sleeping well is earning best." It's a business in which you're treated with respect, since lack of cash makes a man soft as wax; you should see them crawl to me on all fours and promise to pay me back mountains of gold! Why, just the other day God sent me a garment cutter from Berdichev who wants to start his own business. I first met him in my boarding house, a rare young man of sterling character. If only I can open him a line of credit for 10–15,000 rubles, he says, he'll reward me so handsomely that I can give up factoring for good. Although I have yet to find him financing, I trust, with God's help, that I will.

All the factors do well and own horses. A good horse and buggy, you should know, is a big help in making a living, since here in Yehupetz a horse is worth more than a man. But as I'm busy and in a hurry, I'll be brief. God willing, I'll write more in my next letter. Meanwhile, may He grant you health and success. My fondest greetings to your parents and the children, each and every one.

Your husband,
Menakhem-Mendl

P.S. Kopl's bankruptcy would be small potatoes in Yehupetz. No Yehupetz merchant is taken seriously until he's gone bankrupt at least three times. Once the custom was for a bankrupt to leave town, but that's no longer in vogue. It's not even called bankruptcy any more. The expression is, "I'm in arrears." In plain language that means, "Kiss my rear." And as for your query regarding courtasins and conquerbines, they're what's known as *pilagshim* in Hebrew and *Kepsweiber* in German. Believe me, I wouldn't waste a moment's thought on them.

FROM SHEYNE-SHEYNDL IN KASRILEVKE TO HER HUSBAND MENAKHEM-MENDL IN YEHUPETZ

To my dear, learned, & illustrious husband Menakhem-Mendl, may your light shine!

First, we're all well, thank God. I hope to hear no worse from you.

Second, I wish all my enemies would burst from the bellyful your last letter gave me. First you're a sugar-pusher, now you're a money-lender! Where do you get the money from? And if God helps you to a few rubles, must you blow them as fast as you can? Didn't you promise to send me a money order as soon as you had some cash? How could you go back on your word? My mother, bless her, had your number when she said, "Don't hold your breath waiting for him, because nothing good comes from a graveyard." And not from a charming place like Yehupetz either, for which the flames of hell aren't hot enough. "Daughter," said my mother, "always remember this prayer: Protect me, dear God, from a Berdichev tycoon, an Uman fanatic, a Mohilev skeptic, a Konstantin servant, a Kamenetz politician, and a Yehupetz rogue." Was she right or not? But what does his lordship care about his wife and children? Day and night it's Sheyne-Sheyndl do this and Sheyne-Sheyndl do that. I suppose you remember the kopeck that Moyshe-Hirshele swallowed last year. Well, this time he goes, the boy does (did I say boy? he's a demon!), and all but takes leave of this world. One day he's a healthy child and the next he's barely alive, clutching his ear and screaming in a voice I don't recognize. "What is it, my darling?" I say. "What hurts you?" But he only points to his ear and keeps screaming. I poke him, I kiss him, I pinch him, I hug him—he just screams and screams. On the third day I took him to the doctor. The first thing the genius asks is have I looked in the child's ear. "Not only have I looked," I say, "I've drilled with a knitting needle. There's nothing there." "Tell me," he says, "what did you have for your Sabbath meal?" "We had the usual," I say. "Radishes, onions, jellied calf's foot, a noodle pudding—is that enough for you?" "How about beans?" he says. "Did you cook beans or peas or the like?" "What does that have to do with anything?" I ask. "Since when do peas cause an earache?" "If there were peas around," he says, "your child might have played with one and stuck it in his ear. It could have begun to sprout there . . . " To make a long story short, he fetched a machine, tortured that poor child for half an hour, and pulled out a fistful of peas. Maybe you can tell me why the whole world stuffs itself with peas and nothing happens and my son makes medical history! But you know what my mother says: "With the right kind of luck you can break your nose falling on grass . . . "

To get to the point, my dear husband, why lend money to Berdichev bankrupts and swindlers? Take your few rubles and come home! You're sure to find a good business here. "Money," says my mother, "can buy everything but a fever." I am, from the bottom of my heart,

Your truly faithful wife,
Sheyne-Sheyndl

Do me a favor, Mendl. Write me no more about your Yehupetz charlatans and their *Kepsweiber*—I don't want to hear the filthy word. They should all roast! Listen to this instead. The son of Levi Moyshe-Mendes, Berish is his name (that's after his grandfather Reb Berishl, may the old scoundrel rest in pieces), turned up this week with two accomplices at Libe Moyshe-Mordekhai's store and said to Libe's daughter Feygl (Fanitshke she calls herself—what a name!), "Fanitshke, my love," he says, "come let me look at your finger." So Fanitshke shows him her finger and he slips a ring on it and tells his friends, "You're my witnesses that I've taken Fanitshke as my wife according to Jewish law." You should have seen the commotion! Libe fainted dead away. The whole town came running with its mouth open. Everyone put in his two cents. In the end they went to the rabbi, who told Berish to give Fanitshke a divorce. But Fanitshke said she didn't want one. She was, she said, in love with him. The poor girl is hopelessly in-*fat*-you-ated, the two of them planned it together. Just put yourself in place of the father! And I thought I had problems . . .

FROM MENAKHEM-MENDL IN YEHUPETZ TO HIS WIFE SHEYNE-SHEYNDL IN KASRILEVKE

To my wise, esteemed, & virtuous wife Sheyne-Sheyndl, may you have a long life!

Firstly, rest assured that I am, praise God, in the best of health. God grant that we hear from each other only good and pleasing news, amen.

Secondly, finance is strictly for beggars. Lending money is not a bad occupation provided the money is your own. When it's someone else's, all you get is the runaround. And God preserve you from falling into the clutches of a loan shark, one of your garden-variety Berdichev, Vinnitse, or Shpole twenty-percenters, let alone the big bankers, who give you such a hard time that you're better off clipping lottery coupons. . . . In short, I've sent finance to the devil and now am in real estate. Why real estate? Because it's all the rage. If you think buying a house in Yehupetz is like buying a house in Kasrilevke, you're mistaken. The first thing you do here is take a mortgage from the bank; next you take a second mortgage; then you rent out the rooms and have an income. In a word, the house costs nothing and you're its lucky owner! Why, then, you ask, doesn't everyone buy one? Because not everyone can afford the down payment. If, with God's help, the deal I'm working on pans out (I have several in the fire), I'll buy a place for 20,000, not a red cent of which will be mine, and register it in your name. The arithmetic is simple: 15,000 comes from the first bank, 6,000 from the second, and a thousand stays with me. That's enough to live off for a while, even minus the rent and other goodies. Where do you think all the fortunes in Yehupetz come from? But since I'm busy and in a hurry, I'll be brief. God willing, I'll write more in my next letter. Meanwhile, may He grant you health and success. Give my fondest greetings to the children, each and every one.

Your husband,

Menakhem-Mendl

P.S. What you write about Levi Moyshe-Mendes' son and Libe's daughter would be back-page news in Yehupetz. Here falling in love is a must; without it there's simply no match. It's not unusual for a man to throw over his wife for another woman he's fallen in love with, or for a woman to throw over her husband. Sometimes the woman who was thrown over falls in love with the husband of the wife who was thrown over—I mean, with the husband of the wife who threw over her husband. How did the rabbis put it? "What's mine is yours and what's yours is mine." That's Yehupetz!

Yours, etc.

FROM SHEYNE-SHEYNDL IN KASRILEVKE TO HER HUSBAND MENAKHEM-MENDL IN YEHUPETZ

To my dear, learned, & illustrious husband Menakhem-Mendl, may your light shine!

First, we're all well, thank God. I hope to hear no worse from you.

Second, who ever heard of a man walking out on his wife, children, and in-laws, moving to a strange town, and changing his line of work twice a day? First he pushes sugar, then he lends money, and before you know it he's buying houses on the house! I daresay it would be a fine business if only owning a house that you owe more for it than it's worth weren't worse than being trapped in a fire. (Speaking of which, why doesn't one burn down Yehupetz?) Lucky me! As soon as his lordship's chickens hatch, he'll buy me a house in my name. What do I need another house for? Send money and I'd know what to do with it. As my mother, God bless her, would say, "Bring the bread and I'll find the cutting knife . . . "

I suppose I should make my peace with the fact that life has it in for me. Still, I can't help thinking: here I am a Jewish wife like Blume-Zlate, she's no prettier than I am, she's certainly no smarter or cleverer—why do I end up in the doghouse while she gets more full of juices by the day? Dear God, I'd like to see her dry up like an old hag! And yet to be honest, what do I have against Blume-Zlate? What harm has she done me? I wouldn't mind her reaching a ripe old age with her Nekhemye if only God were nicer to me. "Better to wish yourself well than another ill," as my mother says.

It makes my heart ache to see people living such fine lives when I have to sit here like a widow in black, waiting to hear from my fine breadwinner! Each day I think: this could be our lucky one. Perhaps a buried treasure will come your way and you'll build me a palace in Yehupetz! But your fine Yehupetz wife-swappers can break all their bones before I throw away my wig and give up everything to become your *Kepsweib* there. I wish you well from the bottom of my heart,

Your truly faithful wife,

Sheyne-Sheyndl

My mother says, "It's not brains or good looks that a person needs, it's luck." Take Nekhameh-Breindl and my Aunt Dvoyreh's daughter Rokhl. Nekhameh-Breindl glows like the summer sun and Rokhl is sour as vinegar. So what happens? Poor Nekhameh-Breindl is a wallflower and Rokhl finds a husband—a fine, honest fellow, an idiot from

Yampele. That is, he has his brains in his behind, but he comes from a good family. The only thing wrong with it, they say, is that a sister of his has been baptized. And his health is poor, too, which means he needn't fear the draft. They're a lovely couple—she doesn't mind his not being too bright and he doesn't mind her not looking so good. But beauty makes nothing good, my mother says. It's goodness that makes everything beautiful.

FROM MENAKHEM-MENDL IN YEHUPETZ TO HIS WIFE SHEYNE-SHEYNDL IN KASRILEVKE

To my wise, esteemed, & virtuous wife Sheyne-Sheyndl, may you have a long life!

Firstly, rest assured that I am, praise God, in the best of health. God grant that we hear from each other only good and pleasing news, amen.

Secondly, Yehupetz real estate is for the birds. I'm now in country property. Country property is a different kettle of fish. In the first place, you needn't wear out your shoes. You mail a letter, get back an itemized praysee, send your customer for a look—and with God's help, you've rung up a sale. And in the second place, you're not dealing with a lot of poor devils. You're talking landed gentry—princes, counts, grafs. How do I get to rub elbows with grafs? That's a story in itself.

You know I'm not supposed to be in Yehupetz. Well, now and then the police show up at our boarding house to search for bad apples. We're always tipped off in advance by our landlady and away we melt like salt in water—some of us to Boiberik, some to Demyevka, and some to Slobodka. This time, though, the landlady wasn't warned herself. A bad business! There we were, sound asleep in the middle of the night, when there's a knock. The landlady jumps out of bed. The cat's at the door, all mice in the straw! Naturally, there's a rush for the exits. Half of us head for the cellar and the other half for the attic, including me. Next to me is a Jew from Kamenetz, and as we're lying on the floor with aching ribs he lets out a groan. "What's the matter?" I whisper. "I just remembered something," he says. "I left my papers under my pillow. I'm worried sick about my papers!" "What papers are those?" I ask. "Oy," he says, "very important ones. We're talking half-a-million at the least." Well, as soon as I hear half-a-million, I turn on my back and whisper, "What papers can be worth all that money?" "It's country property," he says. "I have property in Volhynia, a big estate with the latest equipment, and horses, and oxen, and more sheep than you can count, and water mills, and breweries, and farmyards, and top-notch gardeners, all in perfect condition!"

I moved closer to him when I heard that. How does a Jew come by such a property? "I didn't grow it in a compost heap," he says. "It belongs to gentry and I'm the agent. I've come to Yehupetz with all the papers—the deed, the praysee, everything. What am I supposed to do now?" "For God's sake, don't do anything," I say. "Who's going to steal your property? Just pray the cops stay out of this attic." After a while I gave him a poke and asked: "Have you found a buyer in Yehupetz?" "No," he says, "not yet. I don't trust the locals. They're the worst kind of liars. You can't believe a word they say. Maybe you know an honest real estate agent, someone reliable?" "Do I?" I say. "It's an honor to be introduced! I'm a real estate agent myself. Not that I've ever dealt in country property—but if God sends me the right buyer, I'll know what to do with him." "I can see," says he, "that I'm talking to an honorable gentleman. Give me your hand and let's shake on it! It will be just the two of us. I'll give you the papers and you'll handle it." In short, we're now partners. He finds the properties and I look for the buyers. And since I'm busy and in a hurry, I'll be brief. God willing, I'll write more in my next letter. Meanwhile, may He grant you health and success. Give my fondest greetings to the children (I hope they're well) and to everyone.

Your husband,
Menakhem-Mendl

P.S. The scare in the boarding house was a false alarm. It was just a neighbor tapping on the window. But see how the Lord provides. If not for the neighbor there would have been no scare, if not for the scare we wouldn't have run to the attic, if not for the attic I wouldn't have met the Jew from Kamenetz, and if not for the Jew from Kamenetz I wouldn't be selling country property. Now wish me success!

Yours etc.

FROM SHEYNE-SHEYNDL IN KASRILEVKE TO HER HUSBAND MENAKHEM-MENDL IN YEHUPETZ

To my dear, learned, & illustrious husband Menakhem-Mendl, may your light shine!

First, we're all well, thank God. I hope to hear no worse from you.

Second, I have a bad cough. Your Yehupetz ladies should catch it from me. I've been drinking goat's milk and went to see the doctor. Quite a living they make from me, the doctors! They should all drop dead and take the pharmacist with them. But at least we now have a second pharmacy in town and can haggle over prices.

Congratulations on your new business with all its counts and country properties! At this rate, you'll soon run out of things to do. One would think someone as successful as yourself would be less critical of your former professions. But it's as my mother says: "When a girl can't dance, she blames the musicians . . . "

I fear, Mendl, that once you've tried everything, you'll be reduced to peddling matches like Aunt Sosie's son Getzl who ran off to America. He thought he would live like a king there and now he writes letters that could break a heart of stone. In America, he writes, you either work yourself to death or die of hunger. No one gives a starving man a crust of bread. A fine place it is, America—it deserves to burn with Yehupetz! Don't say you haven't been warned. "When there's bread," says my mother, "don't hanker after sweets." But perhaps there'll be a miracle and we'll hear better news from you—and sooner received than Getzl's. I wish you nothing but the best,

Your truly faithful wife,
Sheyne-Sheyndl

"Heaven and earth," says my mother, "have sworn to let nothing vanish"—and so along comes a government investigator to sniff out what happened to the money that Moyshe-Mordekhai willed for the public good. Some young rascals ratted on you-know-who but he produced accounts showing he didn't have it. Where could it be? Only the wind knows. I hope to God he rots in jail for what he did!

FROM MENAKHEM-MENDL IN YEHUPETZ TO HIS WIFE SHEYNE-SHEYNDL IN KASRILEVKE

To my wise, esteemed, & virtuous wife Sheyne-Sheyndl, may you have a long life!

Firstly, rest assured that I am, praise God, in the best of health. God grant that we hear from each other only good and pleasing news, amen.

Secondly, I'm now holding over a million's worth of country property. No one has ever seen the likes of it. Where, you ask, does it all come from? Listen to this.

One day while I was at the Exchange with my partner from Kamenetz, we let it be known that we had an estate. A group of agents gathered round, all with country property too, and pretty soon we decided on a joint venture. In a word, we pooled properties—we gave them our listings and they gave us theirs. It's a no-lose proposition. If we sell their properties, we'll make good money, and if they sell ours, we'll make better. Either way, we stand only to gain.

The upshot is that I'm in tight with all the agents and have acquired quite a reputation. I sit with them in Semadenni's at marble tables like Fanconi's and drink coffee and eat French pastries. That's how it works here, too: if you don't order, you're out in the street. Semadenni's is the real Yehupetz Exchange. All the traders in town gather there. It's as loud and noisy as (you should pardon the comparison) a synagogue. The entire place shouts, laughs, talks with its hands. There's a lot of fighting and quarreling too, which usually ends up in court because no one can agree on splitting the commissions. Everyone swears, curses, uses his fists, and so do I. And being busy and in a hurry, I'll be brief. God willing, I'll write more in my next letter. Meanwhile, may He grant you health and success. Give my fondest greeting to your parents and the children, God bless them, each and every one.

Your husband,

Menakhem-Mendl

P.S. One of my properties in Volhynia has a chateau. It has 66 rooms paneled with mirrors and an indoor garden called an orangeade with citrus trees growing all year round. That's quite apart from the horses and carriages, which are a sight to behold—and it's going for next to nothing! If God sends me a customer, I'm in the clover. Of course, country agents tend to exaggerate because their tongues run away with them, but I fear there's nothing to be done about that. You can't make a living by telling nothing but the truth.

Yours, etc.

FROM SHEYNE-SHEYNDL IN KASRILEVKE TO HER HUSBAND MENAKHEM-MENDL IN YEHUPETZ

To my dear, learned, & illustrious husband Menakhem-Mendl, may your light shine!

First, we're all well, thank God. I hope to hear no worse from you.

Second, the devil take all your fine letters! I'm ashamed to show them to a soul. "The worse heartache," says my mother, "is the one you can't bare." I ask you, what kind of business is it to sit all day at Sima-Dina's drinking coffee with French pastry as though it were a Saturday night? (And who the deuce is Sima-Dina, I'd like to know! We once had a healer in Kasrilevke by that name, but she's long passed on to the other world.) You have a shanty with sixty-six rooms? Well, bless my soul! My enemies should die sixty-six times! What is it to the lord of Yehupetz if I break my back day and night for his children? Just yesterday little Leah had a fight with Moyshe-Hirshele and stuck a fork in his face. It was sheer luck he didn't lose an eye. But what good does it do to tell you such things when they go in one ear and out the other? You're a heartless fiend! I could write until I burst while his lordship sits in bloody Yehupetz drinking coffee and watching the traders trade punches at the Exchange. I wish to God someone would give you the punch you deserve! It might knock some sense into you. I am, from the bottom of my heart,

Your truly faithful wife,
Sheyne-Sheyndl

You can flaunt your hoity-toity connections all you want, Mendl, but listen to a true story about our two Kasrilevke doctors, Dr. Kubeybe and

Dr. Lakritz. They fight like alleycats. Not long ago Dr. Kubeybe went and told on Dr. Lakritz for overdosing a child. So naturally, Dr. Lakritz went and told on Dr. Kubeybe for insuring corpses with Fayvl the insurance agent. Then Dr. Kubeybe told on Dr. Lakritz for . . . but they should both fry for our sins and those of Jews everywhere!

FROM MENAKHEM-MENDL IN YEHUPETZ TO HIS WIFE SHEYNE-SHEYNDL IN KASRILEVKE

To my wise, esteemed, & virtuous wife Sheyne-Sheyndl, may you have a long life!

Firstly, rest assured that I am, praise God, in the best of health. God grant that we hear from each other only good and pleasing news, amen.

Secondly, I'm now in lumber. A country property without woodland, it seems, is like a house without a stove. Lumber is the magic word. It's the key to success, men make millions from it.

Naturally, you'll want to know how I came to lumber. Listen to what the good Lord can do. Being in country property and hanging around with all the agents, I ran into a real heavyweight one day. "Well, what have you got for me?" he asks. "Come, let's have a look." I opened my briefcase and showed him listings worth a million-seven and he says, "Excuse me for saying so, but all your properties aren't worth a pinch of snuff." "How's that?" I ask. "It's because," says he, "they don't come with anything. You're selling a lot of earth and sky. Where's the woodland? What do I want with a property that has no lumber? Don't just stand there, man! Give me lumber, lumber!" It was such a shock to think I had been selling worthless property that I couldn't get out a word. "Well, then," I said at last, "show me a nice estate with woodland and I have the customer already lined up." "That will be my pleasure," he says. "I have a forest for you that no man has ever set foot in. It has trees old as the world, oaks high as the clouds. They're the original cedars of Lebanon! And there's a railroad on one side and a river on the other. *Chop-chop, splash,* and your trees are floating to the sawmill!"

Well, who needed to hear more? Off I ran to find a buyer. And don't think God didn't lend a hand! I heard of a customer and sent an agent to sound him out via a second agent who had a third test the water. (Don't worry about that. If the deal goes through, God willing, there'll be enough for us all.) Then I went to see the fellow myself. "For you," I said, "I have a forest as old as the world. There's a railroad on one side and a river on the other—*chop-chop, splash,* and your trees are floating to the sawmill!" He took a fancy to it at once and wanted to know everything: what was the forest called, and exactly where was it, and how many acres did it have, and what kind of trees grew in it, and how tall and how wide were they, and were they hardwood or softwood, and how high off the ground were the bottom branches, and how did you reach the place, and was there a good road to it, and did it snow there in winter . . . there were so many questions I couldn't get in a word. On and on he went until he said: "But why waste words? Bring me a praysee and we'll talk." "What do you need a praysee for?" I said. "It won't take a minute to find the seller. He's better than a thousand praysees." In short, I brought him to my man's room. They took one look at each other and began to laugh so hard I thought they would have a stroke. "So this is the owner of your forest?" asks the first fellow. "And this is your buyer?" says the second. Just then the door opens and in walks a Jew from Belaya Tserkov. In no time the table is cleared, cards are brought out, and the four of us sit down to a hand of whist. Tomorrow we'll try to close the deal. But as I'm busy and in a hurry, I'll be brief. God willing, I'll write more in my next letter. Meanwhile, may He grant you health and success. Give my regards to your parents, and my fondest greetings to each of the children.

Your husband,

Menakhem-Mendl

FROM SHEYNE-SHEYNDL IN KASRILEVKE TO HER HUSBAND MENAKHEM-MENDL IN YEHUPETZ

To my dear, learned, & illustrious husband Menakhem-Mendl, may your light shine!

First, we're all well, thank God. I hope to hear no worse from you.

Second, I don't call this a life. "If this is the transportation," my mother would say, "let me off and I'll walk . . . " I can imagine, God help us, what big businessmen you must be if you can afford to drop a deal worth millions to play whist. I wish you'd waste away from your whist as I'm wasting away from my cough! For God's sake, has it come to this, that a husband who didn't know what a deck of cards looked like is now a cardsharp? Is that what the tender young man I married wants to be in his old age? And you know what you can do with all your forests! What on earth do you know about trees? When did you last sit and watch one grow? My mother, bless her, would say: "What is the rabbi doing raising pigs?" If you ask me, your fine lumber business will go up in smoke like all your other golden occupations. Still, I wish you nothing but the best.

Your truly faithful wife,
Sheyne-Sheyndl

The whole world is talking about you. Not long ago my cousin Kreindl ran into my mother in the marketplace, near the fish stalls, and chewed her ear off. Why, she wanted to know, didn't I divorce you and put an end to it? Mind you, my mother didn't even try keeping up appearances. She didn't argue. All she said was: "The pillow that sleeps two doesn't need a third head. . . . Better an old pot than a new kettle. . . . Friends are like weeds: they pop up without being asked. . . . Criticism starts at home. . . . One man eats garlic and another smells of it. . . . An ox has a big tongue and still can't blow the shofar . . . " She said a few other things too, my mother did. In fact, she left Kreindl speechless.

FROM MENAKHEM-MENDL IN YEHUPETZ TO HIS WIFE SHEYNE-SHEYNDL IN KASRILEVKE

To my wise, esteemed, & virtuous wife Sheyne-Sheyndl, may you have long life!

Firstly, rest assured that I am, praise God, in the best of health. God grant that we hear from each other only good and pleasing news, amen.

Secondly, my woodland has turned out to be a wilderness. There wasn't a tree in it, let alone a forest or a river. It was all one big waste of time, a lot of worn shoe leather! I now see, my dear wife, that lumber is not for me. I'm not made for dealing with liars. They'll sell you castles in the air and stick you six feet in the ground.

What am I doing now? I'm in a new business—sugar mills. That's something you can't beat nowadays. Jews are buying sugar mills and the agents are cleaning up. There's a fellow from Belaya Tserkov who goes every week to Radomishl, sells the Jews there two or three mills, and is back home in time for the Sabbath with 10 or 15,000 rubles in his wallet! What more could you want? Ordinary servants, ex–household help, are dealing in mills. They walk around with gold watches, speak German, send their wives to the best spas, take pills for their livers, and carry on like bluebloods! In a word, sugar mills are the only game in Yehupetz. The whole world is into them and so am I.

You must be wondering how I became involved with a business about which I didn't know a blessed thing, even though it's quite elementary. Listen to how God works. A while back I stopped going to Semadenni's (and not, as you call him, Sima-Dina—he's a man, not a woman, and a nasty one!). It wasn't because we had quarreled but because I was tired of all that coffee and pastry. Besides, I had run out of money. And so I hung out in the street like the other Jews and one thing led to another until I met a mill agent, a fine fellow who knows the business inside out. There's no one in sugar, he says, not even Brodsky, in whose home he doesn't come and go. "Where," he asks me, "do you come from?" "From Kasrilevke," I say. "That is, I'm originally from Yampol and I'm registered in Mazepevke, but I have a wife in Kasrilevke and do business in Yehupetz." "So tell me," he asks, "this Kasrilevke of yours—is it a town or a village?" "A town?" I say. "Kasrilevke is a regular city." "And a Jew can live there?" he asks. Honestly, what a question! "And a river," he asks, "do you have a river?" "Do we have a river!" I say. "The Shtinkeylo flows right through the place." "And a railroad?" he asks. "How far is the nearest railroad?" "The nearest railroad," I say, "is no more than seventy versts off. But tell me, what makes you ask?" "First," he says, "give me your hand and promise to keep this a secret. I tell you, Reb Menakhem-Mendl, we're about to make a barrel of money! I just had an idea that comes to a man once in a hundred years. You see, everyone is out to buy a sugar mill these days but there aren't any mills left. Those Radomishl Jews have bought them all and no one is selling. The latest thing is to build them from scratch—and since Jews are barred from the villages, everyone is looking for a town. You can see for yourself," he says, "that God created Kasrilevke to have a sugar mill—and as I live and breathe, I have the man to build it, an investor with half a million rubles. The problem is finding a site. Do you know anyone in Kasrilevke who can tell us if there's enough beets and room for a mill?" "Do I?" I say. "You bet I do! My whole family lives there—my wife, my children, and my in-laws. I'll write at once. You'll have a thoroughly thorough answer in a jiffy!"

And so, my dear wife, please talk to old Azriel and Moyshe the redhead, since they pal around with Russian gentry. Find out how many beets we can count on and what they'll cost and write me back at once, because it's urgent. We can make a tidy sum from this, a good 10 or 15,000. But being busy and in a hurry, I'll be brief. God willing, I'll write more in my next letter. Meanwhile, may he grant you health and success. Give my fondest greetings to everyone.

Your husband,
Menakhem-Mendl

P.S. I asked my new partner who his investor is and was told it was a Jew from Radomishl. He's all fired up to make the deal because the Radomishl Jews are big on sugar mills. He's even willing to buy an old windmill, he says, as long as it has a chimney that works. I pray to God it's as good as it sounds and we'll make some money from it, even though there are quite a few partners—it's beginning to look like close to a dozen. But I hope this is the real thing at last. You know I put no stock in get-rich-quick schemes.

FROM SHEYNE-SHEYNDL IN KASRILEVKE TO HER HUSBAND MENAKHEM-MENDL IN YEHUPETZ

To my dear, learned, & illustrious husband Menakhem-Mendl, may your light shine!

First, we're all well, thank God. I hope to hear no worse from you.

Second, I must have read your song-and-dance a dozen times and I still don't know what you want. Is there room in Kasrilevke? There's enough room in our new cemetery alone to bury half of Yehupetz. And what is this river you talk about? I hope you and your partners have more luck than we have water in our river. By Passover time we're drinking tadpoles and in summer it's as grassy as a lawn. Let your Yehupetz bluebeards take a sip of it in the month of Tammuz and they'll need their liver pills indeed.

No, Mendl, let their livers rot in Yehupetz and we'll get along without their sugar mills here. "Passover cleaning," my mother says, "comes and goes, but the house remains the same house." Get all that claptrap out of your head. You'll sell as many mills as you've sold forests, country property, Yehupetz real estate, and sugar. I promise you that your partners will clean you out before you know it, because you were born a sucker and a sucker you'll always be. I wish you all the best,

Your truly faithful wife,
Sheyne-Sheyndl

One more thing, Mendl. What's this we hear about registering in Yehupetz to go to the Land of Israel? A forty-kopeck subscription, we're told, will get you there. What's the lowdown? Here in Kasrilevke it's all anyone talks about. The young folk sit up discussing it all night at Yosl Moyshe-Yosi's. In short, things are going from bad to worse. But if you want peace and quiet, my mother says, you should look for it in the grave . . .

FROM MENAKHEM-MENDL IN YEHUPETZ TO HIS WIFE SHEYNE-SHEYNDL IN KASRILEVKE

To my wise, esteemed, & virtuous wife Sheyne-Sheyndl, may you have a long life!

Firstly, rest assured that I am, praise God, in the best of health. God grant that we hear from each other only good and pleasing news, amen.

Secondly, sugar mills are in a slump. It's sellers only. Money is so dear and sugar is so cheap that you can't give the stuff away. The business is kaput. The millers are fighting to stay alive. The investors are gone, the agents are out of work, and so am I.

I suppose you think I'm in a bad way. Never fear, my dear wife. God's in His heaven and Yehupetz is still around, too. You can trust me to land on my feet. In fact, I have reason to believe that I'm about to hit the jackpot, since my latest line promises a return of 100,000 to one. I'm talking ten million rubles, maybe more—the sky is the limit! That's because gold, they say, will soon hit record highs. Well, then, I ask you: what about silver? What about iron? What about copper, tin, quicksilver? I'm not even talking coal and precious stones. There are tracts of land sitting on fortunes—why, you can pick up a gold mine, I'm told, for as little as three-million-five. They're practically free! They're just a bit far away. They're beyond the Uropal Mountains and it takes three weeks to reach them because there aren't any trains.

Whom can I interest in such a proposition? Brodsky, of course! The problem is getting to see him. To begin with, he has a doorman with gold buttons who looks you up and down: let him see a frayed coat and you'll never cross the threshold. And if you're lucky enough to get past the doorman, you can cool your heels on the stairs for hours, hoping to be let into Brodsky's office, only to see him fly by like the wind to his carriage just as your turn is next. Go do something about it! It's only polite to come back and try again the next day . . . and the next day the same thing happens. You have to hand it to him: he's a busy man!

You can see that getting to Brodsky isn't easy. I haven't given up, though. One crack at him and I have it made. But being busy and in a hurry, I'll be brief. God willing, I'll write more in my next letter. Meanwhile, may He grant you health and success. My fondest greetings to everyone and to the children,

Your husband,
Menakhem-Mendl

P.S. Your question concerning the Land of Israel no doubt refers to the Zionites. They're most serious people, though not well thought of on the Yehupetz Exchange. I've gone to a few of their meetings to see what it's all about, but everything was in Russian—and lots of it. You would think it would be no skin off their backs to talk to Jews in a Jewish language! My friends on the Exchange just laugh when I mention them: "What? The Cyanides? Dr. Herzl? You call that a business too?"

FROM SHEYNE-SHEYNDL IN KASRILEVKE TO HER HUSBAND MENAKHEM-MENDL IN YEHUPETZ

To my dear, learned, & illustrious husband Menakhem-Mendl, may your light shine!

First, we're all well, thank God. I hope to hear no worse from you.

Second, my sister Gitl is now a widow with seven orphans. My brother-in-law—may my life be as long as his was short!—has died of the toothache. Of course, his health wasn't too good before that. I hope never to cough up blood the way he did. Still, we thought he'd hang on. Who could guess he'd have a tooth pulled by Shmelke the healer and lie down the next morning and die? It's as my mother says: "Tomorrow is another day—but whose?"

And now poor Gitl is left by herself. Her grief is not to be described. If it had been the other way around, God forbid, and she had died and left Zalman-Meir a widower, I don't suppose he would have wasted any tears on her. No, he would have waited a month and sent to Berdichev for a stepmother. All you men are the same—you're not fit to fasten your wives' apron strings. If you were, would a father of children go chasing pots of gold at the end of a rainbow? A millionaire he thinks he'll be! His lordship is doing so well that he's even made it to Brodsky's front door! I'm afraid that's as far as you'll get. I swear, you'll wear out your boots just standing there! Do you think Brodsky has nothing better to do than fly away with his millions to some blasted place beyond the Uropal Mountains just because Menakhem-Mendl has heard that gold and quicksilver are lying on the ground there? It's the old story of the deaf man hearing the dumb man tell of the blind man seeing the cripple run . . .

I can already see your next letter informing me that your latest bonanza has fizzled out too. Not that you won't dream up something even crazier and write that, since the cow jumped over the roof and laid an egg, you're opening a hatchery. If only you'd get it into your head that you have a wife at home, provided she survives all this, and little children who await you like the Messiah, you wouldn't be running from door to door with your lunatic notions that are sickening to think of.

You haven't learned a thing from your Yehupetz. I'd put a torch to it!

I wish you all the best,

Your truly faithful wife,
Sheyne-Sheyndl

Here's an item for you. Do you remember Meir-Meshulams? He has a daughter, Shprintsl. She's as strong and healthy as a horse—old enough to be married by now, it's true, but still a fine girl. Well, who goes and falls for her but a book peddler, a fellow that goes from house to house with penny novels. Poor Shprintsl took such a fancy to them that she must have read a hundred and now she's tetched in the head. She talks in strange words that no one understands, insists her name is Bertha and not Shprintsl, and says she's waiting for a calvalier to carry her off through the window and the devil knows where, London or Stamboul. . . . You tell me: don't the waffleheads who write such crazy stuff deserve to be strung up?

FROM MENAKHEM-MENDL IN YEHUPETZ TO HIS WIFE SHEYNE-SHEYNDL IN KASRILEVKE

To my wise, esteemed, & virtuous wife Sheyne-Sheyndl, may you have a long life!

Firstly, rest assured that I am, praise God, in the best of health. God grant that we hear from each other only good and pleasing news, amen.

Secondly, we have a great God! Just listen to this.

Now that I'm a regular at Brodsky's, I'm known all over the Exchange. Traders come to me with a thousand different proposals: houses, country property, lumber, railroads, steamboats, factories worth millions, all on account of Brodsky. . . . Well, there are these two partners, neither from these parts. One goes around in a long cape with a hood and the other has a name that's too weird to write. One day they get hold of me on my way to Brodsky's and Long Cape says: "Listen here, Reb Menakhem-Mendl, we'd like a word with you. It's like this. We've heard you're friends with Brodsky. Don't get us wrong. We have nothing against that." "Well, then," I say, "what is it that you want?" "What is it that we want?" they answer. "We want what everyone does: to make some cash. We're traders ourselves, we have businesses. Let's not quibble over who needs who more, because we'd like to make you a fifty-fifty offer. We'll all earn a little less that way, but it will be money in the bank. Better a bird in the hand, as they say." "Look," I tell them, "let's not beat around the bush. Don't be shy and show me your cards." "Praise God," they say, "we have a full deck of them. We have coal in Poltava. We have iron in Kanyov. We have a burned-out mill in Pereyaslav. We have some brand-new machines invented by a Jew from Pinsk. We have a country squire out to trade a forest for a distillery. We have a Jew looking for a large, cheap house in Yehupetz. We have country property, woodland! Bring us the buyers and we have the estate; bring us the estate and we have the buyers." "Nix to that," I say. "I'm through with country property and forests. I wouldn't touch them with a ten-foot pole." "Come, come," says Long Cape. "You know every deal is not the same. Why, I have a property now in the Caucasus, a place sitting on fields of oil—whole geysers are gushing from the ground! They say it's good for a million barrels a day." "Now you're talking!" I say. "That's what I call a business. Count me in."

The three of us went to the Jewish cafeteria. (I've stopped going to Semadenni's because they just chuck you out anyway. The cafeteria is cozier and you can talk all day.) Just as we're about to sign on the dotted line, in walk four more partners: a fellow I know with fat lips, a blond bluffer who sells watches, a bigger one with a red, warty nose, and another man, a widower. I needn't tell you that I wasn't thrilled by that, but Long Cape gave me such a lecture, with so many good points in it, that I agreed to go along. Of course, you can't have partners without quarrels: everyone wanted a bigger share. Still, if we come to terms with the oilmen, God willing, as easily as we did with each other, we won't be doing badly. It's a million-smacker-apiece deal. Let it go through and I'll rent an office on Nikolaievsky Street and be in the big time! But as I'm busy and in a hurry, I'll be brief. God willing, I'll write more in my next letter. Meanwhile, may He grant you health and success. Give my fond greetings to the children, each and every single one of them.

Your husband,

Menakhem-Mendl

P.S. There was something important that I wanted to write you, but I can't remember what it was. I'll have to leave it for the next time.

Yours, etc.

FROM SHEYNE-SHEYNDL IN KASRILEVKE TO HER HUSBAND MENAKHEM-MENDL IN YEHUPETZ

To my dear, learned, & illustrious husband Menakhem-Mendl, may your light shine!

First, we're all well, thank God. I hope to hear no worse from you.

Second, I'll be brief myself, because I have no strength left to write. A body might as well throw peas at the wall. "No bridegroom," my mother says, "hears sad music at his own wedding." Rolling in millions outside Brodsky's door may make you a hero in Yehupetz, but you're not such a big shot here. The millions roll past you to Brodsky and your fields of oil are a lot of water on the brain. All you'll get from them is a good soaking! Listen to me and come home. Forget the past and anything mean I may have said. "Better a slap from a friend than a kiss from an enemy," says my mother. Send a telegram and catch the first coach home. It will be the end of all my troubles.

I wish you nothing but the best,

Your truly faithful wife,
Sheyne-Sheyndl

If you'd like to hear the latest news, the whole town is talking about it. Do you remember Moyshe-Meir's Meir-Motl? He has a daughter named Ratzl and some Ratzl she is—an honest-to-God spitfire, a maddymissell with book-learning who speaks French and plays the pianer and wouldn't give a young man the time of day. You'd never guess she came from a long line of butchers—but a miserly father makes a spendthrift son, my mother says. She's gotten a heap of proposals, Ratzl has, and turned down every one. Nobody is good enough for her. The husband she marries has to have everything: looks, brains, money—a prince from a fairy tale! The matchmakers have tried everything. The last fellow they came up with was a real gem, a young man as rare as a drop-o'-cool fruit, a small-town boy from Avrich. They picked a halfway spot, brought the two of them there, and put them in a room to get acquainted. Right off Ratzl turns to the young man and asks, "So, what's your opinion of Dryfuss?" "Dry-who?" he asks. "Who's that?" "What?" screams Ratzl. "You've never heard of Dryfuss?" "No," he says. "What's his line?" The next thing you know Ratzl runs out of the room and faints and the poor fellow crawls back to Avrich with his tail between his legs. The devil take them both! Just tell me one thing: you keep smart company—who is this Dryfuss and what's the fuss all about?

FROM MENAKHEM-MENDL IN YEHUPETZ TO HIS WIFE SHEYNE-SHEYNDL IN KASRILEVKE

To my wise, esteemed, & virtuous wife Sheyne-Sheyndl, may you have a long life!

Firstly, rest assured that I am, praise God, in the best of health. God grant that we hear from each other only good and pleasing news, amen.

Secondly, Brodsky and I have split up. Not that we've quarreled, God forbid. I simply steer clear of him. Why hang around with Brodsky when I'm about to see Rothschild in Paris?

You must be wondering why I need to see Rothschild. The answer is Caucasus oil. All the oil there belongs to Rothschild, even though he spends his time in Paris. How, then, do we bring the horse to water? Well, I had an idea. There was a big investor on the Exchange named Todres, a real go-getter. Back when the market crashed and we all took up trading, Todres went to Paris and became a millionaire. Now, by a stroke of luck, he's in Yehupetz. I wasted no time, went to see him, and let him know loud and clear that I'm into land in the Caucasus that's gushing with oil and needs capital. Right off the bat he says, "I have the man for you." "And who," I ask, "might that be?" "Rothschild," he says. "You mean to say you know Rothschild?" I ask. "Do I know Rothschild?" he says. "I've lost count of how many deals we've done together and how much I've made from them." "Excuse me for asking," I say, "but would it be too much trouble for you to drop him a line?" "Writing Rothschild," he says, "is no problem. The two of us are thick as thieves. But that's neither here nor there. You have to have an itemized proposal. Otherwise there's no point."

To make a long story short, I went to my partners and came back with a proposal itemized seventeen different ways. What do you say now, my dear wife: is your Menakhem-Mendl a businessman or not? Let God give us the go-ahead from Rothschild and I'm at the head of the class! The only problem is that meanwhile I'm strapped for cash. You should see how hard-up all Yehupetz is. A day doesn't go by without a new bankruptcy. But don't you fret, my dear. It's only temporary. All our trials, God willing, will soon have a happy end. As soon as I get word from Paris, I'll do some shopping for us and for the children, bless them all. And being busy and in a hurry, I'll be brief. God willing, I'll write more in my next letter. Meanwhile, may He grant you health and success. Give my fondest greetings to the children and to everyone,

Your husband,

Menakhem-Mendl

P.S. The story you ask about is an interesting one. It all begins with a Dreyfus who was a captain in Paris—that is, with a captain named Dreyfus. And Esterhazy was a major. (That's higher than a captain, unless it's the other way around.) Captain Dreyfus was a Jew but Major Esterhazy was a Christian and he wrote a memoveranda framing the captain. Dreyfus didn't take that lying down and was sentenced to eternal life on an island in the sea. Along came Zola and made a stink showing that Dreyfus didn't write the memoveranda. It was all the major's fault, Esterhazy's! And so Esterhazy went to jail. Then Zola upped and ran away and a colonel named Picquart raised a rumpus. That made a bunch of generals like Mercier and Roget tell more lies about Dreyfus. Pretty soon the Frenchies were fighting with themselves about bringing Dreyfus back from the island. There was a trial in Rennes with a big lawyer from Paris and they shot him in the back—the lawyer, that is, not Dreyfus. Then they wiped the floor with those generals and Dreyfus was convicted and set free. That's because he was guilty even though he was innocent and go do something about it! I trust it's all clear to you now.

Yours, etc.

FROM SHEYNE-SHEYNDL IN KASRILEVKE TO HER HUSBAND MENAKHEM-MENDL IN YEHUPETZ

To my dear, learned, & illustrious husband Menakhem-Mendl, may your light shine!

First, we're all well, thank God. I hope to hear no worse from you.

Second, you're a madman. You're gushing with oil, you're off to Paris, you're throwing around millions! Next you'll be howling like a dog in the streets. His lordship is one of your rich Yehupetz Jews, the proof being that he's broke and so are they! "If it acts like a donkey and brays like a donkey," my mother says, "it must be a donkey."

Mark my words, Mendl: if you're not brought home in chains, it will be in a straightjacket. One way or another, you'll realize you have a wife, may she live to see the day, who knows better than you. And as for all your shopping, I thank you kindly. Yehupetz's shops should have nothing but customers like you and your lying partners who are worth gadzillions and haven't a kopeck! I only hope I've heard the worst of it. My very best wishes,

Your truly faithful wife,
Sheyne-Sheyndl

May I know no more sorrow in my life than I understood a word about your Dryfuss! How does a Jew get to be a captain? And what's a memoveranda and how do you frame one? And why did Zola run away and why didn't they shoot him to his face? But it's as my mother says: "If you want to learn how to grow cabbages, ask the gardener, not the goat."

FROM MENAKHEM-MENDL IN YEHUPETZ TO HIS WIFE SHEYNE-SHEYNDL IN KASRILEVKE

To my wise, esteemed, & virtuous wife Sheyne-Sheyndl, may you have a long life!

Firstly, rest assured that I am, praise God, in the best of health. God grant that we hear from each other only good and pleasing news, amen.

Secondly, I wish the Caucasus had been swallowed by the earth before I heard of it! I can't show my face at the Exchange. How come? It's very simple. Yesterday I'm there when Todres says to me: "Listen here, my fine friend, just where is this Caucasus of yours?" "Where should it be?" I say. "It's in the Caucasus." "Well," he says, "I've been searching the map for it. Your oil fields are a lot of baloney." "What do you mean by that?" I say. "I mean," he says, "that there's no town called Caucasus anywhere. You won't even find it in the Bible. Just how does a Jew come to another Jew with a business deal made of whole cloth? And meant for whose ears? For Rothschild's! Do you have any idea who Rothschild is?" "Of course I do," I say. "What makes you think I don't? Just don't go blaming me. I only passed on the information."

Off I go to look for Long Cape. I find him sitting in the cafeteria with all the Jews and put him over the barrel. "Suppose you tell me, old man," I say, "where this business of ours is supposed to be." "You're asking me?" he says. "It's in your hands. You're the one bringing the customer." "That's not what I meant," I say. "I'm talking about the oil fields. Where are they? How do you get there? What's the nearest town?" "To tell you the truth," he says, "I don't rightly know. You'll have to ask my partner." So we go and ask Weird Name and he tells us to ask Red Nose. Red Nose says he doesn't have a clue; he only knows what he heard from Fat Lips, which is that Long Cape has a business in the Caucasus; he'll be hanged if he knows where. In a word, the more we tried getting to the bottom of it, the more everyone pointed the finger at someone else until I was left holding the bag. Naturally! Who else would they stick with it?

Do you understand now, my dear wife, what I've been through? With luck like mine I might as well be buried alive. It doesn't matter what I try. At first everything goes hunky-dory, the winning ticket is in my pocket, any day now I'll cash in my chips—and then the wheel gives one more spin and it all blows up in my face. I reckon I'm not meant to strike it rich. Everyone in Yehupetz makes good but Menakhem-Mendl. The world parties and leaves me out in the cold, watching it count the millions I'm not allowed to touch.

But perhaps I haven't found the right combination. No one knows when his luck will look up. It's bound to happen if you wait long enough . . . but as I'm feeling low, I'll be brief. God willing, I'll write more in my next letter. Meanwhile, may He grant you health and success. Give my greetings to your parents and write me how you are. And kiss the children for me and tell me what's new in Kasrilevke.

Your husband,

Menakhem-Mendl

P.S. Misery loves company. The next man's troubles makes your own easier to bear. Take the fellow sharing my room. He was a provisioner who owned stores and houses and now he's in Yehupetz suing the government. He's hoping for a settlement, a big one, but meanwhile he's broke and staying with me. If he wins his case, God willing, he'll keep me in mind.

I have another roommate, too, who's even worse off. He's a writer who writes for the papers and is working on a book; I'm putting him up until he's done. Now and then the landlady pities him and brings him a glass of tea. And there's a third fellow, a real pauper. Why, the writer has nothing on him! I can't tell you myself what he does. He's a part-time agent, part-time matchmaker, and part-time actor, besides being a singer and an exterminator. And a jolly Jew he is, though he's dying of hunger and doesn't have a cent! When you see so many troubles, you forget your own. Please write about your health and the children, bless them, and about your parents and everyone else.

Yours, etc.

FROM SHEYNE-SHEYNDL IN KASRILEVKE TO HER HUSBAND MENAKHEM-MENDL IN YEHUPETZ

To my dear, learned, & illustrious husband Menakhem-Mendl, may your light shine!

First, we're all well, thank God. I hope to hear no worse from you.

Second, what did I tell you, you damned fool? You should kiss every word I write! "The wise man blesses the whip that flogs him," says my mother. A fine businessman you've turned out to be, you and your rotten gang of provisionals, ragpickers, scribblers, singsongers, and mice chasers—what a laugh! I can't think of better company in which to sit in a Yehupetz boarding house throwing rubles out the window.

Well, at least you show signs of coming to your senses. You say you *reckon* you're not meant to strike it rich. Do you still doubt it, Mendl? I've been shouting at you at the top of my lungs to put all that nonsense aside. May my life be as hard and your brains stay as addled as you'll ever see a million rubles. Forget it, Mendl! Forget there's a Brodsky in the world! You'll only be the better for it. "Keep your eyes on the ground, not the clouds"—isn't that what our holy books say? Stop envying the Yehupetz Jews and their parties. Let them party till they croak. They can break every bone in their bodies! As always I am,

Your truly faithful wife,
Sheyne-Sheyndl

Tell me, my dear Mendl, what's gotten into you that you suddenly remembered Kasrilevke? And since when do you worry about my health? A body might almost think you miss us. My mother would say, "Let the calf run free, it will come home by itself when it's hungry." I'm waiting for a telegram telling me when you'll arrive. It's about time. I pray this is my last letter.

♦♦♦ *An Honorable Profession: Menakhem-Mendl Becomes a Writer*

MENAKHEM-MENDL IN YEHUPETZ TO HIS WIFE SHEYNE-SHEYNDL IN KASRILEVKE

To my wise, esteemed, & virtuous wife Sheyne-Sheyndl, may you have a long life!

Firstly, rest assured that I am, praise God, in the best of health. God grant that we hear from each other only good and pleasing news, amen.

Secondly, I've had it with business: no more Exchange, no more deals, no more Semadenni's. They're all a sneaking, thieving swindle! I have a brand-new profession, a much finer and more respectable one. I'm happy to say I've become a writer. In fact, I'm writing already.

How, you ask, do I come by literature? It seems I was born for it.

If you recall my last letter, I mentioned a writer who is staying with me in my boarding house. He writes for the papers and makes a living from it. The way it's done is, he sits and writes and sends it off and gets a kopeck a line when it's printed: the more lines, the more kopecks. Well, I thought it over and asked myself: Good lord, what does he do that I can't? What's the big trick? After all, I went to school just like he did and have a better handwriting—why not give it a try and toss off a line or two for the Jewish papers? What can I lose? No one will chop off my head. The worst that can happen is, I'll get no for an answer.

And so I sat down and wrote a letter to the editor with my autogeography—how I played the market in Odessa and Yehupetz, and how I sold my soul for fool's gold, Londons and stocks & bonds and every horse I could bet on, and how I went from rags to riches and back again, seventy-seven times a millionaire and seventy-eight a beggar. I cut no corners, wrote everything down to the last detail, and sent off ten pages. If they liked my writing, I said, they could have as much as they wanted.

Don't think that a month and a half didn't pass without an answer. The paper wrote that it liked my writing and wanted more. If it was as good as the sample I sent, it would print it and pay me a kopeck a line. What do you say to that? I sat down and figured out that in summer, when the days are long, I can knock out a thousand lines per day. That's a ten-spot right there—and there are thirty days in a month! Not bad, a starting salary of 300 rubles. . . . Straightaway I went out, bought a ream of paper and a bottle of ink, and got to work. And since I'm busy writing, I'll be brief. God willing, I'll write more in my next letter. Meanwhile, may He grant you health and success. Give my fondest regards to your parents and to the children, each and every one.

Your husband,

Menakhem-Mendl

P.S. If with God's help I get ahead with my writing—that is, if I acquire the literary reputation I soon hope to—I'll ask the editors to advance you a few rubles. I wish you, my dear wife, to benefit equally from my new line of work. It's more honorable than business, which is why it pays an honorarium and not a commission. It's an easy way to make a decent living.

FROM SHEYNE-SHEYNDL IN KASRILEVKE TO HER HUSBAND MENAKHEM-MENDL IN YEHUPETZ

To my dear, learned, & illustrious husband Menakhem Mendl, may your light shine!

First, we're all well, thank God. I hope to hear no worse from you.

Second, my precious darling, what can I say? Bullets couldn't stop you, much less words. One might as well shoot at a stone. My mother, bless her, was a wise woman when she said: "A sick man will recover and a black one will turn white before a fool stops being a fool." You can't tell me she wasn't right! I weep to think of all the tricks you've played on me since I've had you for a husband . . . and now, as if all that weren't enough, you decide to become a circus clown. A penny-a-liner! And to think there are even worse fools than you who will pay to read what you write! Who knows what new trouble your scribbling, God forbid, may get us into? From you, I've learned to expect the worst. As my mother says, there's no need to show the beaten dog a stick. . . . Not that this will stop his lordship from chasing wild geese and dreaming of easy street. Far from it! He sits writing in his Yehupetz boarding house and leaves the children and me with the grippe in Kasrilevke. Every one of us is down with it, we've been sick for the past three weeks. . . . And as for the advances that I'll get, I'm much obliged, but you'll be lucky if that honorarity of yours is enough to buy your fine gang a hot meal. You're one rarity of a nincompoop yourself! If you don't want a wife who dies young with a clutch of orphans, give up your littleture and pipe dreams and come home. You'll be a welcome guest. "Better to foul your own nest than another's," my mother says. As always, I wish you the best.

Your truly faithful wife,

Sheyne-Sheyndl

Do you remember Moyshe-Dovid the bill collector? He's been wanting to dump his wife for some time and couldn't think of a way, and so he finally took off for America. Well, she caught up with him at the border and taught him a lesson he'll never forget. I wish he'd get the grippe himself.

FROM MENAKHEM-MENDL IN YEHUPETZ TO HIS WIFE SHEYNE-SHEYNDL IN KASRILEVKE

To my wise, esteemed, & virtuous wife Sheyne-Sheyndl, may you have a long life!

Firstly, rest assured that I am, praise God, in the best of health. God grant that we hear from each other only good and pleasing news, amen.

Secondly, I'm taking literature by storm, praise God. I've already appeared in the papers with all the writers and feel like a new man. The first time I saw my name in print—*Menakhem-Mendl*—I was moved to tears. What for? For there being such fine, honest people in the world! I'm speaking of the editorial board. After all, I'm not the only writer around, there are plenty of others besides me—and yet not only did it read every word that I wrote, it answered me in writing itself, in a letter delivered to my own mailbox, saying it liked my piece very much. It was just a bit on the long side—that was number one. And number two was, it doesn't want me making things up. It wants a *literary description*—its very words—of life in Yehupetz with all its types. That means it wants to know everything.

You couldn't ask for nicer people! And as I wasn't about to be outdone, I rolled up my sleeves and sat down to write and have been writing ever since. This is the third day I'm at it and I'm still going strong. And since I'm busy with my writing, I'll be brief. God willing, I'll write more in my next letter. Meanwhile, may He grant you health and success. My fondest greetings to the children and your parents,

Your husband,

Menakhem-Mendl

P.S. Please let me know whether you've received an advance from the board. I asked it to send you some money. What's a few smackers to it? It can deduct them from my pay.

FROM SHEYNE-SHEYNDL IN KASRILEVKE TO HER HUSBAND MENAKHEM-MENDL IN YEHUPETZ

To my dear, learned, & illustrious husband Menakhem-Mendl, may your light shine!

First, we're all well, thank God. I hope to hear no worse from you.

Second, your lovely letters are making me spit blood. Money from boards I'll be sent! Are you working for a newspaper or a lumber yard? You can put a match to your board and all its money! I need it like last year's snow. To quote my mother: "Spare me your sting and you can keep your honey."

Believe me, your board will turn to sawdust before I see an advance from it. An advanced case of heartburn I'll get! If it's my fate to have a scribbler for a husband, why must you scribble in Yehupetz? Isn't there enough ink in Kasrilevke? There's something fishy going on here. Bite into the apple, says my mother, and you'll find the worm.

No, my dear husband, stop making excuses! Pack up your littleture and come home, because I can't bear the children's sorrow any longer. All they ever ask is, when will papa be here? On Passover I tell them Sukkes and on Sukkes I tell them Passover. And Moyshe-Hirshele misses you most of all. As smart as a whip he is—a lot smarter than his father, that's for sure. I wish you all the best.

Your truly faithful wife,
Sheyne-Sheyndl

What do you say about my Nekhameh-Breindl? She's now on her second divorce. No one knows why. Her husband showed me in secret an arm full of black-and-blue marks. He's willing, he says, to let her keep the dowry and the wedding jewelry—anything to get rid of such a curse. My mother says an ounce of luck is worth a pound of gold, but luck in men is the one thing we lack.

FROM MENAKHEM-MENDL IN YEHUPETZ TO HIS WIFE SHEYNE-SHEYNDL IN KASRILEVKE

To my wise, esteemed, & virtuous wife Sheyne-Sheyndl, may you have a long life!

Firstly, rest assured that I am, praise God, in the best of health. God grant that we hear from each other only good and pleasing news, amen.

Secondly, I've already gone through two bottles of ink and am now on my third. Describing a city like Yehupetz is no mean task. I decided to begin with my boarding house, and first of all with my landlady. Why with her? On account of her husband. He was a soldier, and he's been dead for thirteen years, and she was his second wife. She married him, she says, for the right to live in Yehupetz and she wouldn't wish such a life on her worst enemies. She was, she says, twenty years younger than him and as pretty as a picture. All the men, Jews and Christians, were wild about her . . . and now she's reduced to bringing Menakhem-Mendl a bowl of borscht or meat with horseradish each time he snaps his fingers. She has a son and daughter to support, too, both in high school, neither of whom lifts a finger to help. They sit and wait for her to serve them. She brings them coffee in bed every morning, and they expect to find lunch on the table when they come home from school whether there's food in the house or not. And you should hear the racket they make if it isn't waiting for them! But that's the sort of children they are. One morning the daughter, the high-school girl, woke up and hollered for some soap. She actually ran half-naked with her neck showing into the dining room where we boarders were having breakfast and shouted at her mother in Russian: "What kind of flophouse is this?" Naturally, we gave her a scolding. Did she mean to tell us, we asked, that she was taught to behave that way in high school? "You should be grateful," I said, "that your mother slaves for you. She even shines your shoes while you sleep!" Those were my very words. I was about to give her another piece of my mind when her brother butts in and says: "Mind your own business!" The nerve of him opening his trap at me! I was so annoyed that I wrote it up for the papers, the poor woman and her darling children and the whole scene. I hope he learns his lesson when it's published! Well, it's a big world. You can bet there are plenty of other widows being driven to distraction by their children. Do you see now, my dear wife, what I'm paid to do? And being busy and in a hurry, I'll be brief. God willing, I'll write more in my next letter. Meanwhile, may He grant you health and success. Give my fondest greetings to your parents and the children, God bless them, each and every single one.

Your husband,
Menakhem-Mendl

P.S. An editorial board is not a piece of wood. It's a group of people that gets together to put out a newspaper. The board sends writers to different cities. It needs material and we're paid to produce it. We send it in and it's printed. I hope that makes the newspaper business clear.

Yours, etc.

FROM SHEYNE-SHEYNDL IN KASRILEVKE TO HER HUSBAND MENAKHEM-MENDL IN YEHUPETZ

To my dear, learned, & illustrious husband Menakhem-Mendl, may your light shine!

First, thank God, we're all well. I hope to hear no worse from you.

Second, I read your letter and couldn't believe my eyes. A bad dream, that's all I can say. A grand subject you've found to make a rhubarb from—a widow and her blasted bawdy house! Believe me, if I were you I would have minced no words with that young man and sent that naked hussy to peel potatoes in the kitchen instead of writing them both up in the papers. But I have a husband, it seems, who gets paid to be a stump preacher. My mother says it takes all kinds to make a world, but if you ask me, before sticking your nose into other people's pots you might take an interest in your own. Are you your children's father or not? You should hear Moyshe-Hirshele say his ABC's—all your widows aren't fit to carry his schoolbag! As soon as I'm up to it I'll have a photograph made of him and the others, so that you can see what you've traded for your rotten boards and bawds. I wish you only the best.

Your truly faithful wife,
Sheyne-Sheyndl

FROM MENAKHEM-MENDL IN YEHUPETZ TO HIS WIFE SHEYNE-SHEYNDL IN KASRILEVKE

To my wise, esteemed, & virtuous wife Sheyne-Sheyndl, may you have a long life!

Firstly, rest assured that I am, praise God, in the best of health. God grant that we hear from each other only good and pleasing news, amen.

Secondly, I've finished the landlady and am now writing up the lodgers. In other words, I'm describing the sad cases in my boarding house. If I do say so myself, it's going well. Each boarder is a sorrier story than the next, but the one we call "Touch o' Gold" takes the cake.

All the ink and paper in the world aren't enough for him. He comes from Zhvanitz, married a woman from Ladizhin and another from Soroke, and moved to Yekaterinoslav, where he started his first business. He was in gold—that is, some shady characters relieved him of his money in return for sacks of yellow sand. Well, you can't just go and throw yourself in the river, so he took his walking stick and went to the Odessa Exchange, where he put together some deals, made a few rubles, and advertised for a partner. Sure enough, a fellow turned up, someone in iron—that is, the two of them bought land near Krivorog that was sitting on iron ore. Right off they were offered a few thousand rubles to lease the mining rights, but Touch o' Gold turned it down: it was, he said, either half a million for the whole property or nothing. Well, nothing it was and Touch o' Gold decided to try coal. He found a German engineer—I mean, a Jew who spoke some German—and rented a mine with him. The price was good, too, but the first shaft they dug, don't ask me where it came from, they had a flood on their hands. Two pumps were brought to get rid of the water, but the harder they pumped, the more it kept coming. So Touch o' Gold said to heck with the German and found a Jew in the egg business—stuffed eggs, not fresh ones, because the yolks had been used for something else, I don't remember what. As luck would have it, the egg machine broke and the Jew took off and left Touch o' Gold with a mountain of rotten eggs. After a while they began to stink and Touch o' Gold received a summons. So one dark night he climbed out the window, leaving the eggs behind in Yekaterinoslav, and opened a cigarette paper factory in Kremenchug with the money he still had. It so happened that his new partner loved chess. He loved it so much, Touch o' Gold says, that he played it all day and all night, without eating, drinking, or sleeping. Once the two of them discovered at the end of a long game that all their cartons of cigarette paper were empty. Where had the paper gone? It was anyone's guess. Meanwhile Touch o' Gold heard of a small-town pharmacist who was selling out his stock. He went and bought it for a pittance and stood to make a killing. How was he supposed to know it included a crate of gunpowder? Well, there was all this gunpowder traveling by train when it took a notion to blow up along with the car and the conductor, who barely came out of it alive. How's that for the golden touch! He says he could kill the fish in a river just by looking at it. The man has a comeback for everything! He's a little fellow, a real live wire with burning eyes, a hat pushed back on his head, hands in his pockets, and a mind that's always working on something new. He never runs out of ideas. That's because he's made up his mind to become a millionaire. If he doesn't, he'll light out for America. Once he's there, he says, things will work out. In fact, he wants me to join him. He says people like me keep their heads above water. But I would be crazy to push my luck by giving up a good literary career! And as I'm busy and in a hurry, I'll be brief. God willing, I'll write more in my next letter. Meanwhile, may He grant you health and success. My fondest greetings to your parents and all the children.

Your husband,
Menakhem-Mendl

P.S. I don't understand why I haven't received a response from the editorial board to my first piece. I haven't gotten any money either. By now I've sent off two more pieces. God willing, I'm sure to hear from them tomorrow or the day after.

Yours etc.

FROM SHEYNE-SHEYNDL IN KASRILEVKE TO HER HUSBAND MENAKHEM-MENDL IN YEHUPETZ

To my dear, learned, & illustrious husband Menakhem-Mendl, may your light shine!

First, we're all well, thank God. I hope to hear no worse from you.

Second, dear husband, I beg you in God's name to come home as soon as you get this letter, because my poor father is dangerously ill. The doctors consulted and found that he has, I dread to say, water in his stomach. The pain is unbearable. You can imagine the state that my mother, bless her, is in. She cares nothing for herself, all her thoughts are only of him. "If you had lived with someone in one room for thirty years, you'd feel that way too," she says. And you sit in your lovely Yehupetz, describing cretins I wouldn't mention with my father in one breath! As always, I wish you health and happiness.

Your truly faithful wife,
Sheyne-Sheyndl

For the love of God, be sure to come at once and send a telegram!

FROM MENAKHEM-MENDL IN YEHUPETZ TO HIS WIFE SHEYNE-SHEYNDL IN KASRILEVKE

To my wise, esteemed, & virtuous wife Sheyne-Sheyndl, may you have a long life!

Firstly, rest assured that I am, praise God, in the best of health. God grant that we hear from each other only good and pleasing news, amen.

Secondly, your letter was like a knife in my heart. If I had wings, I'd fly to Kasrilevke. But I can't afford to go anywhere. I'm flat broke and in debt to my landlady. Not only have I run up a large food bill, I owe her for paper and ink. I kept thinking I would hear from the editorial board, but after all my expenses, and all the fine things I wrote my fingers off about, it's been as quiet as a mouse. Not very nice, I must say! If they didn't like what I wrote, they could at least have told me to stop. But I suppose my time and effort don't cost them anything. Anyone else would have raised Cain. To tell the truth, if I had the money for a telegram, I'd cable them to put up or shut up.

There are no words for how heartsick I feel. I can hardly get my pen to write. Who would have thought it? They didn't even have the decency to answer when I asked for a free copy of the paper. I could have made more money chopping wood! I don't know how it is with other writers, but I've been treated like the lowest of the low.

All that's left is to pray to God. *I will lift up mine eyes unto the hills from whence cometh my help*. I'm at the end of my rope, worse than this it can't get—and because I'm feeling low, I'll be brief. God willing, I'll write more in my next letter. Meanwhile, may He grant you health and success and send your father a full recovery. And may I soon see the children healthy and well, because I miss them so that I'm pining away.

Your husband,
Menakhem-Mendl

P.S. This letter has been with me for several days because I had no money to buy stamps. I kept thinking: what do I do now? It seems there's no way of making a living in this world that I haven't tried. The one thing left is matchmaking. There's a matchmaker here in the boarding house, and to listen to him talk, he does all right. It may not be as respectable as literature, but it's a sight better than trading. If only God would pitch in!

Yours, etc.

FROM SHEYNE-SHEYNDL IN KASRILEVKE TO HER HUSBAND MENAKHEM-MENDL IN YEHUPETZ

To my dear, learned, & illustrious husband Menakhem-Mendl, may your light shine!

First, we're all well, thank God. I hope to hear no worse from you.

Second, I don't know what to write. I showed your letter to my mother and she says it's all my fault. The bed you make, she says, is the bed you sleep in. "If it had been me writing to that son-of-a-gun-in-law of mine," she says, "I'd have brought him to his senses long ago. I'd have gone and collared him myself." You're in luck, she says, that my father is on his deathbed and the two of us are falling off our feet.

The money I'm sending is from my mother. I hope you appreciate her kindness. May I never read another letter of yours again! And may Yehupetz sink into the ground like Sodom once you leave it, with all its grand businesses, fortunes, traders, matchmakers, boards, and bawdy houses. I wish you much health and happiness, now and always.

Your truly faithful wife,
Sheyne-Sheyndl

♦ ♦ ♦ *It's No Go: Menakhem-Mendl the Matchmaker*

FROM MENAKHEM-MENDL ON THE ROAD TO HIS WIFE SHEYNE-SHEYNDL IN KASRILEVKE

To my wise, esteemed, & virtuous wife Sheyne-Sheyndl, may you have a long life!

Firstly, rest assured that I am, praise God, in the best of health. God grant that we hear from each other only good and pleasing news, amen.

Secondly, it's no go. The harder I try, the less it works out. As soon as I received the rubles you sent, I paid my bill at the boarding house and packed my things. What can I tell you? I was already on my way to Khvostov, where I planned to change for Kasrilevke.

But God is greater than any of us. Listen to this. I mentioned in my last letter a matchmaker at my boarding house, Leybe Lebelski by name, who likes to boast that he has a fortune in his pocket—a list of the whole world. A while back he announced that he was going on a trip to arrange a match. He had received, he said, an urgent telegram, and was leaving his things with our landlady for safekeeping. Since then we've seen no more of him than you have. And so as I was saying good-bye, the landlady said: "Since you're heading in the same direction, you might as well take Lebelski's papers. Maybe you'll run into the idiot and let him have them." "But what do I want with someone else's property?" I asked. "Never you mind," she said. "It's not money, it's just a bunch of names."

No sooner said than done. And as I was sitting in the carriage, curiosity got the better of me. I opened the envelope and took a peek—a gold mine! Correspondences with other matchmakers, names of satisfied parents, even a list of eligibles in alphabetical order! I give it to you verbatim:

Avritch—Khaveh d/o R. Levi Tankenog, Esq. & Miryem-Gitl. A+ family tree, tall & attractive, seeks young man w/ diploma, offering 4,000.

Balti—Faytl s/o Yoysef Hitelmakher, Esq. Educated, Zionite, certified accountant w/ draft exemption, regular synagogue-goer, cash only.

Boiberik—R. Mendl Lopita. Established, 3x widower, well-preserved ca. 70, seeking first-time bride.

Dubno—Leah d/o Meir Karzik. Good family, short, redhead, speaks French, will pay well.

Glokhiv—Yefim Bolosni. Pharmacist & part-time moneylender, beardless but prefers Jewish women, seeking brunette.

Heysen—Lipe Brosh, b.-in-law Itsi Koymen, consultant Zalman Radimishler's sugar mill, only son, handsome boy w/ devil in eyes, seeks well-feathered nest.

Kasrilevke—Yoysef-Yitzkhok s/o R. Nosn Koyrakh. Father filthy rich & a wild man. Still-waters-run-deep intellectual type, knowledge of Hebrew, Russian, Torginnev & Darwen, seeks poor orphan but must be raving beauty, generous expense account. Pay the piper & I'll dance to your tune.

Khmelnik—Basya Flekl, Esq'ess. Widow & usurer, shrewd old bird, seeks scholar, money unnecessary.

Kremenchug—educated run-for-your-life Cyanide, claims 100 incomes + total recall of Talmud. Chess whiz, can top all you say, talks and writes like the blazes, rumored to have wife already.

Lipovitz—s/o Leibush Kapoti. Wild-eyed Hasid, lives in Odessa, 8th grade matriculation, violin & some Hebrew, presentable.

Mezhbizh—R. Shimn Shepsl Shimmeles, widower w/ 2 never-weds @ 3,000 per, must first remarry himself, seeks never-wed too.

Nemerov—Smitsik, Bernard Moiseyevish, of well-known Smitsiks. Divorced, lives alone, cornet & high connections, seeks first-time bride + 5,000 or divorcee + 10.

Perilok—high-school graduate, s/o Mikhl Fritog, Esq. Religious, Sabbath-observer, not a kopeck less than 20,000, will settle for half.

Radomishl—g.s./o Naftoli Rademishler. Sugar mill, A+ family, half Sadegor Hasid & half Europinion Jew (short ear locks, long gabardine), knowledge of languages & rabbinic law, uncle has 1 m. in bank, seeks sincere, attractive, wig-wearing, Sabbath-candle-lighting wife w/ triple-A family + 200,000 + piano + French + voice & dance lessons + no previous boyfriends.

Shpole—Ilye von Chernobyl, Esq. Currently residing in Yehupetz, sugar & real estate, partner Von Chernobyl & Babishke (the famous millionaire), only daughter, highly accomplished young lady seeking dream man, prefers professor to doctor, looks of Joseph + brains of Solomon + musical ability + triple-A family, money no object. Brodsky-class wealth, no draftables need apply. Cable sent to Radomishl.

Smile—Perele Damme, divorcee w/ 10,000, seeking educated businessman.

Talne—R. Avremele Fayntig. Widower, Bible-quoting Hasid, seeks widow with business.

Tomeshpol—5 first-time brides, 3 presentable, 2 ugly as sin, seeking doctor w/ furnished apt. or lawyer w/ Yehupetz practice, correspondences mailed.

Tsarytin—rich widower, wholesale fishmonger living in Astrakhan, standard commission + 2 first-series lottery tickets. Have asked for 25 R's for mailing costs and/or stamps.

Vinitse—Khayyim Hekht. Solid income, own droshky, net worth 10,000, plays market like fiddle.

Yampeli—Moyshe-Nisl & Beile-Leah Kimbek. Parvenus, hot for respectable match, will double all offers, prompt payment of commission on wedding night + tip.

Zhitomir—Shloymi Zalman Todotayke, Esq. 2 never-weds, both attractive, youngest slightly pockmarked, piano, German, French, seek educated men, no need for independent income.

Well, there I was in the carriage with Lebelski's list, reading it over and over and thinking: God Almighty, how many ways You have made for Jews to make a living! Matchmaking, for example. What could be finer, better, easier, more respectable? What does it take, after all? Nothing but a bit of common sense and enough brains to see who goes with who. Take Avritch, for example. There's an attractive girl there with 4,000 looking for a young man with a diploma—and Balti has an educated Zionite with a degree in accounting and in need of cash. Anyone can see they're made for each other. And Talne has a widower seeking a widow with a business—let him get together with Basya Flekl in Khmelnik, who doesn't mind a poor scholar. Are you with me, my dear wife? If I went into matchmaking, I'd do it my own way. First I'd write every matchmaker in the world. Then I'd draw up a master list and get to work—at first on paper, of course—matching columns. And I'd have partners all over, one in each town, and go fifty-fifty with each. I might even open a central office in Yehupetz or Odessa with clerks to write letters and send telegrams. And I'd be the brains behind it, all the right combinations would be mine!

You can imagine the thoughts that were flying through my head . . . and who the deuce should sit next to me just then but the hairiest old man you ever saw. He was carrying a bag and puffing like a goose and had the strangest way of talking, all friendly-like but most odd. "Young man," he says, "is it conceivable that you might possibly make allowances for an old fellow like myself by troubling yourself to move over a bit, so that," says he, "a Jew like me might have the pleasure of your company?" "Why not?" I say, making room. "Gladly. Where are you from?" "You mean my whences and wherefores?" he replies. "I'm from Koretz. My name is Osher and I'm known as Reb Osher the Matchmaker. With God's help I have been," he says, "for quite a while now, that is, believe it or not, for nearly forty years, a matchmaker." "You don't say!" I say. "That makes two of us!" "If I rightly follow you," he says, "it might not be unreasonable to deduce from your learned remarks that you are a matchmaker yourself. In that case, we're brothers. Howdy-do!" So he says, sticking out a fat, white, hairy hand for me to shake and asking most politely: "And what, if I may have the pleasure of knowing it, did you say your name was?" "It's Menakhem-Mendl," I say. "That," says he, "sounds familiar. I believe I've heard it before, although I can't quite place it. Listen here, Reb Menakhem-Mendl: I have a proposal to make. Seeing as how the tedium of travel is great, and the Almighty has providentially brought the two of us together, would it not be advisable, inasmuch as we now find ourselves under one roof, so to speak, to put our time to constructive use?" "Well, now," I say, "what use might that be?" "What would you say," says he, "to some excellent wine in a shabby bottle?" "Well now," I say, "what wine and what bottle are those?" "Lend an ear," says Reb Osher, "and I will parse the matter for you thoroughly. The matter," he says, "is this. I have in Yarmilinitz a superb piece of goods, the genuine article! Reb Itzikl Tashratz is his name. The man is up to his ears in pedigree. And his wife has even more. The problem is that he wants cash up front. Whatever he gives the young couple to start life with, he wants twice as much from the other side." "Why" I say, "I'll be hanged if I don't have just the thing for you!" And I pull out Leybe Lebelski's list, show him Yampeli, and say: "Here's just what you're looking for. Read it for yourself. *'Moyshe-Nisl Kimbek, parvenu'*—that's new money. *'Hot for respectable match'*—he'll do anything. *'Will double all offers'*—he'll pay twice as much as the other side. Exactly what your man wants!"

Well, Reb Osher thinks it over, sees where Moyshe-Nisl Kimbek promises prompt payment of the commission plus tip, rises from his seat, grabs my hand, and says: "Congratulations, Reb Menakhem-Mendl! We're in business! If I'm not mistaken," he says, "I happened to notice that you have in that basket of yours some egg cookies, a package of tea and sugar, and a few other provisions. I don't suppose it would do any harm to have a snack now. Once we reach Khvostov, God willing, you can look for hot water, because I see you also have a samovar. We'll have tea at the station, where I have reason to believe it will be possible to purchase some 114-proof vodka. With that in hand," says he, "we'll drink a toast on the way to my Yarmilinitz bluebloods and your Yampeli parvenus. This is indeed an auspicious occasion." "Amen to that!" I say. "May your words go straight to God's ears. But it's not quite as simple as all that . . . " Well, he interrupts me, the matchmaker does, and says: "Hear me out, Reb Menakhem-Mendl! You have yet to learn whom you're dealing with. I'm not wet behind the ears. I am the internationally famous matchmaker Reb Osher and I am responsible, God be praised, for more marriages in my life than I have hairs on my head. We should both," says he, "have a ruble for every couple I have seen married and divorced and married a second time and divorced again. One look at your list is all I need to match 'em up. Your Moyshe-Nisl," he says, "will do just fine. I can smell a rat there for sure. Why else," he says, "would he be so desperate for a match and fall all over himself to tip us? Oh, there's a worm here, my friend—a very wormy apple indeed!" "What, then," I ask, "shall we do?" "What we shall do," he says, "is very simple. We shall go our separate ways at once. I," he says, "to Yarmilinitz and my Reb Itzikl Tashratz, and you to Yampeli and your Moyshe-Nisl Kimbek. We have our work cut out for us. Yours will be to squeeze all you can from your wormy apple and mine will be to hold my Tashratz to his word. A Jew selling pedigree can drive a hard bargain."

And so you see, my dear wife, how what began as a joke, a mere lark, turned into a serious venture. Between one thing and another we reached Khvostov, where we had tea and a bite to eat and sat down to talk in earnest. To tell the truth, I was beginning to feel a little queasy. Since when was I a matchmaker? And what was I doing with another man's lists? You might even say I had stolen them. How was it any different from finding a wallet with someone's money? And yet on the other hand, why blow it up out of all proportion? If anything came of it in the end, Lebelski and I would split the take. I wasn't a stick-up man robbing strangers.

In a word, I overcame my doubts and we parted, Reb Osher for Yarmilinitz and I for Yampeli. As soon as I arrived there, we had decided, I would poke around to find out what made Moyshe-Nisl Kimbek so eager for a match. If he and his family made a good impression, I would cable Yarmilinitz to arrange a meeting. Let the boy and girl hit it off and we could break out the champagne! "The main thing, Reb Menakhem-Mendl," says Reb Osher, "is not to stint on telegrams. In matchmaking, you should know, telegrams are half the battle. Parents go wild over them."

It was time to buy our tickets. Having spent his last rubles on telegrams, my new colleague was out of cash. "I tell you," he said, "most people would be happy to earn in a month what telegrams cost me alone." Would you believe it? That's the kind of money there is in matchmaking! And since the train wasn't about to wait, I laid out my last rubles on his ticket. Every business has its expenses. We exchanged addresses, bid each other a fond farewell, and went our ways—he to Yarmilinitz and I to Yampeli.

Arriving in Yampeli, the first thing I did was check out Moyshe-Nisl Kimbek. "All things considered," I was told, "he's no worse than he is." "Has he many children?" I asked. "Many children," I was told, "are for poor Jews. Rich Jews have only one." "What sort of child is it?" I asked. "A daughter," I was told. "Grown-up?" "Enough for two." "With a dowry?" "Double your money." "How's that?" I asked. I poked around—tap-tap here, tap-tap there—and got nowhere, so I put on my good jacket and went to see the man himself.

I could describe his home for you, but what would be the point? It was as full of finery as a rich Jew's home should be, and his family—pure gold! I introduced myself, explained why I had come, and was received royally and served with tea, honey cake, a delicious marmalade, and a bottle of vishniak. The father, Moyshe-Nisl, appealed to me at once: a good-natured fellow, without a mean bone in his body. And I took a liking at first glance to his wife Beile-Leah too, a fine, quiet, pious woman with a double chin. They tried to feel me out about the match. Was the young man of good character? In what direction did his talents lie? . . . How was I supposed to answer when I didn't know myself! But a Jew with some learning is quick on his feet, and so I told them: "Let's settle your side of it first. I need to know how much you're putting up. And I want a look at the principal."

Well, he hears that, Moyshe-Nisl does, and says to his wife: "Where is Sonitshke? Tell her to come." "Sonitshke is getting dressed," says Beile-Leah, getting up and going out and leaving me with Moyshe-Nisl. We helped ourselves to a drop of vishniak, had some more marmalade, and made small talk. What about? Don't ask me. Last year's snow and the price of rice in China! "How long have you been a matchmaker?" Moyshe-Nisl asks, pouring me another glass of vishniak. "Since my wedding," I tell him. "My father-in-law was a matchmaker too. So was my father. In fact, all my brothers are matchmakers. There's practically no one in our family who isn't . . ." I didn't even crack a smile, although I could feel myself turning red. Don't ask me where I dreamed up such malarkey. But what choice did I have? As your mother would say, "If you're knee-deep in mud, keep on crawling." All I wanted was a break from God to pull the match off, earn my share fair and square, and split it with Lebelski. Why shortchange the fellow? It could be argued of course that the whole commission belonged to him—but where would that leave me? Nothing would have happened without me; wasn't my investment worth something too? I wasn't telling all those lies just for my sake. Who could say it wasn't God's plan for Lebelski to lose his lists, for me to find them, and for all three of us to make a bundle?

I was thinking all this when in walks Beile-Leah with the young lady—I mean, Sonitshke: a big, healthy, pretty, generously proportioned girl like her mother. I took one look at her and thought: "My God, that's a ton-itshke of Sonitshke!" She was dressed, Sonitshke was, rather strangely, in a long evening gown that made her look middle-aged, not because she was old but because . . . but you wouldn't believe the size of that child! Naturally, I wanted a word with her to see what kind of creature she was. Some chance I had with a father who wouldn't stop talking! This time it was about Yampeli—and you'll never guess the things he said. Yampeli, he said, was a town of badmouths, of backbiters, of grudge-bearers, of nasty-noses, every one of whom would gladly drown his neighbor in a spoon of soup. He would have gone on and on if his wife hadn't cut him short and said: "Moyshe-Nisl! Haven't you talked enough? Let's ask Sonitshke to play the piano." "Just say the word," says Moyshe-Nisl with a wink at Sonitshke. And so she goes and sits at the piano, Sonitshke does, opens a big book, and bangs away for dear life. After a while her mother says: "Sonitshke! How come you're playing all those haytoads? We'd like to hear The Volga Boatman, *pozhaliste!*" Well, Sonitshke begins playing that piano so fast that you can't even follow her fingers—and all the while her mother is feasting her eyes on her, you can see her wanting to say: "How's that for only two hands!" After a while she and her husband slip out of the room and Sonitshke and I are left alone. Now's the time for a little chitchat, I think—let's find out at least if the girl can talk. I'll be blamed, though, if I could think of a thing to say! I rose, walked around the room, stood behind her, and finally said: "Excuse me for interrupting, Sonitshke, but there's something I'd like to ask." *"Naprimer?"* she answers in Russian, turning around with an angry look. *"Naprimer,"* I say, "suppose I asked: what is your heart's desire? I mean, for example, what kind of husband would you like to have?" *"Viditye,"* she says to me a bit more softly, lowering her eyes. "*Sobstevenno,* I'd like him to have a degree, but I know that's *ponaprasno. Po krayne meri,* he should be an *obrazaveto,* because even though Yampeli is considered a *fanatitcheski* place, we all have a Russian *obrazovanye.* An *utshebe zavadyenye* may be out of the question, but there's not a *barishnye* who wouldn't like to be *znakome* with Zola, Pushkin, or *dazhe* Gorky . . . " So she says to me, my beauty, half in Yiddish and half in Russian, although the Russian was more like two-thirds.

At this point her mother returned. "Everything in good measure!" she says, followed by Sonitshke's father, and the three of us get down to brass tacks: how big should the dowry be, and where will the get-acquainted meeting be held, and when is a good time for the wedding. I was about to go to the station to send a telegram when Moyshe-Nisl takes my arm and says: "Stay a while longer, Reb Menakhem-Mendl! First have a meal with us. You must be hungry." We washed and sat down to table, and had another glass of vishniak, and Moyshe-Nisl Kimbek's mouth didn't shut for a second. It was Yampeli this, and Yampeli that, and Yampeli, Yampeli, Yampeli. "You simply can't imagine," he says, "the kind of town this is. It's a lying, loafing place! Take my advice and don't say a word to anyone. Above all, don't tell them who you are and where you're from and why you're here—and whatever you do, don't mention that you know me. Do you hear that, Reb Menakhem-Mendl? *You don't even know me!*" He must have repeated that ten times.

Well, off I went to send a telegram to my partner in Yarmilinitz as per agreement. The message was perfectly clear: *Goods inspected first-class six thousand cable offer where do we meet.* The answer arrived the next day—strangely phrased: *Up ante ten gets half six suggest Zhmerinka cable back.* Not understanding a word of it, I ran to my Moyshe-Nisl. He reads it and says: "What kind of Jew are you? It's crystal clear! The man wants ten thousand for his three. You can write him back that he's too smart for his own good. It's double or nothing. And tell him," he says, "that he'll be beaten to it if he doesn't get off his rear end."

With that in mind I sent off a telegram: *Double or nothing if not off rear end will be beaten.* Back cables my Osher: *Agree to half twice less one a bargain.* Off I go to Moyshe-Nisl. "It's crystal clear!" he says. "That means your partner's client will put up half as much as I do minus a thousand rubles. In short, my ten gets his four. He's a clever one, your father of the groom—he thinks he can take me for a ride. It's time he learned he's dealing with a businessman! My final offer," he says, "is double plus a thousand. That means his four gets my nine, his five gets eleven, his six gets thirteen. Got that? Let him say, yes or no, if he has a mind to go ahead."

I returned to the station and knocked off a telegram to Reb Osher: *Four gets nine five eleven six thirteen say yes or no if he has a mind.* Back comes a telegram: *We're on our way. Come.*

This last telegram arrived during the night. I don't have to tell you that I couldn't fall asleep. I kept trying to calculate the profit I would make if, with God's help, I found matches for Leybe Lebelski's whole list. Surely, that wasn't too much to ask of God! I had made up my mind that, if we clinched the deal, Reb Osher and I would become full-time partners. He seemed a fine fellow—and a successful one. Of course, I would give Lebelski a fair shake, too. Why shouldn't I? The poor devil was a father with children to support just like me . . .

I rose early, said my prayers, and went to show my customers the telegram. Over coffee and rolls it was decided that the four of us would set out for Zhmerinka that same day. So as not to give away our secret, we arranged for me to take the early coach and the three of them to follow. That way I'd have a chance to find a good hotel and order us a decent dinner.

And so I did. I reached Zhmerinka in advance and found the best hotel, which happened to be the only one in town—a place called the Odessa Inn. Straightaway I had a talk with the innkeeper, a fine, hospitable lady. "What," I asked, "do you have to eat?" "What would you like?" she says. "Do you have fish?" I ask. "Fish," she says, "can be bought." "How about soup?" I ask. "I can put one up," she says. "With what?" I ask. "Rice or noodles?" "Even soup nuts, if you like," she says. "Well, then," I say, "how about a roast duck to go with it?" "Duck," she says, "can be had for a price." "And the drinks?" "What drinks would you like?" "Do you have beer?" "Why shouldn't I have beer?" "And wine?" "Wine," she says, "costs more than beer." "Wine will be fine, my dear woman," I say. "Please make us a dinner for eight." "Eight?" she says. "I count one." "You're a strange one, you are!" I say. "What's it to you? If I say eight, that makes eight."

We're still talking when in walks my partner Reb Osher. He hugs and kisses me like a father and says: "Something told me I'd find you at the Odessa Inn! How about some food?" "That's already taken care of," I say. "I've ordered dinner for eight." "What does dinner have to do with it?" says Reb Osher. "Just because dinner is dinner, must we starve while we're waiting for it? I can see," he says, "that you know your way around here. Suppose you ask for a plate of meat and some vodka. I'm fearsomely faint from hunger!" And he steps into the kitchen to wash his hands, Reb Osher does, and tells the innkeeper what to bring.

Well, we tuck in at a table—and as we eat Reb Osher tells me he's worked wonders by getting his customer up to three thousand. Why, splitting the Red Sea would be easier! "But what are you talking about?" I say. "What three thousand? Four was the minimum we settled on." "Hear me out, Reb Menakhem-Mendl," he says. "I know what I'm about. Reb Osher is not my name for nothing! Let me tell you," he says, "that if my customer had had his way he would have offered a grand total of zero, because he thinks his family tree should be enough. And his is nothing compared to his wife's! They should be paid, they say, for the right to marry them. In short," says Reb Osher, "I had to sweat blood to make him promise two thousand." "Two thousand?" I say. "What two thousand? You just said three!" "Hear me out, Reb Menakhem-Mendl," he says. "I'm an older hand at this business than you are. Not for nothing am I called Reb Osher! Once our parties get together, God willing, and the boy and girl have a look at each other, there'll be dancing in the streets. I've never lost a match yet over a thousand shmegaroos. That's why my name is Reb Osher! There's just one thing that's bothering me." "And what," I ask, "might that be?" "It's the draft," he says. "I've told my customer that your rosy-cheeked youngster can thumb his nose at it because he has an exemption." "Draft?" I say. "What kind of horsefeathers is that?" "Hear me out, Reb Menakhem-Mendl," he says to me. "My name is Reb Osher!" "It can be Reb Osher eighteen times," I say, "I still don't know what you're talking about. Draft, shmaft! What's that have to do with my Moyshe-Nisl? Since when do girls go to the army?" "Girls?" says Reb Osher. "We're talking about your Moyshe-Nisl's boy!" "Since when," I say, "does Moyshe-Nisl have a boy? His daughter is an only child." "Do I correctly understand you to be saying," says Reb Osher, "that you have brought a girl to this match just like I have? But how can that be? We specifically spoke about a boy." "Of course we did," I say. "And it was you who was bringing him." "Just what," says he, "made you think it was me? You should have let me know you had a girl!" "And I suppose you let me know!" I said. He blew his top at that, Reb Osher did, and said: "You know what, Menakhem-Mendl? If you're a matchmaker, I'm a rabbi!" "And if you're one," I say, "I'm a rabbi's wife!" We traded insults for a while—"Know-nothing!" "Liar!" "Moron!" "Glutton!" "Stumblebum!" "Boozer!"—until he hauled off and hit me and I grabbed his beard and gave it a yank. God Almighty, what a scene . . .

You can imagine how I felt. All the expense, the trouble, the time—the sheer disgrace of it! The whole town came running to see the grand partners who had met to marry off two girls. That blasted Reb Osher didn't stick around for long. He took off and left me with the innkeeper and a dinner bill for eight. My luck was that I managed to slip away before the families arrived. I shudder to think of what happened when they did.

Well, go be a prophet and guess that a damned matchmaker who runs around sending telegrams and talking a blue streak is going to match one young lady with another! It's simply no go, my dear wife. Even jumping in the river wouldn't help. And as I'm in a wretched mood, I'll be brief. God willing, I'll write more in my next letter. Meanwhile, may He grant you health and success. Tell the children, bless them, that I miss them and give your parents and everyone my fond greetings.

Your husband,
Menakhem-Mendl

P.S. God never sends the illness without its cure. I left Zhmerinka thinking the sky had fallen in and praying my money would hold out till Kasrilevke—and even then I faced the devilish prospect of a night camped out on the railroad tracks. But there is a great God above! Who should be sitting in my carriage but a real devil of a character, a life ensurance agent, an inspector—and you should have heard the life he promised me if I became an agent too! But exactly what an agent does, and how he ensures a person's life, are complex matters, and as I've already gone on long enough, I'll leave them for the next time.

Yours etc.

♦♦♦ *Always a Loser: Menakhem-Mendl the Insurance Agent*

FROM MENAKHEM-MENDL ON THE ROAD TO HIS WIFE SHEYNE-SHEYNDL IN KASRILEVKE

To my wise, esteemed, & virtuous wife Sheyne-Sheyndl, may you have a long life!

Firstly, rest assured that I am, praise God, in the best of health. God grant that we hear from each other only good and pleasing news, amen.

Secondly, my dear wife, I'm on the run. I've had another setback—a severe one. I can thank my lucky stars I'm not in jail. The devil knows what I might have gotten: forced labor or even Siberia. And yet I'm no guiltier than you are. But it's as your mother says: once a loser, always a loser . . .

Now that I've been snatched from the jaws of disaster, I can sit down and write you about it. You know from my last letter what a state I was in after the splendid match we arranged for two girls. I wouldn't have wished it on anyone. I felt I was at the end of my rope—bye-bye, Menakhem-Mendl! And just then I ran into an inspector who works for the Acquitable Life Ensurance Company, which is a firm that ensures you against dying and does a fine business. He took out a book and showed me how many people he had ensured, and how many were dead or alive, and how they were all better off for it. If you ask how that can be, it's quite simple. Suppose Acquitable sells me 10,000 rubles of life ensurance. That means I pay 2 or 3 hundred rubles a year until I die. If I kick off right away, I'm in luck: 10,000 R's are nothing to sneeze at. And if I don't? Then the luck is Acquitable's. It employs lots of agents, mostly Jews with families that need to eat. Why begrudge them a living?

The problem is that not everyone can be an agent. In the first place, you have to dress well—and well is well: a good suit, a starched collar and cuffs (paper ones will do, but they had better be clean), a nice tie, and, naturally, a top hat. And most of all, you have to speak well. An agent has to be able to talk—to talk up, to talk over, to talk back, to talk down, to talk into, and to talk on until your customer gives in and buys life ensurance. That's why the inspector saw right away that I had the makings of a good agent myself.

But I must explain to you, my dear wife, the difference between an agent and an inspector. An agent sells ensurance while an inspector inspects the agents. And there are inspector-majors who inspect the inspectors and an inspector-general who inspects the majors. That's as high as you can get in Acquitable. It takes an inspector to become a major, a major to become a general, and so on. Whoever makes general is set for life. A general, my inspector told me, can earn 30,000 a year.

To make a long story short, the fellow wanted me to join Acquitable. Nothing would come from my own pocket, he said. In fact, I would even get an advance for clothes and a briefcase. Not bad for starters! I thought it over and asked myself: what am I risking? Either I succeed and make it big, or I don't and the marriage is off. And so I said yes and started a new life as an agent.

Of course, it wasn't as quick as all that. Before becoming an agent you have to see the general, because nothing cuts the mustard without him. And so my inspector took me to Odessa at his own expense to meet the inspector-general himself—a man, I was told, with 20 provinces and 1,800 agents working under him. That's how big he is. That is, he isn't so big himself, he's just made a big deal of. But he does have big eyes that don't miss a trick and a smile for everyone. His name is Yevzerel, and his office takes up a whole building with room after room, each with chairs and desks and files and books and agents going in and out. The place is jumping, the telegrams fly back and forth—it's enough to make your head spin. Getting to hell and back in a barrel is easier than seeing the inspector-general! I was half-dead by the time I was ushered in to Yevzerel, who very kindly offered me a seat and a cigarette and wanted to know all about me.

Well, I told him everything, the whole story: how I was bound for Kishinev, and ended up in Odessa, and dealt in Londons until I moved to Yehupetz, and worked on the Exchange buying and selling Putivils and Liliputs and other stocks & bonds, and traded in sugar, real estate, and lumber, and tried my hand at matchmaking, and even had a fling at writing. There was nothing in the world, I told him, that I hadn't knocked my brains out doing and I still had nothing to show for it. Once a loser, always a loser!

He listened to me, the general did, got to his feet, put a hand on my shoulder, and said: "Do you know something, Mister Menakhem-Mendl? I like you. I like your name and I like the way you talk. I can see you becoming one of our top agents—and I mean top! Take an advance, pick yourself a route, and good luck."

That's just what I did. I was given some rubles, outfitted myself like a king (you wouldn't have recognized me), bought a big briefcase, stuffed it with a wagonful of forms and brochures, and set out for the blue yonder—I mean, for Bessarabia, where the living is said to be good. That's the place to do business, I was told. I could sell ensurance there like hot cakes.

I took a train and then another and another and arrived in a little town, a damned hole in the middle of nowhere. If only it had burned to the ground before I got there! How was I supposed to know it had a reputation for the worst crooks and chiselers? And it was just my luck that it was the anniversary of my father's death, so that I had to stop there to say the mourner's prayer. God preserve you from such a dump! Something told me to stay on the train. But what can a man do when he has to say the kaddish? I looked for a synagogue and found one just as the evening prayer was beginning. When it was over the beadle came up to me. "An anniversary?" he asks. "Yes," I say. "And where might a Jew like you be from?" he asks. "From the big world," I say. "And what might your name be?" "Menakhem-Mendl," I say. "Then welcome!" he says, shaking my hand, as did the rest of them. A circle formed around me and everyone wanted to know who I was. "An agent," I said. "You mean a salesman?" "Not exactly," I said. "I'm in life ensurance. From Acquitable. I ensure you against dying." "What kind of bad news is that?" they asked. So I explained it while they stood gaping as if I were selling them the moon—all but two of them, whom I noticed right away. One was a tall, thin, stooped-looking fellow with a shiny, hooked nose and a habit of pulling the hairs of his beard. The other was short, stout, and dark as a gypsy with a shifty eye that spun like a compass and a way of smiling when nothing was funny. I saw they understood what life ensurance was, because they gave each other a look and one grunted: "It's worth a try."

I could tell they were types you could do business with. And in fact, as soon as I left the synagogue they came after me and said: "Where are you off to, Reb Menakhem-Mendl? Don't run away! There's something we wanted to ask you. Were you really thinking of selling ensurance in a hick town like this?" "Why not?" I asked. "To Jews like the ones you just prayed with?" asks Hook Nose. And Shifty Eye adds: "All they're good for is eating noodle pudding!" "Then what would you suggest?" I inquire. "Find a rich Christian," says Hook Nose. And Shifty Eye adds: "Nothing beats a rich Christian!"

Well, we talked for a while and it's like this: the two of them are friends with a Christian gentleman, a Moldavian landowner they sometimes work for, and they're sure he'd like to be ensured. "Then it will be my pleasure to do it," I say. "I'll even give you a cut. Share and share alike!" It was decided that in the morning, at the early service in the synagogue, they would let me know if he was interested. Their one request was to keep it confidential. I mustn't tell anyone at my inn that we had talked business.

At the crack of dawn I'm up and off to the synagogue. We reach the end of the service—my two friends aren't there. Why hadn't I taken their names and addresses? I couldn't even ask the beadle for them because I was pledged to secrecy. At the last minute, though, just as we were shutting our prayer books, they showed up. I could have jumped for joy! But though I was dying to hear their news, it wasn't the place for it.

They rushed through their prayers and hurried out with me on their heels. "Well?" I asked. "Shhh!" they said. "Not here in the street! You don't know this blamed town. Keep following us. We'll settle things at home and have a bite to eat." And with that Hook Nose makes a sign to Shifty Eye and Shifty Eye vanishes and leaves me alone in the dark alleys with Hook Nose. I walked behind him until we got there.

The room we entered was small, dark, and smoky. Flies crawled on the walls and ceiling; a lamp with a paper shade painted with faded flowers hung above a table covered by a red cloth. By the stove stood a small, grease-stained woman, looking pale and frightened. She gave Hook Nose a questioning look. "Food!" he said, walking by her. In no time there were rolls, appetizers, and a bottle of brandy on the table. Soon Shifty Eye arrived. Waddling behind him was a three-hundred-pound behemoth with a big blue nose, two hairy mitts for hands, and the strangest legs you ever saw. They started out huge and grew so thin toward the bottom that you wondered how they could hold him.

This was the Moldavian gentleman, who spied the brandy bottle and let out a great rumble from his stomach that sounded like: *"Otse dobre dilo!"* And so we each had a swallow of brandy (the gentleman had two) and chatted about the grain crop until Shifty Eye turned to me and whispered: "The man is loaded! He has 10,000 bushels of wheat, to say nothing of oats. Don't be misled by how shabbily he's dressed. He's a terrible skinflint." Meanwhile, Hook Nose is advising the gentleman to keep his wheat in storage until winter when prices will rise. *"Otse dobre dilo!"* says the gentleman, emptying more glasses between mouthfuls of food, which he's putting away as though there's no tomorrow. He blows his nose and lets out a big burp and when he's finished Hook Nose says: "Now we can get down to business!"

Well, I sat that Moldavian gentleman down in a corner and gave him such a spiel that I can't tell you where it came from. I explained how important it was to have life ensurance. It didn't matter, I said, if you were as rich as Rothschild. In fact, the richer you were, the more you needed ensurance, because an old age lived in poverty was harder on a rich man. A beggar, I said, was used to it, but a rich man would rather die first. *"Otse dobre dilo!"* says the gentleman, passing more wind like a bellows. I was still working up a full head of steam when Hook Nose interrupts, using Hebrew words the gentleman can't follow. "That's enough *dabern!*" he says. "Go get some *niyor* and *ksive* what you have to!" So Shifty Eye brings a pen and paper and I write out a policy for the gentleman to sign. He looks at it, he does, and breaks into such a sweat that he can barely write his name. Then I take him to the doctor for a checkup, receive a first payment, write out a receipt, and the deal is done.

Back I go to my inn in fine fettle and order a meal. "So what's new?" asks the innkeeper when he sees me. "What should be new?" I say. "I understand you deserve to be congratulated," says the innkeeper. "What for?" I ask. "For selling a policy," he says. "What policy is that?" I ask, playing innocent. "The one you sold to the Christian," he says. "What Christian is that?" I ask. "The fat landowner," he says. "But how do you know," I ask, "that I sold a policy to a Christian landowner?" "What I know," says the innkeeper, "is that he's a landowner as much as you are." "Then what is he?" I ask. "The bogeyman," says the innkeeper, laughing right in my face. I turned pale, sat down, and begged him to explain what he meant. How did he know what I had been up to?

Well, he finally realized I knew nothing, felt sorry for me, took me to the next room, and told me things about my two associates that made my hair stand on end. They were, it seemed, common swindlers; a worse pair of rascals couldn't be found. "They've broken enough laws," said the innkeeper, "to be sent a long way up the river. It's their good luck that they always find someone else to take the rap. Your rich Moldavian is a bum, a rip-snorting, God-awful drunk, not the man in whose name you wrote the policy. If *he*'s not already pushing up daisies, you can bet he soon will be. Do you get the picture?"

I nearly passed out when I heard that. A lot of good my new clothes would do me if I had to wear them to prison! I ran to the station as fast as my legs could carry me, hoping not to bump into my two friends. May they rot in hell with their Moldavian gentleman, and their lousy town, and their blasted Bessarabia, and their damned Acquitable, and the whole bloody business of death ensurance! Surely God can provide better livelihoods. I only pray I reach my destination safely—and since I have a long way to go, I'll be brief. God willing, I'll write more from Hamburg. Meanwhile, may He grant you health and success. Say hello to the children, bless them. God keep them healthy and strong until we meet again in better times. My fondest greetings to your parents and to everyone.

Your husband,
Menakhem-Mendl

P.S. I forgot to tell you where I'm going. I'm off to America, my dear wife! And not just me. A whole crowd is traveling with me. That is, each of us is heading for Hamburg and from there to America. Why America? Because they say it's the place for Jews. The streets, they say, are paved with gold and money is dished out by the plateful. Why, a day's work is worth a whole dollar there! And the Jews, they say, are lapping up the cream. Everyone says that in America, God willing, I'll be a big hit. The whole world is going because there's no future here, you can't do business any more. And if everyone is doing it, why not me? What's there to lose? I only hope you don't have too a hard time of it, my dear, or think too badly of me. I swear always to remember you and the children, God bless them. I'll work day and night, nothing will get in my way. And if the Lord lends a hand and I do well (and I'm as sure to as day follows night!) I'll buy tickets for you all and send for you. You'll live like a princess there—you'll have nothing but the best—I won't let a hair fall from your head. Upon my word, it's time you saw a bit of the world too! Just don't worry or take it to heart, for there's a great God above looking after us.

Yours etc.

Motl, the Cantor's Son

♦♦♦ *Part One*

THE CALF AND I

I'll bet you anything no one felt as good in the warm, bright days after Passover as me and the neighbors' calf Menye. By me I mean Motl, Peysi the cantor's son. Menye was the name I gave the calf.

Together we basked in the first rays of the sun, which only warmed up after Passover. Together we sniffed the new blades of green grass kicking off their blanket of snow. Together we sprang from our own dark holes to welcome each sweet, bright spring day—me, Motl, from a cold, wet house that smelled of sourdough and medicine, and Menye from a dirty stall that smelled worse, a miserable hutch with crooked walls that let in the snow in winter and the rain in summer.

Let loose in God's world, we said our thank-you's to Nature. I stretched both arms high, opened my mouth wide, and took such a gulp of fresh, warm air that I felt myself growing taller, shooting up and up into the deep blue skullcap of the sky with its wispy clouds and birds that flashed by and were gone with a twitter and a zoom. Without thinking I broke into a song finer than any prayer of my father's. It had no words—no notes—no melody. It was as natural as a waterfall or the sound of the waves, a song of songs, a heavenly rhapsody:

Oy-yoy, Tate!
Oy-yoy, Father!
Oy-yoy-yoy-yoy-yoy, God!

That was my way of telling the world how I felt. Menye had his.

First he nuzzled the ground with his wet, black nose. Then he pawed it three times with his front hoof, raised his tail high, leaped straight in the air, landed on all fours, and let out a muffled "moo." It was such a funny sound that I had to laugh and make it myself. Menye seemed pleased by this, because he repeated the whole act, ending with the same four-legged jump. Naturally, I did the same, mooing and jumping like Menye. It could have gone on forever, a moo from Menye and a moo from me, a jump from me and a jump from Menye, if something didn't land on my neck. It's my brother Elye's hand, all five fingers of it.

"Just look at you, almost nine years old and dancing with a calf! Get into the house, you rascal! Papa will give it to you!"

♦♦♦

Bull! Papa isn't giving me anything. Papa is sick. He hasn't led a synagogue service since Simkhes Toyreh. All night he coughs. We sent for Dr. Blackwhiskers, the doctor with the big mustache and merry eyes. He's a friendly man who calls me "Bellybutton" and tickles me in the stomach. He told my mother to take my father off potatoes and put him on clear broth and milk, a steady diet of clear broth and milk.

My mother listened and covered her face with her shawl when he left. Her shoulders shook. After a while she wiped her eyes, called my brother Elye, and spoke to him in a whisper. They were arguing. My mother wanted Elye to go somewhere and Elye didn't want to. He said loudly:

"I'd rather go to my grave than to them! I'd sooner lie down and die."

"Bite your tongue, you savage! How can you say such a thing?"

Although my mother spoke quietly, she clenched her teeth and shook a fist as though to knock Elye down. But soon she backed off and asked:

"What should I do, son? We have to help your poor father."

"We'll sell something," my brother said, glancing at the glass cupboard.

My mother glanced at it too. She said softly:

"What is there to sell, our souls? That's all we have left. You can't be thinking of that empty cupboard."

"Why not?" Elye asked.

"Murderer!" screamed my mother. "How did I raise my children to be such murderers?"

She turned red, began to cry, dried her eyes again, and gave in. The same thing had happened with my father's books; with the silver collar of his prayer shawl; with our two gold-plated kiddush cups; with her good silk dress; and with all the other things we had sold one by one, each to a different customer.

The books went to Mikhl the book peddler, a man with a stringy beard that he's always scratching. Elye had to go for him three times before he came. My mother cheered up at the sight of him and raised a finger to her lips. Mikhl understood the need for secrecy. He looked at the bookshelf, scratched his beard, and asked in a low voice:

"Well, now, what do we have here?"

My mother signaled me to fetch the books. I didn't have to be asked twice. I jumped up so fast I crashed into the table and got a clout from Elye for behaving like a wild man. Elye went to the bookshelf and laid the books on the table. Mikhl leafed through them with one hand and scratched his beard with the other while pointing out what was wrong with each book. This one had a torn binding. That one was split in the back. A third had no value. When he had gone through every book, backs, bindings, and all, he gave his beard a scratch and said:

"If you at least had a complete set of the Mishnah, this might be worth something."

My mother turned pale as a sheet. My brother Elye flamed and shouted:

"If you wanted a Mishnah you should have said so instead of wasting our time!"

"Hush!" my mother said.

"Who's there?" a hoarse voice asked from the next room.

"No one," my mother answered, sending Elye to my father's bedside.

She settled with Mikhl by herself. It couldn't have been for much because when Elye came back and asked, she told him it was none of his business. Mikhl took the books, stuffed them in his sack, and cleared out.

♦♦♦

Of all the things we sold, the glass cupboard was the most fun.

In the first place, who could take it? It had always seemed part of the wall; how was it going to leave now? And besides, where would my mother now put the bread, the hallah, the dishes, the tin spoons and forks (our two silver spoons and one silver fork had been sold long ago), and where would we keep the matso on Passover? That's what I wondered as Nachman the carpenter stood measuring the cupboard with the big raw nail on the fat finger of his greasy hand. In his opinion it wouldn't fit through the door. The cupboard was this wide, the door was that wide—there was no way of getting it out.

"Then who got it in?" Elye asked.

"Why don't you ask the cupboard?" Nachman said crossly. "How do I know? Someone, that's who."

I felt sorry for that cupboard. I mean, I felt sorry to think we'd be stuck with it. But soon Nachman came back with his two sons, both carpenters too, and it flew through the door as though possessed. Nachman went first, followed by his sons. He gave directions:

"Kopl, that way! Mendl, to the right! Kopl, slow down! Mendl, stop!"

I helped by bringing up the rear. My mother and Elye just stared at the bare wall that was covered with cobwebs and bawled. What a sight!

Suddenly—*cra-shhh!* Just as the cupboard reached the door, the glass shattered. The carpenter and his sons blamed each other. "You've got the hands of a tin rooster!" "And you have the feet of a bear!" "The devil take you!" "It was a black year you were born in!"

"What's going on?" a hoarse voice asked from the other room.

"Nothing," my mother said, wiping her eyes.

♦♦♦

"Now what?"

So my mother asked Elye one morning, looking anxiously at the bare walls. Elye and I helped her look at them. Then Elye looked at me, all worried and pitying-like.

"Go outside," he said sternly. "I need to talk to Mama."

I hopped out on one foot and made straight for the neighbor's calf.

Menye had grown by leaps and bounds and was now a handsome young bull with a cute black muzzle and big round eyes that looked so smart when they asked for something to eat that they were almost human. He liked being chucked with two fingers beneath the chin.

"What's this? Hanging out with that calf again? The two of you are bosom buddies!"

It was Elye again. This time, though, he was nice. He took my hand and told me we were going to Hirsh-Ber the cantor's. I would like it there, he said. There would be plenty to eat. Things at home weren't good. We had to save Papa's life. Elye opened his gabardine and showed me his vest.

"I've even sold the silver pocket watch I was given for my engagement. Brokheh's father will have a fit if he finds out. He'll turn the world upside down!"

It's a good thing Brokheh's father never found out and the world is still right side up. What would poor Menye do on his head?

"Here we are," my brother Elye said. He was getting nicer by the minute.

Hirsh-Ber wasn't a cantor like my father. According to my father, he couldn't even carry a tune. But he knew music and had a choir of fifteen boys and a temper you had to watch out for. I sang him a synagogue number, jerking it out for all it was worth, and he said I was a soprano. "A soprano?" said Elye. "A soprano to beat all sopranos!" Elye bargained, was given an advance, and said I would be living at the cantor's. "Do what he tells you," he said. "And don't feel homesick."

That's easy to say. How was I not supposed to feel homesick? The spring mud was gone, the summer sun was shining down, the sky was crystal clear, and I even had my own pile of logs. The logs weren't ours. They belonged to a rich Jew named Yosi who was building a house and had dumped them next door. Three cheers for Yosi! I made a fort out of them and picked the brambles and puffballs that grew between them. The brambles made good swords and the puffballs went bang when you blew them up and knocked them against your head.

I had a good life. So did Menye. The whole outdoors was ours. And I shouldn't feel homesick?

♦♦♦

After three weeks of living with Hirsh-Ber I've hardly sung a note. I have another job. It's taking care of Dobtshe. Dobtshe is a hunchback. That's why she outweighs me even though she isn't two years old. Carrying her around can break your back. But Dobtshe loves me. She likes to grab me and feel me all over. "Kiko," she calls me, don't ask me why. At night it's "Kiko ki," which means I should stay up and rock her. Love isn't the word for it. At mealtimes it's "Kiko pi," which means I should give her all my food. I want to go home. Even without Dobtshe, the food at Hirsh-Ber's isn't great.

Last night was the night of Shavuos. That's when you can see the sky open up if you stand outside and wait to wish on it. But not with Dobtshe loving me. "Kiko ki!" she said and I had to rock her until I fell asleep myself. That's when I had a visit from Menye. He looked at me with his human eyes and said: "Come!" The two of us headed downhill for the river. As soon as we reached it—*hup!* I rolled up my pants and was in the water with Menye swimming behind me. I made for the opposite bank, as far away as I could get from Dobtshe, Hirsh-Ber, and my sick father.

I woke up with a start. It was only a dream. But I have to get away. How? Where? Home, of course. The problem is that Hirsh-Ber is awake, too. He has a big tuning fork that he tests on his teeth and holds to his ear. He wants me to dress quickly. We have a new number to sing today after the Torah reading.

In synagogue I see my brother Elye. What is he doing here? He usually prays at the butchers' place, where my father is the cantor. As soon as the Torah scroll is taken out, he goes over to talk to Hirsh-Ber. Hirsh-Ber doesn't look very happy. I hear him say:

"Don't forget: as soon as your Sabbath lunch is over!"

"Come, you're going to see Papa," Elye says. The two of us start for home. Elye walks and I skip. I mean, I run. That is, I fly.

"Take it easy! What's the hurry?" my brother asks. I can see he wants to talk to me. "You know Papa is sick, very sick. God knows what will become of him. We have to do all we can for him. There's no one else to help. Mama's dead set against putting him in the public sick ward. She says she'd rather die first. . . . Shhh, here she comes."

♦♦♦

My mother holds out her arms and throws them around me. I feel a tear that isn't mine on my cheek. Elye goes to my father and leaves us standing outside. We're not alone. Around us stand our neighbor Fat Pesye, her daughter Mindl, her daughter-in-law Perl, and two other women.

"A guest for Shavuos! God grant you pleasure from him!"

My mother doesn't lift her swollen eyes. "A guest? A child! He's come to see his sick father. My little boy!"

That's what she says out loud to everyone. She adds quietly to Pesye, who is shaking her head:

"What a town! You would think someone might drop in on him. For twenty-three years he ruined his health by praying his heart out for them. There's nothing left to pay the doctors with. Everything has been sold except the sheets and pillows, God help us! I've boarded the boy with Hirsh-Ber the cantor, done all I could."

I let her complain while craning my neck in all directions. "What are you looking for?" she asks.

"What could a young scamp like him be looking for?" Pesye says. "It's got to be that calf." She turns to me and says like my best friend:

"What can I tell you, my boy? Your calf is gone. We had to sell it to the butcher. What choice did we have? Supporting one dumb critter is hard enough. Two is asking too much."

So Menye has become a dumb critter. A strange woman. Pesye, sticking her nose into everything. What's it to her whether we're planning to have dairy for Shavuos?

"How come you ask?" asks my mother.

"I was just wondering," Pesye says, pressing a pot of sour cream into my mother's hands.

"What in God's world are you doing, Pesye! What do you take us for? God forbid we should be that badly off. You ought to know better."

"I do," Pesye says. "That's why I'm doing it. Lately, knock wood, our cow has been swimming in milk. We have more cheese and butter than we can eat. I set this aside for you. You'll return it when you can."

Pesye talks to my mother while I think of my logs and my calf. If I weren't ashamed I would cry.

My mother says: "When Papa asks how you are, just say: 'Praise God, I'm fine.'"

Elye makes sure I understand: "No complaints and no sob stories, do you hear? 'Praise God, I'm fine,' that's all you say."

Elye leads me to my father's room. The table is covered with bottles, pillboxes, cupping glasses. The window is closed and the room smells like an apothecary's. In honor of the holiday the walls are decorated with green branches. A paper cutout of a Star of David hangs over the bed. That's Elye's work. Sweet-smelling grasses are spread on the floor. My father motions to me with a long, thin finger. My brother Elye gives me a push and I go to him.

I hardly recognize him. His skin is like clay. The gray hairs on his head glisten damply. Each of them looks pasted on. His two eyes are stuck deep in their sockets. His teeth don't look like his own, either. His neck is so thin it can hardly hold up his head. But at least he can sit. He makes a sound like a drowning man, lays his bony fingers on my face, and gives me a smile as crooked as a corpse's. He says:

"I reckon you know enough to say the kaddish, eh?"

Elye bends and pretends to blow his nose while he sniffles.

Just then my mother walks in. Behind her is Dr. Blackwhiskers. He greets me like a younger brother, pokes me in the stomach, and says cheerfully to my father:

"I see you have a guest for Shavuos. Enjoy him!"

"Thank you," my mother says. She signals to the doctor to examine my father and give him his medicine.

The doctor opens the window noisily and scolds Elye for keeping it closed. "I've told you a thousand times he needs fresh air!"

Elye points to my mother to say it's her fault. My mother says she's afraid my father will catch cold. She signals to the doctor again. He takes out a big gold pocket watch. Elye stares at it. The doctor notices and says: "I've got half-past five. What time do you have?"

"My watch isn't running," Elye says, flushing from the tip of his nose to the ends of his ears.

My mother fidgets. She wants my father to get his medicine. The doctor takes his time asking all kinds of questions. When is my brother's wedding? What does Hirsh-Ber think of my voice? I should have a good one, because voices are inherited. My mother fidgets some more. At last the doctor moves a stool to the sick bed and takes my father's hot, dry hand.

"Well, cantor! How has Shavuos been treating you?"

"Praise God." My father smiles like a corpse.

"Aha! You've been coughing less? You slept well?" The doctor bends close to him.

"Not at all . . . ," my father answers, stopping to catch his breath after every few words. "I've been coughing more and sleeping less . . . but God be praised . . . it's Shavuos . . . the day the Torah was given . . . and we have a guest . . . a guest for the holiday . . . "

Everyone looks at the guest. The guest stares at the floor. His thoughts are somewhere else. He's thinking of logs, bramble swords, puffballs that burst like bombs, a calf that has become a dumb critter, the river at the bottom of the hill. He's thinking of the high, bright, deep, blue skullcap of the sky.

LUCKY ME — I'M AN ORPHAN!

I've never been so important. How is that? Because my father, Peysi the cantor, died on the first day of Shavuos. That makes me an orphan.

My brother Elye and I have to say the kaddish. Elye taught me to say it. He's a good brother and a rotten teacher. He whacks me each time he gets mad. He sat me down, opened a prayer book, and had me read:

Yisgodol veyiskodosh shmey rabbo . . .

Elye said I had to learn it by heart. He read it with me a few times and told me to practice. I tried but couldn't get the hang of it.

Everything went fine up to *veyatzmokh purkeney.* I kept getting stuck on those two words. Elye poked me with an elbow and said that either I was dreaming (I was) or thinking of the calf (I was). He's no slouch, my brother Elye. He made me say the kaddish over and over. In the end I got as far as *le'eylo ule'eylo min kol birkhoso veshiroso* and couldn't go a line further. Elye grabbed me by the ear and said Papa should only rise from his grave and see the son he had.

"I wish I could skip the kaddish."

So I said to Elye and got a good box on the ear. My mother came running.

"For the love of God! What do you think you're doing? Have you forgotten the boy is an orphan?"

My mother and I sleep together in my father's bed, which is the only furniture left. She lets me have most of the blanket.

"Cover yourself and sleep, my orphan," she says. "I only wish there was something to eat."

I cover myself and don't sleep. I practice the kaddish. It's the one thing I have to learn, because I've stopped going to school and am no longer in Hirsh-Ber's choir. Orphans are excused.

Lucky me!

♦♦♦

Congratulations! I know the whole kaddish by heart. You should hear me rattle it off in synagogue. Like a house on fire! I have a terrific voice too, a soprano I got from my father. All the boys are jealous. The women cry. Rich Jews like Yosi give me a kopeck after prayers. But Yosi's son, bug-eyed Henekh, is out to get me. He sticks his tongue out whenever I say the kaddish. He's dying to make me laugh. I keep a straight face just to spite him. Once Aron the beadle saw him and chucked him out by the ear. That's what I call a good deed!

Now that I say the kaddish every morning and evening, I don't have to carry Dobtshe around. I'm free as a lark to spend all day by the river, swimming and fishing.

Fishing is something I taught myself to do. I could teach you too if you wanted. You take off your shirt and knot the sleeves and wade into the water up to your neck. You have to wade pretty far. When your shirt is full of mud and weeds, you hustle out and give it a shake to see what's in it. If there are any tadpoles flipping about, you throw them back —that's plain human kindness. Sometimes there's a leech. Leeches are good money. They fetch three and a half kopecks a dozen. That isn't hay.

You can forget about fish, though. There used to be fish but no more. I haven't caught a single one. Leeches are good enough for me. But sometimes there are no leeches either. This summer I'm still looking for my first. Just don't ask me how Elye found out I'd gone fishing. He nearly tore my ears off. It's a good thing Pesye saw him. She watches out for me like a mother.

"How can you pick on an orphan like that?"

Elye was so ashamed he let go of my ear. There's nothing folks won't do for me. Lucky me—I'm an orphan!

♦♦♦

Pesye is in love with me. She keeps asking my mother if she can have me. "What do you care?" she says. "I already have twelve mouths to feed. So there'll be a thirteenth."

She had almost talked my mother into it when Elye butted in:

"Who'll see to it that he says the kaddish?"

"I will, all right? I hope that's good enough for you."

Pesye's no rich lady. Her husband is a bookbinder named Moyshe. They say he's pretty good at it. But being good isn't enough; you need luck too. That's what Pesye tells my mother. My mother disagrees. She says you can be lucky without luck. Look at me. I'm an orphan and everyone wants me. They're actually fighting over me. My mother says they can kill themselves first. She cries and asks Elye:

"What do you think? Should we let him stay with Pesye for a while?"

Elye is nearly a grown-up. That's why she asks him. He strokes his smooth face as if it had a beard and talks grown-up talk.

"By all means! Anything to keep him from growing up a bum."

That means I can live with Pesye if I promise not to be a bum. There's nothing being a bum doesn't include. Tie paper to the cat's tail and you're a bum. Bang a stick on the priest's gate to make his dogs come running and you're a bum. Unplug Leibl the water carrier's barrel so that all the water runs out and you're a bum.

"It's your luck you're an orphan," Leibl says. "Believe me, I'd break every bone in your body if you weren't."

I believe him. He'd never lay hands on an orphan.

Lucky me.

♦♦♦

You'll pardon my saying so, but our neighbor Pesye told a fat lie. She said she had twelve mouths to feed. But by my count, I'm the fourteenth. She must have forgotten blind Uncle Borukh. Or else she left him out because he has no teeth. That doesn't stop him from eating, though. He stuffs his mouth with food and swallows it like a goose. Everyone stuffs themselves at Pesye's. It's unnatural how much they eat. I stuff myself too. But I'm the only one to get kicked beneath the table for doing it. The worst kicks come from Bumpy. He's a maniac, Bumpy is. His real name is Hirshl but he's called Bumpy because of the bump on his forehead. Everyone at Pesye's has a name. There's Log, and there's Tomcat, and there's Ox, and there's Ratface, and there's Petelulu, and there's Give-Me-More, and there's Butternose.

Don't rack your brains over it. I'll explain each one to you. Log is Log because he's heavy and round. Velvl is black and hairy as a cat. Hayyim looks like an ox, so that's his name. Mendl is Ratface on account of his pointy nose. Faytl doesn't talk so well: that makes him Petelulu. Berl is always eating; give him bread with chicken fat and he wants more. Zerakh is Butternose because of a disgusting habit that's not his fault. You can thank his mother for never teaching him to use a handkerchief. But maybe she's not to blame either. Let's not fight over it.

It's a house full of names. Even the poor cat, who did nothing to deserve it, is called Feyge-Leah the Beadle's Wife. That's because Feyge-Leah's a big woman and the cat's a big cat. I don't know how many lickings Pesye's boys have gotten for calling that cat by a woman's name. Go throw beans at the wall! Everyone has a name and that's that.

♦♦♦

I've been given a name too. Don't try to guess what it is. It's Lips. No one, it seems, likes my lips. They say I use them too much when I eat. I'd like to see someone eat without them! Although I'm not the type to take offense, it's a name I hate. That's why they tease me with it. I've never seen such wise alecs in my life. First they called me Motl-Much-Lips. Then they shortened it to Much-Lips. Now it's plain Lips.

"Lips! Where have you been?"

"Lips! Wipe your nose!"

When it gets me down, I cry. Once Moyshe asked why I was crying. I said he'd cry too if his name was Motl and everyone called him Lips. "Who's everyone?" he asked. "Bumpy," I said. He went to give Bumpy a licking and Bumpy said, "It's Log." He went to Log and Log blamed Tomcat.

It went on like that. In the end Moyshe lined them all up, took the binding of a prayer book, and whacked them one by one. "I'll teach you little bastards to make fun of an orphan," he said. "The devil take whoever brought you into this world!"

I'm not making up a word. He made them all pay for it. They took their licks because of me.

What luck I'm an orphan!

WHAT WILL BECOME OF ME?

Can you guess where Paradise is? I'll bet you can't. And do you know why not? Because it's a different place for everyone. My mother thinks it's where my father is. She says that's where the good souls go when they die. And the proof is that if he's not in Paradise, where else can he be? Why else was he made to suffer so much in this world? That's what she says, my mother, wiping her eyes.

Ask my friends, though, and they'll tell you that Paradise is a mountain of crystal as high as the sky. Boys run free as the wind there, never go to school, take baths of milk, and eat honey by the fistful. And listen to this: I know a bookbinder who thinks Paradise is the bathhouse! I swear, that's what I heard our neighbor Moyshe say. It's enough to drive you crazy—especially if like me you think Paradise is Dr. Menashe's garden.

You've never seen such a garden in your life. Not only is it the only garden on our street, and even the only garden in our town, it's the only garden of its kind in the world. There's never been another like it and never will be. I just don't know what to describe for you first: Dr. Menashe's garden or Dr. Menashe and his wife. I'd better begin with the two of them. After all, it's their garden.

♦♦♦

Menashe walks around with a cape all the time, the same as Dr. Blackwhiskers. He has one big eye and one small one and a crooked mouth. I mean, one side of his mouth is longer than the other. It was blown out of shape by the wind. That's what Dr. Menashe says. It beats me how he can be right. Any wind that could do such a thing would have blown my head off long ago.

Most likely, it's just a habit. For example, I have a friend, Berl, who's in the habit of squinting all the time. And I have another friend, Velvl, who always sounds like he's slurping soup. There's nothing you can't get used to if you set your mind to it. And even if Dr. Menashe has a crooked mouth, he's still the best doctor around. He doesn't put on airs like the other doctors but comes lickety-split when he's called. And he makes his own medicines instead of writing out those weird prescriptions. Not long ago (I must have spent too much time in the river) I came down with such a case of the aches-and-shakes that my mother went running to get him. He took one look at me and said with that crooked mouth:

"There's no need to worry. It's nothing serious. The little rascal's caught a cold in his lungs."

And with that he took a blue flask from his pocket and tapped something white into six packets of paper. It was a powder, he said, and I should take my first dose right away. I crumpled the packet in my hand, turning it this way and that. Something told me it would taste awfully bitter. Don't think it didn't. There's bitter and there's bitter, and if you've never made your own chewing gum from the bark of a young tree you'll never know what that powder was like. There must be a law that the more powdery anything is, the bitterer it tastes. God himself couldn't have done anything about it. It tasted like death.

Dr. Menashe said I should take a dose every two hours. He might as well have told me to drink bile. As soon as my mother went to tell my brother, I dumped the other five doses in the tub and filled the packets with flour. My mother had a time of it running to Pesye's every two hours to look at the clock. After each dose she said I was looking better. By the last I was in perfect health.

"Now that's what I call a doctor!" my mother said. She kept me home from school for a day and gave me sweet tea and white bread.

"There's not a doctor can hold a candle to Menashe, God bless him! He has powders that could bring a dead man back to life."

So my mother told everyone, wiping her eyes as usual.

♦♦♦

Dr. Menashe's wife is known as "the Doct'ress." Everyone tells you to steer clear of her. That's because she's mean. She has a face like a man's, a voice like a man's, and boots like a man's. Whatever she says sounds cross. You can guess what people think of her. She's never in her life given a hungry man a slice of bread, even though her house is full of food. There are jams and jellies from last summer, and from the summer before that, and from ten summers before that. What does she need them all for? Go ask her! That's how she is. Some people are hopeless.

Every summer the Doct'ress makes more jam. I suppose you think she cooks it over a coal or wood fire. Not in your life! She uses weeds, pine cones, dead leaves. There's enough smoke to choke the whole street. If you ever come our way on a summer day and smell an awful stink, don't worry—the town's not burning down. It's just the Doct'ress making jam. She makes it from the fruit in her garden. I told you I'd get around to the garden .

♦♦♦

What grows there? Apples and pears and cherries and plums and sour cherries and raspberries and currants and peaches and gooseberries and blackberries and huckleberries and whortleberries and you name it. Even grapes for Rosh Hashanah. If you want a new fruit to bless the new year with, you have to buy your grapes from the Doct'ress. Sure, you can find them in Cracow and Lemberg too, if you look hard enough. But they'll be sour. That's why the Doct'ress gets such a good price for them.

She makes money from everything, even her sunflowers. God help the person who asks permission to pick one! You'd have an easier time pulling teeth. And I'm not even talking about her apples, pears, cherries, and plums. That's taking your life in your hands.

I know that garden like a Jew knows his prayers. I know every tree and what grows on it and if this year's crop is better than last year's. You're wondering how? Believe me, I've never set foot in it. How could I when it's surrounded by a high fence with monster stakes? Worse yet, there's a dog inside. I mean, he's more like a wolf. He's on a long leash, the big brute, and just try getting past him—just let him think you're thinking of trying—and he'll rip and tear at you like the very devil. So how do I know what's in that garden? That's the next thing I'm going to tell you.

◆◆◆

If you don't know Mendl the slaughterer, you certainly don't know where his house is. It's next to Menashe's and looks down on his garden. You can see the whole garden from Mendl's roof. The trick is getting up there.

It's a cinch for me. Mendl's house is next to our own and not as high. Shinny up to our attic (I'll show you how to do it without a ladder), stick your foot out the window, and you're already on Mendl's roof. You can lie there as long as you like on your back or on your stomach. Just don't try standing, because someone might see you and wonder what you're doing. The best time is before sunset, between the afternoon and evening prayers, when I'm supposed to be in synagogue. I tell you, that garden is a Paradise! Adam and Eve's had nothing on it.

When summer comes and the trees blossom with white feathers, you can bet your boots there'll be green raspberries. They're the first fruit to watch out for. Some folks wait for them to get ripe. That's plain dumb. Take it from me, they're better green. You say they're sour? They pucker your mouth? Big deal! Sour food is good for the heart and your mouth's no problem. Just rub the inside of it with salt and keep it open for half an hour and you're ready for more green raspberries.

After the raspberries come the currants. They're red, with little black mouths and yellow seeds, dozens of them on each branch. Run a branch through your teeth and off they come, all juicy and yummy. When they're in season my mother buys a quart for a kopeck and I eat them with bread. The Doct'ress' garden has two rows of currant bushes that shine in the sun. What wouldn't I give for just one branch—for just one currant to pop in my mouth! But all this talk is making me hungry. Let's go on to sour cherries.

Sour cherries don't stay green for long. They ripen in no time. I swear, I've been on Mendl's roof and seen cherries that were green as grass in the morning, rosy pink by afternoon, and red as fire by evening.

Sometimes my mother buys sour cherries too. But how many can she afford? Five cherries on a string. What can you do with five cherries? You play with them until you lose them and can't find them any more.

♦♦♦

If you can count the stars in the sky, you can count the cherries in Menashe's garden. I've tried lots of times and always lost count in the end.

One thing about cherries is that they won't drop from the tree until they're past their prime. You'll never find a fallen cherry that isn't black as a plum. Peaches are different: they fall as soon as they turn yellow. Ah, peaches, peaches! They're my favorite fruit. I've eaten one in my whole life and still remember the taste of it. My father was alive then and our house had all its fixings, the glass cupboard and the little couch and all the books and bedspreads. We were on our way home from synagogue when he reached into his back pocket, the one he kept his handkerchief in.

"Care for some peaches, boys?" he asked. "Here's one for each of you."

Out came his hand with two big, round, yellow, luscious peaches. My brother Elye couldn't wait. He said the blessing out loud and stuffed the whole peach in his mouth. Not me. I played with it, looked at it, sniffed it, and ate it bit by bit with bread. Peaches and bread are a swell combination. I'll never forget that peach.

From Mendl's roof I can see a tree full of peaches. They fall one by one, yellow and red ones, splitting open when they hit the ground. I can even see their big pits. What will the Doct'ress do with so many peaches? She'll make lots of jam and store it in the back of her oven and take it down to the cellar in winter and keep it until it gets moldy.

After the peaches come the plums. Not all at once. You've got two kinds of plum trees in Menashe's garden. The first are the cherry plums; they're small, sweet, hard, and black. Then come the bucket plums. Bucket plums are sold by the bucket. They're thin-skinned, sticky, and watery but not as bad as you think. In fact, I wouldn't mind one right now. But the Doct'ress doesn't give them away. She'd rather make plum jam for the winter. Don't ask me how she'll eat it all.

♦♦♦

We're done with the cherries, plums, and peaches. Now it's apple time. Apples, you should know, are not pears. Even a bergamot, which is the best pear in the world, is worthless until it's ripe. You might as well chew wood. But an apple is an apple no matter how green it is. Bite into a green apple, I grant you, and you've got one sour mouth. Do you want to know something, though? I wouldn't swap you a green apple for two ripe ones. A ripe one takes forever to ripen but a green one is ready to eat the minute it sets on the tree. The only difference is the size. And apples are like people: getting bigger doesn't make them better. Your little apple can taste just as good. Take your Winesap. What doesn't it have that a bigger apple does? And it's going for nothing this year. There's such a glut they'll be trucking them in wagons. I heard that from the Doct'ress herself. She was talking to Ruvn the Apple Jew when the fruit was young on the trees.

Ruvn had come to look at her garden. He wanted to buy her pears and apples on the branch. He's the world's biggest expert, Ruvn is. One look at a tree and he'll tell you what it's worth. He's never wrong either, barring winds, heat waves, weevils, and worms. Those things come from God, there's no way to predict them. Not that I know what God needs apple weevils for. But he must know what he's doing when he takes the bread from Ruvn's mouth. A bit of bread, Ruvn says, is all he asks from a tree. He has a wife and children at home and needs to put something on their table. The Doct'ress promised him not only bread but meat. She should only, she said, be as lucky as he was in getting such trees. Trees? Pure gold!

"You know I have your best interests at heart," the Doct'ress said. "I don't wish better for myself."

"Amen!" Ruvn said with a smile on his kind, red face that was peeling from the sun. "Promise there'll be no winds or weevils this year and I'll give you every kopeck you're asking for."

The Doct'ress gave him a sharp look and said in her man's voice:

"Promise you won't fall and break a leg."

"No one is sent an announcement that he's about to break a leg," Ruvn answered with a twinkle. "And the rich should worry more than the poor because they have more to lose."

"You're a clever Jew," the Doct'ress said in a tone that could kill. "A man who wishes misfortune on others had better watch his tongue before he loses that too."

"You're quite right," Ruvn said with the same smile. "A tongue is a useful thing to have. Unless, God forbid, it belongs to a hungry man on your doorstep."

♦♦♦

Too bad the Doct'ress' garden isn't Ruvn's! Life would be a lot finer then. You've never seen such a witch. Let the measliest, wormiest apple with wrinkles like an old woman's fall from a tree and she'll pick it up and drop it in her kerchief. Where does it go from there? Either to her attic or her cellar. Most likely her cellar, because I've heard it's full of rotten apples. Swiping an apple from her is a good deed.

But how? Sneak into her garden at night when the whole town's sleeping and fill my pockets? A swell idea if not for the dog! And the most annoying part is that there are so many apples on her trees this summer that they're practically begging to be taken. I wish I knew a magic charm to make them jump into my arms.

Well, I thought and I thought and what I finally thought of wasn't magic. It was a long pole with a nail at one end. I had only to hook an apple by the stem and give a yank, and over the fence it would go. Provided it didn't fall, of course. But what if it did? As long as I didn't poke holes in it, the Doct'ress would think it was a windfall.

I swear, I didn't bruise a single apple. I didn't let any fall, either. I know how to handle an apple-swiping pole. The trick is to take your time. You've hooked an apple? Eat it real slow, take a break, and go for another. The birds won't tell on you, I promise.

How was I supposed to know that the witch knew exactly how many apples she had on each tree? She must have counted them and seen some were missing, because the next evening she waited for the thief to show up on Mendl's roof. She had figured out that someone was up there with a pole. Even then I might have gotten away with it if not for the witnesses. An orphan can always beg for mercy—but not when the Doct'ress thought of taking my mother and Mendl's wife and our neighbor Pesye up to our attic with her. It was no trick to spot me through the window, fishing for apples.

"Well? What do you say about your darling son now? Do you believe me?"

It was the Doct'ress. I'd know that voice anywhere. I turned to look and saw all four of them in the attic. Don't think I panicked and threw my pole away. It dropped by itself. It was sheer luck it didn't take me with it. I couldn't look those women in the eyes. If not for the dog, I'd have jumped and killed myself. The worst part was my mother. She didn't stop weeping and wailing.

"Oh, my God! That I should have lived to see the day! Here I thought my orphan was saying kaddish for his father and I find him on the roof stealing apples from a garden! May I be struck by lightning!"

The witch gave it to me good with her man's voice:

"He deserves a beating, the scoundrel! A whipping! A flogging! Let him bleed! Let him learn what it means to be a thie—"

My mother didn't let her finish the word.

"He's an orphan!" she screamed. "A poor orphan!" She kissed the Doct'ress' hand, begged her forgiveness, and swore by all that was holy that I would never do it again. As she lived and breathed!

"Make him swear never even to look at my garden!" thundered the Doct'ress without a drop of pity for an orphan.

"May I hope to die! May my eyes be poked out!" I said. I climbed down from the attic with my mother, who went on crying and scolding after everyone was gone.

"I ask you, what will become of you?" she said. Elye turned pale when she told him what had happened. It must have been from anger, because I heard her whisper that I was an orphan.

"I haven't touched him," Elye said. "I'd just like to know what will become of him. What?"

That's what he said, my brother Elye, gritting his teeth and waiting for an answer. How am I supposed to know? Do you?

MY BROTHER ELYE GETS MARRIED

Congratulations! You haven't heard the news? My brother Elye is getting married.

Hoop-de-doo! You should see the excitement. The whole town is buzzing with it. It's all anyone is talking about. That's what our neighbor Pesye says. She says it will be a grand wedding. Kasrilevke, she says, hasn't seen such a wedding in years.

Why all the fuss? Well, the groom is an orphan and his mother is a widow: that's one reason to celebrate. And you have to give my father credit. My father had a good reputation. Not that anyone ever thought of it when he was alive. But now that he's dead, Peysi the cantor has become a great man. It's awesome, the things people say about him. I've heard them tell my mother that the bride's father should pay for the whole wedding because his son-in-law is Peysi the cantor's boy. Elye is embarrassed by such talk. It makes him stroke his little beard like a grown-up.

He really is one now. He's been one since his beard began to grow. I reckon that came from smoking. Elye took up smoking when my father died. His first cigarette gave him such conniptions that he nearly coughed to death. Now he lights right up and blows smoke through his nose. Big deal! You think I can't do it too? I just don't have any tobacco. I smoke paper, straw, whatever I can get hold of. Did I catch it from Elye when he found out! But how come he can and I can't? It's not my fault if I'm not nine years old yet. I promised him, I even swore on a Bible, that I'd lay off smoking for good. But how long does he expect me to keep my promise? Who doesn't smoke nowadays?

♦♦♦

The world is coming to an end! That's what Pesye says. She just came back in a huff from Elye's father-in-law. It looks bad. He's found out his watch is missing. A good silver watch, a gift to his son-in-law! Still, it's not as though Elye gambled it away. He sold it to pay for medicines and doctors. It's no crime to try saving your father's life.

That's what Pesye said. But Elye's father-in-law is no genius. What, he wants to know, does his watch have to do with anyone's father? It's not his lookout to support all the world's fathers with his watches. Suddenly Elye has all the fathers in the world and they've all been given watches! Pesye says you can't make a fur hat from a pig's tail.

She's talking about Yoyneh the bagel maker. That's Elye's father-in-law. He's a simple soul, a baker. "He should bake bagels in his grave," Pesye says. That's only a joke. Or is it? Who would buy them if he baked them there?

He's a rich man, Elye's father-in-law. Pesye says he's worth a fortune. She told him she would never marry into a family like his because she doesn't like pigs. He put up with it because it's best to hold your tongue when Pesye starts in on you. He was even ready to forget the watch if she'd lay off. But Pesye didn't want to. Pesye wanted Yoyneh to buy Elye a new watch. Who ever heard, she said, of a young man getting married without a watch? Yoyneh the bagel maker couldn't see what business it was of Pesye's if his son-in-law had a watch or not. Pesye said it was her business because Elye is Peysi the cantor's son and Yoyneh is a rich pig. That did it. "Go to hell!" Yoyneh said, slamming the door in Pesye's face. "I'll see you in hell's ovens before me!" Pesye answered. "That's where a baker like you belongs."

My mother was terrified that Yoyneh would break the engagement. Pesye said not to worry. No one ever calls off an orphan's wedding. And who do you think won? We did! Yoyneh the bagel maker bought Elye a new watch. It's silver like the first and even better. He brought it over himself.

I'd give anything to own a watch like that. What would I do with it? First I'd take it apart to see what made it tick. And then? I'll tell you. My mother wished Yoyneh many long years of life in which to buy Elye a gold watch. Then Yoyneh wished my mother many long years of life in which to marry off her youngest son. That's me! I told her I wouldn't mind getting married right now for a watch. She patted my cheek and said with tears in her eyes that a lot of water would flow under the bridge before my wedding. You can search me what my wedding has to do with bridges or why she has to cry.

A day doesn't go by without her crying. She cries the way other people eat or pray. If the tailor brings Elye the wedding suit Yoyneh ordered, my mother cries. If Pesye bakes a honey cake for the wedding, she cries. Now the wedding is tomorrow and she's crying. Maybe someone can explain to me where all those tears come from.

♦♦♦

What a day! It's late summer and the weather is late-summery. The sun no longer makes you sweat or want to jump in the river. It's as soft and kissing-warm as a mother. The sky is spread out like a Sabbath tablecloth. The whole world is celebrating my brother Elye's wedding.

There's a fair in town today. It opened this morning. Fairs are always where you'll find me. I'm crazy about them. Just look at all those Jews, shouting, sweating, swearing, hustling their customers, running around like chickens without heads—a real carnival! The peasants are in no hurry. They walk slowly with their hats pushed back, inspecting the merchandise. They touch it, haggle over it, have a fine time looking for bargains. Women in weird bonnets stick goods in the bosoms of their dresses when they think no one's looking. But the Jews are wise to them and keep an eye out. When they catch one, they try shaking the goods loose. That's when the fur begins to fly.

Once a peasant woman bought a candle in a church and stuck it in her bonnet. Some practical joker lit it without her knowing. The merchants saw and started to laugh. She didn't know what the joke was and swore at them, and the more she swore the harder they laughed. It ended in a Jewish-Christian free-for-all. I tell you, it's a carnival!

The best part of the fair is the horse market. It's full of horses, whips, Gypsies, Jews, peasants, country squires. The noise is so out-of-this-world you could go deaf. The Gypsies shout foul language, the Jews clap their hands, the squires crack their whips, and the colts scamper like crazy. I like to watch horses and listen to horse talk. I'm dying for a colt of my own. I like everything little, puppies and kittens too. Baby pickles, potatoes, onions, heads of garlic, anything that's small. Not piglets, though. I hate pigs even when they're babies.

To get back to the horses: they run around, the colts run after them, and I run after the colts. I'm a ball of fire on my feet. I go barefoot and dress light: a pair of pants, a shirt, and my *tallis koton*. When I race down the hill with it flapping in the wind, I feel I have wings and could fly.

"Motl! For God's sake! Stand still for a second!"

That's Pesye's husband, Moyshe the bookbinder. He's hurrying home from the fair with a bundle of paper. I'm afraid he'll get me in dutch with my mother and Elye will give it to me, so I walk slowly over to him with my eyes on the ground. Moyshe puts down his bundle, wipes my sweaty face with the corner of his coat, and says sternly:

"Isn't an orphan like you ashamed to run around with horses and Gypsies? And on a day like this! Have you forgotten your brother's wedding? Get on home!"

♦♦♦

"Lord-a-mercy! Where have you been?"

That's my mother, clapping her hands and looking at my torn pants, sweaty face, and scratched feet. I have to hand it to Moyshe. He didn't breathe a word about the fair. My mother washes me and dresses me in a new pair of pants with a little brimmed cap for the wedding. Don't ask me what those pants are made of. They go on standing by themselves after I take them off and they make funny noises when I walk. Some pants!

"Rip these and we're finished."

So my mother says and I agree. The world could come to an end before you could rip a pair of pants like those. The most you could do is break them. The cap is an antique with a shiny black brim that you spit on and polish like shoes. My mother stands looking at me, tears of joy on her lined cheeks. She wants me to look good for the wedding. She says to my brother:

"Elye! What do you think? The boy is dressed like a prince, touch wood."

My brother Elye looks at me and strokes his beard. I know what he's thinking. He's thinking that princes don't go barefoot.

My mother pretends not to notice. She's wearing a strange yellow outfit I've never seen before. It looks awfully big on her. I could swear I've seen it on Pesye. She has on her new silk kerchief, too. It still has all its crinkles. Don't ask me to describe it because it keeps changing. It's hot pink in daytime, yellow toward evening, and white at night, but it tends to green in early morning and sometimes it takes on a fine old shade of bright reddish dark greenish sky bluish colorless gray. You can't knock a kerchief like that. It's one of a kind. But it does look awfully strange on my mother. It doesn't stick to her face. To be honest, it looks more like a man's hat. Except even a hat goes better with a face than that kerchief.

Take my brother Elye's hat. It looks like it's growing out of his head. He's shaved his long earlocks—shaved? cut them clean off!—and is wearing a white dress shirt with a stiff, pointy collar and a red and white tie with blue and green polka dots. What a tie! Not to mention his squeaky boots with the high heels. They're supposed to make him look taller, those heels, but they help as much as cupping helps a corpse. Elye is on the short side. Actually, he's not as short as he looks next to that big, tall, red-faced, splotchy-skinned baritone he's marrying. I mean Brokheh, Yoyneh the bagel maker's daughter. A fine-looking couple!

Enough of hanging around the bride and groom, though. I'd rather watch the band. And most of all, the bass fiddle and the kettledrum. That's what I call instruments! If only I were allowed to play them. But I can't even get near them without having a cheek slapped or an ear pulled. Those lowdown musicians would bite off the finger that touched anything.

If she were good, my mother would let me be a musician. She'll never agree, though. It isn't because she's bad. It's because Peysi the cantor's son mustn't be a common wage earner. That's what she tells me when we talk about my future. Everyone's worried about my future: my mother, Elye, Pesye, even Moyshe the bookbinder. Moyshe wants to take me on as an apprentice but Pesye won't agree. She says such work is beneath a son of Peysi's.

But here I am talking about myself and forgetting the wedding! The ceremony is over and we're seated at the tables. The women and girls are dancing a quadrille. I blundered into it with my stiff pants and bounced off the dancers like a rubber ball. You should have heard what people said. "Get a load of the cavalier!" "He has two left feet and trips over both!" "I wish he'd trip right out of here!" Pesye began to shout (she was already as hoarse as a frog): "Are you crazy or are you crazy? The boy is the groom's brother!"

That put them in their place. Naturally, I was taken and seated at the bride's table. Three guesses who they sat me next to! Three hundred wouldn't be enough. It was the bride's little sister, Yoyneh the bagel maker's daughter Alte! She's just a year older than me and has two braids tied under her chin with a ribbon. She looks like a bagel twist herself.

Alte and I sat near the bride and groom and ate from one plate. Elye kept an eye on me to make sure I sat straight and used my fork and wiped my nose with my napkin and didn't eat like a slob. To tell the truth, I didn't enjoy that meal one bit. I don't like being stared at. And to top it all off, Pesye lost her marbles. "I wish you health and happiness!" she shouted across the room to my mother. "Just take a look at these two lovebirds! A match from heaven!"

That brought over Yoyneh the bagel maker, all duded up. Pretty soon the rumor is going around that Alte and I are a couple. Yoyneh has this half-smile on his face. I mean, he's smiling with his top lip and crying with the bottom one. Everyone is looking at us. Alte and I stared at the floor and poked each other in the ribs. I held my nose to keep from laughing and turned as white as a blister. Another second and it would have burst and made a fine scene. Luckily, the band struck up a dreamy tune and all the wedding guests went into a trance.

I looked up and saw my mother in her weird yellow dress and silk shawl. She was crying again. You tell me: is she ever going to stop?

I LAND A SWELL JOB

My mother has news for me. I have a job! Not to worry, though: I haven't been apprenticed to a tradesman. Her enemies won't see the day when Peysi the cantor's son becomes a common laborer. My new job is an easy one, a good one. I'll go to school every day and spend the night at old Luria's house. Old Luria, my mother says, is a rich man. The problem is that he isn't well. That is, there's nothing wrong with him: he eats, drinks, and sleeps like a normal person. He just doesn't sleep at night. At night he never shuts his eyes. His children are afraid to leave him alone then. Someone, they say, should be with him. It can even be a child if he's trustworthy. In fact, a grown-up would be bothersome. A child is no more noticeable than a cat.

"You'll get five rubles a week and your supper," said my mother. "A good supper, too, a rich man's food! The leftovers from his table alone could feed our whole family. I'll pick you up at school every day and bring you to old Luria's. You won't have to do any work there. And you'll eat well and have a comfortable bed. Plus five rubles a week. I'll be able to make some new clothes for you. I'll even buy you a pair of boots."

That sounds pretty good, doesn't it? So why cry? But that's my mother for you. It doesn't count unless she's cried.

♦♦♦

I go to school but I don't really learn. Sitting in a classroom isn't for me. Mostly, I help the rabbi's wife around the house and play with the cat. The housework is a lark. I sweep the rooms, help carry wood, and run errands. It beats learning any day. Nothing is worse than that. *Kometz-*

alef-aw, kometz-alef-aw, kometz-alef-aw—how many times can you listen to the same old thing?

The cat, now—there's someone with brains! People say cats are dirty. Take it from me, it isn't true. A cat is a real clean animal. And don't believe what they say about them getting into trouble. They're as easy as pie to get along with. A dog will suck up to you and wag its tail. A cat just sits licking itself and shuts its eyes and purrs when you pet it. I like cats.

But try to explain that. Talk to the boys at school and they'll tell you the craziest things about cats. Touch one, they say, and you have to wash your hands. Hold one and you'll lose your memory. They're full of it. Still, they'll give a cat a good kick every time they walk past one. I can't stand seeing that. They just laugh at me, though. That's because they have no feelings for animals. They're murderers. And they call me Peglegs because of my new pants. They call my mother names too. "There goes your crymama," they say.

That's her now, coming to bring me to my swell new job.

♦♦♦

As we walked to old Luria's my mother complained how "sad and dreary" life was. (Just plain sad isn't enough for her!) God had given her two children and now she would be left without both. My brother Elye, she said, had married well—he was swimming in chicken fat, knock wood—but his father-in-law was a lout. A baker, God help us! What could you expect from a baker? She kept grousing, my mother did, all the way to my swell new job at old Luria's. Old Luria, she told me, lived in a palace. That's something I'd always wanted to see.

Meanwhile, all I was seeing was the kitchen. But that wasn't bad, either. The stove was so white that it sparkled, the dishes sparkled too, and so did everything else. We were asked to have a seat. My mother remained standing. Not me! After a while a woman dressed like high society arrived. She spoke to my mother and pointed at me. My mother nodded and dabbed her lips. Before leaving, she told me to be good. Then she cried a little and dried her eyes. In the morning, she said, she would come to take me to school.

I was given my supper: soup with hallah bread—hallah in the middle of the week!—and meat, a whole bunch of it.

After supper, I was told to go upstairs. The cook showed me where that was. Her name was Khaneh and she was dark with a long nose. The stairs had soft padding. I'd have loved to walk on them barefoot.

Even though it wasn't dark, the lamps were already lit. There were more of them than you could count. The walls were hung with all kinds of things, even pictures with little people in them. The chairs were made of leather. The ceiling was painted like our synagogue's. But I don't mean to compare them. Old Luria's ceiling is nicer.

I was shown into a big room. It was so big that if only I had been alone, I'd have run from wall to wall and rolled on the nubby rug that covered the floor. It looked perfect for rolling on. For sleeping on, too.

♦♦♦

A tall, nice-looking man with a high forehead, gray beard, silk house robe, velvet skullcap, and embroidered slippers: that was old Luria. He was sitting over a big book from which he didn't look up. He just went on reading while chewing his beard, tapping his foot, and humming to himself. A strange Jew, old Luria! I couldn't tell if he knew I was there. Most likely he didn't, because no one had introduced us and he didn't glance my way. The door shut behind me. All at once he called out, still without looking up:

"Come over here, please. I'd like to show you something in the Rambam."

Who was he talking to? Me? No one ever said "please" to me. I looked around. There was no one else in the room. Old Luria growled again in a deep voice:

"Please come and have a look at the Rambam."

I wanted to know what that was and stepped up to him. "Are you talking to me?"

"You, you! Who else?"

So he said, old Luria, looking at his big book and taking my hand and running my finger across the page to show me what was written in the Rambam. Once he got started, his voice grew higher and shriller. He actually turned red from excitement. He jabbed the air with a thumb, poked me in the ribs, and said: "Well, what do you say to that? Not bad, eh?"

It could even have been very good. How was I supposed to know? I kept my mouth shut tight and let him carry on. The more he did, the tighter I kept it.

A key scraped in the door. It opened and in came High Society. She went over to old Luria and spoke in his ear. He must have been deaf to make her shout like that. She told him to stop bothering me because it was my bedtime. Then she took me by the hand and led me to a couch with springs. The sheets were white as snow. The blanket was soft as silk. What heaven!

The woman tucked me in, left the room, and locked the door from outside. Old Luria rose and paced back and forth with his hands behind his back. He looked down at his slippers and hummed to himself and had this strange frown on his face. I was so sleepy my eyes shut by themselves. Suddenly he came over and said:

"You know, I'm going to eat you."

I opened my eyes and stared.

"Get up! I'm going to eat you."

"Who? Me?"

"You! You! I have to eat you. It's only logical."

That's what he said to me. Then he went back to frowning and pacing, head down and hands behind his back. He was talking more softly now, as though to himself. I held my breath and listened. He kept asking questions and answering them:

"The Rambam says the universe was created. What is the proof? The proof is that every consequence has its cause. And how can this be demonstrated? It can be demonstrated by the power of my will. In what way? By eating him! What are the counterarguments? Compassion? But compassion has nothing to do with it. It's purely a matter of will. The will must will something. And I will to eat him. I *will* eat him, I must! . . ."

♦♦♦

A fine state of affairs! Old Luria was going to eat me. What would my mother say? I shook so hard from fear that the couch moved from the wall. Little by little, I worked my way into the space that this made and dropped to the floor. My teeth were chattering. I wasn't long for the world. How could he do such a thing? I cried for my mother, the silent tears rolling down my cheeks and into my mouth. They tasted salty. I had never wanted her so badly. And I missed my brother Elye, though not as much as I missed our neighbor's calf Menye. I thought of my father too. I was still saying the kaddish for him. Who would say it for me when I was eaten?

I must have slept well because I awoke with a start. I touched the wall and then the couch and peeked out to see where I was. The big room was full of light. The nubby rug was still on the floor and the pictures were still on the walls. Old Luria was reading the big book he called the Rambam. I liked that name. It sounded like a bell.

Suddenly I remembered the night before. Suppose he still wanted to eat me? I dove back into my hiding place as quietly as I could. Soon a key scraped and the door opened. It was High Society with Khaneh the cook, carrying a tray. On it was coffee, a pitcher of hot milk, and fresh butter rolls.

"Where's the young man?" Khaneh asked, looking around.

She spotted me.

"A proper rascal you are, I declare! What are you doing down there? Come with me to the kitchen. Your mother is waiting."

I leaped from my hiding place and bounded barefoot down the padded stairs, singing *ram-bam, bim-bam, ram-bam, bim-bam* all the way to the kitchen.

"Where are you rushing off to?" I heard Khaneh ask my mother. "Let the boy have some coffee with a butter roll. And you might as well have some, too. No one will hold it against you. We're not about to run out of food."

My mother thanked her and sat down. We were brought hot, delicious coffee and fresh butter rolls.

Have you ever eaten sugared egg cookies? That's how good those rolls were. Maybe better. And the coffee! I can't begin to describe it. A taste of Paradise! My mother perked up with each sip and gave me half her butter roll.

You would have thought Khaneh had been knifed. "What are you doing?" she cried. "Eat, eat! There's plenty for everyone!"

She handed me another roll. That made two and a half. While I ate I listened to them talk. It sounded pretty familiar. My mother spoke about being a widow with two sons, one swimming in chicken fat and the other the poor little fellow sitting next to her. I tried to picture Elye in a pond of fat. How big was it? How did it get there?

Khaneh listened and shook her head. After a while she began to gripe about her own luck. She had always been her father's favorite and now she had to cook for others. Her father had been a wealthy man until he was ruined by a fire and took sick. Next thing, he died. To think of him rising from the grave and seeing his Khaneh slaving away at a stranger's oven! Not that she had any reason to complain. She had a good job. The one thing wrong with it was old Luria. He was a bit . . . but I never found out what old Luria was a bit of. Khaneh put a finger to her forehead and now it was my mother's turn to shake her head.

Then my mother talked some more and the head that shook was Khaneh's again. When we left, she gave me another butter roll. I showed it to the boys at school and they stood watching me eat it with big eyes. A person would think they'd never seen a butter roll before! I gave each of them a little piece and they licked their fingers after eating it.

"Where did you get that from?"

I popped the last piece in my mouth and chewed and swallowed it while sticking my hands in my stiff pockets and doing a barefoot jig. If it had had words, they would have been:

"What a bunch of beggars! A butter roll, big deal! You should try it with coffee some time. Then you'd know what a taste of Paradise is!"

SWIMMING IN CHICKEN FAT

Now that old Luria's is history, all that keeps my mother going is my brother Elye. Thank God he's still swimming in chicken fat! That's what my mother says, wiping her eyes as usual—this time with a bit of pleasure. Elye, she says, is set for life. Not that his wife is anything to write home about. (I happen to agree with that.) But Elye has a rich father-in-law, Yoyneh the baker. Yoyneh doesn't do the baking himself. He has bakers for that. He buys flour and sells bagels. On Passover he bakes matsos for all Kasrilevke. He's a fiend about his bakery. In fact, he's a fiend, period. Watch out for him.

He's a maniac, Yoyneh is. Once he nabbed me while I was with Elye. I had just helped myself to an egg bagel—a hot one, fresh from the oven. Don't ask me what got into him, but all of a sudden he had the face of a murderer with these I'll-settle-your-hash-for-you eyes. I never went back to his bakery. I wouldn't go there again if you paid me. What kind of Jew grabs you by the collar and boots you through the door with three swift kicks?

I told my mother, who went running to give Yoyneh a piece of her mind. Elye saw her and stopped her. He actually took Yoyneh's side! He said I was a disgrace who did nothing but eat bagels all day long. If I had to eat bagels, Elye said, he would give me a kopeck to buy one. My mother told him he had no pity for an orphan. Elye said being an orphan didn't give you the right to anyone's bagels. My mother told Elye to pipe down. Elye said he would shout as loud as he pleased and let the world know I was a thief.

That's one word my mother can't stand. She turned every color and told Elye to remember there's a God above. God is not to be trifled with. There's nothing he doesn't see. He's the father of all orphans and stands up for them and Yoyneh the bagel maker wouldn't be worth the price of a bagel without him. That's what she told my brother Elye. She took my hand and slammed the door and we went home.

♦♦♦

Didn't I say don't trifle with God? Listen to what happened to Yoyneh. I've already told you he didn't do his own baking. He had workers, two men and three women.

Well, something began to go wrong. I mean, a lot of things did. Yoyneh's customers started complaining that his bagels had feathers and ribbons and cockroaches and bits of glass in them. Then some Christian found a big black hairball. A Christian is no joke, especially when he threatens to go to the police.

There was an investigation to see whose hair it was. The men blamed the women and the women blamed the men. The women said they were blondes, all three of them. The men said that no man had such long hairs. Then the women started to quarrel among themselves and more charming facts came to light. One of them had baked a sock band in a hallah. Another had dropped a bandage into some dough. A third had used a ball of dough as a pillow. Naturally, she denied it. She swore to God it was a lie, and anyway, she had only done it once or twice. It was Yoyneh's fault for not giving her a pillow.

The town was in an uproar. Yoyneh was making in his pants. All his hollering to high heaven didn't help. No one wanted to touch his bagels. Everyone said they weren't fit for the dogs. It couldn't have happened to a nicer fellow.

♦♦♦

Yoyneh was no pushover, though. He fired the bakers, men and women alike, and hired others in their place. On Saturday he had an announcement made in all the synagogues that he had a new staff and would be personally responsible for the hygiene. He even offered a ten-ruble reward for any hairs found in his bagels. Business picked up again. Everyone was looking for a hair. No one found one and anyone who did was told by Yoyneh that he had planted it himself. Just what you'd expect from a slick operator! But God was keeping score and struck again.

One fine morning Yoyneh's new bakers woke up, took their things, and walked out. They wouldn't come back for love or money—not unless he raised them a ruble a week, let them sleep at home, and promised to stop knocking their teeth out. That was something he had a habit of doing when he was sore.

Yoyneh lost his temper. In all his years of running a bakery, no one had ever told him who to slug. And a raise was out of the question. For every worker he fired, he said, ten were waiting in line to be hired. Hungry workers were not a rare commodity.

But when Yoyneh went to look for more bakers, he couldn't find a single one. No one wanted to work for him. All the bakers had banded together. They said he had to take back the workers he had fired and meet all three of their demands: (1) A ruble raise; (2) Sleeping-at-home rights; (3) No more knocking out teeth.

It was a grand sight to watch Yoyneh froth at the mouth, bang on the table, and curse a blue streak. Revenge is sweet. But that's nothing compared to what came next.

♦♦♦

It was a hot summer day. The melon season had just begun. That's the best time of the year. After it come the High Holy Days. Forgive me for saying so, but I could do without them. I'd rather have fun than be high and holy. And what's more fun than a market full of melons? Wherever you look, there's a honeydew or a watermelon. The honeydews are yellow inside. The watermelons are red with little black pits and sweet as honey.

My mother's not wild about watermelon. She says honeydew is thriftier. A watermelon, she says, fills your stomach with water while a honeydew is breakfast, lunch, and dinner for two. She's dead wrong about that. If I were the Tsar I'd eat nothing but bread and watermelon all year round. I don't even mind the seeds. Give your melon a shake and they fall right out and you can eat all you want. Boy oh boy!

But all this talk of watermelon has gotten me off the subject. I was telling you about Yoyneh the bagel maker. Was he in for it! No one dreamed it was coming. There we were at the table, my mother and I, eating bread and honeydew, when who opens the door and walks in but Elye, holding my father's Bible. His wife Brokheh is dragging after him. In one hand she has a fur stole with a tail and in the other a pour-through. That's a kind of noodle sieve. Elye is white as a sheet. Brokheh is red as fire.

"Mother-in-law, we've come to live with you," Brokheh says.

"We barely made it here alive, Mama," says Elye.

The two sit themselves down and have a good cry with some help from my mother. I try imagining what could have happened. A fire? A fight? Forget it! Yoyneh the bagel maker is bankrupt. That means he's gone bust. His creditors came, wrote down the worth of all he owned, and carried it off down to the last feather. They took everything in his house, the house included, and rubbed his nose in the dirt. I mean they begged his pardon for cleaning him out and told him to scram.

"God almighty!" my mother said, wringing her hands. "What happened to all his money? He was a wealthy man."

My brother Elye started explaining that Yoyneh wasn't as wealthy as all that. Before he could get very far, though, Brokheh butted in and said the opposite. She should only be worth, she told my mother, what her father had been. So what happened to all his money? He spent it on her wedding.

The wedding cost a fortune. Brokheh likes to talk about it. In fact, it's all she ever talks about. There's never been, she says, a wedding like it. The pastries, the roasts, the tortes, the honey cakes, the strudels, the breads, the jams and the jellies—all for her wedding!

Now the wedding is over and Brokheh owns a fur stole and a noodle sieve. Naturally, she and Elye can forget the dowry Yoyneh promised them. Elye can also forget his good Sabbath clothes, his prayer shawl, and his linens. His silver watch, too. A shipwreck would have left him with more. My mother is beside herself. A calamity! Who would have thought it? Everyone envied her son's marriage. Someone must have put a hex on her—or else she did it herself with her big mouth. Either way, she's the main victim.

"When the chicken fat runs out, all that's left is an empty hole. You'll live with me, son, until God has pity."

That's what my mother said, offering Brokheh her bed—the one piece of furniture we had left.

MY BROTHER ELYE'S SOFT DRINK

> One ruble gets you a hundred!
> Buy our book for a ruble plus postage and earn
> a hundred or more a month. Don't waste another minute!
> Step right up and see what's in it!

That's what my brother Elye read in a newspaper soon after leaving his father-in-law's. He had been promised three years' free board by Brokheh's parents and had barely lived with them for three months. But I've already told you all that. I don't like to repeat myself unless asked.

But this time even asking wouldn't help because I'm too busy making money. I have to make the rounds with a soft drink manufactured by my brother Elye. He learned to make it from the book advertised in the paper. The minute he read about it he sent off his last ruble and told my mother her worries were over.

"Mama! Thank God we're saved! From now on we'll be in money up to here."

Elye raised a hand to his throat.

"What happened?" my mother asked. "Have you found a job?"

"Better than that," Elye answered, his eyes bright. He told my mother to wait until the book arrived.

"What book is that?" she asked.

"A book to end all books!" Elye said. Would she settle for an income of a hundred rubles a month?

My mother laughed and said she'd settle for that much a year—in the bank. Elye told her to think big and went off to the post office. He went to the post office every day to ask for his book. A week had gone by since mailing the ruble and there still was no sign of it. Meanwhile, we had to live. "You can't just spit out your soul when you've had enough," my mother said.

Now why would anyone want to do a thing like that?

♦♦♦

The book at last! We unwrapped it and Elye sat down to read. Hoo-ha, the things that were in it! Every way of making money you could think of. There was a hundred-ruble-a-month formula for the best ink. Hundred-a-month directions for the finest shoe polish. A hundred-a-month mouse-cockroach-and-bug killer. Hundred-a-month recipes for liqueurs, lemonade, soda water, barley beer, and other drinks.

Elye chose barley beer. In the first place, from drinks you could make even more than a hundred a month; the book said so itself. And besides, why fool around with ink, shoe polish, and cockroach killers? The one question was which drink to choose. Liqueurs called for capital like Rothschild's. For soda water you needed a special machine, a thingamajig that cost a fortune. Barley beer was the best bet.

Barley beer is a drink that costs next to nothing to make and sells well—especially in a hot summer like this one. We have a Jew in our town, Borukh the barley beer maker, who's made a pile from selling it in bottles. Borukh's barley beer is world famous. It explodes from the bottle as though shot from a gun. Only Borukh knows its secret. Some say he doctors it with gunpowder. Others say raisins. Or hops. Comes summertime, he doesn't have enough hands to count his money with.

The barley beer Elye makes from his book isn't bottled. It doesn't explode, either. But it is special. I can't tell you how it's made because Elye won't let anyone watch him making it. He pours the water and shuts himself up in my mother's room and measures out the other ingredients. No one—not me, not my mother, not even Brokheh—is allowed in. But if you can keep a secret, I'll tell you what's in it. That much I know.

Here goes, then: one lemon peel, some treacle, a sort of vinegar called crumby tartar, and lots of water. Water is the main ingredient. It takes the place of the barley. You stir everything with a corncob, or just a plain stick, and the barley beer is ready. Then you pour it in a jug and add some ice. It's the ice that does it. Elye's drink isn't worth beans without it. You won't find that in the book. I learned it the hard way. I tried drinking some warm barley beer and thought I was going to die.

♦♦♦

The first batch of barley beer was finished. Now I had to sell it. Who else was there? It was beneath Elye's dignity. After all, he's a married man. And we could hardly let my mother run around the market and shout: "Barley beer! Jews, get your barley beer!" The job was mine by unanimous decision. That was fine with me. In fact, I was tickled pink. Elye showed me what to do. I had to hold the jug in one hand and a glass in the other and chant:

Jews, have a drink,
A kopeck a glass!
It's cold and it's sweet!
Get our brew while it lasts!

I've told you I have a good voice, a soprano I got from my father. I just confused the words, so that they came out:

Sweet barley beer,
A kopeck a Jew!
It's cold and it's fresh!
Be the last for our brew!

I don't know if that's what did it, or if our barley beer was really that good, or if it just happened to be a hot day, but I sold out my first jug in half an hour and went home with fifty kopecks in my pocket. Elye gave the money to my mother and refilled the jug. Five or six rounds a day like that, he said, six days a week, and we'd clear our hundred rubles a month. The overhead was next to nothing. The only expensive item was the ice.

That's why I had to sell the barley beer quickly—to make the ice last for the next jug. I walked as fast as I could. I mean, I chanted and ran, followed by a flock of little parrots. I didn't pay those children any mind. I just wanted to empty my jug and refill it.

I can't tell you how much I made that first day. All I know is that Elye, Brokheh, and my mother couldn't do enough for me. For supper I was given a slice of honeydew with my watermelon, plus two whole bucket plums. And I'm not even talking about the barley beer. We drank barley beer like water. Before I went to bed my mother sat me down and asked me if my feet hurt. Elye laughed. He said a big boy like me wasn't bothered by sore feet.

"Sure," I said. "If it was up to you, I'd be on them selling barley beer all night."

They all laughed at my sass. My mother had tears in her eyes. That's nothing new. Mothers are made to cry. Or do I just imagine mine isn't the only one?

♦♦♦

Knock wood, we're going great guns. One day is hotter than the next. What scorchers! Everyone is dying of the heat. The children are dropping like flies. A glass of barley beer is a lifesaver. Honest to God, I'm making ten rounds a day. My brother Elye shut one eye and looked into the barrel with the other and said we were running low. That gave him the idea of adding water. He didn't know I thought of it first.

I may as well admit it's a dodge I hit on. You see, every day I drop in on our neighbor Pesye and give her a glass of our brew. Her husband Moyshe gets two glasses for being such a good fellow, and each of their children gets a glass too. Why not let them know we make a good product? Uncle Borukh also gets a drink; after all, the poor man is blind. And then there are all my friends and acquaintances—you can't expect me to charge them. That's a lot of free barley beer. I make up for each glass I give away by adding two glasses of water.

We all do the same. If Elye has a drink of barley beer, he adds water right away. That's common business sense. Why lose a kopeck? Brokheh is no different. Each time she downs a few glasses of Elye's barley beer (it's shocking to see how she likes the stuff), she waters the jug. Even my mother, who won't take a glass unless she's offered it, makes up for it at once. There's never a drop less that way.

We're raking it in. My mother has already paid off a few debts and taken some things out of hock. We have a table and a bench next to the bed, and meat, fish, and white bread on the Sabbath. God willing, I've been promised a pair of new boots for the New Year. I wouldn't trade places with anyone.

♦♦♦

Go be a prophet and guess that our barley beer will end in the slops bucket! Worse yet, I have a police record. Listen to this.

One day I dropped in with my jug on Pesye. Her whole family was there and dying for barley beer and I drank a glass or two myself. That left me twelve or thirteen glasses short, so I went home to fill up. Only instead of taking water from the water barrel, it seems that I took it from the washtub, twenty glasses' worth. Then I headed back for the street, singing a new song I'd made up:

Jews, have a taste
Of Paradise:
Cold barley beer
With lots of ice!

Along comes a Jew, hands me a kopeck, and asks for a glass of barley beer. He swallows it in one gulp, makes a face, and says:

"Young man! What kind of drink is this?"

Let him ask! Two more customers are already behind him, waiting their turn. One takes a big sip, the other a small one. Both spit it out, pay me, and walk off. Someone else complains that the barley beer tastes of soap. Another hands me back the glass and says:

"What is this stuff?"

"A drink," I say.

"A drink? You mean a stink!"

The next person to taste my barley beer throws it in my face. By now I'm surrounded by a crowd of men, women, and children, all waving their hands and talking a mile a minute. A Russian cop sees the fuss and comes over to check it out. Sure enough, someone rats on me. The cop looks at the barley beer and wants to try some. I give him a glass and he chokes on it.

"Where did you get this swill?" he asks.

"From a book," I say. "My brother made it. He's the manufacturer."

"Who's your brother?"

"Elye."

"Elye who?"

"Don't *daber* about your *akhi,* you little fool," a Jew says to me in a Yiddish mixed with Hebrew to keep the cop from understanding.

There's a hullabaloo. More people push into the crowd. The cop grabs my arm and wants to book me and my barley beer. The commotion grows louder. "An orphan! A poor orphan!" people shout.

Something tells me I'm in bad trouble. I look around the circle. "Jews, have pity!" I cry.

Someone tries slipping the cop a coin. He won't take it. An old man sidles up and says to me:

"Motl! Take your *yad* from the *yovon*'s and pick up your *ragloyim* and make a *pleyte*."

That's just what I did. I wrenched my arm free, took to my heels, and made a beeline for home. I arrived there more dead than alive.

"Where's the jug?" Elye asks.

"At the stationhouse," I say and fall sobbing into my mother's arms.

WE FLOOD THE WORLD WITH INK

What a dope I am! Just because I sold a batch of not-so-great barley beer I was sure I'd lose my head. False alarm! "Why make a fuss?" Pesye said to calm my mother. "As if Yente doesn't mix candle wax in the goose fat she sells or Gedalia the butcher didn't feed the town non-kosher meat for a whole year!"

You should have seen my mother. She takes everything to heart. That's what I like about Elye. He doesn't let a barrel of barley beer get him down. As long as he has his book he's not worried. I mean *One Ruble Gets You a Hundred.* He took a look at it and decided to make ink.

You can't go wrong with ink, Elye says. Everyone uses it. The world's getting smarter all the time. Who isn't learning to write nowadays? He even went and asked Yidl the scribe how much he spent on ink. A fortune, Yidl said. Yidl must have sixty girls in his writing classes. The boys don't go to him. That's because he paddles them with a ruler. He doesn't do that to the girls. Who ever heard of paddling a girl?

I wouldn't mind being a girl myself. I wouldn't have to say the kaddish for my father. I'm tired of it. It's always the same old thing. I wouldn't have to go to school, either. I haven't told you that I'm back in school half time. You could put what I learn on the edge of a knife, but I make up for it by getting whacked. You think it's the rabbi who does it? It so happens to be his wife. What's it to her if I feed her cat? You should see the poor thing. It's always hungry. It's always crying like a person. The sight of it's enough to break your heart. But that's what the rabbi's wife doesn't have. What does she want from that poor cat? Let it get within a mile of some food and she screams loud enough to send it running to kingdom come. Not long ago it disappeared for days on end. I thought it was dead. But it was only having kittens.

Let's get back to Elye's ink.

♦♦♦

My brother Elye says the world has changed. Once, when you wanted to make ink, you had to buy gall-apples, slice them, cook them forever, throw in some vitriol, and add sugar for shine. A production! Nowadays, Elye says, ink's a pleasure. "All it takes," he says, "is a bottle of glycerin and some powder you buy at the apothecary's. You mix them with water, bring it to a boil, and you have ink." That's what he says, Elye.

He went to the apothecary and came back with a bunch of powder and a bottle of glycerin. Then he shut himself up in my mother's room. Don't ask me what he did there. It's supposed to be a big secret. Everything's a big secret with Elye. He can't ask my mother for a mixing bowl without his voice dropping to a whisper. All I know is that he mixed the powder with the glycerin in a big new pot that he bought, stuck it in the oven, and whispered to mother to put the chain on the door. No one knew what he was up to. My mother stared at that oven as if it was about to explode.

Next Elye rolled the barley beer barrel into the house and told us to take the pot from the oven, pour its contents into the barrel, and add more water. "Stop!" he said when the barrel was half full. He checked with his book and whispered that he needed a pen and paper. "Proper stationery," he told my mother. He dipped the pen in the barrel, wrote something on the paper, and finished it off with a flourish. Then he showed it to my mother and Brokheh. They took one look and said:

"It writes!"

Elye put us back to work pouring water. After a while he raised his hand and said "Stop!" again. He dipped the pen in the barrel, wrote something else, and showed that to my mother and Brokheh too. They looked and said:

"It writes!"

We kept it up until the barrel was full. There wasn't room for another drop of water. Elye raised his hand, said "Stop!" one last time, and we all sat down to eat.

♦♦♦

After dinner we filled the bottles. Elye had brought home bottles from all over the world. There were big bottles and little bottles and beer bottles and wine bottles and vodka bottles and plain ordinary bottles. He had also bought some used corks on the cheap and a new funnel and a tin dipper. He whispered to us to put the chain on the door and the four of us set to work.

We hit on a pretty good system. Brokheh rinsed the bottles and handed them to me, I stuck the funnel in them, and Elye ladled out the ink. We had a grand time getting ink all over our hands and faces. By the time we were through, Elye and I were as black as two devils.

I can't remember when my mother last laughed so hard. I'm not even talking about Brokheh. Brokheh nearly split her sides. Elye doesn't like being laughed at. He wanted to know what was so funny. That just made Brokheh laugh harder. She was having a fit a minute. I swear, I thought she would croak. My mother begged us to stop and wash up.

But Elye didn't want to call it quits. Washing up was not on his mind. Bottles were. We had run out of them. He whispered to Brokheh to buy more. Brokheh looked at him and burst out laughing. Elye didn't like that one bit. He whispered to my mother and she went to get more bottles while we refilled the barrel. Not all at once. After each bucket of water Elye raised his hand and said, "Stop!" Then he dipped the pen in the barrel, wrote a few words, and said:

"It writes!"

After a while my mother came back with a new bunch of bottles. We filled them until there were none left.

"How long do we keep this madness up?" Brokheh asked.

My mother muttered something against the Evil Eye.

Elye lost his temper and shouted:

"I asked for a wife and got a cow. God pity you!"

♦♦♦

Don't ask me how much ink we have. It wouldn't surprise me if it's a thousand bottles. The problem is what to do with them.

Elye has tried everything. Selling a bottle at a time, it seems, is no way to get rich. That's what Elye said when Moyshe dropped by one day. Moyshe was so alarmed by all those bottles that he jumped a foot in the air. He and Elye had the strangest conversation. Here it is, word for word:

Elye: What's the matter?

Moyshe: What's in those bottles?

Elye: What do you think? Wine!

Moyshe: Some wine! It's ink.

Elye: If you knew it's ink, why ask?

Moyshe: What are you going to do with all that ink?

Elye: Drink it.

Moyshe: Be serious. Are you going to sell it by the bottle?

Elye: What do you take me for, a lunatic? I'll sell ten, twenty, fifty bottles at a time. You know wholesell?

Moyshe: Of course I know wholesell. Who will you wholesell?

Elye: Who? The rabbi.

My brother Elye went to a big wholeseller. The wholeseller asked to see our ink. But when Elye brought him a bottle, he didn't want to look at it. It didn't have a label, he said. A bottle, he said, needed a label with a pretty picture. "I make ink, not pictures," Elye said. "Then make yourself scarce," said the wholeseller.

Next Elye went to see Yidl the scribe. Yidl said a word that wasn't nice. He had enough ink to last him the whole summer. "How many bottles did you buy?" Elye asked. "Bottles?" Yidl said. "I bought one. When it runs out I'll buy another."

Are we ever in a business! Leave it to a scribbler like Yidl. First he spends a fortune on ink, now a bottle lasts him forever.

My brother Elye is going out of his mind. What will he do with all that ink? It doesn't look like wholeselling will work. He's decided to retell. I wish someone would tell me what that means.

I'll bet you do too.

♦♦♦

My brother Elye bought a large sheet of paper. He wrote in big letters:

Ink Sold Here
Wholesale and RETAIL
Good and CHEAP

The words "retail" and "cheap" took up most of the sheet. Elye poured himself a drink of water and hung the sign on our door. Through the window I saw people stop to read it. Elye watched them and cracked his knuckles. That's something he does when he's nervous. After a while he said, "You know what? Go outside and hang around to see what they're saying."

I was out of the house like a shot. Half an hour later I was back. Elye whispered: "Well?"

"Well what?"

"What are they saying?"

"What is who saying?"

"The people in the street."

"They say it's a nice sign."

"That's all?"

"That's all."

Elye sighed. My mother asked him what the matter was. "You're being foolish," she said. "Did you expect to sell out your whole stock in a day?"

"All I want is one customer," Elye answered with tears in his eyes.

"Don't be foolish. Wait, son. With God's help you'll have a customer."

My mother went to set the table. We washed and sat down to eat. The bottles took up so much room that the four of us had to squeeze together. We had just blessed the bread when a young man came flying through the door. A very odd young man he was, too. He's someone I know. His name is Kopl and his father is a ladies' tailor.

"Is this where they sell ink?"

"Yes. What can we do for you?"

"I'd like some ink."

"How much do you want?"

"A kopeck's worth."

My brother Elye was fit to be tied. If not for my mother, he would have punched Kopl in the nose. But he controlled himself and poured out a kopeck's worth of ink. Fifteen minutes later a girl walks in. Don't ask me who she was. She asked my mother while picking at her nose: "Do you make ink?"

"Yes. What can I do for you?"

"My sister wants to borrow some ink. She has to write a letter to her fiancé in America."

"Who is your sister?" asks my mother.

"Basye the seamstress' daughter."

"Eh?! My, how you've grown! I never would have recognized you. Have you brought an inkwell?"

"Where would I get an inkwell? My sister wants to borrow a pen, too. She'll return it."

My brother Elye is gone from the table. He's in my mother's room. He's pacing back and forth there and whispering, biting his nails and staring at the floor.

♦♦♦

"What made you make so much ink? You must have thought you were supplying the whole world. Did you think there was an international ink shortage?"

That's Moyshe the bookbinder. He's a strange Jew, Moyshe. He can't resist rubbing it in. He's not a bad type, but he can be an awful pain. There's nothing he likes better than sinking his teeth in you. Did Elye give it to him! He should mind his own business, he said. Did he want to bind another *selikhe* in a Haggadah?

That hit where it hurt. Once Moyshe was asked by a coachman to rebind an old Passover Haggadah. As luck would have it, he glued in a High Holy Day *selikhe* by mistake. When the coachman came to the *selikhe* in the middle of the Seder, his voice changed to a funeral dirge. The whole table burst out laughing. The next day he showed up at Moyshe's house ready to tear him limb from limb.

"You bastard, what have you done? How could you stick a *selikhe* in my Haggadah? I'll beat the living daylights out of you!"

That was one swell Passover!

Excuse me for getting sidetracked. I'll return to our booming business in a jiffy.

OUR INK BUSINESS COMES TO A SAD END

Elye had a problem. What to do with all that ink?

"Ink again?" asked my mother.

"It's not the ink." Elye said. "The devil can take the ink! It's the bottles. We've sunk capital in them. We have to get our money back."

He can make money from anything, Elye. There was nothing to do but pour the ink down the drain. The problem was where. It was embarrassing.

"We have no choice," Elye said. "We'll do it at night. No one will see us in the dark."

We waited for it to get dark. Just out of spite, the moon came up bright as a lantern. (Have you ever noticed that when you need it it's never there?) You would think someone had sent for it specially—that's what Elye said as we carried out the bottles. He told me to spill them in different places to keep from making a lake, so I walked behind him and emptied each of them somewhere else. By the neighbor's wall—*splash!* By the neighbor's fence—*splash!* By the neighbor's goats chewing their cud in the moonlight—*splash!*

"That'll do for tonight," Elye said, and we went home.

It was dark and quiet except for the crickets. Through the open door of our house we heard the cat purring by the oven. All the sleepyhead ever does is snooze and warm herself. Then we heard footsteps. A ghost!

It was my mother. She never sleeps. She's up at all hours, sighing, groaning, wringing her hands, talking to herself. Each night she gets a little off her chest. Who is she talking to? There's a new sigh every minute.

"Ah, God! Dear God!"

♦♦♦

I lay half asleep on my mattress, listening to the hubbub outside. The voices sounded familiar. Little by little I opened my eyes. It was broad daylight. The sun was shining through the window, calling to me. I tried remembering last night . . . of course! The ink!

I jumped out of bed and dressed quickly. My mother was in tears. (When wasn't she?) Brokheh was furious. (When wasn't she?) Elye stood in the middle of the room with his head down like a cow being milked. What was the matter? Plenty!

All hell had broken loose when the neighbors rose that morning. Help! Murder! One man had ink on his wall. Another had ink on his new fence. Someone's white goats had turned black. We might have wriggled out of it even then if not for the slaughterer's socks. A new pair of white socks, hung by his wife on the neighbor's fence—ruined! I ask you: who told her to go hang his socks there?

My mother promised to buy her a new pair if she calmed down. *And the wall? And the fence?* It was agreed that my mother and Brokheh would take two brushes and some whitewash and paint over the stains.

"You're lucky to have such good neighbors. If that ink had ended up in the Doct'ress' garden, you would know what the fear of God was!" So Pesye said to my mother.

"Who says you need luck to be lucky?" my mother answered, looking at me.

Search me what that means.

♦♦♦

"I've learned my lesson," Elye said. "Tonight we'll take the rest of the bottles to the river."

That's quick thinking or else I'm not a Jew! I'd like to see you show me quicker. All the junk in the world ends up in the river anyway. Folks do their wash there, scrub their horses, clean their pigs. The river and I are old friends. I've already told you how I catch fish in it. I couldn't wait to start dumping ink.

As soon as it was dark we filled a pillow case with bottles, carried it down to the river, poured out the ink, took home the empties, and filled the pillow case again. It took us all night. I've never had a grander one.

Just picture it. The town is fast asleep. The sky is full of stars. The moon is shining on the river. It's so quiet it's a joy.

The river has a life of its own. It's liveliest after Passover, when the ice breaks up and it rips and tumbles along. After that it starts to shrink. By the end of summer it's fallen asleep. The mud at the bottom goes *bulla bulla bulla* and the frogs sit and talk from bank to bank. It's a poor excuse for a river then. Honest, I can cross it with my pants on.

All our ink made that river a little bigger. A thousand bottles of ink is no joke. We worked like oxen and slept like the dead in the morning. My mother was sobbing when she woke us.

"I'm ruined! What have you done to the river?"

Kasrilevke had been struck by a disaster. There was nowhere to do the wash, nowhere for the horses to drink, nowhere for the water carriers to get their water—and everyone was blaming us. That was my mother's wake-up news. We didn't wait to hear any more. We didn't want to find out how an angry water carrier took his revenge. We lit out, my brother Elye and I, for Elye's friend Pinye.

"Let them look for us there if they want to!"

That's what Elye said, taking my hand and running down the hill to Pinye's. Pinye is someone you should meet. He's worth being introduced to. He's a pretty quick thinker himself.

THE STREET THAT SNEEZED

Would you like to know our latest business? It's mice. My brother Elye spent the whole week reading *One Ruble Gets You a Hundred.* Now he's an expert on exterminating mice, cockroaches, and other pests. Rats too. Just let him loose with his powder and the mice are done for. If they don't run for their lives, they'll lie down and croak on the spot. Don't ask me how he does it. It's a secret. Only the book and Elye know. Elye keeps the book in his breast pocket. The powder is in a packet of paper. It's pink and grainy like snuff and called "shemeritsi."

"What's that?"

"Turkish pepper."

"What's Turkish pepper?"

"Any more whats out of you and I'll make a door handle of your head."

That's what he said to me, Elye. He doesn't like to be bothered when he's working. I stopped asking and watched. He had another powder too. It was also good against mice, he said, but it had to be handled with care.

"It's death itself," Elye told my mother, Brokheh, and me a hundred times. Especially me. If I knew what was good for me, I'd keep away from it.

Our first experiment was on Pesye's mice. Pesye has more mice than you can count. You know her husband, Moyshe the bookbinder. Their house is full of books. There's nothing a mouse likes better. I mean, it's not so much the books that the mouse likes. It's the glue in the bindings. A mouse will eat a whole book just to get at the glue. Mice cause Moyshe a lot of damage. Not long ago they made a hole in a High Holy

Day prayer book, right where it said "God is King" in big letters. By the time they were done with God, nothing was left but the top of the "K."

"Just let me at them for one night," my brother Elye begged the binder. Moyshe didn't want to. He said: "I'm afraid you'll ruin the books."

"How can I ruin them?" Elye asked.

"I don't know. But you will. They're not mine."

Go talk to a bookbinder! It wasn't easy to get him to agree to even one night.

♦♦♦

The first night didn't go too well. We didn't catch a single mouse. Elye said that was a good sign. It meant the mice had smelled the poison and run away. Moyshe wagged his head with a one-lipped smile. You could see he didn't believe us.

Pretty soon the news got out that we were expert exterminators. It started with Pesye, who went to the market that morning and told the whole town we were the world's best mice-ridders. Pesye is out to make a name for us. Back in the days when we made barley beer, she touted it all over Kasrilevke. Then we switched to ink and she spread the word that we made an ink to beat all. Not that it did any good, because who needed ink? But mice are something else. Everyone's got them. There's hardly a house without them.

Of course, every house has a cat too. But how many mice can a single cat take on? And especially, if the mice are rats. Cats scare a rat as much as the Book of Esther scares Haman. I've even heard it said that the cats are more frightened than the rats. At least that's Bereh the shoemaker's opinion. The stories he tells about rats are terrifying. Some people think he exaggerates. But even if he's telling only half the truth, that's enough. He says his rats once ate a pair of new boots in a single sitting. He swears to it by so many oaths you'd have to believe him even if he was a Christian. He saw it with his own eyes, he says. Two big rats came out of their hole at night and ate the boots. He was too frightened to come close, since they were as big as dogs, so he whistled, stomped, and shouted "Scat!" to drive them off. Nothing worked. The rats went on chewing even when he threw a shoe heel at them. Then he threw the cat and they jumped on her and ate her. No one believes him. It's a fact, though. Bereh said it under oath.

"Just give me one night with them," Elye told Bereh. "You won't have a single rat left."

"My pleasure," Bereh said. "I do appreciate it."

♦♦♦

We spent the whole night at Bereh the shoemaker's. Bereh sat up with us. Does he have some swell stories! He told us about the war against Turkey. Bereh served in the Russian army. He was stationed in a place called Plevne and the Turks were shooting at him with cannon. To give you an idea of the size of them, one cannon ball is bigger than a house. Each cannon fires a thousand balls per second—and just for the record, you can go deaf from a single one.

One night, Bereh says, he was standing guard when he heard a big bang and went flying high above the clouds, where he saw a cannon ball burst into pieces. It was sheer luck, he says, that he landed on soft earth and didn't squash his brain. My brother Elye listened with his eyebrows. I mean, his eyebrows were the only part of him that laughed. That's a strange way to laugh, let me tell you. But Bereh didn't notice. He kept telling the grandest stories, one scarier than another. We stayed up all night. Rats? We never saw any.

"You're a wizard!" Bereh said to my brother in the morning. He went and told the whole town that we had a magic charm that drove his rats away in one night. Blow him down if he hadn't seen it with his own eyes! My brother Elye said abracadabra and the rats jumped from their holes, lit out down the hill, and swam across the river the devil knows where.

♦♦♦

"Are you the exterminators?" Every day a new customer shows up and asks us to charm away his mice.

Elye is an honest man. He doesn't like to fib. He says we use a powder not a charm. The mice smell it and run.

"A powder, a charm—just get rid of my mice! How much does it cost?"

Elye doesn't like to bargain. He has one price for the powder and one price for his work. Both get higher every day. It's not Elye who raises them, it's Brokheh.

"What are you waiting for?" she says. "If you're going to eat pork, do it till the fat runs down your chin. And if you're an exterminator, get paid like one."

"What about honesty? What about God?" my mother asks.

"Honesty? So much for honesty!" (Brokheh gives the oven a kick.) "God? So much for God!" (Brokheh gives a pillow a smack.)

"Brokheh! What are you saying?! What's gotten into you?!"

My mother shrieks and wrings her hands.

"Leave the fat cow alone!" Elye says, pacing and playing with his beard. He's got a pretty nice beard by now. It's grown like nobody's business. The more he plays with it, the faster it grows. It grows kind of funny, though. I mean, it's all on his chin and his throat. The rest of his face has no hair. I'll bet you've never seen a beard like that.

Call Brokheh a fat cow and you'd normally end up seeing stars. But this time she kept her mouth shut. That's because Elye is making money. When Elye makes money, Brokheh treats him like a king. And being his assistant, I'm somebody too. Brokheh used to call me "Tagalong." And "Stumblebum." And "Beggarguts." Now I'm Mottele.

"Mottele! Fetch me those shoes."

"Mottele! Bring a quart of water."

"Mottele! Take out the garbage."

Make money and you're treated differently.

♦♦♦

The thing with Elye is that he likes to think big. If it's barley beer, it's by the barrel. If it's ink, it's a thousand bottles. If it's rat poison, it's a whole sack. "What do you need all that poison for?" Moyshe asked. Did Elye give it to him! Leave it to Elye to go off and saddle me with that sack instead of locking it in the closet.

I suppose you want to know what made me ride it like a hobbyhorse. Well, I've always wanted a horse. How was I to know the sack would burst and yellow stuff would pop out of it? I could have passed out just from the smell. As soon as I bent to clean up, I began to sneeze. I sneezed as though I had a snuff box up my nose. Hoping the sneezing would stop, I ran outside. Some chance!

Just then my mother passed by. "What's the matter?" she asked, seeing me sneeze. All I could say was *Ah-chooo!* And *Ah-chooo* and *Ah-chooo* and *Ah-chooo.*

"Lord-a-mercy! Where did you catch such a cold?" my mother asked, wringing her hands. Since I couldn't stop sneezing, I pointed to the house. She went inside and came back sneezing worse than me.

Along came my brother Elye and saw us both. "What's going on?" he asked. My mother pointed to the house. Elye went to have a look and came running out sore as hell.

"Who broke the . . . *Ah-chooo! Ah-chooo! Ah-chooo!*"

I hadn't seen Elye so angry in ages. He went for me with both hands. If he hadn't been sneezing so hard, I'd have ended up a cripple.

Now Brokheh passed by and saw the three of us sneezing like crazy.

"What's with you?" she asked. "What are you all sneezing for?"

What can I tell you? No one could say a word. We just pointed to the house. Brokheh went inside, ran out red as a beet, and laid into my brother Elye:

"How many times do I have to . . . *Ah-chooo! Ah-chooo! Ah-chooo!*"

That brought our neighbor Pesye. All we could do was point to the house. A minute later she ran out of it.

"What kind of . . . *Ah-chooo! Ah-chooo! Ah-chooo!*"

Pesye stood waving her arms. Moyshe came to see why, stared at the five of us, and burst out laughing.

"You're a sight for sore eyes!"

"Maybe you could . . . *Ah-chooo! Ah-chooo! Ah-chooo!*" We all pointed to the house.

Moyshe went inside. He came out laughing even harder.

"I can tell you what your problem is. I took a pinch of it. It's shemi . . . *Ah-chooo! Ah-chooo! Ah-chooo!*"

He grabbed his sides and started to sneeze. With each sneeze he took a hop, landing on the tips of his toes and balancing there for a second before taking off again with the next sneeze. In no time all our neighbors and their wives and their children and their cousins and their uncles and their aunts and their friends were sneezing too, lined up from one end of the street to the other.

My brother Elye was good and worried. What worried him most was the thought of all those sneezes being blamed on him. He grabbed my hand and we ran to Pinye's house. It took half an hour to stop sneezing. Then Elye told Pinye the whole story. Pinye listened like a doctor to a patient. When Elye was finished he said:

"All right. Now show me the book."

Elye took the book from his pocket and handed it to Pinye. Pinye began reading the first page. *One ruble gets you a hundred! With nothing but your own two hands, you'll soon be making a hundred rubles a month as though by magic* . . . He took the book and threw it in the oven. Elye lunged for it. Pinye grabbed him and said:

"Easy there! Where are your manners?"

Before long Elye's book was a heap of ashes. Only one page was not completely burned. You could still make out the word "Shemeritsi" on it.

OUR FRIEND PINYE

You may remember my wanting you to meet Pinye. I said he was a quick thinker. Before I introduce him, though, I'd better tell you about his grandfather, his father, and his uncle. Don't worry, I'll make it short. I'll start with his grandfather.

You've never heard of Reb Hesye the glazier? That's Pinye's grandfather. He's a glazier, mirror maker, painter, and tobacconist all in one. Nowadays he makes and sells snuff. As long as you're alive and kicking, he says, you should work and be independent. He's a tall, thin fellow with red eyes and a monster nose, broad below and curved like a shofar on top. I'll bet it got that way from taking snuff. He's still pretty sharp, even though he's a hundred years old. Some say he has more brains than both his sons put together. That's Hirsh-Leyb the mechanic and Shneyur the watchmaker.

Hirsh-Leyb the mechanic is Pinye's father. He's tall and thin like Reb Hesye with the same monster nose, even though he doesn't take snuff. He's an oven mechanic. That means he makes ovens. They all say he has a good head on his shoulders. It sure is a big one with an enormous forehead. Hirsh-Leyb, they say, could learn any trade and be tops at it. There's nothing he can't figure out. He even says so himself. One look at anything is all he needs.

Hirsh-Leyb taught himself to make ovens. He did it by watching Ivan Pichkor the oven maker and almost dying of laughter. The poor goy, he said, didn't know the first thing about ovens. Hirsh-Leyb went home, took apart his old oven, and built a new one from the same bricks. It smoked so badly that he nearly choked, so he took it apart and made another. A couple of tries later he was a famous mechanic.

Hirsh-Leyb has invented an oven that holds its heat for eight whole days. If he had the materials, he says, he could build it. Just give him the right sort of tiles and he'll make an oven you'd pay to see. An oven, he says, takes more brains than a watch. That's a dig at his brother Shneyur.

Hirsh-Leyb's brother is younger and even taller and has the same nose. He's a watchmaker. With a mind like his, they say, he could have been a rabbi or a teacher or a slaughterer. That's how good a student he was. But he wanted to be a watchmaker. Why a watchmaker? It's like this.

To listen to Shneyur, he was always figuring things out, even as a boy. For example, he thought a lot about locks. Why did one lock open with three twists to the right and another with three twists to the left? What made a clock tick? How come it chimed when the hour hand reached twelve?

The first time Shneyur saw a cuckoo clock, he nearly went out of his mind. It had been given to his father by a retired colonel in payment for some work. Every hour a door opened and out came a bird and said, "Cuck-koo!" It looked real enough to be alive. Even the cat was fooled. It went for that bird every time it appeared.

Shneyur swore he would find out how that clocked worked. One day when no one was home he took it down from the wall, unscrewed all its screws, and emptied out its insides. His father beat him so hard that he was given up for dead. To this day, he says, you can see the marks. That didn't stop him from becoming a watchmaker, though. I don't know if he's the best there is, but he's cheap and he's fast.

Shneyur has repaired my brother's watch many times. He fixes it at least once a week. Elye has a funny watch. When it isn't running faster than a madman, it's four hours slow or has stopped completely. Go get it to start again! Elye would look for another watchmaker if he wasn't afraid of hurting Pinye's feelings. Pinye says it's the watch's fault, not his Uncle Shneyur's. It's simple logic, he says. If the watch were a normal watch, any watchmaker could fix it. Since it isn't, what difference does the watchmaker make?

You can't argue with that.

♦♦♦

Pinye has a head like his father's and his uncle's. He has their nose too. His whole family is nosey. His Aunt Kreine's daughter Malka has a nose that's beyond belief. Actually, it's more the face that her nose is on. It isn't quite human. It looks more like a bird's or an animal's. She's ashamed to go into the street with it. Lord-a-mercy!

Although Pinye looks like Malka, he's a man. It doesn't matter so much what a man looks like. Still, you can't help laughing at the sight of him. Besides being tall and thin with a pair of long ears and a neck like a gander's, he's nearsighted. He's always bumping into you. Watch out for your feet when he gets up to leave a room. One pants leg is hiked up, one sock is falling down, his shirt is rumpled, and his tie is never where it should be. He talks with a wheeze and sucks on candies. He always has something in his mouth.

Pinye is quite a fellow. There's nothing in the world he doesn't know. Folks say he knows more than the rabbi. He can put the biggest genius in his little pocket, Pinye can. You should see his handwriting too! And he's a whiz at rhymes. Pinye can rhyme anything. He's rhymed our whole town—the rabbi, the slaughterer, the beadles, the butchers, his own family, everyone.

Pinye's rhymes can make you die laughing. They're passed around and learned by heart. I even remember a few myself. Here's one:

Shmuel-Abba the beadle
Is certain to eat all
He can when he sits down to dinner.
He grabs what he's able
To take from the table
And doesn't get up any thinner.

And Nechameh his wife?
As I value my life,
I'd rather we didn't discuss her.
Her brain's smaller than that
Of the rabbi's old cat—
The devil take her and cuss her!

The whole town buzzed with this poem. One man even set it to music and sang it at his Sabbath meal. The song went round until it got back to the beadle and his wife. They sent for Hirsh-Leyb the mechanic and asked with tears in their eyes what Pinye had against them. Hirsh-Leyb went home, locked and bolted the door, and gave Pinye a licking. He whipped him so hard that Pinye gave his word of honor never to write another rhyme in his life.

♦♦♦

Pinye hasn't rhymed a word since. He says the rhymes don't come any more. That's because he has problems. It all started with his wanting to get married. I mean it wasn't Pinye; it was his father, who wanted to make a man of him. He arranged a match with the daughter of a miller and the miller set Pinye up in the flour business.

Elye envies Pinye for having his own business. Pinye just laughs. It may be a business, he says, but it's no business of his. What kind of work is messing around with flour? At most it's a job for some young moron of a miller's son. He's not to blame, Pinye says, if he can't sit still in a store. His mind keeps flying off. His whole family is like that. They're high flyers.

That's what Pinye says. He doesn't want to run a store. He'd rather enjoy a good book. That makes his father-in-law the miller sore. There's nothing the man can do about it, though, because he's afraid of ending up in Pinye's rhymes. And his daughter is delicate, an only child. Taybl, her name is. She has a face like a Cossack's but she's as good as gold. My mother says she hasn't a drop of gall. It beats me how anyone can count the drops. Taybl minds the store while Pinye stays at home. Elye and I drop in on him there. He tells us everything. Pinye likes to gripe about his fate. He's boxed in, he says. He can't breathe. If only he could get away, he would be a different man. A year to see the world is all he asks. So he says to Elye. Elye is the one person he trusts. He shows Elye letters from important people. The important people write Pinye that he has it in him. Pinye thinks he has it in him too. I look at him and think: God almighty, just what does he have there?

♦♦♦

Pinye came to tell Elye a secret. I can't hear about a secret without wanting to find out what it is. I'd find out every secret in the world if I could. I eavesdropped and here's what I heard:

Pinye: How much longer are we going to hang around here?

Elye: That's just what I ask myself.

Pinye: I read about a fellow who lit out with nothing but the shirt on his back. For half a year he slept in the streets and went hungry.

Elye: And then?

Pinye: We should only have his luck.

Elye: You don't say!

Pinye: Today Rothschild is a pauper next to him.

Elye: Is that a fact?

Pinye: You bet it is! Would I pull your leg? I've talked things over with Taybl.

Elye: What does she say?

Pinye: What should she say? She's ready to come with me.

Elye: She is? And your father-in-law?

Pinye: Who's asking him? Would he be happier if I left Taybl behind? You can see I'm itching to go. I can't waste another day here.

Elye: You think I can?

Pinye: Then let's take off.

Elye: With what?

Pinye: The ship tickets cost nothing, you dope.

Elye: What do you mean, nothing?

Pinye: You pay in installments. That's nothing.

Elye: But what about getting to the ship? There are railroad tickets, all kinds of expenses.

Pinye: How many tickets do we need?

Elye: You tell me. How many?

Pinye: It's simple arithmetic. Taybl and me makes two. Brokheh and you makes four.

Elye: And my mother.

Pinye: That's five.

Elye: And Motl.

Pinye: Motl can travel half fare. Maybe even for free. We'll say he's under six.

Elye: Are you crazy?

I couldn't keep quiet a second longer and jumped for joy. The two of them turned and saw me.

"Beat it, you pest! Can't you see this is an adult conversation?"

I took off on the run, jumping and slapping my legs. Just imagine: me, a traveler! Ships . . . trains . . . tickets . . . half fares! Where were we going? Who cared! What difference did it make? Somewhere—that's all that mattered! I had never gone anywhere in my life. I had no idea what traveling was like.

Of course, that's a bit of an exaggeration because I did once take a ride on the neighbor's goat. I paid for it by falling off and getting a bloody nose and a whipping. But I wouldn't exactly call that traveling.

I walk around in a fog. I've lost my appetite. Every night I dream of traveling. In my dreams I have wings and can fly. Hurrah for Pinye! I think a thousand times more of him now. I would kiss him if I weren't embarrassed. What a Pinye Pinye is!

Didn't I tell you he was a quick thinker?

WE'RE OFF TO AMERICA!

We're off to America! Where is that? Don't ask me. I only know it's far away. It takes forever to get there. You have to reach a place called Ella's Island where they take off your clothes and look at your eyes. If your eyes are all right, come right in! If they're not, you can go back to where you came from.

I'd say my eyes were pretty good. The only trouble they ever gave me was when some boys from school ganged up on me and blew snuff in them. Did they catch it from Elye! Since then I've had perfect vision. The problem, Elye says, is my mother. Who knows what all that crying has done to her eyes? She hasn't stopped since my father died. Elye tells her:

"For the love of God! Think of the living, too. They'll send us back because of your eyes."

"Don't be silly," my mother says. "I'm not doing it on purpose. The tears come by themselves."

That's what she says, my mother, wiping her eyes with her apron and going over to the pillows by the wall. She's redoing them all. America, it seems, has everything but pillows. It beats me how anyone sleeps there. They must get headaches all the time.

Brokheh is giving her a hand. I don't mean to boast, but we have a lot of linens. Not counting the bedspreads, there are three big pillows and four babies. My mother is making the babies into another big one. That's too bad because I like the babies better. Some mornings I play with them. They make a fine hat or even a cake.

"When we get to America, God willing, we'll turn them back into babies."

So my mother says, showing Brokheh what to do. Brokheh would rather stay put. It's hard for her to leave her parents. Had anyone told her a year ago that she would be going to America, she would have laughed in his face.

"And if anyone had told me a year ago that I'd be a widow . . . "

My mother starts to cry. Elye loses his temper.

"There you go again! You'll be the ruin of us!"

♦♦♦

As if that weren't enough, along comes our neighbor Pesye, sees us working on the pillows, and hands us a sob story of her own:

"So you're really going to America? God speed you and bring you happiness! He's capable of anything, God is. Look at my only daughter Rivl, who went to America with her husband Hilye. They write that they're breaking their backs and making a living. It doesn't matter how many times I've asked them to send us a long letter with all the whats, whys, and wherefores. All they ever write is: 'America is a country for everyone. You break your back and make a living . . . ' But who am I to complain? I should be thankful they write at all. At first there wasn't so much as a howdy-do. We thought they had sunk to the bottom of the sea. Then at long last comes a letter saying, thank God, they're in America. They're breaking their backs and making a living. . . . Well, I suppose that's something to knock your brains out and redo all the pillows and travel across the ocean for!"

"I'm asking you for the last time. Stop being a wet blanket!"

That's from my brother Elye. Pesye turns on him.

"A wet blanket? Still wet behind the ears, *you* are—and such a smart one! He's going to America to break his back and make a living! To think of all the times I nursed you, held you in my arms, took care of you . . . Why don't you ask your mother about the fish bone you swallowed one Friday night as a boy? If not for the three good whacks I gave you on your back, you couldn't break it in America now."

Pesye would have gone on if my mother hadn't calmed her: "Please, Pesye darling! Pesye dear! Dearest Pesye, please be strong!"

She started to cry again. Elye hit the ceiling. He threw down the pillow he was holding, ran outside, and yelled as he slammed the door:

"To hell with it all!"

♦♦♦

Our house is empty. It looks deserted. The little room is full of bundles and bedclothes. They're piled to the ceiling. When no one is looking I climb to the top and sled down. Life has never been so good.

We've stopped cooking. For our meals Elye brings a dried fish and an onion from the market. What could be better than fish with onions?

Sometimes Pinye eats with us. He has more on his mind than ever. It doesn't stop working for a second. Going to America has made a nervous wreck of him. That's what my mother says. One pants leg is too high and one sock is too low. His necktie hangs every which way. He bumps his head each time he enters the house. My mother tells him:

"Pinye, bend over! You don't realize how tall you've gotten."

"He's nearsighted, Mama."

That's Elye's excuse for him. The two of them have gone off to finish the paperwork on the house. We sold our half of it to Zilye the tailor long ago. But don't expect a quick closing from a tailor. What a wafflehead that Zilye is!

First he starts coming three times a day to look at the house. He taps the walls, he smells the stove, he crawls into the attic, he looks at the roof. Then he brings his wife—Menye is her name. Just the sight of her makes me laugh. Pesye's calf was called Menye too, and this Menye reminds me of that one. Menye the calf had a white face with big, round eyes and so does the tailor's wife.

Next Zilye began bringing all kinds of experts, most of them tailors like himself. Each found something wrong with the house. That's when it was agreed to bring Pinye's father, Hirsh-Leyb the mechanic. Hirsh-Leyb knows all about houses. He's honest and can be trusted.

Hirsh-Leyb came and inspected the house from every angle. He threw back his shoulders, tilted his head, adjusted his hat, scratched his chin, and declared:

"This house will stand for a hundred years."

A tailor friend of Zilye's said:

"Sure! Redo it in brick, prop it up with some good beams, put in four new walls, give it a tin roof, and it will stand until the Messiah comes."

You couldn't have made Hirsh-Leyb madder if you had cussed him to his face or sprayed him with soda water. All he wanted to know was: "Where does a sneaking, lowdown, lying louse of a needle pusher get off opening his big fat mouth in front of a mechanic like me?"

I got my hopes up too soon, though. Just when I was sure there would be a swell fight, everyone and his uncle turned up to make peace between Hirsh-Leyb and the tailors. We bargained, settled on a price, sent out for vodka, and drank toasts to a safe voyage and our making lots of money and coming back, God willing, from America.

"Hold on there!" Elye declared. "What's the big hurry to come back from America?"

That started a conversation about America. Hirsh-Leyb was ready to bet a pot of gold that we would be back in no time flat. If he weren't worried about Pinye being drafted, he would never agree to his going. America? Feh!

"Begging your pardon," said Zilye the tailor, "but what's so feh about it?"

"America," Hirsh-Leyb said, "is a lowdown land."

"Begging your pardon," said Zilye, "but what's so lowdown about it?"

"That's obvious," Hirsh-Leyb said.

"If it's so obvious, you might explain it," said Zilye.

But although Hirsh-Leyb tried explaining, he was too soused to put two words together. So was everyone. We were all in a grand mood, myself included. All except my mother, who kept wiping her eyes with her apron. Elye saw her and whispered:

"You're a heartless woman! Don't you even care about your own eyes? Murderer!"

♦♦♦

It was time for the good-byes. We went from house to house, parting from every relative, neighbor, and friend. We spent a whole day at Yoyneh the bagel maker's. Brokheh's parents made us a swell dinner. The whole family sat around a table.

I sat next to Brokheh's sister Alte. I've already told you about her. She's a year older than me and has two braids. Since Elye's wedding we're supposed to be a couple. Whoever sees us together says, "There go the bride and groom." That's why we're not embarrassed to be seen talking. Alte asked me if I would miss her. Of course I would, I said. Then she asked if I would send her letters from America. I said of course to that too.

"But how can you? You don't know how to write."

"So what?" I said, sticking my hands in my pockets. "You think you can't learn in America?"

Alte looked at me and smiled. Don't ask me what was so funny. She's just trying not to be jealous. Everyone is. Even bug-eyed Henekh would like to drown me in a spoon of water. He stopped me and said with his buggy eyes:

"I hear you're going to America."

"Yup."

"What will you do there, walk the streets with a tin cup?"

He's lucky my brother Elye wasn't there. Elye would have given him a tin cup all right! I wasn't going to start up with a bum like that. I stuck out my tongue and ran to Pesye's to say good-bye to her and her gang.

That's some gang Pesye has! I've told you about them. All eight of them stood around me in a circle. They wanted to know if I was glad to be going. It didn't take long to answer that. Are they green with envy! The greenest is Bumpy. He can't take his eyes off me. He keeps sighing and saying:

"So you're going to see the world."

Yup. I'm going to see the world. I can't wait!

♦ ♦ ♦

We're off! Leyzer the coachman is here with his "eagles"—three horses fast as lightning who wouldn't stand still for love or money. They paw the ground, snorting and foaming. I can't make up my mind whether to watch the horses or help with the bundles. In the end I compromise by staying with the horses while watching the bundles being carried out. They fill Leyzer's wagon. There's a mountain of pillows on it. And no time to waste, because it's forty-five verst to the station.

We're all here: me and my brother Elye and his wife Brokheh and his friend Pinye and Pinye's wife Taybl and their whole family—Hirsh-Leyb the mechanic, and Shneyur the watchmaker, and Taybl's father the miller, and the miller's wife, and Aunt Kreine and her birdfaced daughter, and even old Reb Hesye. They've all come to say good-bye to Pinye. On our side there's Yoyneh the bagel maker with his wife and sons. It's a pity I haven't introduced them all. Now it's too late because we're off to America. They stand around giving advice. Watch out for thieves in America!

"There aren't any thieves there."

That's what Elye says, patting the secret pocket sewed by my mother in a place where no one would dream of looking. The money from the sale of our house is there. It's squirreled away safe and sound.

"Don't you worry," Elye says. He's tired of having to give the whole world an account of our money.

It's time to say good-bye. We look around . . . where is my mother? Nowhere, that's where! Elye is about to have a fit. Leyzer is chafing at the bit. He says we'll miss our train if we don't get cracking. But wait—here she comes! Her face is red and her eyes are swollen. Elye pounces on her.

"What's the matter with you? Where have you been?"

"Saying good-bye to your father in the graveyard."

Elye turns away. No one knows what to say. I haven't thought of my father since the day we decided to go to America. I feel an ache inside. We're going and he's staying in the graveyard.

But there's no time to think of that. Someone gives me a push and tells me to climb aboard. How am I supposed to climb a mountain of pillows? By using Leyzer's shoulders as a ladder!

Suddenly there's such a weeping and a wailing that you might think the Temple had been destroyed. The loudest is my mother. She throws her arms around Pesye and says: "You've been a true sister to me. Truer than a sister!" Pesye doesn't cry. Her big Adam's apple just bobs in her throat and tears big as beans run down her fat cheeks.

Everyone is done kissing except Pinye. Watching Pinye kiss is better than going to the theater. Each kiss lands in the wrong place, that's how nearsighted he is. If his lips don't wind up in your beard or on your nose, his head bangs into yours. He can't take a step without tripping. You could die laughing.

Praise God, we're all in the wagon. I mean we're on top of it. My mother, Brokheh, and Taybl are sitting on one mountain and Elye and Pinye are facing them on another. Leyzer and I are in the driver's seat. Although my mother wanted me next to her, Elye said I'd be better off by the driver. You bet I am! I can see the whole world and the whole world sees me. Leyzer reaches for his whip. There's a last round of good-byes. The women cry.

"Be well!"

"Have a good trip!"

"Write and tell us how you are!"

"The best of luck!"

"Don't forget us!"

"A letter a week! Write at least once a week, for goodness' sake!"

"Give our love to Moyshe, and Basye, and Meir, and Zlote, and Khaneh-Perl, and Soreh-Rokhl, and all their children!"

"We'll be sure to! Take care! Be well!"

We all shout back from the wagon. We're moving, I swear! Leyzer gives each of his eagles a crack of the whip. The wheels are turning. The wagon bumps and jolts. I jump with such joy I nearly fall off my seat. Something is tugging at my heart. I'm so happy I could sing. We're off, off, off to America!

RUNNING THE BORDER

Traveling by train is a dream. Traveling by wagon wouldn't be bad either if your ribs didn't rattle so much. Leyzer's eagles were really fast as lightning. By the time we reached the station we felt struck by it. No one could climb out under his own power.

I had the easiest time because I was next to the driver. Although the seat was so hard that all my bones ached, I jumped right down from it. That's more than I can say for Elye, Brokheh, Pinye, Taybl, or my mother. The women were in a bad way. They had to be carried out one by one after unloading the linens. Leyzer did it himself.

He's one mean cuss, Leyzer. Does he have a mouth! But he's a good, faithful driver, even if he did throw us out of his wagon with all our things and leave us stranded in the station while he went off to look for a return fare.

Our first problem was the ticket agent. He made a fuss over our bundles. I mean it was more the pillows than the bundles. What was it to him how many we had? My mother tried talking to him nicely. She explained that we were going to America. The big oaf said that for all he cared, we could go somewhere else. I won't repeat the word he used.

"The goy can be handled," Elye said. "We'll grease his palm."

He said that to Pinye. Pinye is our leader. He's our best brain and speaks Russian. He just happens to have a temper. So does Elye, but Pinye's is hotter. He had a talk with the goy in Russian. In Jewish it went like this:

"Listen here, little man! A black year take you if we aren't going to America with every last pillow and pillowcase. Here's for a glass of vodka—and now shut your trap, you swine!"

Naturally, the goy didn't want to. He called Pinye some names of his own. "Dog's puss!" "Pig's ear!" "Christ-killer!" "Jew's ass!" We were afraid of a scene, even the police. My mother wrung her hands and said to Pinye:

"Who asked you to open your big mouth?"

"Relax," Pinye said. "The goy will settle for an apology and half a ruble."

And so he did. Both men apologized. Pinye kept talking a blue streak in Russian and the goy kept cursing like all get-out and carried our things into a big hall with high windows called the waiting room.

That's when the real fun started. The goy said we wouldn't be allowed on the train with so many pillows and rags. (He must have meant the quilts. I ask you: just because the lining is torn and a bit of padding is falling out, does that make a quilt a rag?) We had to talk to the stationmaster. Who did? Why, Pinye of course.

Pinye went with the goy to the stationmaster. I tagged along. With the stationmaster Pinye took a different tack. He waved his hands and tried to sound reasonable. I've never heard such crazy words in all my life. *Columbus . . . Civilization . . . Alexander von Humboldt . . . Slonimski . . . Mathematics* . . . I can't even remember them all. Pinye must have won the argument, because the stationmaster didn't answer back. A lot of good it did, though. We had to put our pillows in the baggage car and take a stub for them. My mother was beside herself. What were we going to sleep on?

♦♦♦

My mother needn't have worried. There was nowhere to sleep. There was nowhere even to sit. The car was so crowded you could hardly breathe. There were lots of passengers besides us, Jews and Christians, all fighting for a place. Because of the pillows we arrived at the last minute and barely found room on the floor for the women and bundles. My mother sat at one end of the car and Brokheh and Taybl at the other. They had to shout the whole length of it. That made everyone laugh. Elye and Pinye were left hanging in the air. Pinye is so blind that he kept bouncing off the other passengers.

I was fine. In fact, I was terrific. Despite the crush, I found a window to stand by. What didn't I see through it! Houses, trees, people, fields, forests, all whizzing by. I can't begin to describe it all. You should have seen that train fly! You should have heard those wheels turn! And the smoke! And the whistles! And the chug of the locomotive!

My mother was afraid I'd fall out the window. "Motl?" she kept screaming. "Motl!" A young toff with blue sunglasses made fun of her. "Motl?" he screamed in the same singsong. "Motl!" He had the Christians rolling in the aisles. The Jews pretended not to hear. It bothered my mother as much as last year's snow. She only screamed "Motl? "Motl!" even louder. Then she wanted me to eat something. We had all kinds of good things: radishes and onions and garlic and cucumbers and hard-boiled eggs, a whole egg for each of us. I hadn't feasted like that in ages.

The only spoiler was Pinye. Pinye had to stick up for the Jews. He didn't like the Christians laughing at the way we ate garlic with our onions. He stood up straight and told the toff in Russian:

"I suppose eating pig is better!"

That made those Christians mad. One of them blew his stack. He hauled off and let loose with such an uppercut that Pinye's head rang like a bell. Pinye isn't the type to take that lying down. He threw two punches back. Being blind, he hit the wrong man. Luckily the conductor came along. What a scene! Everyone was shouting. The Jews blamed the Christians: a Christian had crushed a Jew's toe with a suitcase. A Christian had thrown a Jew's hat out the window. The Christians said it was a lie: the Jews were making it up. But the Jews had witnesses—Christian ones. One was even a priest. A priest, said the Jews, doesn't lie. That's only, said the Christians, because we had bribed him not to. The priest stood up and gave a speech.

Meanwhile a few more stations went by. Some passengers got off at each. The car began to empty out. Pretty soon our women were sitting on a bench with all their bundles just like princesses. The best seats were Elye's and Pinye's. We were having a fine old time when Taybl noticed that Pinye's cheek was swollen. Pinye swore he didn't feel a thing. That is, his cheek hurt but it was nothing. Pinye doesn't like to talk about such things. He'd rather ask the other passengers where they're going. Some said to America. America? A celebration!

"For heaven's sake," Pinye said, "why keep it a secret? We're going to America too." Pretty soon we were friends. Everyone knew where everyone came from and was bound for.

"You're going to New York? We're off to Philadelphia."

"What's Philadelphia?"

"A city like New York."

"Hold on there! Comparing Philadelphia to New York is like comparing Eishishok to Vilna! Otvotsk to Warsaw! Drazhne to Odessa! Semyonevke to Petersburg!"

"My, my! A person might think you've been everywhere."

"You bet I have! I can tell you every place I've been in."

"You'll have to wait until I can take the day off. Right now, tell me, all of you: how are we going to run the border?"

"You'll run it the same as us, the same as everyone."

They all went into a huddle to talk about running the border. I wasn't sure what that meant. How fast could my mother run? But there was no one to ask. Not my mother, because what does a woman know? And not Elye, because he doesn't like being pestered. (A boy like me, he says, should mind his own business.) And not Pinye, because he was too busy talking. So was everyone. Everyone was telling everyone some story about a border. One man says the best border to run is Novoselitz. Another says you can't beat Brody. Says a third, "Ungeny's not bad either." That brought down the house. "Ungeny! You call that a border? Next you'll tell us Rumania is a country! You can have the damn place!"

"Hey! It looks like we're at the border now . . . "

♦♦♦

I had always thought a border looked special. Not at all. The town we were in had the same houses, the same Jews, the same Christians, even the same marketplace with the same stores and stands as Kasrilevke.

Brokheh and Taybl went to shop in the market. My mother wouldn't let me out of her sight. Maybe she thought I would run the border without her. Elye and Pinye went off to talk to two strangers.

My mother said the strangers were called agents. That meant they would run the border with us. They didn't look like they could run very fast. One had a green overcoat, a white umbrella, and eyes like a thief's.

The other was better quality with a top hat. A third person, a woman, played peekaboo behind them. She was all pious-and-respectable-like and wore a wig. She kept dropping God's name as though they were best friends and asked my mother where we planned to spend the Sabbath.

My mother said we would be across the border by then. "Amen!" the woman answered with a long face. "God grant it!" She was only afraid, she said, that we were being taken for a ride. The agents we were dealing with, she said, were no better than thieves. They would walk off with our money and leave us high and dry. If we wanted to run the border, she said, we should run it with her. With her, she said, it would be a breeze. Search me how she planned to run with that big wig.

By now Elye and Pinye were back. They looked pretty down in the mouth. It seems the two of them had quarreled. Each was blaming the other for having to spend the Sabbath in this place. And that wasn't the worst of it. The worst was that the two agents were threatening to rat on us. The next thing I know my mother is crying and Elye is scolding her for ruining her eyes. Because of her eyes, he says, we'll never make it to America!

♦♦♦

Elye and Pinye have broken off talks with the agents. "We've changed our minds," they told them. "We're not going to America after all." Was I depressed! I mean I thought it was true. But it was only a trick. Leave it to Pinye. He told the agents a fib to get rid of them while negotiating with the woman. She took an advance and told us to be ready tonight. The night will be dark and moonless. That's the best time for running the border. I can't wait to see how you run it.

We spent all day arranging our things. Everything had to be repacked and left with the woman. She'll send it across the border after us. People, she says, come first with her. Then she gave us instructions. At midnight, she said, we should walk out of town until we come to a hill. At the hill we turn left and walk as far as the next hill. At the next hill we turn right and walk some more to a tavern. We wait there while one of us goes inside. There'll be two Christians drinking vodka at a table. The password is "Kaimove"—that's their name. As soon as they hear it, they'll come with us and lead us to a forest.

"Four more Christians," the woman said, "will be waiting for you in the forest. Wake them up if they're asleep. Apart from that you mustn't make a sound. Anyone hearing you will shoot. There are soldiers everywhere. The four men will lead you downhill through the forest until you're on the other side."

Hills, taverns, forests—it sounded pretty grand to me. My mother was afraid. So were Brokheh and Taybl. We men laughed at them. A woman is scared of a cat.

The summer sun set. We said the evening prayer, ate our dinner, and waited for it to get good and dark. At the stroke of midnight we set out, all six of us.

The men went first. My mother, Brokheh, and Taybl followed as usual. The woman with the wig had given good directions. We left town, came to a hill, turned left, came to another hill, turned right, and reached a tavern. One of us went inside. Who? Pinye, of course. We waited half an hour, an hour, two hours—no Pinye. Brokheh and Taybl wanted someone to look for him. Who? Elye, of course. My mother didn't like the idea. "Then I'll go," I said. She liked that even less.

But here's Pinye! "Where have you been?" "In the tavern." "Where are the Christians?" "Asleep." "Why didn't you wake them?" "Who says I didn't?" "Why didn't you give them the password?" "Who says I didn't?" "And?" "And nothing." "But that's not good." "Who says it is?"

♦♦♦

Elye had a brainy idea. He and Pinye would enter the tavern together and try waking the Christians. Two are better than one.

That's what they did. Half an hour later they all came out. The two Christians looked still asleep. They were drunk and cursed to wake the dead. The women were scared out of their wits. You could tell by how they sighed and groaned. Every minute my mother said "Oh, God, please" in a tiny voice.

We walked on. Where were the men waiting in the forest? Suddenly the Christians stopped in their tracks and asked how much money we had. We were too terrified to say a word. My mother was the first to find her tongue. We had no money, she said. "You're lying!" said the men. "All Jews have money." They took out two long knives, waved them in front of us, and said: "Fork up or we'll slit your throats!" We stood there like dumb, frightened lambs until my mother told Elye to open his secret pocket and hand over the money.

That's when Brokheh went and fainted. My mother saw her and screamed, "Help!" Taybl heard my mother and screamed too. A second later—*rat-a-tat-tat!* Shots echoed through the forest. The two men took off on the run. Brokheh picked herself up. My mother grabbed me by one hand and my brother Elye by the other and shouted:

"Run, boys! The God of Israel be with you!"

So this was running the border! Where did she get the strength from? We kept tripping over tree roots and falling. Each time we got up and ran some more. My mother turned around and asked in her tiny voice:

"Pinye, are you running? Brokheh, are you running? Taybl, are you running? Run, run, the God of Israel is with us!"

I can't tell you how long we ran. The forest was already behind us. Dawn was breaking. We were sweating like mad, even though a cool breeze was blowing. We came to a street. Another street. A white church. Gardens. Yards. Little houses.

A Jew was coming toward us, driving a goat. He had the longest earlocks I've ever seen, a long, tatty gabardine, and a green shawl around his neck. We stopped to say hello. He stared at us. Pinye struck up a conversation. The Jew had a strange way of talking. I mean he talked our language, but he didn't talk it like we do. Pinye asked if we were near the border. "What border?" the Jew asked. It seemed the border was far behind us.

"In that case, why are we running like lunatics?" So Pinye said, sounding like a different Pinye. He turned around, squared his shoulders, made a finger, and shouted in Russian:

"Take that, you lousy Ivans!"

We all began to laugh like mad. The women laughed so hard they collapsed on the ground. My mother raised both her arms. "Thank you, dear, dear God," she said, and burst out crying.

WE'RE IN BRODY!

Would you like to know where we are? Smack in the middle of Brody! That means we're getting near America. It's a fine place, Brody is. You don't see such streets and people back home. Even the Jews are different. I mean they're the same Jews, they're just more so. Their earlocks are longer, their hats are weirder, their gabardines have belts and hang to the ground, their shoes have no socks, and their women wear fancy wigs. And you should hear them speak German—I tell you, that takes the cake! They say *beheimeh* instead of *beheymeh* and *sheigetz* instead of *sheygetz*. And the way they sing their words! A person might think they were chanting the Torah.

We got the hang of it pretty quick. Pinye was the quickest. He was talking perfect German in no time. He says that's because he studied it back home. But Elye says he never studied a word and picked it up just as well. I'm learning it too. The only one who doesn't cotton to it is Brokheh. She goes on speaking Jewish. She's on the slow side, Brokheh is.

My mother doesn't want to speak German either. She says she wants to talk the way she's used to. Why twist her tongue for no good reason? She has it in for German. Back in Kasrilevke, she says, she thought all Jews who spoke it were honest. Now she sees that the German Jews are no saints. One even shortchanged her in the market. It seems you can be a thief in German too.

Brokheh joins the conversation. "I'll say you can! Why, each is a worse thief than the next! At least back home we knew the thieves were Christians."

"Back home, my dear, the Christians knew it too."

My mother has a story about that. We had a Christian neighbor named Khimke, a fine woman and a thief like all her kind. If she came to visit and my mother left the room, Khimke made sure to leave it too. That's how afraid she was of stealing if left alone.

♦♦♦

Everything is different with the Germans. Even their money is different. They've never heard of kopecks and rubles. They have groschen and schillings. One ruble is worth a bunch of groschen. My mother calls them "buttons" and says they aren't real money. Elye says they melt like snow between your fingers. He goes off each day to a corner, unstitches his secret pocket, takes out a ruble, and sews the pocket back up. The next day he opens it again and takes out another ruble.

The days go by and our baggage hasn't arrived. It looks like the woman who ran us across the border has pulled a fast one. First her pals stick us up in the forest and now we're stuck without our things. My mother wrings her hands and cries: "Our pillows! Our quilts! How will we go to America without them?"

Pinye has an idea. He's going to file, he says, a *zayavlenye,* which is a protest, with a *proshenye,* which is a petition, to the *natshalnik,* who is the commander of the border post. Or else he'll cross the border himself and find the woman with the wig. He'll make her rue the day she was born. He'll give her what for, Pinye will.

It's all a lot of hot air. All the *zayavlenyes* and *proshenyes* in the world won't do any good. And Pinye won't cross any borders because Taybl won't let him. Not for all the Tsar's gold, she says. Running the border once was enough for her. To tell the truth, it was enough for us all.

We tell our story to everyone: how we met the woman with the wig, and how she told us how to run the border, and how we were taken to the forest, and how we almost had our throats slit, and how Brokheh has a habit of fainting, and how my mother screamed and the soldiers shot and the men ran away and our lives were saved.

That's my mother's version. Elye has his own. Before he gets very far with it, Brokheh butts in with hers. But Brokheh, Taybl says, doesn't remember because she passed out. Taybl tells it her way and is interrupted by Pinye, who says Taybl doesn't know a thing. And so Pinye tells the whole story from the beginning. We tell it over and over each day, mouthing the words and nodding as we listen. Everyone says we were lucky and should say a special prayer of thanks.

♦♦♦

Life on this side of the border is good. In fact, it couldn't be better. There's not a stitch of work to be done. Either we sit in our inn or go for walks in the city. I've told you what a fine place Brody is. I don't know what Brokheh has against it. Every day she has some new complaint. This here is no good, and that there isn't clean, and something else smells bad, and back home it was different. Once she let out a scream in the middle of the night. We all jumped out of bed.

"What is it? Thieves?"

"What thieves? Bedbugs!"

In the morning we went to complain to the innkeeper. He couldn't make head or tail of it until Pinye explained to him in German what the matter was. Never in his life, said the innkeeper, had he heard the likes of it. Not in the whole kingdom of Austria. We must have brought the bedbugs from Russia.

Did Brokheh blow her top! A Jew like our innkeeper, she said, is worse than a Jew who's been baptized. It beats me why she said that, because the innkeeper seems like a fine fellow. He talks with a lopsided grin and likes to give friendly advice about where to go and who to buy from and who to steer clear of. Sometimes he even comes along.

Mostly, we buy clothes. We've become spiffy dressers. Pinye says it isn't nice to dress like bums. A tourist, he says, should dress respectably. And especially in a country where everything is dirt cheap. The first thing he bought was a top hat. After that he bought a new tie and a frock coat, the kind that comes down to the knees.

You'd have to be made of cast iron to keep a straight face when Pinye wears his new clothes. He's tall, he's thin, he's nearsighted, and he walks with a bounce, remember? And his nose! My mother says he looks like a circus clown. Elye says it's more like an organ grinder. Pinye says he'd rather be an organ grinder than a bum.

Elye says he could dress like a German too if he wanted. It's no trick to throw away your money, he says. In America we'll need every penny. Pinye says money won't be a problem there. In America, he says, every man is worth his weight in gold. He nagged until Elye bought a top hat and a frock coat too. Now when we walk down the street talking German, we could pass for natives if not for the women. I mean my mother, Brokheh, and Taybl. They follow us everywhere. My mother is afraid of getting lost and Brokheh and Taybl tag after her like calves. Don't ask me what they're afraid of. The six of us are always together. Everyone stares at us. You would think no one had seen a Jew before.

"The Germans are the world's biggest fools," Elye says. "They'll believe anything they're told."

"Provided it doesn't involve money. They're money-mad. Why, they'd sell their souls for a groschen. And their father for a schilling and God himself for two!"

That's Brokheh. Taybl agrees. None of the women like the Germans. You can search me why they don't. I like them fine. I could stay here forever if we weren't going to America. Where else do you have such houses? And the people! They're swell folk. There's nothing they won't sell you. Even the cows here are different. I'm not saying they're smarter than our Russian cows, but they're more human, that's for sure.

Try telling that to the women, though. They'll only answer that everything was better back home. Nothing is good enough for them, not even our inn. They don't like its owners. "They skin you alive," Brokheh says. "They make you pay for a glass of hot water, even for a pinch of salt. If we don't leave this place soon, we'll end up begging in the street."

That's what she says, Brokheh. Brokheh says a lot of things. She says Elye is an old maid. She says Pinye is the joker in the deck. Anyone else in Taybl's place would have smacked her long ago. But Taybl is without a drop of gall. She doesn't talk back to Brokheh. No one does, not even me. She's a terror, Brokheh is. She calls me "Crumb-bum" and "Motl Chop-Chop." Since we've been on the road, she says, I've grown a fine pair of chops. I wouldn't give her the satisfaction of answering. My mother can't stand it and cries. Elye hates that. He says her eyes are ruined. With eyes like hers we'll never make it to America.

♦ ♦ ♦

I have news! We've heard from our pillows. The woman who ran us across the border is in jail. Pinye is delighted. He says the police should be congratulated. "So congratulations," says my mother. "Now where are my linens?" "The same place mine are," Pinye says. We may as well face it. We'll never see them again.

It's time to move on. Elye acts as though it's the end of the world. My mother tries to cheer him. "Don't be foolish," she says. "Would you be happier if they had taken all our money in the forest and slaughtered us in the bargain?" Pinye says she's right. A Jew, he says, should see the bright side. Brokheh sticks her nose in and says, "I've always said Elye was an old maid."

We have to make plans. How do we get to America? Everyone suggests something else. One person says via Paris. Another says London. A third tells us Antwerp is closer. We can't make up our minds. My mother is scared of Paris because it's so big. Brokheh doesn't like the sound of Antwerp. Who ever heard of a city named for ants? That leaves London. Pinye thinks it's our best bet. He's read in a book called "The Atlas" that London is quite a place. It's the hometown of Moses Montefiore and Rothschild.

"Rothschild? He's from Paris!"

So says my brother Elye. The one thing he and Pinye agree on is that they always disagree. If Pinye thinks it's daytime, Elye is sure it's the middle of the night. They don't exactly quarrel. It's more like boxing. They can go at it for hours if no one stops them.

Once they had it out over the German word for horseradish. In Kasrilevke we said *khreyn,* but did the Germans say *khron* or *khran?* They went at it hammer and tongs until they decided to buy some horseradish in the market and show it to our innkeeper. "Hey there, Mr. Germany," they said, "we'd like to ask you something. Tell us the truth: this here fruit—do you call it a *khron* or a *khran?*" "You're talking Jewish," answered the innkeeper. "In German it's a *Meerrettich.*"

Did you ever hear such a crazy word in all your life? He'll do anything to annoy us, that innkeeper. He makes everything sound like something else. He calls a hair *a har,* which means a gentleman, and a gentleman *a her,* which means "Over here!" And how does he say "over here"? *Hier-hier!* And you wonder why we call the Germans cabbageheads?

♦♦♦

You'll have to excuse me for going on about the Germans and their language and forgetting all about America. America, it seems, is still a ways off. First we have to get to London. And before that, there's Lemberg. In Lemberg, we're told, there's something called an Emigration Committee. We're hoping it can help us. Why shouldn't it when it's helped others—and especially after all we've been through, what with losing all our bundles and linens and all? My mother is planning what to say to it. "Just don't cry!" Elye tells her. "Think of your eyes! Don't you want to get to America?"

That's what he says, Elye, and goes off to pay our bill. A minute later he comes back pale as a ghost. What's wrong? The bill has thrown him completely. There's nothing that isn't on it. The six Sabbath candles we lit—six groschen. The *havdalah* candle to end the Sabbath—four groschen. "What *havdalah* candle?" Elye asks. "The one you heard me say the blessing over," says the innkeeper. "But why four groschen?" Elye asks. "If you'd rather make it five, let's make it five," says the innkeeper. Next comes something called his "commission." What kind of bad news is a commission? It's his fee, he says, for coming with us to buy clothes.

Brokheh hears that and gives her hands a clap. "Mother-in-law! What did I tell you? These Germans are worse than the robbers in the forest! Your biggest Russian pogromchik is a saint compared to them. You say the name of this place is Brody? I tell you it's Sodom!"

Being compared to a Russian pogromchik didn't faze that German as much as hearing Brody called Sodom. Did he fly off the handle! The Russians, he said, had the right idea. If you asked him, there should be more pogroms. If he were the Kaiser of Russia, he would slaughter every one of us.

I've told you our friend Pinye has a temper. He can be pretty peaceful until it explodes, but just say a wrong word to him then and you're taking your life in your hands. He drew himself up to his full height, Pinye did, went over to that innkeeper, and shouted right in his face:

"Go to hell, you stinking kraut! And your father, too!"

The kraut made Pinye pay for that. He gave him two such juicy slaps in the face that the sparks flew. What followed was grand. All Brody came running. It was Jew against Jew, a real slugfest. Do I love it when the fur begins to fly!

We took off for Lemberg that same day.

THE LEMBERG COMMITTEE

Lemberg, mind you, is nothing like Brody. First, there's the town itself. It's clean, airy, pretty—a sight for sore eyes. I won't say it doesn't have streets like Brody's in which you have to hold your nose and wear galoshes even in good weather. But it does have a park in the center of it where everyone goes walking, even the goats. On Saturdays the Jews promenade in their fur hats and no one says a word. It's a free country. And the people! Pure gold!

My mother says Lemberg and Brody are like day and night. Elye says he wishes we had come to Lemberg first. Pinye says that's illogical, since Lemberg is only better than Brody because it's further from the border and nearer to America. "You call that logic?" Elye says. "Show me Lemberg on the map and show me America!" When it comes to maps, Pinye says, he's studied geography and can teach Elye a thing or two. "Then why don't you tell me where the Committee is," Elye says. "What Committee?" "The Emigration Committee!" "What does that have to do with geography?" "A big expert like you," Elye says, "should know that too."

So Elye says. But the more people in the street we stop to ask, the more have never heard of the Emigration Committee. A weird town!

"They know. They're just not telling!"

That's Brokheh's opinion. She's down on everything, Lemberg too. She thinks the streets here are too wide. Now isn't that something to be ashamed of!

That's women for you. Nothing ever suits them.

◆◆◆

We've found the Committee. It's in a tall building with a red roof. First you wait outside for a while. It's a pretty long while. Then someone opens a door and you climb some stairs and see a lot of people at the top of them. Most are emigrants from Russia like us. Many look hungry and have babies. The ones without babies look hungry too. Each day they're told to come back the next morning. The next morning they're told to come back the next day.

My mother has made friends with some of the women. Many have had bad luck too. They tell each other about it and feel luckier. Some have been through pogroms. That's horrible to hear about. Everyone is going to America and no one has a way of getting there. Some folks have been sent back to Russia. Some have found work in Lemberg. Some have been sent on to Cracow. Where is the Committee? You're at it. Who is the Committee? May you know as much sorrow in your life as anyone knows that!

A tall man with a pockmarked face and kind, smiling eyes appears.

"He's from the Committee! He's a doctor."

The doctor pulls up a stool. Every few minutes a new emigrant steps up to him with some new problem. The doctor listens and says he's only one person. He wishes he could help. "On a Committee of thirty members," he says, "I'm the only one who ever shows up. What can I do all by myself?"

The emigrants don't want to hear that. How long can they go on like this? They've used up all their money. Either give them tickets to America, they say, or send them back to Russia.

The doctor explains that he can only send them as far as Cracow. In Cracow there's another Committee. Maybe it can do more than this one.

The emigrants protest that they're at their wits' end. The doctor takes out his wallet and hands them a coin. The emigrants pocket it and go away. New emigrants take their place. They tell the doctor they're hungry.

"What can I do for you?" he asks.

“We want to eat,” they say.

“Here’s my breakfast,” he says. “Eat.”

He points to some rolls and a cup of coffee that have been brought him. Honestly, he says. Have his breakfast. What can a man do all by himself? The emigrants thank him. The food isn’t for them. It’s for their children.

“Next time bring them too,” says the doctor with a twinkle in his kind eyes. He turns to the next emigrant.

“What can I do for you?”

♦♦♦

It’s my mother’s turn to tell the doctor her case history. How she had a husband. And how this husband was a cantor. And how the cantor fell ill. And how he grew worse until he died and left her a widow with two children, one grown up and one a little boy. (That’s me!) The older one was recently married. He was swimming in chicken fat. Then the fat ran out and left a hole. His father-in-law went bankrupt and he was nearing draft age, so we decided to go to America.

“Mama, what kind of sob story are you giving him?”

That’s my brother Elye. He starts again from the beginning:

“Draft, shmaft—the thing is, we’re going to America. I mean me, and my mother, and my wife, and my little brother” (that’s me!), “and that fellow over there” (he points to Pinye). “We had to run the border. I mean we couldn’t get an exit permit. The thing is, my friend and I were draft age . . . ”

“Allow me!” Pinye says, shoving Elye aside and telling it his way. Even if Elye is my brother, I have to admit that Pinye tells it better. For one thing, he knows Russian. Does he use some swell words! This is how it went:

“If I were to present you with a short *vozglyad* of the entire *polozhenye,* you would have a *totshke zrenye.* We’re going to America less because of the *voyenske povyonost* than because of the *samastoyatelnost.* Here, you see, we’re extremely *styesnitelni,* not merely in terms of *progres,* but also regarding *vozdukh,* as Turgenev observed. And *vovterikh,* that’s especially so since the *yevreiski vopros,* not to mention the pogroms, the Constitution, and *tomu podovne,* as Buckle says in his *History of Civilization . . .* "

But I don't do Pinye justice. That was only the beginning. He was just warming up when the doctor cut him short, took a sip of his coffee, and said with a smile: "Well, what can I do for you?"

That's when Elye muscled in and said to Pinye: "How come you never stick to the point?"

That made Pinye pretty sore. He walked away, tripping over his own feet and saying crossly: "You think you talk better? So talk!"

Elye stepped up to the doctor and began the whole story again.

"The thing is, we came to the border. I mean we started negotiating with the agents. Those agents, let me tell you, are real bastards. Right away they give us the runaround. They double deal, they rat, they finagle. And then along comes this woman. I mean a decent, pious, one-hundred-percent type! So we bargain with her and arrive at a price for running us across the border. The thing is, we're supposed to go first and our belongings will follow. She found two Christians to go with us . . . "

"Just listen to him! He's already up to the Christians! What's the big rush?"

That's Brokheh jumping in to tell it her way. It's the same story but a little different. The woman told us to walk to a hill. There we turned right and walked to another hill. Then we turned left and walked to a tavern. Pinye went inside and found two men drinking vodka. He gave them a password and they took us to a forest. It's a lucky thing that she, Brokheh, has a habit of fainting . . .

"Shall I tell you something, my dear woman? I'm about to faint myself. Please get to the point and tell me what I can do for you."

My mother steps back up to the doctor and says: "The point is that all our things were stolen."

The doctor: "What things?"

My mother: "Our linen. Two bedspreads, four large pillows, and two more made from the babies."

The doctor: "That's all?"

My mother: "And three quilts, two old and one new. And some clothing and—"

The doctor: "That's not what I meant. I meant, is that the worst that happened?"

My mother: "You'd like worse?"

The doctor: "But what is it that you need?"

My mother: "Linens."

The doctor: "That's all?"

My mother: "It's not enough?"

The doctor: "You still have your tickets? Your money?"

My mother: "That much we have. Our ship and railroad tickets, both."

The doctor: "Then you have a lot to be thankful for! I envy you. Let's change places. Don't think I'm joking. I'm perfectly serious. Take my breakfast, take my emigrants, take my Committee, give me your tickets—and I'm off to America today. What can I possibly accomplish here, all by myself with so many poor souls?"

That doctor was . . . but none of us could say what he was. There was no point in hanging around Lemberg. Every new day, Elye said, only meant running up more bills. It made more sense to go to Cracow. Cracow was full of emigrants. Wasn't that what we were too?

WITH THE EMIGRANTS

If you're traveling to America, stick with the emigrants. It's the best way to go. Come to a new city and you needn't look for a place to stay, since there's already one waiting for you. That's because of the Committee. It's the Committee that sees to such things.

Our first night in Cracow we were put up in a room, unless you prefer to call it a stall or a closet. In the morning someone came from the Committee to take our names. My mother didn't want to give them. She was afraid of the draft. I'm telling you! Everyone had a good laugh. Since when does the Austrian Kaiser work for the Russian army? Next we were taken to a dormitory. That's a big room with lots of beds and emigrants. "It looks like our Kasrilevke almshouse," said my mother. "Mother-in-law," Brokheh said, "let's get out of this town."

I've already told you that the women are like that. Nothing pleases them. They're always finding fault. They didn't care for Cracow from the start.

Elye doesn't like Cracow either. He says it isn't Lemberg. Lemberg was full of Jews. Not that there aren't plenty of them in Cracow too, but they're a funny sort of Jew, half-Polacks who curl their mustaches and talk Proshepanye. That's according to Elye. Pinye thinks otherwise. Cracow, he says, is more civilized.

Pinye swears by something called civilization. I'd give a lot to know what that is.

♦♦♦

The Committee has put us up in a great place. I mean, it's great for making friends. You keep meeting new emigrants. You sit with them, eat with them, and swap stories with them. Some of the stories are pretty hairy: one person escaped a pogrom by a hair, another beat the draft by a hair, another made it across the border by a hair. Everyone talks about their agent. "Who was yours?" you're asked, "the dark one or the blond one?" "He wasn't dark and he wasn't blond," comes the answer. "He was a bastard."

Usually we get to tell our story too, the whole blessed miracle: how we found some agents, and how we met the woman with the wig, and how she tried to swindle us, and how her Christian pals brought us to a forest, and how they asked for our money and said they'd cut our throats. It was a stroke of luck that Brokheh likes to faint and my mother began to scream. Then a shot rang out and the Christians took off and before we knew it we were on the other side.

Everyone listens and nods and says, "Whew!" One emigrant, a tall, mean-looking fellow with cotton in his ears, asked us:

"What did she look like, that woman with the wig? Religious and pious-like?"

Told that she did, he turned to his wife and said: "Soreh! Did you hear that? It's the same woman!"

"She should catch the cholera! I wish to God they all did!"

That's what Soreh said, telling a fine tale of how the woman with the wig set them up, fleeced them of everything, and tried selling them fake tickets to America.

Another emigrant sat up when he heard that. He was a tailor with dark eyes in a pale face and he said: "Fake tickets? Listen to this!"

But before he could tell his story, a fellow named Topolinski said he had a better one. In his town, he said, was a bureau that sold tickets from Lubow to America. A young man was talked into buying one and laid out sixty rubles for a piece of paper stamped with a red eagle. He traveled to Lubow and tried boarding a ship—*Just where do you think you're going?* Did someone say ticket? A colored candy wrapper!

♦♦♦

I'm getting tired of hearing about tickets. I like emigrants, but tickets are something else. I'd rather spend my time with a boy my age I met on the train to Cracow. His name is Kopl and he has a harelip. He got it from falling off a ladder. He swears it didn't hurt, even though there was lots of blood. And as if splitting a lip wasn't bad enough, he was also given a tanning from his father. If you haven't already guessed, that's the mean-looking man with the cotton in his ears. And Kopl's mother is the woman called Soreh. His parents, he says, were once rich. They were rich until the pogrom.

I asked Kopl about that. The emigrants are always talking about pogroms, but I could never figure out what one was. He said: "You don't know what a pogrom is? What a dummy! They have them everywhere. Anyone can start one and they last for three days."

"But what are they? A kind of fair?"

"What kind of fair? Some fair! It's breaking windows. Smashing furniture. Ripping pillows. The feathers fly like snowflakes."

"But why?"

"Why yourself! Because, that's why. And they don't just wreck houses. They smash shops and loot and rob and shoot and throw it all in the street and douse it with kerosene and set it on fire."

"You're kidding."

"I'll bet you think I'm making it up! And when there's nothing left to rob, they go from house to house with axes and clubs and iron pokers, singing and whooping. The police go with them and they shout, 'Kill the kikes, boys!' If they catch you, they beat you up and cut your throat and fill you with holes . . . "

"Why me?"

"What do you mean, why you? Because you're a Jew."

"But how come?"

"How come yourself! It's a pogrom."

"So what if it is?"

"Get out of here, you dunce! It's hopeless talking to you."

That's what he said, Kopl, turning away and sticking his hands in his pockets like a grown-up. It made me sore to see him act so high-and-mighty. I didn't say anything, though. I just thought, "Wait and see, you big shot, you'll need me yet," and I let a few minutes go by. Then I went back to him and started a conversation. I asked him if he knew German. He just laughed at that. "Who doesn't know German? It's the same as Jewish."

"Oh, yeah? Well, if you know it so well, suppose you tell me how you say horseradish."

He laughed so hard he nearly choked.

"What do you mean, how do you say horseradish? Horseradish is horseradish!"

"That shows how much you know."

"So how do you say it?"

I'd be darned if I could think of it myself, so I went and asked Elye. "Horseradish?" he says. "How would you like some right in your puss?"

Elye must have been in a bad mood. He gets that way when he has to take money from his secret pocket. Pinye laughed at him. Then they began to fight. I looked for a place on the floor between our bundles and went to sleep.

♦♦♦

Nothing has come of our stay in Cracow. We haven't even seen the Committee. The emigrants have told us it's a waste of time. As soon as you get there, they say, the runaround begins. First, they write down how old you are. Then they send you to the doctor for an examination. Then they tell you to come back. When you do, they ask, "What are you here for?" "We were told to come," you say, "so we came." That gets you a scolding for wanting to go to America. "Where are we supposed to go?" you ask. "In what holy book is it written," they answer, "that you have to go anywhere?" You tell them a little story about a pogrom. "It's your own fault," they say. "Look at how one of your young Russians stole a roll in the park the other day." "Maybe he was hungry," you say. "And what about your Russian who attacked his wife in the street yesterday?" they ask. "The police had to be called." "She's not to blame," you say. "She happened to spot her husband, who had run away from home. She caught him and made a scene when he tried getting away." "But why do all your Russians dress in rags?" they ask. "That's all they can afford," you say. "Give them better clothes and they won't wear rags." All they give you is another lecture.

That's what the emigrants tell us. We're fortunate, they say, not to have needed any favors until now. My mother says we wouldn't need one now either if not for our linens. She'd be as happy as the Kaiser's wife if not for them. What will we do in America without them?

That's what she says, my mother, wringing her hands and crying. My brother Elye yells:

"Already? Crying again? It seems you've forgotten that we'll soon be in America and you have to take care of your eyes!"

If you think that means we're getting close, think again. We have a whole lot of traveling still ahead of us. Don't ask me where, but I knew the names of some of the places from the emigrants: Hamburg, Vienna, Paris, London, Liverpool . . .

Hamburg's a town they'd like to see go up in flames. It's worse than Sodom, they say. As soon as you arrive, you're made to take a bath. Being arrested would be more fun. You won't find scoundrels like Hamburg's anywhere. That's what all the emigrants say, so we've decided to head for Vienna. In Vienna, we've heard, there's a Committee that acts like one.

Committee or not, we're going to Vienna. Ever hear of the place? Be patient and I'll tell you all about it.

GOD IS A FATHER AND VIENNA IS A TOWN

"Vienna—what a town!"

That's my brother Elye. Pinye goes him one better:

"A town? A city to beat all!"

Even the women, who never like anything, have to admit Vienna is a city. My mother has taken out her silk scarf in its honor. Brokheh wears her Sabbath dress with her black lace shawl and long earrings. With her freckled face she looks like a ginger cat.

You've never seen a ginger cat dressed in black? Well, I have. Our neighbor Pesye's boys used to dress their cat up. You may remember her—Feyge-Leah the Beadle's Wife, her name was. Once they put a black skullcap on her. They tied it to her head with two bands, attached a dust rag to her tail, and let her loose. The skullcap was so big it slipped over her eyes and the dust rag drove her crazy. Feyge-Leah ran around like mad, bouncing off the walls and smashing things. Did those boys catch it!

Bumpy caught it the worst. That's Hirshl. He's one crazy kid, Hirshl is. You may as well whip a wall. I miss him the most. Maybe we'll meet up in America. We've heard that Pesye, Moyshe, and the whole gang are going there too. First they laugh at us, then they follow us.

Everyone is going to America. That's what Yoyneh the bagel maker writes. He's also on his way. In fact, he's already at the border. It's not the same border we ran. Ours has a bad reputation. They steal your linens there. They steal them in other places too, but they don't hold you up at knifepoint. True, we've heard of borders where you're stripped naked and robbed of everything. You aren't killed, though. That only almost happened to us. Except that we would have died of fright first. It was our luck someone fired a gun. I must have told you about that. We can hardly remember it any more.

Not that our women aren't still telling the world about the miracle that happened at the border. But Elye and Pinye never let them finish. They think they can tell it better. Pinye wants to write it up for the papers. He's even begun a poem about it. I've told you he writes poems. This one goes:

The town of Radzivil's the size of a yawn
With a border that has to be run before dawn—
And while you are running it thieves run away
With all that you have and leave you to say:
"Thank God that it didn't turn out to be worse!
We might have ended our lives in a hearse
With a slit in our throats and a slash in our purse!"

Pinye says that's just the first stanza. It will improve as it goes along. He has a poem about Brody too. And about Lemberg and Cracow, all in rhyme. He's the very devil for rhymes, Pinye is. He's even written some about Taybl. I know them by heart:

My beautiful Taybl
is charming and able,
a wife from a fable,
God love her!
She'd be perfect if on-
ly she'd leave me alone
and go home to her father and mother!

How's that for poetry? You should see Taybl blush when she hears it. Taybl blushes all the time. Brokheh sticks up for her and calls Pinye "the monster." My mother calls him "the shlimazel." They can't stand his being a poet.

With Elye it's the opposite. Elye is jealous of Pinye. He says that rhymes and songs go over big in America. Pinye has only to shmaltz them up a bit and he'll make a fortune. There are even magazines and newspapers that will publish them in Jewish.

Pinye agrees he'll be a success. He feels he's made for America and

America for him. That's why he can't wait to sail the ocean. Meanwhile, we're stranded in Vienna.

♦♦♦

What are we doing in Vienna? Nothing. We walk the streets a lot. What streets! And the houses! And the shop windows! They shine like mirrors. And the things that are in them! Toys. Clothes. Kitchenware. Jewelry. We stop in front of each, guessing what everything costs. The women wish they had half of it. Pinye laughs and says: "I'd settle for ten percent."

"What's wrong with half? Don't be stingy!" So says Elye, stroking his beard. Elye's beard has grown by leaps and bounds on the way to America. It looks more like a broom now. I'd love to sketch it.

I once drew Pinye's portrait on some paper. And I drew Brokheh with a piece of chalk on a table. Did I get a licking! Brokheh said it was the spit and image of her. She hollered for Elye and he whacked me. He would have murdered me long ago if not for my mother. I get whacked each time he catches me drawing.

I've liked to draw since I was little. At first I drew on the walls with coal. I got whacked for that, too. Then I drew on the doors with chalk and got whacked again. Now I draw with pencil and paper. Elye says: "What's this, more of your doodles?"

I get whacked even harder for sculpting. I like to make little pigs out of bread. Elye lets me have it when he sees them. Pinye comes to the rescue and says: "What do you want from him? Let him sculpt! Let him draw! He may grow up to be an artist."

Elye lets Pinye have it too.

"An artist? You mean a paint smearer? You want him to decorate churches? To doodle on walls? To go around with stained hands like a greasy coachman? He's better off singing for a cantor. God willing, I'll apprentice him as soon as we get to America. He's a soprano."

"Why not teach him a trade?" Pinye says. "Americans work with their hands."

That's all my mother needs to hear.

"What? A common tradesman? Over my dead body will that happen to Peysi the cantor's boy!"

She starts to cry. Pinye defends himself:

"A strange woman you are! Doesn't it say in the Talmud that Rabbi Yohanan was a shoemaker? And that Rabbi Yitzchak was a smith? You don't even have to go that far. My own uncle is a watchmaker and my father is a mechanic!"

That only made it worse. My mother couldn't stop sobbing.

"I suppose that's what my husband spent his life being such a good Jew for, a cantor! I suppose that's why he died young—for his little boy to be a tailor or a shoemaker! And in America yet!"

"There you go again! Have you forgotten that in America you'll need your eyes?"

That's Elye. After a while my mother quiets down.

♦♦♦

I don't care what I'll be in America. I just want to get there. I'm dying to see the place. I've made up my mind to learn three things there: swimming, writing, and cigar smoking. I mean I can do all three already. But I'll do them better in America.

Even if I had been the world's greatest swimmer, I still wouldn't have had anywhere to swim. There's no way you can swim in our river. Lie down in it with your belly in the mud and your feet stick up in the air. Some river! America, they say, has an ocean. If you fall asleep floating in it, the devil knows where you'll wake up.

I can write, too, even though I never studied it. I can print all the letters in the prayer book. I make them look so real you can hardly tell the difference. It's more like drawing than like writing. But I'd like to be able to write fast. That's what they do in America. They do everything fast there, slam-bang. Everyone is in a hurry. I've heard that from the emigrants we've traveled with.

I know almost everything there is to know about America. People travel in trains beneath the ground and make a living. Just don't ask me how they do it, because I have no idea. I'll find out soon enough. I'm a quick learner. One look at anyone and I have him down pat.

Once I did a take-off of Pinye. I did the little hip-hop he walks with, and the way he looks at things like a blind man, and how he talks a mile a minute and smacks his lips. Brokheh nearly split her sides. My mother laughed until she cried. Only Elye didn't think it was funny. He doesn't let me do anything, Elye. I can't figure him out. He says he loves me and he would beat me to death if my mother gave him half the chance. She tells him:

"If you want to be a child beater, have one of your own."

Let someone else lay a hand on me, though, and Elye will tear his eyes out.

Once an emigrant gave me the "governor." You don't know what a "governor" is? You stick your thumb down a person's throat and sock him so hard in the stomach that he's ready for the Angel of Death.

The boy who gave me the governor was ten years old. Did he have a pair of hands!

I could have wished they'd dry up and fall off. He came up to me one day and asked me what my name was. "Motl," I said. "Motl Piss-in-the-Bottle," he says. "How come you're calling me that?" I ask. "Because," he says, "my name is Motl too and you're a jerk. How would you like a governor?" "Why not?" I say. "Come a little closer then," he says, "and I'll give you one." I came closer and he gave it to me. You should have seen me hit the ground. My mother began to scream. Along came Elye and beat the pants off him.

After that we became friends. Besides the governor, I learned all kinds of other things from him. Ventriloquism, for example. You don't know what that is? It isn't something you can learn. You have to be born with it. You shut your mouth, stand perfectly still, and bark like a dog or oink like a pig. I scared my family but good with it. Everyone began looking for a dog beneath the beds and tables. I bent down to look, too, and kept on barking. I tell you, it was a scream! In the end my brother Elye caught on and gave me a hiding. Since then I've given up ventriloquism.

♦♦♦

We would have left Vienna long ago if not for the Alliance. Who's the Alliance? I can't rightly tell you. All I know is that everyone talks about him. The emigrants are mad at him. They say he isn't doing enough. The Alliance, they say, has no pity. They say he doesn't like Jews. Elye and Pinye go see him every day. They come back sweating as though from a steam bath.

"The Alliance should burn," Elye says.

"Like a candle!" says Pinye.

"I'll talk to the Alliance myself," my mother says, taking me by the hand.

We all went together: my mother and me and Elye and Pinye and Brokheh and Taybl. I pictured the Alliance with a beard, a long black coat, a big black belt, and a red nose. Why a red nose? But why does the Judge have mean, beady eyes, fat lips, a couple of teeth, and a riding crop? Do you think I've seen him? Still, whenever Elye says, "Go tell it to the Judge," that's how I imagine him.

So off we went . . . and went . . . and went. Brokheh had a stitch in her side from all that walking. She wished the Alliance would break a leg. We barely made it. But what a house the Alliance lived in! Every Jew should only own one like it, even if it didn't have a front yard. Vienna doesn't go in for front yards. It goes in for weird huge windows and monster doors that are always locked. "They must be afraid we'll walk off with the furniture," Brokheh says. By now she's down on Vienna, too.

There's nothing Brokheh hates more than ringing doorbells. Myself, they don't bother me as long as someone answers. But the Alliance doesn't open so quickly. You can ring till you croak, that's how much of a hurry he's in. And don't think you're the only one. Lots of other emigrants are waiting for him too.

"Ring a little harder. Maybe you'll have better luck."

That's what they said, those emigrants, and laughed. They seemed in a pretty good mood. More and more kept arriving. Pretty soon there was a big crowd of men, women, and children. I like crowds. It would have been a swell scene if only the children had stopped bawling and their mothers had stopped screaming at them.

Thank goodness the door was opened at last. Everyone charged through it so fast you could have been trampled to death. It's a good thing a red-faced Jew with no hat or beard was there to toss us back out like rubber balls. One woman with a child was thrown so hard that she'd still be looking for her teeth if Elye and I hadn't caught her. First, though, she did three somersaults in the air.

It took a while to get into a room. That's when the real party started.

Lordy, lordy! Everyone was shouting all at once. Everyone made a rush for the desks. More hatless, beardless Jews were sitting behind them, laughing and smoking cigars. I couldn't tell which was the Alliance. Neither could my mother. She asked:

"Who here is the Alliance? I've lost everything. All my linens were stolen at the border. My children and I were nearly killed. And they were orphans already, the poor dears! You see, my husband died young, he was a cantor all his life . . . "

That's all she managed to say. Someone grabbed her and showed her the way out. I couldn't understand a word he said. My mother screamed:

"Stop speaking German! Speak Jewish and I'll pour out my bitter heart! I want to see the Alliance."

"Mother-in-law! Let's get out of here. If God brought us this far without the Alliance, He'll bring us the rest of the way. He's a merciful father." That was Brokheh's opinion.

"You're right, my child," my mother answered. "Let's go. God is a father and Vienna is just another town . . . "

THE WONDERS OF ANTWERP

Did you ever think there could be a city called Antwerp? Well, there is, and we're heading for it. How come? Because Yoyneh the bagel maker is sailing from it to America. When Brokheh heard that her father would be in Antwerp, she did cartwheels to get us to go there too. First she doesn't want to hear of the place because it makes her think of ants. Now she's in love with it.

Pinye says it's time for us to part. He wants to go to London. That's a place he has a yen to see. It's almost America, London is. The people there speak English, have blond hair, and live in castles. It's another world.

"You can have your Englishmen and your blond castles. We're sailing from Antwerp!"

That's Brokheh. Taybl turned the color of a red Indian. I've told you she blushes more than she talks. "What's wrong?" Pinye asked. "I don't like the English," Taybl said. "What do you know about them?" Pinye asked. "You've never seen a single Englishman." "And you?" Taybl said. "I suppose you have!"

The long and short of it is that we're all sailing to America from Antwerp. We can sail from Hotzeplotz for all I care, as long as we get there. Pinye and I want to reach America the most. We're sure we'll make it to the top there.

Pinye is peeved at Elye. "We keep traveling and getting nowhere," he says. "Who's holding you back?" Elye answers. "You're a free agent—go where you want!" "How," Pinye asks, "can I go where I want when your mother has to make the acquaintance of every Committee in the world?" "If you're so smart," my mother says to Pinye, "suppose you tell me what we'll do in America without linens." Pinye has no answer to that. He's decided to stick with us.

The truth is he can't stand to leave us. Brokheh and Taybl can't live without each other. Not that they don't fight and call each other names. They're at each other's throats all the time. If not for my mother, they would have stopped being friends long ago. But they always make up in the end. Brokheh can flare up like a match—she says so herself. Catch her on a bad day and you'll get egg all over your face. A minute later she's all sweetness and light. You'd never guess she was just tearing your hair out.

Brokheh and I have been feuding since the wedding. She knows I don't like her. What annoys her the most is my making fun of her. I can't look at her without her thinking that I'm laughing. I've told you I like to draw. Well, not long ago I drew a huge foot with chalk, a real monster. Leave it to Brokheh to decide it's hers! How come? Because no one else, she says, has such big feet. She wears size thirteen galoshes, that's a fact. She ratted to Elye and he yelled:

"More doodling, eh? Up to your old tricks again!"

I swear, even a foot by him is a doodle! He can drive you crazy, Elye can. But it's true that the drawing bug is getting worse. I go around with a crayon I got from the boy who gave me the governor. I've told you about him. His name is Motl too. He's Big Motl and I'm Little Motl. I swapped for it by drawing his portrait on the train to Antwerp, fat cheeks and all. I made him promise not to show it to anyone, because I didn't want Elye laying into me. So naturally Big Motl goes and waves it in Elye's face.

"This looks like my brother's work! Just wait till I get my hands on the little doodler!"

That's what Elye said, running off to look for me. He didn't find me because I was hiding behind my mother, doubled up with laughter. A mother is the world's best hiding place.

♦♦♦

Thank God we're in Antwerp! We barely made it in one piece, but here we are. What can I tell you? It's some city! I don't mean it compares to Vienna. Vienna is in another class. It's a lot bigger and prettier. There are more people there too. But is Antwerp ever spick-and-span! It's no wonder, either, what with how they wash the streets and scrub the sidewalks and clean the houses. I swear, I've even seen them soaping down the walls! I don't mean everywhere. It's not as bad in the emigrants' hotels. In fact it's a pretty swell scene there, the kind of damp, dirty, smoky, crowded place that I like.

Yoyneh the bagel maker hasn't arrived yet. Neither have Pesye and her gang. They're still roaming around Germany. "A hellhole," the emigrants call Germany. They tell one horror story after another. Our stolen linen is chicken feed compared to what some people have lost there.

In Antwerp we've met a woman from Mezhbezh. She's alone with her two children because her husband is already in America. She was on the road for a year, traveling all over and fighting with every Committee on the way. And now that she's made it with her last ounce of strength, she isn't being allowed aboard ship.

Bad eyes? Not at all! Her eyes are fine. She's just a little touched in the head. I mean she's perfectly normal except for the things she says now and then that could make you die laughing. Ask her, for instance, "Where is your husband?" and you'll get the answer, "In America." "And what is he doing there?" "He's the emperor." "But how can a Jew be an emperor?" "In America," says the woman from Mezhbezh, "all things are possible." You get the idea. And she has another strange notion too. She won't eat and doesn't want us to. We mustn't touch the dairy products, she says, because in Antwerp they all have meat in them. "What about the meat?" asked my mother. "You call that meat?" says the woman. "Why, you can eat it with dairy!" We all roared except for my mother. She never laughs when she can cry. "Shame on you," she said, wiping her eyes.

"Well, well, it's about time! You haven't cried for a whole day! How will they ever send us back to Russia if you don't cry your eyes out?"

That's my brother Elye. My mother's eyes were dry in a minute. She feels sorrier for that woman's children than she does for the woman herself. Don't ask me why. As far as I can see, they're having a grand time. They laugh as hard as we do at the crazy things their mother says. By now I know them pretty well. They say she doesn't want to go back to Russia. She wants to join their father the emperor. (Ha-ha-ha!) The officials try tricking her into thinking she can get there by train. (Ha-ha-ha!) They keep telling her the train back to Russia is the Antwerp-America express. (Ha-ha-ha!)

♦♦♦

The things I've seen in Antwerp are not to be described. Every day new people turn up here. They're mostly poor or crippled or have eye problems. "Trachoma," it's called. Whatever it is, America doesn't want it. You can have a thousand diseases, be deaf, dumb, and lame—it's all right if you don't have trachoma.

Where does it come from? You either get it from too much crying or catch it from someone else. You can even catch it from a stranger. I heard that from a girl named Goldeleh. I may as well tell you her story.

I met Goldeleh at Ezrah. Since you don't know what that is either, I'll start with it.

Ezrah is an organization for emigrants. We went looking for it as soon as we hit Antwerp. It's like the Alliance in Vienna. The difference is that they don't toss you out the door. You come when you want and sit where you want and talk as much as you want. Whatever you say is written down in a book. The young woman who writes it is named Fraulein Seitchik and she's nice. She even asked me my name and gave me a candy. I'll tell you about her some other time. Now I'll get back to Goldeleh.

She comes from Kutno, Goldeleh does. She arrived in Antwerp a year ago with her father, mother, brothers, and sisters. It was Sukkes time and they couldn't have had a finer holiday. Not that they were living it up. They stayed in the same miserable quarters as everyone. But they had tickets to America and new clothes fit for a king. Each of them had two new shifts and a pair of new shoes.

Now Goldeleh is down to one shift and no shoes. She'd be going barefoot, she says, if not for Fraulein Seitchik. Fraulein Seitchik gave her the shoes from her own feet, a perfectly good pair. Goldeleh showed them to me. They're pretty swell shoes, even if they are kind of big on her.

To make a long story short, Sukkes came and went and it was time to board ship. First, though, they went to see the doctor. The doctor looked them over and said they were all in good health and could go to America. Except for Goldeleh. Goldeleh had trachoma.

It took a while for that to sink in. At first the family didn't grasp that Goldeleh would have to stay behind in Antwerp while the rest of them went to America. Then they were hysterical. Goldeleh's mother passed out three times. Her father wanted to stay in Antwerp. But it wasn't possible, since they couldn't get a refund on their tickets. In the end they sailed for America and left Goldeleh to get over her trachoma.

Since then a year has passed and she hasn't gotten over anything. Fraulein Seitchik says it's because she cries so much. Goldeleh says that's not the reason. The reason is the calamine. The doctor smears her eyes with the same calamine he gives everyone. If only she had her own calamine, Goldeleh says, her eyes would be fine by now.

"What about your parents?" I ask.

"They're in America. They're making a living. I get mail from them. Every month they send me a letter. Hey, can you read? Read them to me!"

She takes a pack of letters from her blouse and asks me to read them out loud. I tell her I'd like to but can only read prayer book print. Goldeleh laughs and says I'm no better than a girl. To tell you the truth, she's right. I'd give anything to learn to read real writing. Big Motl reads like nobody's business. He reads Goldeleh all her letters. I'm jealous of that, even though they're all the same:

"Dear, darling Goldeleh, we hope you are well!

"When we think of you here in America, our little girl who has been parted from us and lives in misery among strangers, we can't swallow our food. Day and night we weep for the bright little star that our eyes long to see . . . "

Excetra. Big Motl reads and Goldeleh cries and dries her tears. Fraulein Seitchik scolds us for making her cry. She tells Goldeleh she's ruining what's left of her eyes. Goldeleh laughs while the tears run down her cheeks and says:

"It's the doctor and his calamine. They're worse for my eyes than crying."

It's time to say good-bye to her. I promise we'll meet again tomorrow.

"God willing," Goldeleh says, looking like a pious old woman.

Big Motl and I go for a walk in Antwerp.

♦♦♦

Big Motl and I have another friend. His name is Mendl. He's stuck in Antwerp too. Not on account of his eyes, though.

Mendl lost his family in Germany. On the train crossing Germany, he says, there was nothing to eat but salt herring. He was burning with thirst and got off at a station to look for water and the train pulled out and left him without a ticket or a kopeck to his name. Since he didn't speak the language, he pretended to be deaf and dumb. He wandered from one end of Germany to the other until he ran into a party of emigrants who felt sorry for him and took him to Antwerp. There he turned to the people from Ezrah. They've written America to try finding his parents.

Now Mendl is waiting for an answer and a ticket. I mean a half-fare one, since he's not a grown-up. Actually, he's more of one than he lets on. He's already thirteen, though he never had a bar mitzvah. He doesn't even own a prayer shawl or tefillin. How could a boy his age not have his own tefillin, one of the emigrants wanted to know. "I'd rather have a pair of boots," Mendl said. That got him a dirty look. "You little brat!" the emigrant told him. "After all that's been done for you, where do you get the cheek?" He made such a fuss that everyone chipped in and bought Mendl tefillin.

Antwerp has everything. It even has a Turkish synagogue. Don't think that means Turks pray in it. It's prayed in by Jews. They just do it in Turkish. Everything is so upside down you can't understand a word. Mendl took us there. He, me, and Big Motl are thick as thieves. We roam the streets together. This is the first place we've been to where my mother isn't afraid to let me go off by myself. Antwerp is different, she says. The people here are human beings, not Germans. And everyone speaks Jewish.

That's because there are so many emigrants. What would we do without them? It's like living in your own home. Soon we'll even have guests. Next week, if all goes well, Yoyneh the bagel maker will arrive with his household. And Pesye and her gang are due any day now, too. Things are looking up. God willing, I'll tell you all about it.

THE GANG'S ALL HERE

You've already met Pesye's gang. The youngest, Bumpy, is my age. He's nine, going on ten.

I like Bumpy. The best thing about him is that he's no crybaby. You can clobber him all you want—he takes it like a sponge. He's bullet proof! Once he tore a prayer book that Moyshe was binding. Moyshe took his cutting board and whaled into Bumpy so hard that he laid him up in bed for two whole days. It was touch-and-go if Bumpy would pull through. He wouldn't even eat, that's how bad it was. Pesye gave him up for dead. Moyshe was beside himself. No more Bumpy!

No more Bumpy, my eye! Don't think that on the third day he didn't jump out of bed and eat like a horse. They're big eaters, Pesye's gang. "The hungry horde," she calls them.

Pesye's a great lady. She's just a little on the fat side. In fact, she has three chins. I once drew all three on some paper. Bumpy snatched it and showed it to her. Did she laugh! Elye found out and gave me one of his lickings. It's a good thing Pesye was around. "Don't make a big deal of it," she said to Elye. "Boys will be boys." That's Pesye! I love her.

I don't love all her hugging and kissing, though. She was all over me from the minute she arrived in Antwerp. Pesye hugs everyone, especially my mother. You would have thought it was my father come back to life, the way my mother cried when she saw Pesye. She kept it up until Elye warned her that she'd never make it past the doctor.

Everyone in Antwerp has to see the doctor. The first question you're asked is either, "Have you been to the doctor yet?" or, "Well, what did the doctor say?" If you don't go by yourself, you're sent by Ezrah. Our first time there my mother began telling her whole story—how her husband was a cantor, and how he caught cold and fell ill, all the way to our stolen linen. How could we go to America without it?

Fraulein Seitchik wrote it all down. My mother was just warming up when someone asked:

"So you're going to America?"

"Where else?" we answered. "To Yehupetz?"

"Have you been to the doctor?"

"What doctor?"

"Here's his address. He'll check your eyes. That's the first order of business."

My brother Elye heard "eyes," looked at my mother, and turned white as a sheet.

♦♦♦

We hurried off to the doctor. Everyone except my mother. She'd see him another time. Elye was worried about her. All that crying hadn't done her any good.

The doctor examined our eyes, wrote something down, signed it, and put it in an envelope. We thought it was a prescription and were scared. "What's wrong with our eyes?" we asked, but he just pointed to the door. We reckoned that meant it was time to leave and took the prescription to Ezrah. Fraulein Seitchik opened the envelope, read it, and said:

"Good news! The doctor says your eyes are fine."

Good news was right! But what about my mother? She was crying even now. "What are you doing?" we asked. "The doctor will flunk you!"

"Don't I know it! What do you think I'm crying for?"

So she said, my mother, putting a hot compress on her eyes. It was given her by a barber-surgeon, an ugly puss of an emigrant with weird teeth, a dandy's gold watch chain, and a name that sounded like the looks of him: Beeber!

Beeber came to Antwerp with Pesye and Moyshe. He met them on the way and ran the border with them. They didn't have adventures like ours. No one tried killing or robbing them. Still, they had a rough time. You should listen to some of their stories.

Were they put through the grinder in Hamburg! It could make your hair stand on end. Why, Sodom is a resort town next to Hamburg. They treat emigrants no better than convicts there. If Beeber hadn't saved the day, they would never have gotten out of it alive. He's a terror, Beeber is. Did he put those Germans in their place—and without knowing a word of German! But he does speak a swell Russian. I've heard it said he knows more Russian than Pinye.

Pinye says Beeber's stories would be even better if they were true. He didn't cotton to Beeber from the start. He's even written a poem about him. When Pinye takes exception to someone, he puts it in rhyme. I can recite it for you:

Beeber the medic
Can give you a headache
By telling a story
Ten times or more. He
Swears it's all true,
But between me and you,
Even his small talk
Is just so much tall talk!

♦♦♦

Beeber has promised to cure my mother's eyes. He'll see to it, he says, that no one finds anything wrong with them. He learned the trick of treating eyes back in Russia. And he's been in Germany and watched the doctors there. They can make the blind see, that's how good those German doctors are.

"Are you sure they don't do the opposite?" Pinye asked. Beeber blew his stack (he has a temper, Beeber does) and gave Pinye hell. Pinye, he said, is a wise guy. Wise guys don't get far in America. Americans, Beeber said, don't like monkey business. They say what they mean and mean what they say. A man's word is sacred there. America is built on truth and honesty and justice and integrity and humanity and loyalty and compassion and . . . "You're sure that's all?" Pinye asked. That only made Beeber madder. It's a shame the conversation was interrupted.

How come? Because someone came to tell us people were looking for us. Who can it be? Guests! Special guests! Yoyneh the bagel maker and his family have arrived. A new gangful! We go through the whole song-and-dance. First Brokheh kisses her parents. Then Elye kisses his in-laws. Then Pinye kisses his friend-in-laws. Then Beeber kisses them too. "Who's this?" Yoyneh and his wife want to know. "I'm Beeber," says Beeber. Pinye begins to laugh. My mother cries. Elye squirms. He glares at my mother and tugs his beard. But there's nothing he can say. If you can't spare a few tears for your in-laws, for whom can you?

"How did you run the border? Who stole your things and where?"

That's our first question. They have a bunch of stories for us. But I don't have the patience to listen. I go off to a corner with Alte.

Remember Alte? She still has two braids and looks like a bagel twist but she's gotten older. I told her about Goldeleh, and about my friends Mendl and Big Motl, and about Ezrah and Fraulein Seitchik, and about the doctor who looks at your eyes. From there I went on to Vienna, and the Alliance, and Cracow and Lemberg, and running the border and saving our lives. I didn't leave anything out.

Alte listened and told me her own story. Her father had been wanting to go to America for some time. Not her mother Riveleh, though. That is, it was Riveleh's family that was against it. They said you had to slave in America and Riveleh wasn't used to hard work. But after she and Yoyneh went bankrupt and their creditors started knocking on the door, there was nothing to do but sell everything and go.

There was one thing Riveleh refused to part with: a chemise Yoyneh had bought her back in the days when business was good. "What do you need a chemise for? Who wears them in America?" Yoyneh asked. "What do you mean, what do I need it for?" answered Riveleh. "For years I dreamed of a chemise, and now that I have one you want me to sell it?" Day and night that chemise was all they talked about. Riveleh's family took her side. She and Yoyneh fought all the time. It almost led to a divorce.

Who won? Riveleh, of course. The chemise wasn't sold. They packed it and took it to the border. Comes the border—no more chemise.

That's what Alte told me. I didn't care about the rest. Once I heard the chemise was gone, I lost interest. I took Alte for a walk around Antwerp. She wasn't impressed. She had seen bigger cities, she said. I took her to the emigrant hotels and introduced her to my friends. That didn't cut much ice either. She carries on like a grown-up, Alte does. She thinks a lot of herself.

Later that day we all walked to Ezrah, our gang and Yoyneh's. When we got there we ran into Pesye's gang. Goldeleh was there too. She wanted to make friends with Alte but Alte didn't want to. Goldeleh asked me why Alte was so snooty. I told her it was because we were engaged at my brother's wedding. Goldeleh turned red as fire. She slipped away and went to wipe her eyes.

♦♦♦

Listen to our latest bad luck. We took my mother to the doctor. He looked at her eyes and said nothing. He just put another slip of paper in an envelope. We took it to Ezrah. Fraulein Seitchik was the only one there. She gave me a big smile (she always does when she sees me) but stopped smiling the minute she opened the envelope. "How are you today?" my mother asked. "How should I be, *meine Frau?"* said Fraulein Seitchik. "This isn't good. The doctor says you can't go to America."

Brokheh, as you know, likes to faint. Down she went. Elye's face didn't have a drop of blood in it. My mother turned to stone. She couldn't even cry. Fraulein Seitchik went to get some water. She revived Brokheh, comforted Elye, consoled my mother, and told us to come back the next day.

All the way to our hotel Elye lectured my mother. How many times had he told her not to cry! She couldn't answer him. She just looked at the sky and said: "Dear God, do me and my children a favor and take me from this world right now!" Pinye claimed it was all that lying Beeber's fault. We snapped at each other all day.

In the morning we went back to Ezrah. We were advised to go to London. In London my mother's eyes might be cleared—if not for America, at least for Canada.

Where was Canada? No one knew. Someone said it was even farther than America. Elye and Pinye began to fight. "Pinye!" Elye said. "Where is this Canada? I thought you were a geographer." Pinye said Canada was in Canada. To be exact, it was in America. That is, Canada and America were the same place, with a difference. "That makes no sense," Elye said. "Sense or not, it's a fact," answered Pinye.

Pesye, Moyshe, and their gang were sailing for America. We went to see them off at the ship. Whew, what a scene! Men, women, children, bundles, pillows, sacks of linen, people running, yelling, sweating, eating, swearing! Suddenly, there's a noise like some huge animal's: *HOOOOOOOOOOO!*

That's the signal that the ship is leaving. Everyone is hugging, kissing, crying—a regular opera. They're all saying good-bye and so are we. We kiss Pesye's whole gang. Pesye tells my mother not to worry. They'll soon see each other in America. My mother makes a gesture with her hand and fights her tears. Lately she's been crying less. She's been taking a pill against it.

All the passengers are aboard. We're left behind on the pier. Am I jealous of Bumpy! Just the other day the shoe was on the other foot. There he is on deck with his torn cap, sticking his tongue out at me. That's his way of saying he'll be in America before me. I give him the finger to hide how low I feel. That means: "Bumpy! You should break all your bones if I'm not in America before you know it!"

Honestly, don't worry. I'll get there soon enough.

THE GANG BREAKS UP

Day by day the crowds of emigrants get smaller. Antwerp is emptying out. Every Saturday a new shipload sails for America. My friend Big Motl is gone too. I don't know what it was about him that Elye didn't like. I guess it started with Brokheh.

Brokheh has a way of overhearing things, especially when they're funny. She thinks everyone's laughter is her business. You can be laughing at Pinye for stuffing his pockets with candies or at Beeber for the whoppers he tells—Brokheh is sure the joke is on her or her family.

Mind you, she was right this time. We put on a play about Riveleh and her chemise.

One day my mother had enough. "Oy, in-law!" she said to Riveleh. "Imagine if I talked about my stolen linens as much as you do about your chemise."

"As if there's any comparison," Riveleh answered in her gruff voice.

"I suppose you think I stole them myself," says my mother.

"How should I know?" Riveleh says. "I never slept on them."

"In-law!" my mother says. "What kind of talk is that?"

"As you say good morning to me," says Riveleh, "so I'll say good evening to you."

"But how have I offended you?" my mother asks.

"Who says I'm offended?" says Riveleh.

"Then why did you say there's no comparison?" my mother asks.

"Because," Riveleh says. "I'm talking about my chemise and you come along with your stolen linens."

"I suppose you think I stole them myself."

"How should I know? I never slept on them."

And around it went again. Who needs tickets for the theater?

♦♦♦

Big Motl and I stayed up half the night rehearsing our play. It was Big Motl's idea. "You'll be your mother and I'll be Riveleh," he said. "I'll be gruff and you'll whine."

We dressed for the parts. Big Motl put on a wig and I wore a kerchief. We sent invitations to Mendl and Alte and Goldeleh and all the other boys and girls in our gang. Act I went like this.

Little Motl (whining): Oy, in-law! Imagine if I talked as much about my stolen linens as you do about your chemise!

Big Motl (gruffly): As if there's any comparison!

Little Motl: I suppose you think I stole them myself.

Big Motl: How should I know? I never slept on them.

Little Motl: In-law! What kind of talk is that?

Big Motl: As you say good morning to me, so I'll say good evening to you.

Little Motl: But how have I offended you?

Big Motl: Who says I'm offended?

Little Motl: Then why did you say there's no comparison?

Big Motl: Because I'm talking about my chemise and you come along with your stolen linens.

Little Motl: I suppose you think I stole them myself.

Big Motl: How should I know? I never slept on them . . .

Go guess that just as Big Motl said "slept on them" the door would open and in would walk Brokheh and Riveleh and Yoyneh the bagel maker with all his sons and my mother and Elye and Pinye and Taybl and Beeber with his yellow teeth and still more people—a regular mob! That rat Brokheh had brought the whole world to string me up. But the whole world didn't have to. Elye did it himself. He gave me such a box on the ear that I woke up hearing bells the next morning.

"The two Motls must be separated," Brokheh declared. Make no mistake about it, Elye warned me: he would beat me like an egg white if he caught me with Big Motl again. But if you're waiting to hear what that feels like, you've forgotten that there are mothers who would sooner lose both bad eyes than see their son treated like an egg white.

♦ ♦ ♦

My mother's eyes aren't getting any better. That means things are getting worse. A million dollars couldn't buy her passage to America.

It's time to leave Antwerp. The doctors here are a lowdown bunch. They look at your eyes and go berserk if they find one little trachoma. They haven't a drop of pity. We'll have to get to America some other way. The question is how.

There are plenty of possibilities. But we're running out of cash. A lot has gone to the doctors and Beeber—all on account of my mother's eyes. I've talked it over with Elye and Pinye. "Let's go to London," they say.

I'd rather go to America. Pesye and her gang must have arrived there long ago. I'll bet they're already making a living. Bumpy must be walking around with his hands in his pockets, as happy as a nutcracker. Yoyneh, Riveleh, and their kids, including my fiancée Alte, decided not to wait for us either. They've sailed to America too.

Was that a day! We didn't let my mother go to the ship because she was sure to cry her eyes out. A lot of good that did! It just made her cry harder. We were robbing her of her only pleasure, she said. Crying is the one thing that does her good.

No one was even listening.

♦ ♦ ♦

Do you know who's glad that Yoyneh the bagel maker's family is gone? You'll never guess. Goldeleh! She nearly jumped for joy when she heard the news. That's because she doesn't like Alte. She said, her face burning like an oven: "I don't want to see your red-braided bride again! She's stuck-up."

"Since when are Alte's braids red?" I said. "They're brown."

That just made her angrier. She burst into tears and shouted: "They're red! Red! Red!"

When Goldeleh loses her temper, watch out! Usually she's sweet as sugar. I feel like a brother to her. She tells me how hard she works to pay for her room and board. She cleans the rooms in her hotel, feeds the chickens, and puts the landlord's twins to bed. (First his wife couldn't have children, now she has two.) Every day she goes to the doctor. He treats her eyes with the same calamine he gives everyone.

"If only I had my own. I'd see my mama and papa again."

It breaks my heart to see the tears in her infected eyes. I tell her: "You know what, Goldeleh? When I get to America and make a living, I'll send you calamine from there."

"You will? Swear to me by all that's holy!"

I swear to her. If all goes well and I make a living, I'll send the calamine.

♦♦♦

It's final. We're sailing for London on Saturday. We're already preparing for the trip. My mother, Brokheh, and Taybl have been going from hotel to hotel, saying good-bye to the emigrants. They've had some heart-to-heart talks.

Compared to some people, we're not doing badly. You wouldn't believe the down-and-outers we've come across or how they envy us. To listen to them talk, they all were once rich, lived in the lap of luxury, fed every beggar in the neighborhood, and married their sons and daughters to the upper crust. Now they're a sorry bunch of drifters, every one of them.

I'm sick and tired of their stories. Once, if I heard about a pogrom, I listened to every word. Today I run the other way. I'd rather hear something funny. There just isn't anyone to tell it. The last person was that bull artist Beeber. He's in America now.

"Lying his head off," Pinye says.

"Don't worry," says Elye. "He won't get away with it. Americans don't like types like that. A liar is worse than a pork eater there."

So Elye says. "What makes you so sure?" Brokheh asks. That's when the shouting match begins. Pinye sides with Elye and Taybl sides with Brokheh. Whatever the two men say, the two women say the opposite.

The Men: America is a land of unvarnished truth!

The Women: America is a land of barefaced lies!

The Men: America stands for truth, honesty, and compassion!

The Women: America stands for theft, murder, and skulduggery!

It's a good thing my mother is around. "Children," she says, "we're still in Antwerp. Why fight over America?"

She's right. We're in Antwerp. Not for long, though. In a few days we'll be in London. Everyone is moving on, all the emigrants, the whole gang.

How will Antwerp manage without us?

SO LONG, ANTWERP!

No place has been as hard to leave as Antwerp. It's not so much the city as the people. I mean it's not the people either, it's the emigrants—especially my gang of friends. Some have left before us. Bumpy, Alte, and Big Motl are all making a living in America by now. Only Goldeleh and Mendl (Brokheh calls him "the wild pony") are still here. Who will Ezrah have to help when we're all gone?

I'll miss Antwerp. It's a swell city. Everyone here deals in diamonds. They carry them around in their pockets. Everyone cuts them, faces them, polishes them. Some of our gang have decided to stay on and become diamond cutters. They wouldn't go to America for the world. They want to make a cutter of me, too. My brother Elye thinks it's good work. So does Pinye. If they were younger, they say, they'd learn it themselves.

Brokheh laughs at them. She says diamonds are for wearing, not for cutting. Taybl agrees. She'd love to own a diamond herself. She spends her days looking at the shop windows and saying how the stones are cheap as dirt. That's all she and Brokheh talk about. They're so diamond crazy they see diamonds in their dreams. Pinye thinks it's a big joke. He thinks all jewelry is. So is anyone who cares about it. You can bet he's written a poem. It goes:

Antwerp's your true diamondland!
Diamonds gleam on every hand!
Everyone a millionaire!
Not a poor man anywhere!
Diamonds on such clearance sales
They're even in the garbage pails!

Diamonds glitter! Diamonds flash!
All that's missing is . . . some cash.

I can't remember the rest.

♦♦♦

You would need the brains of a genius to remember all of Pinye's poems. Elye scolds him. He says that if that poem about Antwerp reaches Ezrah, we'll be thrown out the door. We're counting on Ezrah to finance the next leg of our trip.

We go there every day. It's our second home. Fraulein Seitchik knows us all by name. She loves me like a son. She's a sister to my mother. You can see why even Brokheh admits she has a Jewish soul. All the emigrants are in love with her. Best of all, she speaks Jewish. Everyone else in Antwerp talks a kind of German called Flemish. You couldn't beat it out of them with a stick. Pinye can't understand why, with so many Jews around, people don't learn a Jewish language. But not even the beggars would agree to that. They'd rather die of hunger as long as it's in Flemish.

Brokheh has had it with Flemish. She's itching to get to London. She just wishes someone would drop a diamond in the street before we leave. Just one little stone from a hole in someone's pocket! Her eyes shine when she talks about it.

It beats me why she's so wild about diamonds. I'd trade all the diamonds in the world for a paint box and a brush. Not long ago I drew a ship with a pencil. I drew a gang of emigrants on it, each with his own face, and gave it as a present to Goldeleh. Goldeleh showed it to Fraulein Seitchik, who hung it on the wall for all to see. Elye saw it too and whacked me. "More doodles! Are you going to stop your doodling or not?" He hasn't hit me so hard in ages. I told Goldeleh, who told Fraulein Seitchik, who came out of her office to bawl Elye out. She gave him a whole speech about my drawing. He listened and went home and hit me harder. He says he'll beat every last doodle out of me.

♦♦♦

We made our last visit to Ezrah today. Don't ask me what we did there. Elye got into an argument. Pinye talked with his hands. Brokheh butted in and my mother began to cry. The people at Ezrah tried talking to us, mostly in that German of theirs. There were three of them, all trying to see who spoke it better. May I hope to die if I knew what they were saying. My mind was already aboard ship—at sea, in London, in America. Suddenly Goldeleh comes running, all out of breath.

"You're going?"

"Yes."

"When?"

"Tomorrow."

"Where?"

"To London."

"And from there?"

"To America."

"And I'll be left behind with my bad eyes! God knows if I'll ever see my mama and papa again."

That's what she said, Goldeleh, and burst into tears. It broke me up. I didn't know how to comfort her. All I could think of was: "God Almighty! What do you have against this little girl? What did she ever do to you?" I took her hand and stroked it and said:

"Don't cry, Goldeleh. You'll see. As soon as I make a living in America, I'll send you calamine for your eyes. And I'll send you a ticket too, half fare because you're under ten, and you'll come to America. Your mama and papa will be waiting for you at Ella's Island. So will I. You'll look for me and there I'll be—look, I'll be holding this pencil. That's how you'll recognize me, Motl. You'll get off the ship and give your parents a hug, but you won't go straight home with them. You'll give them your things and come with me to see America. I'll show you everything, because I'll know it cold by then. Then I'll bring you to your parents' and we'll have a bowl of hot soup."

Goldeleh didn't want to hear any more. She threw her arms around me and kissed me. I kissed her too.

♦♦♦

Leave it to Brokheh! She's always popping up where you least expect her. Just when I'm saying good-bye to Goldeleh, she has to put in an appearance. She didn't say anything. She just went "A-haaaa!" in a voice ten feet deep. Then she wrinkled her nose and pursed her lips in this weird way and said "A-hemmm!" and went off to look for Elye. I don't know what she told him. I only know that as soon as we left Ezrah, I got two slaps that made me see stars.

"But why?" asked my mother. "What was that for?"

"He knows what it's for," Elye answered and we went back to our hotel.

It's time to pack. What a scene! I like to watch people pack. My brother Elye is a whiz at it. As soon as there's packing to do, he pulls off his coat and gives orders. "Hand me the dirty laundry! . . . Mama, the teapot! . . . That hat, Brokheh, quick! . . . Pinye, those galoshes! You're blind as a bat, they're right under your nose! . . . Motl, what are you standing like a dummy for? Pitch in! All he can do is doodle, doodle, doodle!"

That's me! I jump up and grab all I can and throw it at him. Elye yells that I'll catch it. My mother sticks up for me: "What do you want from the child?" Brokheh objects to my being called a child. My mother remembers I'm an orphan and starts to cry. Elye shouts:

"Go ahead, cry, cry your eyes out!"

So long, Antwerp!

LONDON, YOU SHOULD BURN!

In all my life I've never seen a carnival like the one in London. I mean, it isn't *in* London. It's London that's the carnival. The clamor, the yammer, the hooting, the tooting, the people—like ants! Where are they all coming from and going to? They must be hungry or running to catch a train. Why else would they knock you down and step all over you?

I'm talking about Pinye. Pinye, you'll recall, doesn't see so well. That's why he goes around with his head in the sky and his feet dragging after him. He looks like an absentminded angel. His mind is always somewhere else.

Pinye's introduction to London came in the railroad station. We had barely crawled out of the train when disaster struck. He was first on the platform, one pant leg hiked up, one sock falling down, his necktie jerked to one side—in short, the usual Pinye. I had just never seen him so excited. He was on fire as though with a fever. The weirdest words came tumbling out of him: "London! England! Disraeli! Buckle! History! Civilization . . . !" You couldn't get him to calm down.

Two minutes later our friend Pinye was on the ground, being walked on as though he were a plank. It's a good thing Taybl looked for him and screamed: "Pinye, where are you?" Elye leaped into the crowd and pulled him out, as pale and crumpled as an old hat.

That was for starters. Act Two came later that day, in a neighborhood with the Jewish name of Vaytshepl. That's a place where you can buy fish and meat and prayer books and apples and barley beer and sugar cakes and herring and prayer shawls and lemons and wool and eggs and bottles and pots and noodles and brooms and whistles and pepper and rope, just like back home. It has everything. It even has your Kasrilevke mud. It smells the same too, only worse.

It did our hearts good to see Vaytshepl. It did Pinye too much good. "Why, it's Berdichev!" he shouted. "Children, I swear, we're not in London at all, we're in Berdichev!" The next thing I know he's been given such a Berdichev that I thought it was the hospital for sure. Since then Taybl doesn't let him take a step in London without her.

Vaytshepl made me think: good God, if this is London, what is America like? But as far as Brokheh is concerned, London can go up in flames. She hated it the minute she laid eyes on it. "You call this a city?" she says. "It's hell on earth! It should have burned to the ground a year ago."

Elye tries pointing out London's good sides. It does as much good as chicken soup does a dead man. Brokheh pours fire and brimstone on the place. She has fire on the brain, Brokheh does. Taybl backs her up. My mother says, "Dear God, have mercy and make London our last stopover!"

The three of us, Elye, Pinye, and me, think the world of London. We like the hustle and the bustle. What's it to us if the town is always cooking? Let it boil! Our problem is that we have nothing to do here. We can't find a Committee. Either no one knows of one or no one wants to tell us. This person has no time, that one is busy. Everyone is in a hurry.

The reason we need a Committee is simple. We have nothing left to get to America with. Elye is broke. The proceeds from our house have gone up in smoke. Pinye laughs and says to Elye, "Your secret pocket has lost its secret."

That gets Elye mad. Elye doesn't like wisecracks. He's a brooder, Elye is. He and Pinye are opposites. Pinye calls him "Mr. Family Conscience." What I like about Pinye is that he's always in a grand mood. The good thing about the English, he says, is that they don't speak German. The bad thing is that they speak something worse. Brokheh would trade three Englishmen for one German. Who ever heard of a country, she says, that has money called "aypens," "toppens," and "troppens?"

♦ ♦ ♦

I've told you we're looking for a Committee. Finding a Committee in London is like finding a needle in a haystack. But there's a great God above. One day we're out walking in Vaytshepl. I mean one evening. That is, it was daytime. The point is, there's no daylight in London. It's evening all day long. Anyhow, along comes a Jew with a short jacket, a fine hat, and eyes on the lookout for something.

"If I'm not mistaken, you're all Jews!"

That's what he says, the man with the fine hat. Pinye answers: "You bet! They don't come any more Jewish than we do."

"How would you like to do a good deed?" says the Jew.

"Such as what?" Pinye asks.

"I have an anniversary of a death today and can't get to synagogue to say the kaddish. I need nine Jews to pray with me. Is this young man bar mitzvah?"

He meant me! I liked being called a young man and taken for thirteen.

We followed the Jew up some steps to a dark room full of ragged children and smelling of fried fish. No one else was there. That still left us seven Jews short. The man offered us a seat and ran back down. He came and went a few times until he had rounded up ten men.

Meanwhile I talked to the children and watched the fish fry on the stove. The English call it fishink tships. A tship is a boat for catching fish. It's not a bad dish, fishink tships. One thing is for sure: it's a lot better than Brokheh says it is. The truth is that I wouldn't have minded a piece of it. I'll bet Brokheh wouldn't have, either. We had hardly eaten all day. Lately, our only food has been herring and radishes. They sell swell black radishes in Vaytshepl. But the Jew didn't have the brains to invite us for dinner. Maybe he didn't think we were hungry. At the end of the prayer he thanked us and said we could go.

Elye didn't want to give up. He kept looking at the fishink tships with his mouth watering while asking the Jew if he knew of a Committee. The Jew kept one hand on the door knob and talked with the other. There was a Committee all right, he said. He just couldn't say a good word about it. That is, it wasn't really a Committee. Or rather, it wasn't one Committee. It was several. The London Committees didn't hand out cash so fast. Whoever wanted help had to bring papers and documents proving they were emigrants for America. That was because a lot of Jews in London were just pretending to be emigrants. And once you brought all the documents, you were given a ticket back to Russia. The London Committees weren't big on America.

That made my brother Elye sore. You already know he has a temper. It doesn't take much to set Pinye off either. He began to shout:

"But that's impossible!! How can they send us back to Russia? This is the land of the megneh kahteh."

Don't ask me what that is. The man let us out the door and said: "You can talk all you want. Here's the address of a Committee. You'll see for yourselves."

♦♦♦

The smell of fishink tships followed us down the stairs. Although we were all thinking about food, no one mentioned it but Brokheh. Did she let loose with a mouthful! She hoped to God, she said, that the people upstairs would choke to death on their stinking fish that you could smell a mile away.

That didn't go down well with my mother. "What do you have against that poor family?" she asked. "They're fine folk. Look at the hole they live in—and they still remember to say the prayers for the dead."

"Mother-in-law!" answered Brokheh. "They should roast in hell with their prayers and their fishink tships! If you kidnap strangers on the street, the least you can do is offer their child a piece of fishink!"

She meant me. One minute I'm a bar-mitzvah boy and the next I'm a child again. Happy times are here if Brokheh is taking my side!

The six of us went off to the Committee. The Jew's parting advice was to take a tram. The problem with London trams is that they don't like to stop. You can flag them down till you're blue in the face, they just fly right past you. It doesn't help to run after them either, because you'll never catch them. Luckily an Englishman saw us waving at them and took us to a place where he told us to wait.

Sure enough, we didn't have to wait long. In a minute a tram pulled up and we climbed aboard, Elye and Pinye and my mother and Brokheh and Taybl and me. Along comes a conductor selling tickets. *"Skolke vifl?"* asks Pinye. "Aypens," says the conductor. Pinye gives him aypens. "Not aypens! Aypens!" the conductor says, getting sore. Although Pinye just laughs, Elye loses his temper. "Aypens or not aypens!" he shouts. "Which do you want?" The conductor yanks a cord to stop the tram and chucks us into the street like a madman. You might think we had tried robbing his change belt. How were we supposed to know that eight pence wasn't ha'-pence?

"Well? Does London deserve to burn or not?"

That's Brokheh. We went the rest of the way on foot.

♦♦♦

The London Committee was the same jolly scene as every other Committee we had been to. The same emigrants filled the same courtyard like rubbish and the same men smoked the same cigars and said, "Next!" The only difference was that the other Committees spoke German and had whiskers and this committee spoke English and was clean-shaven. The women had big teeth, wore hairpieces with curls, and were so ugly they made you want to puke—and there they sat, mocking us with their eyes and pointing at us with their fingers and fidgeting at having to deal with us.

Back in the street two girls stopped Elye and told him to go to a bahbeh shahp. We didn't know that meant he should get a haircut. What weird people! They go around full of grease stains from the smelly fishink tships they eat in the street and don't like hair! There are plenty of drunks lying in the gutters here, too. That's something you never saw back home. England would be a fine country, Brokheh says, if only someone would put a torch to it.

"What good would that do?"

That's Elye. Did he get it from Brokheh! She's something when she lets rip. Either she isn't talking to you or else you have to stop your ears and run for your life. I quote:

"How dare you stick up for this God-accursed, gray-skied, barecheeked, twirly-curled, greasy-stained, beer-breathed, beggarly city of old maids and fishink tships and charming Vaytsheplakh and thieving conductors and Jews who pray for the dead and don't give you the time of day? Fire is too good for it!"

That's what she said, Brokheh did, all in one breath, praying with her hands clasped together:

"London, I wish you would burn!"

God Almighty! When will we get to America?

♦♦♦ Part Two

CONGRATULATIONS! WE'RE IN AMERICA!

Congratulations, we're in America!

That's what they tell us, anyway. No one has seen America yet because we're still on Ella's Island. Why did they name it for Ella? "Because Ella had no fella," Pinye says. Pinye can't resist a rhyme.

Pinye is peeved at Ella's Island for keeping us poor immigrants here while the rich ones go ashore. That's something you would expect from a thieving Russky, he says, not from a free country like America. In America rich and poor are supposed to be equal. Pinye starts spouting words: "Columbus . . . Shakespeare . . . Buckle . . . Civilization . . . " He's decided to write a poem sending America to the devil but he doesn't have pencil or paper.

Elye says that if Pinye doesn't like America, he can turn around and go home. I've told you they never agree. "Mr. Summer and Mr. Winter," Brokheh calls them. Elye doesn't take that sitting down. "Fat cow" and "Nanny goat" are two of his names for Brokheh. (Some of the others aren't fit for print.) My mother tells Brokheh that whoever doesn't want to get scratched should stay out of a fight between tomcats.

♦♦♦

What are we doing on Ella's Island? We're waiting for our friends and acquaintances to get us out. We've been in and out of so many places since leaving London and boarding ship that we know all the questions by heart. "What are your names, please?" "Where are you going?" "Whom do you know in America?"

We give the same answers each time. Once there was a Jew named Peysi the cantor. Peysi died and left a widow: that's my mother. My mother has a son: that's Elye. Elye has a wife: that's Brokheh. He also has a friend: that's Pinye. Pinye has a wife: that's Taybl. And there's me, Motl, and my friend Mendl. Brokheh calls him Teeny because he's already in his teens.

Whom do we know in America? Why, half the country and just about every Jew! To begin with, there are our neighbors Moyshe the bookbinder, Fat Pesye, and their gang. We list their full names for the immigration officials: "There's Pinye-Log, and Velvel-Tomcat, and Mendl-Ratface, and Hayyim-Ox, and Faytl-Petelulu, and Berl-Give-Me-More, and Zerakh-Butternose, and Hirshl-Bumpy. Bumpy is called Bumpy because—"

The immigration officials stop us. "All right, we've had enough children. Let's have some adults."

We give them some adults. "There's Yoyneh the bagel maker, a mean Jew if ever there was one. That's one. There's Yoyneh's wife, Riveleh-Chemise. That's two. The chemise was stolen at the border . . . "

My mother hears "border," remembers her linens, and begins to cry. Elye scolds her. My mother tells him she's in America. Now that she needn't worry about her eyes, she'll cry all she wants.

♦♦♦

It's a miracle they let her in with those eyes—to say nothing of surviving the sea voyage. The times we saw the Angel of Death face to face! The times we said good-bye to life!

Everything seemed fine and dandy when we boarded the *Prince Albert*. My friend Mendl and I explored the ship from prow to stern. We couldn't have been more thrilled. Picture living in a three-story house on water! You take a turn around the deck with your hands in your pockets and you're traveling to America. You stop to have a drink and you're traveling to America. You sleep in a bed at night and you're still traveling to America. And the people—a whole city! They're all traveling to America like you and everyone knows everyone in no time. You find out more about a person in a day than you normally would in a year.

Whew! The number of women my mother, Brokheh, and Taybl have made friends with! That's nothing, though, compared to Elye and Pinye's new friends. They talk on and on. The women discuss household things: kitchens, pantries, laundry, linens, socks, pillowcases. The men talk about America, jobs, Columbus, anti-Semitism, pogroms.

A person might think they couldn't live without pogroms. I've told you I don't like to hear about them. The minute someone starts on a new one, I'm off. I take Mendl by the hand and we go for a walk in the streets of the *Prince Albert*.

The *Prince Albert* is a big, fine-looking ship. It has marble stairs, brass railings, and lots of iron and steel. And the crew! Some are stewards and some are sailors, a whole bunch of them. They run around all over. Mendl and I are green with envy. We promise each other that we'll go to sea when we grow up.

The one thing wrong with the *Prince Albert* is that you're not allowed everywhere. Try going beyond the steerage deck and you're chased away. The sailors are a rotten bunch. And the first-class passengers are no better for letting the sailors behave like that. Are they afraid we'll bite them? Mendl doesn't like it one bit. He can't understand why a ship needs different classes. America has no classes, he says. If I don't believe him I can ask my brother Elye.

Elye hates those kind of questions. It's better to ask Pinye. Pinye loves to talk about such things. He'll bombard you with words. Get Pinye started and he's like an alarm clock that keeps going until it runs down.

♦♦♦

I found Pinye sitting on deck with his nose in a book. Pinye doesn't read with his eyes. He reads with the tip of his nose. That's because he's nearsighted. When I was practically on top of him I said: "Pinye, I have a question."

Pinye took his nose from the book.

"What's up, little man?"

"Little man" is Pinye's name for me. I mean it's his name when he's in a good mood. He's almost always in a good mood, even when he's fighting with Elye or Taybl is sulking.

I asked Pinye if Mendl was telling the truth.

You should have seen him catch fire and shoot sparks! Why, America, he said, is the only country in the world with real freedom and equality. Only in America can you be sitting with the President on one side of you, and a bum, a down-and-outer, on the other, and next to the bum is a millionaire. Civilization! Progress! Columbus!

Pinye cut loose with his biggest words. A Jew standing next to us, a stranger, mixed in:

"If it's such a wonderful country and everyone is so equal, how come there are down-and-outers and millionaires? You're not being logical."

But let Pinye fight his own battles. I had found out what I wanted to know. Mendl was right. There are no classes in America. Classes are bad. So are first- and second-class passengers. Just don't ask me why. What have they ever done to me?

Mendl says: "Who do those fat cats think they are shutting themselves up with a lot of shiny mirrors? Do they think they're too good for the likes of us lower-deckers? Aren't we human too? Don't we all pray to the same God?"

In the end, they got their comeuppance. It happened on the night of Yom Kippur, when the upper crust had to stoop and join us in steerage.

♦♦♦

Since the *Prince Albert* sailed after Rosh Hashanah, we spent Yom Kippur at sea. Our last meal before the fast was roast potatoes. All our meals were potatoes, because the *Prince Albert* had no kosher kitchen. There was also bread and tea with sugar. I tell you, it wasn't half bad. I could live on nothing else for a whole year. Brokheh says too many potatoes make you fat. But what doesn't Brokheh say? When did Brokheh ever like anything?

She didn't like the *Prince Albert* either. She said it was too slow. Who ever heard, she said, of a single trip taking ten days?

We tried explaining that it was because of the ocean, not the ship. Pinye pointed out that there's three times more water than land in the world. Elye said it's only two times. He knows his geography, he said. The world is two-thirds water and one-third land. That means twice as much water. "Three times," Pinye said. "Twice," insisted Elye. "Three times!" "Twice!" They fought for a while and made up.

Who would be the cantor on Yom Kippur? My brother Elye, of course. Not that he was ever a cantor before, but his father was a famous one.

And he has a good voice and knows Hebrew—what more could anyone want? Pinye had the whole ship begging Elye to sing the Kol Nidrei. He spread the word that the young man with the blond beard—that's Elye—is a musical wonder. You should hear him pray! Not to mention the little man who is his brother (that's me!) and sings a mean soprano. It's enough to make God himself take voice lessons.

♦♦♦

It didn't matter how much Elye tried begging off or swore he had never been a High Holy Day cantor. Nothing in the world could get him out of it. He was practically dragged to the prayer stand—I mean to a round table covered with a white sheet. Pinye said to me:

"Let's go, little man. Get to work!"

We gave those passengers a Kol Nidrei to remember!

But the Kol Nidrei was nothing compared to the prayers that came after. There wasn't a dry eye in the house. It started with some sighing and throat-scraping. Then came the quiet sniffles. That led to the blowing of noses, which grew so loud after a while that the whole place was bawling its head off. Everyone was thinking of where he had been a year ago—in his own town by his own prayer stand in his own synagogue with its own cantor and choir boys.

Now we were vagabonds, so many head packed together in a cattle drive. Believe me, even the first-class spiffs with their shiny top hats couldn't hold back their tears. They had their silk handkerchiefs out and were pretending to mop their brows, but I could see them crying sure enough. The stewards and sailors stood at a respectful distance, watching the Jews rock back and forth in their white prayer shawls. They must have been thinking that all that sorrow did us good. Elye gave it all he had while I pitched in with the harmonies. My mother stood in the women's corner in her good silk shawl, holding her prayer book and weeping her heart out.

She was blissful. At last she was in her element.

♦♦♦

The next morning we rose early to start the service on time. We might as well have stayed in bed. Not only couldn't anyone pray, no one could walk or even stand. Our heads were spinning too fast to see straight. We felt so bad we wanted to die. As a matter of fact, that's what we thought we were doing.

What was the matter? I'm too tired to go on now. I'll tell you about it tomorrow.

CROSSING THE RED SEA

I was telling you about the humdinger that hit the *Prince Albert* that Yom Kippur. It was a bad one. We'll never forget it.

It didn't start out like much, just a strip of black cloud at the edge of the sky soon after Kol Nidrei. My friend Mendl was the first to notice it. That's because all the other Jews were still yammering below and reciting Psalms after the prayers. Mendl and I had gone for a walk around the ship and were sitting quietly in a corner. It was a calm, warm night and we were feeling happy and a little sad. I don't know what Mendl was thinking. I was thinking about God. I was thinking how big he must be, sitting up there in charge of everything. How did it feel to be prayed to and praised by so many Jews pouring out their hearts to you?

My mother says God hears and sees everything and knows my every thought. I was hoping she was wrong, because just then I was thinking of a juicy apple, a sweet pear, and a nice glass of cold water. The potatoes were giving me heartburn.

Elye would kill me if he caught me drinking on Yom Kippur. He wanted me to fast the whole twenty-four hours, even though I wasn't thirteen. "We'll see about that," my mother said. Now she was looking for me everywhere. A sailor showed her where Mendl and I were sitting in the prow. "Motl?" she yelled. "Motl!"

"What is it, Mama?"

"You know what it is! Go to sleep! Have you forgotten you have to get up early tomorrow? It's Yom Kippur."

Not that I wanted to, but I went to bed.

♦ ♦ ♦

The sky was black when we woke in the morning. The sea was angry and wild, its waves higher than the ship. They tossed the *Prince Albert* up and down like a toy. The sailors staggered like poisoned mice. The stewards clung to the railings. The passengers hugged the walls and reeled with each step.

All at once it began to pour buckets. The thunderclaps came one after another. God was whipping on his chariot—and on his holiest day! Bolts of lightning flashed across the dark sky. The *Prince Albert* groaned and rolled with the waves. The rain pelted down. It felt like a second Noah's flood. But hadn't God sworn that the first was the last?

"Crossing the Red Sea was nothing compared to this," said my brother Elye.

"Nothing!" Pinye echoed. It was the first time I had ever heard them agree.

The comparison caught on. Before long everyone was looking out the portholes and talking about the Red Sea. I mean everyone who didn't run to the deck to puke his empty guts out. Yom Kippur? Prayers? Who could even remember what day it was?

♦ ♦ ♦

The first to break down in our family was Brokheh. For a while she screamed she was dying. Then she began swearing at Elye. What ever made him think of going to America? She had known all along that Siberia was better. Why, Siberia was gold next to America!

My mother came to Elye's defense. She tried explaining that all things came from God and had to be borne. It said in the Bible . . . but my mother never said what it said in the Bible because just then she turned green. One look at her made Taybl sick too.

Pinye thought it was funny. "Just look at them!" he declared. "Women are one big laugh." He jammed his cap down sideways and stuck his hands in his pockets. "They're ninnies! What do I care if there's a storm and the ship is rolling? I use my brains and figure out what to do. When the ship rolls that way, I bend this way; when it rolls back this way, I bend that way. It's called keeping your equilibrium."

As Pinye was showing us his equilibrium, my brother Elye started looking pretty bad. Soon the two of them rushed outside to chuck up whatever was still in them. So did the other passengers. Then everyone dragged himself off to his bunk and collapsed like a bale of hay. And we weren't across the Red Sea yet!

Mendl and I held out the longest. Mendl had been taught a trick by a fellow emigrant, an old sea hand who liked to give advice. He had been to America three times. The trick, he said, was to stay on deck with your eyes on the horizon while pretending you were riding a sleigh. Before long the old sea hand was sprawled out like a corpse and Mendl and I were soaked to the bone. We couldn't walk a straight line back to our bunks. We had to be taken by the hand and led there.

♦♦♦

How long did crossing the Red Sea take? Maybe a day and maybe two or three. I can't rightly say. All I remember is how good it felt to be alive when it was over. The sky was pure as gold. The sea was smooth as glass. The *Prince Albert* skimmed the water looking like new, churning foam and spray in all directions. The passengers revived and flocked to the sunshine to enjoy a bright new day.

Soon word got around that land was almost in sight. Mendl and I were the first to spread the good news that we had spied it. At first it was a yellow speck on the horizon. Then the speck grew bigger and clearer. Ships appeared in the distance. Lots and lots of them with tall, thin masts.

All our troubles were forgotten. The passengers hurried to put on their best clothes. The women made themselves up. Elye combed his beard. Brokheh and Taybl went to get their good scarves. My mother put on her silk shawl. Mendl and I had nothing to do. But there was no time anyway. We were docking in America. All eyes shone with joy. The Jews who crossed the Red Sea must have felt the same way. That's why they started to sing.

♦♦♦

"Hail to thee, Columbus! The Old World greets thee, O land of freedom—O blessed, golden land!"

That was Pinye's hello to America. He even doffed his cap and made a deep bow. Being half blind, he crashed nose first into the sooty head of a sailor. It's a lucky thing the sailor was a decent goy. He just looked at Pinye's bloody nose, grinned, and grunted into his mustache. It must have been one swell American curse.

Suddenly there was a commotion. The steerage passengers were requested to return to their places. At first the sailors were polite. Then they weren't. Whoever didn't move fast enough was made to.

There we were, young and old, men, women, and children, Jews, Christians, Gypsies, and Turks, with an iron chain on the door and no air. All we could do was stare through the portholes. It was worse than being seasick. We looked at each other like prisoners. "Why now? Why us?" my friend Mendl demanded with blazing eyes.

The first- and second-class passengers were being let down a long gangway that must have had a hundred steps. But what about us? Didn't we get off here too?

"The likes of us can be made to wait," said a Jew, a leech of a tailor from Heysen.

As leeches go he wasn't a bad sort, a snazzy dresser who wore fancy glasses, thought a lot of himself, and liked chewing your ear off. He liked to argue too and had already had a few fights with Pinye. It was all Elye could do to break them up. In the end the tailor had declared himself so insulted that he stopped talking to Pinye entirely. Not only had Pinye called him "Needle Pusher," "Thread Eater," and "Seamsterman," he had thrown in "Fabric Filcher" too.

Now that we were behind bars, though, the tailor talked nonstop even to Pinye. Half of what he said was in Hebrew:

"*Meh onu umeh khayeynu*—what do folks like us count? *Moshul kekheres hanishbor*—we're just so much scrap in their eyes. Except that real scrap isn't thrown away so easily . . . "

Did he get it from Pinye! What kind of comparison was that? He should wash his mouth with soap, the tailor should, for talking that way about America! He really gave it to him, Pinye did. You can't say a bad word about America when Pinye is around. Not that the tailor thought he had said anything bad. All he had said, said the tailor, was that America was a fine place but not for us. We were going nowhere fast.

That was too much for Pinye. He shouted: "What do you think they're going to do, salt us away in a herring barrel?"

"No," said the tailor from Heysen with a triumphant sneer. "They're not going to salt us away. They're going to take us to a place called Ella's Island and pen us up there like calves until someone comes to get us out."

Pinye didn't let that pass in silence: "Get a load of this tailor boy! He's a regular fountain of bad news. There's nothing he doesn't know. Who hasn't heard of Ella's Island? And who doesn't know it's an island and not a cattle pen?"

The hotter under the collar Pinye became, the more the tailor from Heysen feared for his life. In the end he backed off and turned away, although not before grumbling: "Well! Just imagine! You would think I had stained his best suit! Dared criticize his precious America! Pshaw! Just wait a while and you'll see . . . "

IN DETENTION

You can't blame Pinye for being so annoyed at Ella's Island that he's writing a poem about it while fighting all the time with Elye. Mostly, though, he keeps his disappointment with America to himself. He doesn't want the tailor to see it. But he's burning up inside, even if he keeps a stiff upper lip. "How can it be?" he asked Elye in a low voice when we were taken to Ella's Island. "Where do you get off locking people up like so many criminals?" The tailor from Heysen was right.

Actually, it isn't as bad as all that. Not only are we not in a cattle pen, we're in a big bright building with plenty of free food and drinks. We couldn't be treated any better.

Until we got here, though—whew! One by one we had to walk a long hallway with lots of doors on each side. At each door we were stopped by some grouch with shiny buttons who double- and triple-checked us. The first held our eyelids open with a slip of cardboard while examining our eyes. Then the others examined the rest of us. They marked us with chalk and signaled us to go right or left. When all the lefts and rights were finished we came to the big building and started to look for each other. We had gotten separated in the confusion and really were as scared as calves bound for the slaughterhouse.

♦♦♦

Scared of what? Mainly of my mother's eyes. They were still red from crying. Wouldn't you know that in the end they were hardly looked at!

"That's your blessed father helping from heaven. The light shine on him in Paradise!"

So my mother said, hugging us and crying for joy. She was so happy she didn't know what to do with herself.

Elye acted like a new man. All the time we had been on the road, he took his worries out on me. The slaps flew like chips of wood while Brokheh cheered him on. Now he was a different person. He even gave me an orange from his pocket. Everyone on the *Prince Albert* was given an orange every morning. Some stuck theirs in their pockets for later. Not me. Who could resist eating it right away?

Pinye was good and proud of himself. He said:

"Well? Who was right? Didn't I tell you all those stories about being sent back for crying were spread by America's enemies? A bunch of fat-mouthed, lying, hot-aired, no-good bums! It wouldn't surprise me to hear them say that all Jews in America had to be baptized. Where's that damned tailor from Heysen?"

Pinye and America were friends again.

♦♦♦

In all the commotion no one had noticed that one of us was missing. That was my friend Mendl. The first to realize it was Brokheh. She clapped her head and said:

"Oh my God! Where is Teeny?"

"Lord almighty!" cried my mother. We jumped up to look for him, but Mendl was nowhere to be found. He might as well have fallen overboard.

Later we learned it was his own fault. He had been tripped up in the questioning. At first he played deaf and dumb the way he had in Germany. Then he talked a lot of malarkey. One minute he said he was ten, the next thirteen, and the next he broke down and told the truth—which was that he was lost. That is, his parents had lost him in Germany and we had adopted him. He didn't even know their address. Not that he was asking for any favors. He would find them himself. He knew what they looked like and he would recognize them.

Now Mendl was being held in a room with some other boys who would all be sent back to Europe.

♦ ♦ ♦

As soon as we heard the news, we rallied to Mendl's side. My mother raised a cry. The immigration officials, she said, would be responsible for making Mendl an orphan. What would they tell his parents when they met them?

"Take a deep breath," advised the tailor from Heysen. "You're not out of the woods yet yourselves."

"Well, well, if it isn't Haman again!" Pinye declared. He looked about to go for the tailor's throat. The tailor pretended not to notice. You would think he had been asked to give a public address, the way he piled stone after stone on our hearts with each trouble ahead that he listed. First, he said, we would be asked the names of friends and acquaintances. Then we would have to shell out money for telegrams and wait for them to come. We wouldn't be released until they vouched for us and signed a guarantee.

Naturally, Pinye exploded. With a glance at Elye he asked the tailor how come he was such an expert on Ella's Island. The tailor replied that he was an expert because he had met an emigrant aboard ship who had been to America three times.

He must have meant the old sea hand. He's picked up all kinds of tidbits from him. He can even speak English and is already half an American. "Tshikn"—"kitshn"—"shuggeh"—"misteh"—"butsheh" —"bridzh": those are just some of the words he knows. He won't tell us what they mean, though. He says we'll have to find out for ourselves. Pinye waved a hand and walked away as if to say: "Let the dog bark if it wants to."

♦ ♦ ♦

Don't think that tailor from Heysen didn't know what he was talking about. He had it right down to the last detail. After getting the third degree from the doctors, we were asked who we knew in America. "Who don't we?" my mother answered, eager to list all our friends and acquaintances. She's a pleasure to look at now that they've let her in. She glows like a young woman. I haven't seen her this way in ages.

My brother Elye interrupted. He should do the talking, he said, because he had the addresses written on a piece of paper. That made Pinye declare that the officials wanted names, not addresses. Brokheh cut Pinye short. Both the names and addresses, she told him, belonged to our friends, not his. Pinye got sore. "Since when are Fat Pesye and Moyshe the bookbinder more your friends than mine?" he wanted to know. "I don't give a damn about Pesye," Brokheh said. "I'm talking about my father, Yoyneh the baker."

Elye was right. They wanted addresses, not names. The fun and games began all over again.

Naturally, when it comes to reading addresses Pinye thinks he's a world beater. He grabbed the paper from Elye, plastered it to his nose, and read aloud like a chanting rabbi. No one understood a word, especially since it all came out backwards. Elye snatched the paper back and handed it to a Shiny Buttons. The Shiny Buttons looked at it and said: "Awl reit." No one knew what that meant except the tailor from Heysen. Awl, he explained, meant everything and reit meant to write. In short, everything was written on the paper.

We shelled out change for two telegrams. One went to Moyshe and Pesye and the other to Yoyneh. Then we sat down to breakfast. The food wasn't so hot. Brokheh said the tea could be eaten with a soup spoon. Still, it was free. Everything is free on Ella's Island. At least we weren't waiting on an empty stomach.

♦♦♦

Waiting was easier said than done. Our eyes were falling out by the time we saw our first acquaintances. They were Pesye and Moyshe. I mean we didn't exactly see them, because we were in detention. We were told that a fat woman and her husband had come for us. It was maddening not to see them while they were being grilled outside. Someone suggested bribing a guard to have a look. Pinye said America wasn't Russia. In America, he said, there were no bribes. "When it comes to bribes," said the tailor from Heysen (there was nowhere that man didn't turn up), "America and Russia are the same town. The rabbis say that money can even buy a father for a bastard." For once Pinye had no answer.

The tailor from Heysen was right again. It cost us a kvawdeh, which are four to a dahleh, to get to see Pesye through some bars. She smiled at us with her sweaty face and double chin and my mother bobbed her head back. They both had tears in their eyes. Moyshe the bookbinder peered out from behind Pesye's broad back. He had on a real hat instead of his old workman's cap.

A minute later Yoyneh the baker turned up, looking as ornery as ever. He hadn't changed a bit except for his beard, which—lord-a-mercy!—was gone. Riveleh-Chemise was there too. We wanted to shout hello, to hug, to kiss, to ask all kinds of questions. I was dying to hear about Bumpy and the rest of the gang, and about Brokheh's little sister Alte. (You may remember we were engaged.)

Go sue! We're still in detention. All we can do is look through the bars like prisoners or animals in the zoo.

I feel sorry for Pinye. He can't look us in the eye. It's a bad day for America. The way he goes around moping, you might think America was his personal property. He's so mad that he's begun a poem that goes:

I sure would like to see in hell a
Stinker by the name of Ella.

That made my brother sore because Ella sounds like Elye. Pretty soon he and Pinye were fighting. Then Brokheh got into the act with one of her sayings. "There's no need to show a beaten dog the stick," she said. Don't ask me what that means.

AN OCEAN OF TEARS

Even without all the tears cried by my mother since my father died and we started wandering, you would think we had enough problems of our own. But no, she has to cry for the rest of Ella's Island too! Every minute there's a new sob story. My mother takes each one to heart. She wrings her hands, buries her face in them, and weeps to herself.

"You have no cause, Mama," Elye says.

I agree. What's there to cry about? Our homeless days are over. We've made it across the ocean. In an hour or two we'll be free men in America.

But how can she resist? All the misery around her is like an ocean of tears.

I could talk all day and night and not get to the end of the hard luck we've seen on Ella's Island.

For instance, here's a case for you. A family of six, two parents and four children, are being held in detention. How come? Because one of the children, a twelve-year-old girl, can't count backwards. Although she said "twelve" when asked how old she was, she couldn't say how old she was a year ago. "Count from one to twelve," she was told. She did. "Now count from twelve to one." She couldn't. Ask me and I'd have breezed right through it: twelveeleventennineeightsevensixfivefourthreetwoone. Big deal! But they won't let that poor girl into America.

Her family is taking it hard. Their suffering could break a heart of stone. The mother stares at her daughter and sobs. Brokheh and Taybl can't stop wiping their eyes.

♦♦♦

Or how about this one. There was a woman with us named Tsivye. Her husband had disappeared, ditched her long ago. She sent letters trying to trace him and heard one day that he was in Sinsineteh. That's a city in America. Well, off she goes to look for him. Aboard ship she's told that when she gets to New York she should find someone to say he's her husband. That way they'll let her in.

The advice came from my old sea hand—I've told you about him. The tailor from Heysen put in his two cents too. The old sea hand arranged for a friend in New York to pretend to be the woman's husband. But during the questioning the swindle came to light. The friend turned out to have another wife and was no more Tsivye's husband than I'm her uncle.

I'm telling you, was there a scene! All Ella's Island was up in arms. It gave Pinye a chance to settle scores with the tailor from Heysen. He couldn't pass up a dig:

"Well, Mr. Needle Pusher, didn't I tell you America wasn't Russia? In America there's no monkeying around. God bless Columbus!"

Did Pinye catch it from my mother! Brokheh gave it to him even worse. Even Taybl let him have it. They all but scratched his eyes out for laughing at such heartache. My mother treated Tsivye like a sister just to put Pinye in his place. But they'll send her back to Europe all the same. Her phony husband is in for it too. They're both in detention. My mother is beside herself.

♦♦♦

And then there's the young wife, all peaches and cream, on her way to join a husband in Bawstin. She was traveling with a child as pretty as a picture, a curly-haired little girl named Ketzeleh. I mean that was the nickname given her by her grandmother. Her real name was Keyleh. She could run and talk and sing and dance even though she wasn't three years old. The *Prince Albert* was full of children, but Ketzeleh was the favorite. Everyone wanted to kiss her, hug her, play with her. Ketzeleh, come here! Ketzeleh, come to me!

Ketzeleh's mother practically became one of our family. She never left my mother's side. She told us her whole story and read us the letters her husband had written her. She hadn't seen him for over three years. He had never seen his own daughter. He dreamed day and night of her, thought only of seeing his Ketzeleh.

At this point in the story Ketzeleh's mother always broke into tears, my mother wiped her eyes, and I laughed, took Ketzeleh in my arms, and fed her pieces of apple and orange. I put them in her mouth and kissed her tiny warm fingers and she laughed back and stroked me with her little velvet hands.

If only I had had a box of paints! I would have painted Ketzeleh with her silky curls, her pretty blue eyes, and her face of an angel. My friend Mendl laughed at me for spending so much time with a china doll. I swear, that's what he called her.

Well, we're almost in America when Ketzeleh goes and gets sick. She . . . but it gives me the shivers just to think of it. That little girl took part of me with her when she went. I can't talk about it. I don't want to tell you what they did with her body. I'll just tell you about her mother on Ella's Island.

She didn't cry. She had the same glassy stare for everyone. She didn't answer when she was spoken to. It seemed she'd gone out of her mind.

Now they're sending her back. My mother is moving heaven and earth for her. My brother Elye can't take it any more. He's had a bellyful of her tears. Pinye must be hiding. You don't see him anywhere.

♦♦♦

Don't think it's only us Jews who have a hard time on Ella's Island. Plenty of Christians do too. There was a gang of Italians with us on the *Prince Albert,* all wearing corduroy pants and wooden shoes. They sounded like a herd of horses when they walked. They were fine fellows, all of them, and crazy about us. They even had their own name for me. Piccolo Bambino, they called me and gave me nuts and raisins from their pockets. You bet I didn't mind. I couldn't talk to them because they knew as much Jewish as I know Italian, but I liked listening to them talk to each other. They hit their "r"s real hard. *Buona serrrra! Mia carrrra! Prrrrego, signore!*

Well, as luck would have it, one of them blurted out something dumb during the questioning. He told the truth, which was that they were coming to work for a bridge contractor who had signed them up in London. In America, it seems, that's not allowed. Now they're being sent back to Italy. They go around talking with their hands and buzzing their "r"s: *Santa Marrrria!* It doesn't do any good. We all feel sorry for them. They have tears in their own eyes, too.

♦♦♦

Mazel tov! There's a wedding on Ella's Island. Who's the lucky couple? Wait and I'll tell you.

The bride is from Chudnov, an orphan called Leah, a lovely, dark-haired, sweet-tempered girl. She spent the whole voyage with Brokheh and Taybl. The three of them were always together. They told me she was traveling by herself and didn't know a soul in America. She had worked from childhood on, managed to save some money, and decided to emigrate. Chudnov was not for her. Her father was killed in a pogrom and her mother died of sorrow, leaving her on her own. But she could sew and stitch and knit and iron—she had golden hands, my mother said. Everyone felt sure she would do well in America. They were sure she would find a husband there, too. The best! Leah blushed and lowered her eyes when they talked about that.

Leah's problem was that she had no one in America to vouch for her. And a husband was available on the *Prince Albert*. His name was Leyzer Bach and he was a carpenter on his way to an uncle in Chicago. Leyzer was a big, clumsy fellow with blond hair and thick lips, but I liked him because of his songs. He has a beautiful voice. And since he had an uncle to vouch for him, it was decided that he should marry Leah. Need I add that the suggestion came from my friend, the old sea hand?

That's what they did. When questioned at immigration, Leyzer said he was Leah's husband and Leah said she was Leyzer's wife. You would think that would do it, wouldn't you? But they're on to such games at Ella's Island. A husband and wife need a marriage certificate. Leah cried her heart out. "Don't be silly," she was told. "You'll get a divorce in New York and be the same Leah you always were."

But what if Leyzer didn't agree to divorce her? And on the other hand, was being sent back any better? In short, the two had a wedding.

A sad one, without any music. But it did have a real rabbi and real tears. Lots of them. A whole ocean.

Only one person is satisfied. Would you like to guess who it is? It's the tailor from Heysen. He's had his revenge. Now everyone knows he knows best. Each time he walks past us, he strokes his beard and looks at Pinye through his snazzy glasses. But Pinye keeps cool. He sticks his long nose in a book and ignores him. Pinye doesn't give a damn.

♦♦♦

Between our own and other people's troubles, it's hard to get excited about being in America. All we've seen and heard on Ella's Island has worn us out. Now we stand staring at the big noisy city in the distance.

Would you like to know what we're like? A flock of sheep huddled in a field by some railroad tracks and staring at the trains that rush by and vanish! I could kick myself for not having a pencil and paper to draw us and the rest of Ella's Island. Some people sit on their bundles, moaning and groaning. Others keep their sorrows to themselves. Or else cry buckets. Whole oceans of tears.

ON SOLID GROUND

If you've never been at sea for ten days and locked up on Ella's Island with every conceivable human misery, you don't know what it's like to be on solid ground again.

It felt so good that I could have done three somersaults if not for my brother Elye. But even a mope like Elye looked reborn. "I can't believe we're in America!" he declared, rubbing his hands. "Praise be," my mother said with a look at the sky. She let out a sigh. "The living have lived to see the day. The dead are with the dead."

She was thinking of my father. There's no place or time she forgets.

♦♦♦

Pinye is delirious. I hate to say it, but he's gone clean off his rocker. He stood facing the ocean, raised his right hand in a fist, and delivered a speech:

"Now hear this, all you bums, jackasses, drunkards, hooligans, and Jew-hating bastards! We want to thank you for having arrived in this freest, happiest of lands! Without your persecutions and pogroms we would never have heard of Columbus or Columbus of us! You'll have a long wait before you see us again! You'll see the back of your own ears first! One day you'll realize there was a people called the Jews whom you didn't know how to appreciate! You'll come to a bad end like Spain when it expelled us! You'll howl like homeless dogs! You'll long for us! You'll offer to pay gold for each Jew, you'll beg us to come back! Like hell we will, do you hear me?"

Who knows how long Pinye might have kept it up if Yoyneh the bagel maker hadn't laid a hand on his shoulder and said:

"Pinye, for crying out loud! Who are you talking to, the stones? Come on, we'll miss the ferry. Do you want to spend another night on Ella's Island?"

We took our bundles and headed for the ferry.

♦♦♦

But it wasn't as quick as all that. You've probably forgotten that someone was left behind—my friend Mendl. The officials refused to release him and we weren't going anywhere without him. My mother said she could never have a good night's sleep in America if Mendl was sent back to be an orphan.

Our luck was running into an outfit called Hakhnoses Orkhim. That's "Hospitality" in Jewish. It had a representative on Ella's Island, a fine, friendly fellow we were told to see. Right away we told him about Mendl. Naturally, we were all talking at once. He made us stop and choose a single speaker.

We fought for a while and chose Brokheh. Why Brokheh? Because neither Elye nor Pinye can resist interrupting each other and my mother talks pretty well but too much. She can't say a thing without beginning from the creation of the world: how I had a father, and how his name was Peysi, and on and on. No one could expect the Hakhnoses Orkhim man to sit through all that, and so we asked Brokheh to get to the point. As Moyshe the bookbinder likes to say: "Just sign on the dotted line."

Brokheh told Mendl's story in a nutshell and the man from Hakhnoses Orkhim got to work. He ran off somewhere, came back, and ran off again. It wasn't easy, but the second time he came back with Mendl.

♦♦♦

The man from Hakhnoses Orkhim took Mendl by the ear and gave him a talking to. "Listen here, young fellow," he said. "We're vouching for your good conduct. That means you're in our custody for the next two years. We intend to keep an eye on you. Step over the line and you go back to where you came from!" He wrote down our names and those of our friends and acquaintances and all our addresses, and we were free to go where we pleased and do what we wanted.

I suppose you think that made an impression on Mendl. A lot you know him! He's not the type to be fazed. That's what I like about him. Today, when I think of him and all that happened and was still to happen in America, it seems like one of God's miracles. But America is a place for the underdog. It lets the little man rise to the top. It all but brings the dead back to life.

Let's get back to the ferry.

♦♦♦

A ferry is a boat on which you put everything—bundles, bags, even a horse and wagon. While all of us were answering each other's questions, Mendl and I went to have a look around. Although it took my mother a while to notice that we were missing, she made up for it when she did. She must have thought we had fallen overboard.

They found us at the top of the stairs to the upper deck, staring at a monster statue of a woman who looked like a wet nurse. There wasn't much time to look her over, because we could already hear my mother's screams and see Elye approaching. He was mad as hell. We would have been in bad trouble if Brokheh hadn't gasped just then in a strange voice, "Oy, Mama, I don't feel so good," and run to the railing. You might have thought we were back on the *Prince Albert*. But leave it to the tailor from Heysen! (The man never left us for a minute.) Right away he starts lecturing Brokheh, "You should be ashamed of yourself, a big, strong woman like you! Can't you tell a river from an ocean?"

Brokheh said she didn't know it was a river. It looked like an ocean to her. Pinye told her you could tell by the smell. Only an ocean, he said, smelled of fish. "Who says?" asked the tailor from Heysen. "I wasn't talking to you," Pinye said. "I'm not going to argue with a fabric filcher."

That brought in Moyshe the bookbinder. Moyshe had news for Pinye. We were in America now, not Russia. In America a tailor was as good as the biggest swank—maybe better. In America the tailors had a yunye. A yunye was a workers' guild. It just wasn't like a Russian guild at all.

"We bagel makers have a yunye too," said Yoyneh. "Our yunye is as big as the tailors'."

"How can you even compare the two?" Moyshe asked. In no time they were having a grand fight about which yunye was bigger. We were all pretty sick of yunyes by the time Pinye shouted:

"We're almost in New York!"

We all looked at the city, which was getting bigger and bigger. Wow, what a place! What monster houses! They were the sizes of churches, every one. And the windows, thousands of them! If only I had pencil and paper.

♦♦♦

Ka-boom ka-boom! Wham-bangety-bang-bang! Bang! Ring-a-ling-a-ling-a-ling-a-ling! Hey hey hoo ha hey! Ddddrrrrrrrrr! Whoooosh! Chakka-chakkachakkachakka-chakka! And *ka-boom bangety-bang* again! Plus the squeals of a trussed pig: *oink- oink- oink-oink-oink!*

Those were the sounds of our first minute in New York. Nothing, it now seemed, could have been more peaceful than a storm at sea. The real shock was dry land in America. A mob scene, a madhouse!

My mother panicked. Like a hysterical hen, she pecked and clucked and spread her wings over her chicks. "Motl!" she screamed, flapping her arms. "Mendl! Elye! Brokheh! Taybl! Where are you? This way! Over here!"

"For God's sake, Mama," Brokheh said. "What are you screaming for?" And Elye added: "They'll send us back on the first boat to Europe if you don't stop making such a fuss!"

"I'd like to see the day!" Pinye said, sticking his hands in his pockets and jamming his hat down sideways. "Every last Russky will croak before I do! Have you forgotten that God made America for poor, oppressed people like us?"

We were in the middle of a huge crowd. In another minute Pinye would have ended up on his back like in London. As it was, he got an elbow in the ribs. It gave him such a jolt that his cap went flying and was carried away by the wind. We spent so much time chasing it that we missed the stritkah. That's what they call a tram in New York. But we didn't have to wait long for another. We piled into it with our bundles, filling the empty seats, and off we went to the city.

"Thank God we're rid of that leech of a tailor!" Pinye said.

"Don't be so quick to celebrate," Elye said. "With God's help you'll yet run into him in the streets of New York."

THE STRITS OF NEW YORK

The ride through New York was pretty awful. The worst part was changing from the stritkah to the eleveydeh. That's a stritkah that runs on a long, narrow bridge above the ground. It flies like a bullet. You're sure you're going to die.

You think that's all? Wait, I'm not through. You crawl out of the eleveydeh and walk down some stairs to a cellar and get into another stritkah called a tsobvey. The tsobvey rushes through the cellar until you feel faint. Elye says tsobvey is short for tsobveydeh and calls the eleveydeh an elevey. Brokheh swears she's never taking either again. She'd rather walk than ride through the clouds or the earth like a lunatic. "Spare me your ups and you can have your downs," she says.

She's a weird one, my sister-in-law. If I had my druthers, I'd ride the eleveydeh and the tsobvey all day long. So would my friend Mendl.

♦♦♦

You would think that having been around the world, in Lemberg, Cracow, Vienna, Antwerp, and London, we would know what a tram ride was like. For sheer torture, though, there's nothing like suffocating in a crowded New York tsobvey. You stand shoulder to shoulder, hanging on to a strap to keep from falling, and two new passengers get on for every passenger who gets off. You hang there until you're stiff because each seat has plenty of takers—and if you do find an empty one, you end up sitting with a big black goy on either side of you, Negroes with monster lips and huge white teeth who chew their cud like cows. It took me a while to find out that that's called tshooinkahm. It's a kind of candy made of rubber. You have to keep chewing because you're not allowed to swallow it and you're not allowed to spit it out. Small boys, old men, and cripples make a living selling it.

I must have told you about our friend Pinye's sweet tooth. Well, he got hold of some tshooinkahm, swallowed a whole pack, and had such conniptions that he nearly died. The doctors had to pump out his stomach.

But I'm getting ahead of myself. Let's return to our first ride in New York.

♦♦♦

Everyone kept talking while we rode the eleveydeh and the tsobvey. But talking is not the right word. There was so much noise, such a racket, such a rattle of wheels and shrieking of rails and clanking of cars, that you couldn't hear your own voice. You had to shout as if speaking to a deaf man. In no time we all were hoarse. My mother kept begging:

"Pesye, my sweet . . . Pesye, my darling . . . dear, dear Pesye . . . let's talk later!"

For a moment we fell silent and then we shouted our lungs out again. We were only human, after all, good friends and neighbors who hadn't seen each other in ages. How could we keep quiet? There was so much, so much to talk about!

After shouting about this and that, we got around to discussing where to go and whose house to put up at. It took some arguing to decide that Pinye, Taybl, my mother, and I would stay with Pesye, and Elye and Brokheh would go to Yoyneh and Riveleh's. Pesye wanted Mendl to come with her too. Nothing doing, Riveleh said: Pesye had enough mouths to feed. Pesye didn't like that one bit. A mouth, she said, never has too many teeth and a mother can't have too big a family.

"You know what? Let's ask the dinner guest in person."

So said Moyshe the bookbinder and asked Mendl which he preferred: his and Pesye's place or Yoyneh the bagel maker's. Mendl said he would stick with me. I wouldn't have expected any less.

♦♦♦

"The next steyshn is our stahp," Yoyneh announced.

It had to be explained to us that a tsobvey has steyshns and that your stahp is the steyshn you get off at.

"In-law! When did you learn to talk the language?" my mother asked Yoyneh. Riveleh answered:

"I promise you, in-law, you'll be talking it in a week too. Because if you go out into the strit and ask for a meat store, you won't get the time of day."

"What should I ask for, then?" asked my mother.

"You have to ask for a butsheh shahp," Pesye said.

"A plague take them all!" exclaimed Brokheh. "I don't care if they burst. When I want meat, I'll ask for it. Meat, meat, meat, meat, meat!"

♦♦♦

All of a sudden it was Yoyneh's stahp. He grabbed Riveleh, Elye, and Brokheh and rushed from the car. My mother rose to walk her son and daughter-in-law to the door. Pinye got up to say good-bye to Elye and arrange their next meeting. Before he knew it, Yoyneh's family was on the platform and the conductor was shutting the doors. The tsobvey gave a lurch. Pinye was still trying to figure it out when his feet slid out from under him. A second later he was lying in a Negro woman's lap. The woman flung him off with both hands and he went sprawling while the cap flew from his head. The tsobvey car burst into laughter. Mendl and I laughed too. Did we catch it from my mother and Taybl. Go have a face of stone like Brokheh!

♦♦♦

All things come to an end. We arrived at our stahp and climbed down to the strit. If I hadn't known we were in America, I would have guessed we were in Lemberg or Brody. The Jews were the same, their wives were the same, the noise was the same, and even the garbage was the same. Everything was just louder and more confusing. The buildings were taller, too, a whole lot. Six stories is a joke in New York. There are buildings that are twelve. And twenty. And thirty. And forty. And even more.

We stood there in the strit with all our bundles. We had to go on foot the rest of the way. The Americans call that vawkink. We vawked. Moyshe vawked ahead on his short legs and Pesye vawked after him, so fat and heavy she could barely keep up. Pinye and Taybl vawked behind

Pesye. Pinye's vawkink is a scream. He dances more than he vawks, his long, thin legs getting in his way, one pants leg rolled up, the other falling down, his cap perched sideways and his tie pointing east-by-northeast. A weird-looking fellow! He's just begging for someone to draw him.

Mendl and I vawked farthest back, stopping at every shop window. It gave us a good feeling to see that the magazines were all in Jewish and that there were all sorts of other Jewish things: siddurs, and tallis kotons, and yarmulkas, and mezuzahs, and matsos. Matsos in the middle of winter, months before Passover—talk about a Jewish town! But we couldn't stop for long because my mother kept shouting: "Follow me!" We followed her.

♦♦♦

Anyone who's never seen a New York strit has missed something grand. What don't you find there? Jews peddle their wares. Women sit and talk. Babies sleep in little wagons called kerredshiz. Every kerredsh looks alike. The babies drink milk from tiny bottles. The children play. There are thousands of games: button games, hoop games, ball games, curb games, rawlehskeyt games. A rawlehskeyt is a shoe on four wheels. You put it on and roll away.

The noise the children make is deafening. The strit belongs to them. No one would dare tell them to leave it. In fact, America is a land made for children. That's what I love about it. Just try laying a hand on a child! My brother Elye learned that the hard way. He was taught a lesson he'll never forget. Here's what happened.

One day Mendl and I were playing tshekehz in the strit. Tshekehz is a game you play by shooting little round pieces of wood. Along comes my brother Elye in the middle of the game, grabs my ear, and gets set to whack me like in the good old days.

But before Elye can haul off and hit me, up pops this tall kid. He pushes me out of the way, rolls up his sleeves, and says something to Elye in American. Since Elye doesn't understand much American, the kid spells it out with a punch in the nose. Pretty soon there's a circle around us. Elye tries explaining in Jewish that it's his job as my brother to teach me good manners. The circle answers back that America doesn't work that way. In America you pick on someone your own size, brother or no brother.

I ask you: how can you not love such a place?

♦♦♦

I've been talking so much that I've forgotten to tell you that we've reached Pesye and Moyshe's house. I walk through the door and look around—not one of the old gang is there. There's no sign of Bumpy or anyone. Where are they all? Just wait until you hear.

THE GANG AT WORK

The gang was at work, every one of them! But before I tell you what each of them does, let me tell you how a Jewish bookbinder lives in America.

First, the apartment. Back home in Kasrilevke, Fat Pesye would have been afraid to live so high. You climb what must be a hundred stairs until you come to a mansion with a bunch of what Americans call rumz. There are big rumz and little rumz, each with beds and mattresses and curtains on every window. There's a kitshn too, which is where the cooking is done. Instead of an oven there's an iron plate with holes; you turn a knob and fire shoots up as if by magic. And there's water from the walls, all the hot and cold water you could want. You turn a faucet and out it comes.

♦♦♦

Later that day Elye and Brokheh came to see how we were doing. Pinye took them to the kitshn, showed them the faucets, and gave them one of his speeches:

"Well, Elye, what do you say about Columbus now? Show me the Russky who's worth his little finger! All they have back in Russia is vodka and pogroms. They deserve to croak, every one of them."

Elye didn't let him get away with that. "You may be big on Columbus now," he answered Pinye, "but you sang a different song on Ella's Island."

Pinye said that Ella's Island wasn't America. It was the border between America and the world. Baloney, Elye said. They were starting to fight when Brokheh stepped in. The two of them, she said, knew as much about it as they knew what happened in the grave. The whole argument wasn't worth a plugged penny.

You'll excuse me for getting sidetracked. I was telling you about Moyshe and Pesye's apartment. I'll get back to it and their boys, the whole gang.

♦♦♦

You can bet that Moyshe and Pesye never dreamed of so many bedrumz, let alone a deininkrum. That's a word we can't figure out. A bedrum, fine, it has a bed in it—but what's a deinink? Why not call it the eedinkrum?

Moyshe the bookbinder hears us discussing it and says: "Why lose sleep over it? Who cares as long as we've got a fine place, thank God, and my boys all have work, and we're making a living in America?"

I look at him and think: God Almighty! How a man can change! Back home you never heard him say a word. It was always Pesye, Pesye, Pesye. All Moyshe ever did was make glue and paste books. Now he's grown a head taller. What making a living doesn't do for a man! All his children are bringing home money too. I'll tell you what each does and how much he earns. I hate to admit it, but my mother is jealous that Pesye has so many boys.

♦♦♦

Pesye's oldest boy used to be Log. In America he's Sem. Why Sem? Search me. All I know is, he's earning well. He's got a dzhahb with a peyprbahks fektri. If that's Chinese to you, I'll set you straight.

A peyprbahks fektri is a place where they make cartons. Don't think it's such a big dzhahb. Log doesn't make the cartons. He just brings them to the kahstemehz. That's called a dehlivri boi. Log takes a bondl of cartons under each arm, ten dozen to a bondl, and runs through the strit dodging kahz. The trick is to keep the cartons from getting crushed. Log makes a dahleh-and-a-half a week and is hoping for a reyz. That means more money. He says he can make as much as three dahlehz. His bawss tells him that if he sticks around he'll teach him to be a carton maker. "Be a gud boi and you'll be awreit," he tells him. In Jewish you would say, "If you're nice, I'll let you eat in my sukkeh."

Moyshe and Pesye's second son, Velvel Tomcat, now goes by the name of Villi. He's a dehlivri boi too and works for a grawsri staw. That's a place that sells food and other stuff. Tomcat's dzhahb is harder than Log's. He gets up at an hour when even God is still asleep and arranges and packs all the awdehz. An awdeh is a bondl brought to a kahstemeh with rolls, butter, cheese, eggs, sugar, milk, and krim. Sometimes Tomcat carries the awdeh all the way to the tahpflaw, which is the apartment under the roof. He has to be quick. There's no time to catch his breath, because he's expected back in the staw to sweep and clean. By noon he's finished and free for the day. He doesn't make a whole lot, just fifteen cents a day, except for Fridays. Fridays he gets a kvawdeh plus a hallah to take home.

♦♦♦

Log and Tomcat are the two oldest in the gang. Their younger brothers can't work mornings because of skul. That's American for heder. It's free and so are the books. You better go or else.

Pinye went crazy when he heard that. Back in Russia, he says, they don't allow Jews to go to school and here they don't allow them not to! If you miss skul you're arrested by a trunt ahfiseh. "Those Russkies should be buried alive just for that," Pinye says.

Skul being only half a day, you can work the other half. All Pesye's boys do. Ratface works in a drahgstaw. That's an apothecary's. He washes bottles and goes to the pawstuffis for stemps. In America you can buy stemps in a drahgstaw. Ratface makes a dahleh-and-a-kvawdeh a week.

"That doesn't grow on trees," Moyshe the bookbinder says, pocketing Ratface's pay.

Faytl Petelulu is now Filip. After skul he sells the Jewish noospeypehz. He runs up and down Ist Brawdvey—that's a street—shouting: "Ekstreh! Ekstreh!" Every peypeh has a name. Petelulu makes fifty cents and more a day. It goes to the family. Everyone makes a living and Moyshe pays all the bills.

Even my friend Bumpy is earning money. He just isn't Bumpy any more. He's Herry and he goes to skul too. Afternoons he minds a stend on Rivinktn Strit that belongs to a woman from Kasrilevke. He helps her sell rice, barley, millet, peas, beans, nuts, raisins, almonds, figs, dates, carob pods, and pickles. It's not a whole lot of work.

Mostly he guards against pilfering. You get a kahstemeh buying barley, you have to make sure she doesn't help herself to a handful of raisins or pop a date in her mouth. Bumpy helps himself too. He told me how he once pinched so many raisins that he had a stomach ache for three whole days. His pay comes from carrying bags for the kahstemehz. Some of them give him a pehni or two. Once he even made a nikl—that's five pehnehz in one shot. He can clear a dahleh a week. Back in Kasrilevke the only money he ever saw was on Purim, when the children tricked-or-treated. But Purim came once a year. Bumpy earns money every day.

"Columbus, you should be sculpted in gold!" Pinye says. Once he saw Bumpy at his stend as he was walking down Rivinktn Strit, bought three cents' worth of carob pods, and gave him a pehni tipp. A tipp is extra money from a kahstemeh.

♦♦♦

Moyshe the bookbinder keeps busy, too. He's not binding books any more. In America, he says, it costs a fortune to rent a staw, buy equipment, and find kahstemehz. And he's too old to work as a hiyud hend. He took some advice he was given (that's one thing Jews have a lot of) and opened a book stend on Essiks Strit. He's making a living from it.

Pinye likes that idea so much he's thinking of copying it. A man, he says, should deal in what he likes. Pinye takes to books like a fish to water. Once he sticks that long nose of his in one of them, you can't tear him loose from it.

♦♦♦

Yoyneh the bagel maker has also left his old line of work—and for the same reason. You have to be a millionaire to open a bakery. Besides, he says, you have to join the yunye and he's too old. Yoyneh is afraid he'd get his skull cracked in a streik if he worked for a non-yunye man. (In America there are streiks every day.) In the end he listened to some advice too. The advice was to make something else. Such as what? Such as knishes! Homemade knishes filled with cheese and sauerkraut.

Believe it or not, Yoyneh is doing not badly. Not badly at all. His knishes have a reputation all over the Loaweh Ist Seid. If you walk down Essiks Strit and see a window that says HOMEMADE KNISHES SOLD HERE in big Jewish letters, you'll know it's him. And if you see another sign across the street that says HOMEMADE KNISHES SOLD HERE, you'll know it's the competition. Don't give it your biznis. Buy your knishes from Yoyneh. You'll know it's him because he's mean. And if you don't, you'll recognize Riveleh. She has a double chin like Pesye and a coral necklace. You'll recognize Brokheh too by her big feet. The little girl with the braids and freckles is her sister Alte. We once were engaged. I'll tell you about Alte some other time.

WE LOOK FOR A DZHAHB

We can't complain. We're welcome guests at Pesye and Moyshe's. Life is pretty good there. We all have a swell time, especially on Sundays when the gang is off. That's when we live it up. We all get together, my friend Mendl too, and go to the theater.

It's called the moofink pikshehz. It costs a nikl and you can't believe the things you see. If I were the Tsar's son I'd go to the moofink pikshehz every day and never leave. So would Mendl. Bumpy, too—I mean Herry.

Not my brother Elye. Elye thought the moofink pikshehz were silly. He said they were for children. "If they're for children," I said, "I'd like to know what Pinye and Taybl are doing there. And how about Brokheh?" But Elye has an answer for everything. A woman, he said, has a child's brains and Pinye likes to be annoying.

Elye went on like that until one Sunday he came with us. Now he wouldn't miss a moofink piksheh for the world. We all go together, the grown-ups too, Moyshe, Pesye, Yoyneh, and even Riveleh. Everyone except my mother. How can she go to the theater, she says, when her husband is buried in the ground? Her enemies shouldn't live to see the day!

♦♦♦

Life is not bad at all. But how long can we go on being house guests? It's time to look for a dzhahb. In America you have to make a living. That's what Elye says. He goes around looking worried. Every day he drops by to talk things over with my mother. Brokheh joins them. So does Pinye. Pinye is full of plans and projects. None is worth a hill of beans. I mean they're good plans, it's just that Elye doesn't like them. And if he does, Brokheh doesn't.

For instance, Pinye had the idea that he, Elye, Brokheh, and Taybl should go to work in a shahp and be tailors. In America a tailor sews on a machine and is called an ahpereydeh. For a high-class dzhahb like an ahpereydeh's, Brokheh said, she didn't have to leave Kasrilevke. "I suppose selling knishes on Essiks Strit is higher," said Elye. Did that make Brokheh mad! Who was Elye to be talking about knishes? It was time he realized that her father's knishes were all that kept us from starvation.

♦♦♦

I'd love Pinye just for the things he says. It's a joy to sit back and listen once he gets going. Now he jumped from his seat, waved his arms, and cut loose. I remember every word:

"O you primitive people! Deep in your hearts you're still living in exile, in the dreary land of the accursed Tsar! America is not a pigsty to wallow in like Russia! Every millionaire and every billionaire started out working long and hard here, if not in a shahp than in the strit. Ask Rahknfelleh! Ask Kahnegi! Ask Mawgn! Ask Vendehbilt! Where were they when they were young? Do you think they didn't work the strit? Do you think they didn't run around selling peypehz and polishing shoes for a nikl? Take the king of kahz, Mr. Fawd, and ask him if he wasn't once a plain dreiveh! Take the greatest Americans, Vashinktn, Linkn, Rawzvelt—I suppose you think they all were born prehzident! Take Prehzident Vilsn! You'll pardon my saying so, but he was once a lousy heder teacher."

That was too much for Elye. He interrupted and said:

"Eh, Pinye, show some respect! You're talking about a man who is second only to God. He's king of America."

Watch out for Pinye when he's got up a full head of steam! He only laughed at my brother.

"Ha, that's a good one! King of *what?* King of *where?* There are no kings in America. It's a free country, a democracy!"

"Fine, so the king of America is called a prehzident," Elye said. "So what?"

"So plenty! A king is no more a prehzident than a horse is a house. A king is a king and a prehzident is a prehzident. A king is born a king and a prehzident is elected. If we elect him, Vilsn will be prehzident for four more years. If we don't, it's back to the heder. For your information, I could be prehzident myself one day."

"You? Prehzident?"

"Me! Prehzident!"

In all the years I've known Elye, I've never seen him laugh like that. Elye, as you know, is a worrier. He doesn't laugh much, and when he does it's with half a mouth. This time he laughed so hard that he scared my mother to death.

Not that it wasn't funny. It was enough just to look at Pinye with his hands in the pockets of his pants that were too short, his shiny new American shoes that were too big, his tie that Taybl couldn't get to sit straight, his American cap that kept falling off, and most of all, his nearsighted eyes and long, pointy nose that stared right into his mouth. Good God, *this* was the future prehzident of America? A superman couldn't have kept a straight face.

Elye finished laughing, turned to my mother, and said: "All right, our future is taken care of. We'll sew clothes in a shahp. And Pinye doesn't have to worry because he's going to be prehzident. But what about the boys?"

He meant me and Mendl. He couldn't stand the thought of our doing nothing. It made him sore to see us playing bawl or tshekehz in the strit. Each time he reached for my ear, he had to remember that I wasn't his size.

"The boys should be your biggest problem," Moyshe said.

That was Moyshe's way of telling us that we hadn't outstayed our welcome and had plenty of time to think about a dzhahb.

♦♦♦

Don't imagine we lived like spongers. My mother helped Pesye in the kitshn with the cooking, baking, washing, and cleaning. Taybl made the beds and swept the rumz. Pinye worked with Moyshe at his book stend.

Moyshe couldn't depend too much on Pinye, though. That's because as soon as Pinye sees a book, he's into it nose first and bye-bye Pinye. That's not the worst of it. The worst is that he's a scribbler himself. He's gotten hold of a funtinpen that never runs out of ink and paper is cheaper in America than borscht. He sits at Moyshe's stend and scribbles away.

"Are you studying penmanship?" Elye asks.

Pinye doesn't answer. He takes what he writes and sticks it deep into the breast pockets of his jacket. His pockets are so full that he looks like a stuffed animal.

♦♦♦

Until we find dzhahbz, Mendl and I help the gang as best we can. I work with Log (I mean Sem) carrying cartons while Mendl is partly with Tomcat (that's Villi) in the grawsri staw and partly with Filip (that's Petelulu) selling the Jewish peypehz. For our pay we get tickets to the moofink pikshehz on Sundays and an eiskrim senvitsh and a sawdeh. Then we take a vawk in the pahk. There are lots of pahks in New York, all free. What a country! I go where I want and do what I like.

For a while I hung out at the stend of my old friend Bumpy—I mean Herry—in my free time. But Bumpy's bawss didn't like seeing me there. She knew he sometimes ate a carob pod or a couple of raisins and almonds on the sly. The two of us, she said, were more than her stend could afford.

So I don't go there any more. But Bumpy always has something for me in his pocket when he comes home at night. Once Brokheh caught me chewing and ratted to Elye. Elye asked what I had in my mouth. "Tshooinkahm," I said. Brokheh said tshooinkahm chewers made her nauseous. "They remind me of cows," agreed Elye. Pinye objected to the comparison. He said:

"How can you take the greatest, the smartest, the freest people on earth and compare them to cows? Just tell me this: where would we be now if Columbus hadn't discovered America?"

"In an America discovered by someone else," Elye answered. He said it just like that, without even having to think about it.

◆◆◆

Hallelujah, we have dzhahbz! No more twiddling our thumbs. Our freeloading days are over. We're working in a shahp. I don't mean me and Mendl. We're too young. I mean Elye and Pinye. What's a shahp and what do you do in one? That's the next thing I'm going to tell you.

WORKING IN A SHAHP

Don't ask me exactly what working in a shahp is like because I don't rightly know. I'm not allowed in one because I'm under thirteen. I only know what I hear at night from Elye and Pinye. Do they have stories!

They come home bushed and hungry and we sit down to sahpeh. That's a word Brokheh hates like a Jew hates pork. Another word she can't stand is vindeh. Ask her to open a vindeh and she'll say, "Vindeh is what comes before spring." She has it in for stahkinks too. It doesn't sound like anything she would want to wear on her feet. And dishehz is no better. Why can't we say *posude* the way we used to? Or take *lefl*—you would think it was a good enough word. But no, we have to call it a spuhn! "Still, I suppose," Brokheh says (she always has some new saying), "that if America is a kahntri, and steyk is a food, and a *gopl* is a fawk, English must be a language."

♦♦♦

Elye and Pinye work in different shahps. Elye is an ahpereydeh. Pinye is a presseh. An ahpereydeh sews on a machine. That's something you have to learn. The machine doesn't run by itself.

How did Elye get to be an ahpereydeh when our family never had a tailor or a machinist all the way back to our great-great-grandfathers? We've always been rabbis, cantors, beadles—that's what my mother says. Who would have thought we'd fall so low? But this is America. In America there's nothing you can't do. You can be anything.

Take a rabbi, for example. A rabbi is supposed to have studied for years. But in America there are rabbis called revrindz who were ordinary butchers back in Russia. Elye met a revrind who does circumcisions. In the old country he was a woman's tailor.

"You must be joking," Elye said.

"This is America," answered the revrind.

♦♦♦

So how did my brother learn to run a machine? The same way the ladies' tailor learned to do circumcisions. It took him a while to get the hang of it. First they gave him some leftover fabric to practice with. The next morning they told him to start sewing. You probably think he made a mess of it. Actually, he did pretty well. He did a lot better than Pinye.

That's not because Pinye is lazy. Nothing is further from the truth. Pinye is ready for any drudge work that will help him make a living in America. His problem is being nearsighted and in a rush. They sat him down next to Elye and gave him some leftovers too—and right away he has an eksehdent and sews his left sleeve to the machine! He's lucky he didn't sew his hand to it. Did everyone split their sides! All the ahpereydehz were hooting and hollering. Grinhawn, they called Pinye. A grinhawn is someone just off the boat who doesn't know which end is up. It's a bad name to be called, a lot worse than a thief. And that wasn't all. Listen to this.

♦♦♦

In Elye's shahp where Pinye tried learning to sew, there happens to be an old friend of ours: Pinye's bugaboo, the tailor from Heysen. It was just Pinye's luck to meet up with him again—and what a meeting! The tailor from Heysen is a big shot in that shahp. He's not an ahpereydeh, he's a kahdeh. That means he cuts the fabric that the ahpereydehz sew. And he thinks he's too good even for that. He doesn't plan to hang around long because he has his sights set on being a dizeineh. A dizeineh is big time. He can make fifty, seventy-five, a hundred dahlehz a week! When you strike it rich, you strike it rich. As Brokheh puts it: "God gives everyone a lot. He gives some a lot of money and some a lot of trouble."

Pinye ran into the tailor from Heysen his first day in the shahp. The tailor took off his snazzy glasses, stuck out a hand, and said: "Hallaw, homeboy! Hah duh yuh doo?" Pinye is so blind that he didn't recognize the joker until he mentioned the *Prince Albert*. Then, says Pinye, he felt three holes in his heart. You might ask what the tailor from Heysen ever did to Pinye. But Pinye can't stand the looks of him. He wouldn't work with him in one shop if he were paid a thousand dahlehz an hour. That's what made him sew his sleeve to the machine. He was that flustered.

In short, Pinye's not cut out to be an ahpereydeh. He's found a dzhahb in another shahp as a presseh. Right now he's an assistant presseh. Once he learns the ropes, he'll be up for promotion. He can rise pretty high, he says.

How high is that?

"It's anyone's guess," Pinye says. "The sky is the limit. Not even Kahnegi, Vendehbilt, or Rahknfelleh knew how far they would go."

Meanwhile Pinye is having a hard time. His problem is always being in a hurry. He doesn't see too well, either. Every night he comes home dragging his tail.

One night he came with a burned nose. What happened? He burned it on his own iron. How do an iron and a nose get together? Pinye blames the nose. He was bending over to look for some fabric when it ran into the iron.

"A shlimazel! If he fell into a snow bank, he'd crack his skull on a rock."

I don't suppose I have to tell you that's from Brokheh. She has a big mouth, Brokheh does.

♦♦♦

Brokheh isn't satisfied. Neither are my mother and Taybl. Have you ever seen a satisfied woman?

They don't like the men's slaving to make a living in America. A dzhahb in a shahp is no treat. It starts at seven-thirty every morning and you have to allow an hour for travel, plus time for morning prayers and a bite to eat. You can figure out for yourself when that means getting up—and you want to be on time, because you're docked half a day's pay for each five minutes you're late. How does anyone know how late you are? Leave it to America! Every shahp makes you tell it when you come to work. It's called pahntshink deh klahk.

The klahk hangs on a wall. Elye says it's called a klahk because it goes klik-klahk. A klahk that fits into your pocket, he says, is a vahtsh. "So why is it called a vahtsh?" I ask. "What should it be called?" Elye says. "A tahk," I say. "Why a tahk?" Elye asks. "Because it goes tik-tahk," I say. Elye got mad and told me I'd learned to think backwards from Pinye.

I'm glad Pinye wasn't there. They would have fought over vahtsh just like they did over brekfish. Elye said it's called brekfish because you eat herring. "In that case," said Pinye, "why isn't it called brekherrink?" "What a dope you are!" Elye said. "Don't you know a herrink is a fish?" Pinye saw that Elye had him there and said: "You know what? Let's ask an American."

Well, right away they stop a smooth-shaven Jew in the street and say to him: "Brother! How long have you been in America?"

"Thirty years," says the man. "How come you ask?"

"We have a question," they say. "Why do Americans call the morning meal brekfish?"

The Jew looked at them and said: "Who says it's called brekfish?"

"Then what is it called?"

"Brekfist! Brekfist! Brekfist!" The Jew shouted three times in their face and turned to go. First, though, he added:

"Grinhawnz!"

♦♦♦

It doesn't look like we'll grow old in the shahp. Elye says there are problems with the fawmin. Every shahp has a fawmin who's in charge. In fact, every floor has a fawmin. The fawmin on Elye's floor is a rat. He's an old ahpereydeh who was promoted. The workers say he's worse than the bawss. There's a rumor that he's tinkered with the klahk to make you seem late when you're on time. A real bastard! And Pinye has even nicer things to say about his shahp. You're not allowed to look at a noospeypeh there, not even during the lunch break. You're not allowed to smoke. You're not even allowed to talk. Pinye says it's so quiet that you could hear the flies buzz if it weren't for the noise of the machines.

The good thing is that the irons are gas-heated. The bad thing is that the gas stinks. It stinks in Elye's shahp too. Elye's bawss calls it gaass. Pinye's bawss calls it gez. So now they argue about that too.

To make a long story short, the gez gives the workers such a headache that they have to keep taking breaks. The bawss makes up for that on pehdeh, when he docks the lost time from their pay. And you can add being docked for coming late and leaving early, not to mention days that you're sick.

It's more than anyone can take. There's going to be a streik.

WE'RE ON STREIK!

I tell you, going on streik beats all! What it's like is . . . well, suppose you send your child to the heder and the teacher hits him so hard that you take him out and look for another teacher. Meanwhile, there's no school.

Elye and Pinye have stopped going to the shahp. The apartment is a different place now that they're home again. It's like a week full of Sundays. I've told you that working in a shahp means getting up at the crack of dawn and falling into bed at night. That's because of awvehteim. Awvehteim is staying to work in the shahp when everyone else goes home. Pinye and Elye don't work awvehteim because they have to, they do it for the extra pay. A lot of good it does when pehdeh comes around and they see all they've been docked for! "They're bandits," Elye says.

"You're an imbecile," says Brokheh.

If she ever worked in a shahp, Brokheh says, no one would spit in her kasha. She'd have the bawssehz and the fawminz eating dirt. You better believe it. If anyone can do it, it's Brokheh.

That's why Brokheh was pleased as punch when all the shahp hands called a streik. Every last garment worker in New York laid down his scissors and iron and walked out. You should have seen the excitement! I'm talking homes, strits, hawlz. A hawl is a big room where all the garment workers get together for a mitink. They talk and they talk and they talk.

You hear words you've never heard before. Dzhenril streik . . . yunyin . . . awknahzayshn . . . hiyeh vedzhehz . . . beddeh voikink kahndishinz . . . skebz . . . streikbrehkehz . . . pikits and a lot more like that. I can't make head or tails of any of it. My friend Mendl says he understands it all. Just don't try asking him to explain. "When you're older, you'll get it too," he says. Maybe I will.

Meanwhile, I sit watching the action with itchy fingers. What wouldn't I give to get it down on paper—how everyone looks, and what everyone does, and the things everyone says!

Take Elye, for instance. He doesn't say a thing. He just goes from group to group, listening and biting his nails. I get a kick out of watching him nod. He agrees with everyone.

Do you see that garment worker over there, the one with the wen on the side of his head? He's just grabbed Elye by the lapel and is shaking him while saying it's all a big waste of time. The streik won't get us workers anywhere. The sosayshn uv menefektshehz is too strong. Elye nods. I'll bet he knows what a sosayshn uv menefektshehz is as much as I do.

Now someone new goes over to him, a man with a face like a duck's who sputters when he talks. He takes hold of Elye's jacket button and sputters away, stopping every few sentences to say: "No, sir! We'll fight to the end!" Elye nods again. It's too bad Brokheh isn't here. She'd give him a piece of her mind, don't think she wouldn't.

♦♦♦

Pinye is a different story. If you've never heard Pinye speak at a mitink, you've missed something grand. He puts his heart and soul into it and lets loose with the most terrific words and names.

You have to see it with your own eyes. When it comes to boring an audience of thousands, Pinye is in a class by himself. He begins with Columbus, runs through the entire history of the United States, and would go on all night if anyone let him.

"Who's the spikkeh?" someone asks.

"A grinhawn!"

"What's he want?"

"What are his demands?"

"What's he sounding off about?"

"Sharrap!" a man shouts at Pinye. Pretty soon a whole chorus is shouting:

"Sharrap!"

Sharrap is not a nice word. In Jewish you would say, "Go peddle your wares around the corner!" But words don't scare Pinye. He runs on like an unplugged barrel. You can stop it with your finger, stuff a rag in it—nothing helps. You either wait for the last drop to trickle out or roll the barrel away. That's what two young pressehs did to Pinye. They took him gently by the arms and led him off the steydzsh.

Not that that stopped him. He talked all the way home. And when we got there he started in again on my mother, Brokheh, and Taybl. He actually had some good points, Pinye did. But try talking to a woman. When he's finished, Brokheh comes up with one of her gems:

"What does it matter to the turkey if it's slaughtered for the Purim dinner or the Passover seder?"

Maybe you can tell me what that means.

♦♦♦

The days go by. The streik continues. The workers are tough as steel. Every day there's another mitink in a different place. The menefektshehz, they say, are tough too. They're not giving in. But they will. Everyone's sure of it. There's nothing the workers can't accomplish. This is America.

There's always the last resort. It's called a mahtsh. Thousands of streikehz get together and parade through the streets with their flags. Let's hope it works. We'll be in bad shape if it doesn't.

Mendl and I think it's a swell idea. We'll mahtsh in the front row. But go tell that to an old woman like Brokheh! She says we're just playing soldiers. "You'll ruin your shoes," she tells us. You should hear what Pinye has to say about that.

♦♦♦

There's no turning back now. Mendl and I have put on our good suits. It's as exciting as the Fawt uv Dzhulei. That's an American holiday.

They shoot fiyehkrekehz in the strit and people get killed. What's a few dead on the Fawt uv Dzhulei? It's the day America beat its enemies.

Suddenly the grand mood is spoiled. A man has been killed on Kenell Strit. Pinye brings us the news. He was there and saw it happen. The man had it coming, he says. He was a gengsteh.

"What's a gengsteh?" my mother asks. "A thief?"

"Worse!" Pinye says.

"A murderer?"

"Worse!"

"What's worse than a murderer?"

"A gengsteh is worse than a murderer," Pinye says, "because a murderer murders for murder and a gengsteh murders for pay. They get money to beat up the streikehz. One of them attacked a girl. There was a fight. People jumped on him and hit him."

That's all we can get out of Pinye. He runs around the apartment on his long legs, pulling his hair and breathing fire and shouting:

"O Columbus! O Vashinktn! O Linkn!"

Then he turns around and runs out.

♦♦♦

Naturally, the next victims are Mendl and me. My mother won't let us into the strit for all the money in the world. Not us, not Elye, not Brokheh, not Taybl! If people are getting killed there, she says, it's no place to be. She's gotten us so worried that Taybl is crying like a baby. It's anyone's guess where Pinye is.

My mother turns to Taybl. There's a great God above, she says. He'll see to it Pinye is all right. With God's help he'll come home safe and sound. He'll be a good father to his children, God willing.

Taybl is childless. She's taking medicine and hoping for the best.

"Lots of children," my mother says.

"Amen to that!" I say and get a whack from Elye. That means I should mind my own business.

♦♦♦

Thank God, Pinye is back! He has good news. The gengsteh who was killed is alive. He'll be a cripple for life. He lost an eye and broke an arm. “It serves him right,” Pinye says. “It will teach him not to be a gengsteh.”

My mother feels sorry for the gengsteh. “What difference does it make what he is? There’s a God in heaven, it’s his job to settle accounts. Why should anyone lose an eye and break an arm? Why should a gengsteh’s wife and children have a cripple for a father?”

The streik drags on. There isn’t a stitch of work. Elye is frantic. My mother tries comforting him. The God who brought us to America, she says, won’t let us down now.

Yoyneh the bagel maker and Pesye and Moyshe and all our other good friends come by every day to cheer us up. They say it’s not the end of the world. Where is it written in the Bible that in America you have to be a garment worker? And to show you how right they are, listen to this.

KASRILEVKE IN NEW YORK

Before I tell you about other ways of making a living in America, I'd better tell you about our friends and acquaintances in New York, because it's thanks to them we've risen in the world. Touch wood, we have plenty of them!

All Kasrilevke has moved to America. After we left, folks say, it was one disaster after another. First there was a bad pogrom, then a fire—the whole town burned to the ground. We found out about it from my mother. Leave it to my mother to be the first to hear of any calamity. She heard the news in synagogue. Kasrilevke, you should know, even has its own synagogue in America.

We hadn't been in New York a week when my mother asked about a place to pray. New York has lots of synagogues. There's one on every strit. That first Saturday she went with Pesye.

Pesye's synagogue turned out to be our own. I mean the people were all from Kasrilevke. They call it the Kasrilevke Synagogue Association, or the Kasrilevke shul for short. We know everyone who prays there. Would you like to guess who that is? Eighteen brains wouldn't be enough for you.

First of all, there's the cantor—I mean Hirsh-Ber, the man in whose choir I sang. You may remember my carrying around his lame daughter Dobtshe. She died back in Russia, in the pogrom, and Hirsh-Ber came to America with his wife and children to make a living.

He isn't just a cantor here. He's a circumciser and a titsheh too. A titsheh titshiz children. Mostly he pinches them when no one is looking. That's because in America he isn't allowed to hit them. They say Hirsh-Ber is doing well. He's changed a whole lot. Well, maybe not all that much, but he dresses differently. If he had worn a hat in Kasrilevke like the one he wears here, he'd have had the whole town running after him. His jacket is shorter too. And he's cut off his earlocks. He hasn't touched his big beard, though. He's the only one who hasn't.

Your American hates a beard more than a Jew hates a pig. Once some Christian boys—loahfehz, they call them—stopped Hirsh-Ber in the strit and tried shaving his beard off. It was his good luck that some Jews came along and rescued him from the loahfehz. Since then he tucks his beard into his overcoat whenever he walks in the strit.

♦♦♦

Bereh the shoemaker is here too. That's the man whose rats Elye tried getting rid of. I've told you he likes to spin yarns. No one else would dream of the things he makes up. In fact, he's one lying Jew. In America that's called a blahfeh.

Bereh is the same Bereh as always. If a third of what he said about his shoes were correct, he'd be pretty well off. He says he's the biggest shoemaker in America. The whole country, he says, wears his boots. The prehzident himself has ordered a pair—he swears it with such oaths that you'd have to believe him even if he wasn't a Jew. My brother Elye says it's as true as his story of the cat-eating rats. In short, he's blahfink. In Jewish you would say, "He's rattling the teapot."

I like "rattling the teapot" a lot better. I like it so much that I drew it. I mean I drew Bereh the shoemaker shaking a big teapot in the air. Everyone died laughing. Even Elye gave it half a smile. He doesn't whack me for doodling any more. He just grumbles and says, "If you have nothing to do, I suppose you may as well do it."

♦♦♦

Who else should I tell you about? Rich Yosi is in America too. Once we all dreamed of having a fraction of his money. Now he doesn't have it himself. How's that? The pogrom did him in. I don't mean he was hurt or anything, but he did lose everything he had. His furniture was smashed, his linens were torn, and all the goods were stolen from his store. He and his family escaped by hiding for three days in the cellar and nearly starving to death. But that wasn't the worst of it. The worst was that his debtors went bankrupt. That made him go bankrupt himself. Who would have imagined Rich Yosi running away from his creditors? He cleared out in the middle of the night—for America.

Do you remember Yosi's bug-eyed son Henekh, the one who laughed at me for going to America? Now he walks the strits of New York. He looks the other way when he sees me. It's beneath him to talk to me even now. Wasn't Haman the proud one too! My friend Mendl says he'll make him black-eyed Henekh. Mendl doesn't like swellheads.

And to take the cake, Menashe the doctor is here with the Doct'ress! You know all about their garden with its peaches, cherries, apples, and pears. Well, it went up in smoke. The whole place burned to a crisp. You wouldn't recognize the two of them. They're old and gray. Menashe wheels a pushcart with apples and oranges and the Doct'ress peddles tea. "It could break your heart," my mother says, all teary-eyed.

"It couldn't have happened to a nicer woman," says Elye.

I agree. The Doct'ress got what she deserved. They don't come any meaner. She wouldn't have given a rotten apple to a beggar! She thinks I've forgotten catching it from her in the attic. Not till the day I die.

♦♦♦

All the time we were roaming around Europe, the pogromchiks were robbing and torching our Kasrilevke Jews. The half house we sold to Zilye the tailor was burned too. Now Zilye is in New York. He's still a tailor, but in Russia he was his own bawss while in America he works for someone else. Sometimes he's an assistant presseh and sometime he's an ahpereydeh. He takes home, so he says, seven or eight dollars a week. That's not enough for a living but you can triple it because his three daughters work making shoits.

I asked Elye why it's called a shoit. Elye said that's one English word he can't explain. "Why just one?" said Pinye. "I suppose you can explain all the others." "As a matter of fact, I can," Elye said. "Then suppose you explain butsheh," said Pinye. "It comes from butsherink a cow," Elye said. Next Pinye asked why a tailor was called an ahpereydeh. "He's called an ahpereydeh," Elye said, "because . . . because . . . because get off my back! Since when do I have to explain every word in America to you?"

“Shhh, stop shouting! What good are you to anyone? Come here, little man,” Pinye said to me. “If there’s anything you want to know, don’t ask your brother. He’s no wiser than you are.”

Brokheh stuck up for Elye. “A corpse,” she said, “knows more than both of you together.”

♦♦♦

But I’ve gotten off the subject. That was who we know in America. All of Kasrilevke is here, except for Pinye’s family. They say it’s on its way too.

Pinye’s father Hirsh-Leyb the engineer and his uncle Shneyur the watchmaker have written that they would have left for America long ago if only they had money for the tickets. They’ve asked Pinye to lend it to them. We’re saving our pehnehz. As soon as they add up to a dahleh, we’ll make a down payment on the tickets. God willing, they’ll pay us back. They should do well here. Hirsh-Leyb writes that he’s invented a new stove. It hardly needs any wood. In fact, it needs none at all. How is that? It’s Hirsh-Leyb’s secret. And Shneyur has thought up a new clock that America will go wild for. What sort of clock is it? I’ll tell you what he wrote Pinye.

At first glance you might think it was just an ordinary clock. So what’s so special about it? Well, look at the dial and you’ll see a moon with twelve stars. That’s by night. By day you’ll see the sun—and that’s not the half of it. When the clock strikes twelve a door opens and out steps an officer with a sword and a marching band. The officer lifts his sword and the band plays a march and marches back through the door, which shuts behind it.

What’s your guess? Will Shneyur’s clock make a million in America? He’s been working on it for quite a few years. It was almost finished when the pogromchiks smashed it to pieces. But so what? He’ll make another. Let him get to America and he’ll be awreit.

I still haven’t told you how we’re now making a living. But I’d better leave something for the next chapter.

MAKING A LIVING

The first to start making a living again was Elye. He can thank my mother for that. Every Saturday she prays in the Kasrilevke shul. It's a good place to meet people. It was there that she met Missiz Prehzident. (In America the head of a synagogue is a prehzident too.) She's a fine lady who thinks well of my mother. Brokheh says that's because my mother can follow the prayers and knows what the cantor is saying, which is more than can be said for most women.

Brokheh says the only reason women go to synagogue in America is to show off their deimindz. She's sorry to say they're a bunch of fat cows who can't even read the letters in the prayer book. Eating and gossiping is all they're good for.

My mother doesn't let her get away with that. "My dear daughter-in-law," she says, "that's gossip too." Brokheh says it's not gossip as long as it stays in the family.

But let's get back to Missiz Prehzident and her husband, the prehzident of the Kasrilevke shul.

Maybe you've heard of Hibru Neshnel Delikatesn. It's a company that sells kosher salami, frankfurters, pickled tongues, and corned beef. It has stores all over town. If you're hungry, you step into one and order a haht dawg with mustard or horseradish. My friend Mendl and I once ate three haht dawgz apiece and could have polished off a few more if we had the cash . . . but that's not what I wanted to tell you.

♦♦♦

What I wanted to tell you was that the prehzident of our shul is an owner of Hibru Neshnel Delikatesn. My mother used her connections with his wife to get Elye a job.

Elye is a selzmin. He's also a vaydeh. That means anyone wanting a haht dawg tells him to bring it. At first he objected to that. "What's the big idea?" he asked. "Since when is a Jew with a beard, a cantor's son and a bagel maker's son-in-law, supposed to be someone's servant?"

Pinye gave him what for.

"Listen to you! Do you think you're still in that dump of a Kasrilevke? You're in America, that's where you are! Lots of fine young men like you have sold noospeypehz here, peddled metshehz, polished shoes in the strit. Take Kahnegi! Take Rahknfelleh! Take Vendehbilt! Read about Dzhordzh Vashinktn and Eybrim Linkn and all the other great Americans! You'll see that even Peysi the cantor's son can sell haht dawgz."

That's when Pinye caught it from my mother. As long as he stuck to Kahnegi and Rahknfelleh, she let him have his way. But hearing Dzhordzh Vashinktn and Eybrim Linkn mentioned in one breath with my father was too much for her. For all she knew, she told Pinye, Vashinktn and Linkn were honorable men and good Jews. Still, she would thank Pinye to leave my father out of it. He belonged where he was, in Paradise, putting in a good word for us all.

"Amen!" I said and got a whack from Elye.

To make a long story short, Elye has a dzhahb and makes a living. He sells haht dawgz and waits on tables for five dahlehz a week plus two meals a day, which are also worth something. Not to mention working in a store where the whole world buys delikatesn! Every day he makes new friends with some of New York's finest. We're hoping he'll go far. He's liked by his boss and respected by the kahstemehz. They like being served by a young man who's not your ordinary flunky.

There's just one problem with my brother. You wouldn't want a beard like his. Without it he'd be awreit. And not only does he have a beard, it gets bigger and longer each day in America. Mostly it gets bigger. Pinye says he should give it a trimm. That's what Pinye did. He went to a bahbeh shahp and sat in a tsheh and leaned back and said nothing because he didn't know any English. Along came the bahbeh, grabbed Pinye by the nose, soaped Pinye's face, ran a razor over it, and told him to stand up. Pinye stood and looked in the mirror and didn't know who he was looking at. His cheeks were as smooth as a noodle board! There wasn't a hair or whisker on them. The face in the mirror grinned back at him.

Was he in a pickle! What was he going to tell Taybl? And in fact she fainted twice and felt so sick she took to bed. But that was only the first time. By now she's gotten used to it. Her Pinye goes to the bahbeh for a shave every week and looks like a real American. He speaks English too and no longer swallows his tshooinkahm. If only his collar were straight, his tie stayed in place, and one pant leg wasn't higher than the other, he'd be a real dzhentlmin. That's also called a spawt.

♦♦♦

In fact, Pinye could make a living like everyone if he didn't knock his brains out thinking of ways to get rich. (He comes from a brainy family, Pinye does.) He's kind of making a living already. The trouble is that he goes from dzhahb to dzhahb. You have to hand it to him, though. No dzhahb in the world is beneath him. He'll do anything he's asked to earn a dahleh. Tell him to sweep the strit and he'll sweep the strit. Tell him to shovel coal and he'll shovel coal. Selling noospeypehz is fine too. America, Pinye says, is a free country. The only dzhahb to be ashamed of is a thief's. An American wouldn't steal a bar of gold if you left it in front of him. He wouldn't lie or cheat, either. Pinye is sure of that. He's written a poem about America. I don't remember it all, but here is some of it:

> This country of Columbus
> Is a place for every one-'f-us,
> The only one that's giving
> Jew a chance to make a living.
> From New York City to Seattle
> You won't hear a teapot rattle,
> Nor a blahfeh nor a liar
> From California to Ohio.

It went on like that and ended:

> America's a country where a person can go far.
> That's why it's got a prehzident and not some stinking tsar.

Elye just laughed and said that "liar" and "Ohio" didn't rhyme. Pinye said, "Here's another poem for you. If you know a man named Shmiel, have him over for a meal, and if you know a man named Leyzer, tell him to go to hell. You say Leyzer and hell don't rhyme? Then he can go to hell without a rhyme!"

♦♦♦

In case you're wondering whether Brokheh and Taybl are making a living too, let me tell you they're in the necktie biznis. That's my mother and her synagogue's doing again. A woman she knows there is an awreitnitshke named Kreyndl. Back in Kasrilevke, Kreyndl was a housemaid who worked for Rich Yosi. That's a story in itself.

In Kasrilevke lived a butcher named Meylekh who had a young assistant, Nekhemye. This Nekhemye fell in love with our Kreyndl and wanted to marry her. He just didn't have with what. And so he hit on a scheme. The next time Meylekh the butcher sent him to the fair to buy a cow, he took the money and Kreyndl and lit out for America. He's done pretty well here and now he's an awreitnik with a tie factory.

It so happened that Kreyndl the awreitnitshke had a memorial day for her mother and struck up an acquaintance with my mother in the Kasrilevke shul. When she heard my mother was Peysi the cantor's widow, she offered to help. My mother said the only help she needed was work for her children. Well, one thing led to another and pretty soon the awreitnitshke talked to the awreitnik and got Brokheh and Taybl dzhahbz in his fektri. It's up on Brawdvey. After they had worked there for a while, my mother used her influence and they were allowed to take home piecework instead.

It didn't last very long. Brokheh and Taybl kept busy until the end of the sizn. Then came slekteim and they were out of work. We tried not to let it get us down. As my mother says, "God is a father. He punishes with one hand and heals with the other."

That's something I don't get. Why punish and then heal? You could save yourself the trouble by skipping both.

My mother also says, "God sends the cure with the ailment."

I'll tell you what she's thinking of. Just let me stop to catch my breath.

GOD'S CURE

It's like this.

My brother Elye has quit working for Hibru Neshnel Delikatesn. It wasn't a job for him. He's Peysi the cantor's son, remember? He's well bred and has a good voice. In fact, he'd make a fine cantor himself. What kind of job is bringing people haht dawgz?

Bringing haht dawgz is no disgrace. But there are all kinds of people in the world. Some are well bred themselves. You take a young man from a good home—he orders his haht dawgz, eats them quietly, pays the bill, and bei-bei.

But not everyone comes from a good home. Sometimes you get a rude moron who makes you sizzle. His haht dawgz aren't hot enough. Or else you've forgotten the mustard. And he doesn't say, "Excuse me, please, I'd like another awdeh." He whistles or snaps his fingers and shouts, "Hey, vaydeh! Maw dawgz!"

Elye isn't used to such language. He loses his temper and refuses to answer. The moron doesn't like that and shouts louder, "Hey, professor! Come over here!"

"Since when am I a professor to you?" Elye asks.

That causes the moron to shout so loud that the bawss comes running and says to Elye: "Vahts deh meddeh vid yu?" Elye doesn't answer him either. "I'm asking you a question," says the bawss. "Ask me proper and you'll get an answer," Elye says. "What's proper by you?" asks the bawss. "Proper is Jewish," Elye says. "And talking English makes me a monster?" asks the bawss. "It might," Elye says.

"In that case," says the bawss, "I'm giving you the sek. In proper Jewish, you can stay in bed tomorrow."

♦ ♦ ♦

"I'd rather starve than sell haht dawgz."

That's what my brother Elye says. Pinye disagrees. America, he says, is a free country. You need to take things in stride.

Don't argue with Pinye unless you want to hear about his millionaires. I mean Kahnegi, Rahknfelleh, and Vendehbilt. Elye asks:

"What makes you think you know all about them?"

"What makes me think I know all about the Tsar?" Pinye answers.

"All right, what makes you think you do?"

"If you read as many novels as I have," Pinye says, "you'd know all about him too."

Novels are the books that Pinye reads at Moyshe's stend. Although they're written in a plain, simple Jewish, they're harder to understand than the Bible. Moyshe lends them out. He makes a living from it. One book can have a hundred readers. Most are women. Women are crazy about novels. On Saturday mornings Brokheh gobbles them up like hotcakes. My mother and Taybl listen to her read out loud. My mother falls asleep and Taybl sits there sighing. Sometimes she bursts into tears. She has a tender heart, Taybl does. If I were allowed to draw on the Sabbath, I'd sketch Brokheh reading while my mother sleeps and Taybl cries.

But here I am talking and I still haven't told you about God's cure!

♦ ♦ ♦

First, though, let me tell you about the ailment. It's no joke for a young man like Elye to be out of work. Elye isn't Pinye. If Pinye needs money, he'll take a shovel and shovel snow. Elye says he would shovel it too, but not in the strit. "I suppose you're waiting for a home delivery," Pinye says. Elye gets sore and answers:

"I can see you're in a grand mood."

"Of course I am. I'm in a grand mood every time I remember I'm in America and not in Pogromland."

"Your great-grandmother must be thrilled," Elye says. He's so depressed he decides to go to synagogue.

And that's where God sends his cure, right there in the Kasrilevke shul. Listen to this.

♦♦♦

I've told you how, the same summer we were walking the streets of Vaytshepl, there was a whale of a pogrom in Kasrilevke, plus a fire in the bargain. The hooligans stole all they could, smashed what they couldn't, and burned what they couldn't smash. It wasn't so bad if you were poor. What did you have to lose apart from a few pillows? In fact, you thanked God if you were still in one piece, because not everyone was. Little children were torn limb from limb or left to die of hunger. That's if you were poor.

But the rich! One day you're rolling in clover and the next you're a beggar without a shirt on your back. Just thinking of it can send a chill down your spine, that's what our Kasrilevke Jews say.

There's only one thing I don't get. How come no one gets a chill thinking of the poor people and their children being torn apart? My friend Mendl doesn't get it either. That's how our Kasrilevke Jews are, he says. Let a poor Jew die of hunger and it's nothing. Let a rich Jew become a poor Jew and it's the end of the world.

Well, one of our filthy rich Kasrilevke Jews went by the name of Moyshe-Noyekh. He not only owned his own house with its own yard and its own garden, he was so important that he went around all summer in his underwear. I don't mean only in his underwear—he wore a dressing gown over it. But you won't find a poor Jew dressed like that. You have to be a big deal not to care what anyone thinks of you.

Anyway, we all knew that Moyshe-Noyekh had inherited three shops from his mother, all smack in the middle of the market. He had his own cow too, a real milker. Not that three shops weren't enough to get by on. They were more than enough. But Moyshe-Noyekh's wife Nekhameh-Mirl (we called her Dekhabeh-Birl because her nose was always stuffed) milked so much milk from that milker that she could have paid all their bills just from that. Of course, to keep the Evil Eye away, she told everyone that her "bilk cow" didn't give a drop of "bilk." That didn't fool Kasrilevke, though. Everyone knew it was a lie. The bilkless bilk cow was full of milk.

Would you believe a Jew like Moyshe-Noyekh running for dear life to America in his birthday suit? It could break a heart of stone. And what was he supposed to do when he got there? You couldn't expect him to work in a shop. Nor his children. And so the Kasrilevke Synagogue Association took one look at him and made him the beadle of the Kasrilevke shul.

A beadle in America is not small potatoes. He lives better than a businessman in Kasrilevke. He can get rich from memorial days alone. They're very big on them here. All year long no one has time to pray. "Teim iz mahnee," as they say. But comes the anniversary of a death and off to synagogue everyone goes. And after prayers the family goes to a restaurant for a memorial banquet. You can bet the beadle gets thrown a few bones then, to say nothing of bar mitzvahs. When a bar mitzvah comes along he's in the gravy.

Back in Kasrilevke, becoming bar mitzvah meant putting on tefillin and praying with the grown-ups. In America it's a national holiday. They take the young man, put a prayer shawl on him, call him up to the Torah like a bridegroom so that he can chant in a voice like a rooster's, and listen to him spout a speech he's learned by heart—all in English. God forbid he should say a Jewish word! When he's done he gets blessed by the rebbei, who's as beardless as a Catholic priest. There are presents and the beadle gets his share.

In short, Moyshe-Noyekh has a swell dzhahb. His only problem is having to make the rounds of the synagogue members every month to collect the dooz they've pledged. What kind of dzhahb is it for an ex-rich Jew to go collecting from house to house? Dekhabeh-Birl actually wept as she said to my mother, "I'b tellid you, every tibe by husba'd bakes the rou'ds, it's a pudishbed."

That gave my mother an idea. Why didn't Moyshe-Noyekh ask my brother Elye to be his collector? It would be a load off Moyshe-Noyekh's mind and Elye would make a living.

Needless to say, Moyshe-Noyekh welcomed the idea. It was Elye who balked at first. It didn't appeal to him. Not until Pinye stepped in. He gave Elye a tongue-lashing as only he can. Did he let him have it!

"It's beyond me how you can be so snooty! What makes you think you're any better than Kahnegi, Rahknfelleh, and Vendehbilt?"

Excetra, excetra.

Leave it to Pinye!

♦♦♦

Who would have thought that a little dzhahb collecting synagogue dooz would lead in the end to a big dzhahb? And not one big dzhahb but two—one Elye's collecting for a foinitsheh biznis and one Pinye's collecting for an inshurinks kahmpeni. Wait a minute and I'll tell you what they do.

WE'RE KEHLEHKTEHZ!

One good thing about America is that everything gets delivered to your home. And you can buy it in installments for a dahleh a week and fix up your house like a lord's. It's called foinishink deh epahtment.

Don't ask me what kind of word foinitsheh is. Elye says it comes from "fein" and "tsheh." Pinye says that's ridiculous. In the first place, the word should be "feinitsheh." And second, why a fine chair and not a fine mirror? Elye answers that only an idiot would say feinitsheh instead of foinitsheh. He says that's the law of foinetiks.

They went at it so that they nearly came to blows. Luckily, Brokheh came along and put an end to it. She made them agree to ask an American—I mean a Jew who isn't a grinhawn.

It turned out that the word is neither feinitsheh nor foinitsheh. It's firnitsheh. Go figure.

♦♦♦

No one in America pays cash—not unless you're a Jew like Dzheykip Shif. They say he's the richest man in America. That's according to Elye. Pinye disagrees. Kahnegi, he says, is richer. And Vendehbilt puts Kahnegi in his little pocket and Rahknfelleh makes them both look like pikers. "That's a good one!" Elye says. "You're talking real estate and I'm talking cash. Shif's got more cash than all of them together."

That was too much for Pinye. Elye, he shouted, didn't know what he was talking about. Rahknfelleh gives away more cash in a year than all Shif's property is worth.

Elye hit the ceiling. "Pinye," he cried, "you're an anti-Semite!" Shif,

Elye said, is a Jew, even if Rahknfelleh is richer. If we Jews don't stick up for each other, who will?

"I don't care if Shif is ten Jews!" Pinye said. "Does that mean I have to lie for him? You're forgetting, Elye, that we're in America. In America no one likes a blahfeh."

"If you're talking about lies," Brokheh said, "I'd like to see one of my enemies drop dead for every lie told each day in New York City. And that's not including Bruklin, Brawnzvil, and the Brahnks."

She stopped that argument cold.

♦♦♦

If you're going to charge a dollar a week for firnitsheh, you need someone to go get the dahleh. That's your kehlehkteh. There are plenty of them.

Every kehlehkteh has his own route with its own houses. He knocks on the door and says "Gud mawnink." Then he says "Iz ah vehry neis dey," takes your dahleh, writes out a receipt, and says "Gudbei." That's all there is to it. You don't even have to take off your hat. It isn't the custom. You can walk whistling into the richest man's house with your boots on, or with a cigarette or tshooinkahm in your mouth, and no one will say a word. That's America.

♦♦♦

Elye likes his new dzhahb. It's a lot better than selling haht dawgz in a delikatesn and he makes more money. Some weeks he brings home eight dahlehz, and some ten or twelve. It depends on the veddeh. If the veddeh is good, he vawks. If it's bad, he has to take the stritkah. That costs a nikl. Elye doesn't like to part with his nikelz. He's tight with his money. He isn't like Pinye.

Pinye is a big spender. He almost never vawks. That's because he's nearsighted and could be run over. Actually, he says, he's more absent-minded than nearsighted. He's always thinking about something. He can't let a minute go by without reading a book or a noospeypeh. Even when he's writing, he'll stop to think in the middle of a sentence. He doesn't hear what you say to him then. All of a sudden he'll grab a pencil, or a pen and some ink, and fill both sides of ten pages. Nobody knows what he's writing or plans to do with it, not even Taybl. When Elye asks him, he says:

"You're too young to know."

We've grown older and still don't know.

♦♦♦

Nevertheless, Pinye makes a living. He's a kehlehkteh too. Not for firnitsheh. Pinye kehlehkts for leif inshurinks. Actually, it's more like death inshurinks. Everyone in America has it: husbands, wives, children, parents, brothers, sisters. It costs a nikl to a dahleh a week, no cash down. The more inshurinks you have, the more you pay. There are families in which everyone, from the little babies to the grandparents, carries death inshurinks. If there's anyone who doesn't, it's up to the kehlehkteh to see that he does.

I can't tell you exactly how death inshurinks works. All I know is that it's a dzhahb Elye turned down. He'd rather be a firnitsheh kehlehkteh. Inshurinks means talking. And talking some more. And talking more than that. Pinye is good at it. He could talk a wall into falling down. Pinye could sell death inshurinks to the dead.

Pinye couldn't care less who you are. He has an answer for everything. If you already have inshurinks, you need more. If you don't, you better take it out. If you don't take it for yourself, you can take it for your wife, child, cousin, or nekstdawrikeh. Once Pinye gets you in his clutches, you're done for.

Nekstdawrikeh inshurinks isn't really for your next-door neighbor. It's a way of earning a few hundred dahlehz from the inshurinks kahmpeni if he dies. And your nekstdawrikeh does the same: if you die first, the money is his. You both pay the kahmpeni a kvawdeh a week. The kahmpeni comes to get it. I mean the kehlehkteh does. That's Pinye. He kehlehks your kvawdehz and keeps half for his kehmishn.

♦♦♦

That's kehlehktink. Taking out inshurinks for the first time is called reitink ah pahlisee. If Pinye is the eydzhent who reits it, he earns fifteen-to-one. That means that if the primyim is a kvawdeh a week, he gets fifteen kvawdehz from the kahmpeni in one shot. You can figure out for yourself what two or three pahliseez a day add up to. That's a heap of kvawdehz. It's like coming into an inheritance.

"God help us," Brokheh says to Pinye. "You're flooding the house with money!" You should see Taybl blush as she watches Pinye shake the nikelz and kvawdehz from his pockets.

"So, what did you think?" Pinye answers, making separate piles of the kvawdehz and the nikelz. "That Kahnegi, Vendehbilt, and Rahknfelleh were born millionaires?"

♦♦♦

If I had a fresh sheet of paper, I'd take some charcoal and sketch. This is what I'd put in my picture:

A table. At the head of it sits my mother, her arms crossed on her chest. To one side of her is Brokheh—big and tall, with monster feet. To the other side is Taybl—a skinny little quarter of a chicken. Both are at work, one sewing and one knitting. My brother Elye sits at the table's end, a grown man with a beard. In one hand he's holding ah bahntsh kahdz and in the other some dahleh bilz. They're what he kehlehkted today.

Pinye is hunched across from him, smooth-shaven, a real American. He's emptying his pockets of kvawdehz and nikelz. Being nearsighted, he brings every kvawdeh and nikl to his nose. Two piles rise high on the table, one of kvawdehz and one of nikelz. Pinye goes on counting. He reaches into his pockets for more coins. You can see that his pockets are still bulging. They look ready to burst.

♦♦♦

Nothing lasts forever. And no one is ever satisfied. We're tired of going from door to door for kvawdehz and nikelz. Better your own slice of bread than the next man's loaf. That's what Brokheh says.

The first to sour on kehlehktink was Elye. He was fed up with the biznis. I mean it wasn't the biznis, it was the kahstemehz. Some stopped paying. "You can take your firnitsheh back," they told him. "We need it like a hole in the head." Others were full of complaints. Why did the bed squeak? Why did they see two faces in the mirror? Why didn't the chest of drawers open and close? How come the stool weighed a ton and was hard as nails to sit on?

Some kahstemehz disappeared. They had moved to another epahtment and go find them. Even worse were the ones who wanted to keep up the payments. They liked the firnitsheh, they just didn't have the money. The man of the house was sick. Or out of work. Or on streik. What was Elye to do? Nobody wants to lose a kahstemeh. And so he paid for them out of his own pahkit. There was no end to it. You can imagine what it was like.

♦♦♦

You think Pinye likes his dzhahb any better? Think again! It's easier to cross the Red Sea, he says, than to land a kahstemeh. You talk to some idiot for three days and three nights, you explain what inshurinks is all about, you finally get him to fill out an eplikayshn—and the next day he's changed his mind or been ridzhekted. That means some lowdown doctor wrote the truth. He saw the fellow naked and didn't like what he saw.

The biggest disaster for an inshurinks eydzhent is a leps. A pahlisee lepsiz when a kahstemeh stops paying. Now it's the eydzhent's turn to pay the kahmpeni fifteen times the primyim. If not for all the lepsiz, Pinye says, he'd be a rich man. And it's just his luck that several kahstemehz have lepst together. You would think they planned it that way.

"They can all go to hell, the kahstemehz and the inshurinks and the lepsiz and the kahmpeni!" Pinye says. It's time he and Elye struck out on their own. They've each managed to save a few dahlehz. That's enough to start a biznis.

It's official. We're going into biznis!

WE GO INTO BIZNIS

Whatever you're looking for, you'll find it in the noospeypehz, even if it's bird's milk. Work? It's in the peypehz. Workers? They're there, too. A husband or a wife? Also. A biznis? Try the peypehz again. That's what we did for days until we came across the following edvehteizmint:

> Sigahz–Stayshenree–Kendee–
> Sawdehvawdeh Stend For Sale.
> Across from a Skul. On Account of
> Family Trahbelz. Gehrehntid Gud
> Biznis. Hahry!

Leave it to Brokheh to think of everything that could go wrong. For one thing, she said, how did we know the edvehteizmint was telling the truth? And besides, why crawl into bed with a bunch of family trahbelz? It was probably some husband and his wife. Why get involved in a divorce case?

Maybe you think it was only this edvehteizmint that Brokheh didn't like. Believe me, there were a hundred of them. She found something wrong with each. She was against whatever Elye was for. Just because he had gone and shaved off three-quarters of his beard, she said, he shouldn't think he was such a big shot. "So what if I did?" Elye said. "Your father shaved off all four!"

That brought Pinye into it. "You know what?" he said. "I'll give you odds that out of one hundred million Americans, you won't find half a dozen with beards. Call me a blahfeh if I'm wrong."

"What does that have to do with anything?" my mother asked. "If ducks go barefoot, that means I can't wear shoes? Let's change the subject."

It was bad enough, she said, that Peysi the cantor's son had wiped the beard off his face. To think her enemies had lived to see the day! Why make it worse by talking about it?

♦♦♦

Our new sawdehvawdeh stend had several strong points. One was that Elye was an experienced soft drink manufacturer. Since he made the sirip himself, we could afford to sell a big glass of plain sawdehvawdeh for a pehni and a glass with a flavor for two. And we bought the cheapest kehndeez and could sell them for a pehni a handful.

They were so cheap we ate them ourselves. I mean Mendl, Pinye, and me. All three of us worked at the stend and took kehndee when no one was looking—that is, when Brokheh wasn't there. The trouble was that she was there all the time, helping out with the biznis. Everyone helped, my mother and Taybl too. You might think so many biznismen serving a kahstemeh all at once would frighten him to death, but it worked out pretty well. Kahstemehz like a crowded establishment.

♦♦♦

The best time for our biznis was summer. A hot summer day in New York is worse than a furnace in hell. Everyone wants to cool off with an eiskrim. For a pehni we sold a senvitsh with two chocolate crackers and eiskrim in between. Half of that was our profit. It wasn't our biggest item, though. The real moneymaker in a sawdehvawdeh stend is a drink called seideh. It's sweet and sour and has bubbles that tickle your tongue. All the experts say it tastes like champagne. Even though it's an American drink, Elye knows how to make it.

There's nothing Elye can't make. Don't let Pinye tell you otherwise. He keeps teasing Elye that the only good thing about his seideh is that it's cold. Apart from that, Pinye says, it's for the birds. "If it's for the birds," Elye says, "how come you drink it all day?" "What's it to you what I drink?" Pinye answers. "How much can one person drink? If I drank it from morning to night, it still wouldn't come to a nikl's worth."

That's when Brokheh butts in. A nikl, she says, is money too. So of course Taybl has to stick up for her husband. Pinye, she says, is a full partner in the biznis and can be allowed a nikl's worth of seideh. It's a good thing my mother was there and said: "Why, I wouldn't touch that seideh if you paid me! It looks like bread kvass and tastes like death!"

We all laughed so hard that we stopped quarreling.

♦♦♦

Biznis was even better when the vawdehmehln season began. We cut the mehlehnz into slices and sold them for a pehni a slice. If the mehln was a good one, we made a nice profit and had enough left over for supper. You have to finish a vawdehmehln the day you open it because the next morning it's nothing but red frizz. Mendl, Pinye, and I prayed every day that the kahstemehz would leave some for us.

Some items have a sizn. As soon as summer was over, the seideh and vawdehmehln disappeared. Others sell all year round, like sigahs and sigehrehts. We kept up a good biznis in them.

There are all kinds of sigehrehts. Some are one for a pehni and some are two. Mendl, Pinye, and I sometimes cop a few toofehz. Who has to know?

In America it's called smawkink. Once I was smawkink a toofeh with Mendl, a puff for him and a puff for me. It would have been fine if God hadn't created Brokheh. She smelled the smoke and ratted to Elye, who gave me a smawkink I'd rather forget. It wasn't so much the smawkink that upset him as its being Saturday. It seems that if Peysi the cantor's son is caught smawkink on the Sabbath, you're allowed to beat him to death. Even my mother agreed that this time the dog deserved the stick. That's why I gave up smawkink. I can't even stand the smell any more.

♦♦♦

Our stend also sells peypehz, Jewish dailies and magazines. We don't make much on them but it gives Pinye something to read. Once his nose is in a peypeh, that's it. Noospeypehz affect him like magnets, he says. He'd like to write for the peypehz himself. He's even been up to Ist Brawdvey, where they're printed. He won't tell us what he did there. I sure hope he didn't bring them his poems.

I'll bet he did, though, because whenever a new batch of peypehz arrives, Pinye grabs them and goes through them with a fine tooth comb. His hands actually shake. After a while he jumps up and rushes off to Ist Brawdvey. "What's on Ist Brawdvey?" Elye asks. "Biznis," Pinye tells him. "I thought our biznis was here," Elye says. "You call this a biznis?" Pinye says. "Seven people eating their way through one stend—some biznis!" "Where do you get seven?" Elye asks. Pinye counts them on his fingers. He and Taybl are two. Elye and Brokheh are four. My mother is five. And the two little men—that's me and Mendl—make seven.

That upset my mother. Mendl and me, she said, make our living fair and square. We deliver the peypehz to our kahstemehz before the stend opens in the morning and help out after skul. (I've forgotten to tell you we go to skul now.) She gave it to Pinye, my mother did.

Half of what she says is in American by now. She just gets everything backwards. Instead of cooking a tshikn in the kitshn, she cooks the kitshn in a tshikn. But she laughs at herself along with everyone. "*Abi ir veyst az bei mir* a tshikn iz a kitshn *un* a kitshn iz a tshikn, vahts deh difrins?" she asks.

You tell me. What language is that?

HALLAW, HOMEBOY!

Early one morning my friend Mendl and I were delivering the peypehz to our kahstemehz when there was a clap on my back and someone said:

"Hallaw, homeboy!"

I turn around—it's Big Motl, the same boy who hung around with us in Cracow, Lemberg, Vienna, and Antwerp. I've told you how he taught me to give a governor and be a ventriloquist. He left for America before us and was already doing awreit in New York while we were still pounding the streets of Vaytshepl. That is, he found a dzhahb at a klinnehz.

"What kind of a dzhahb is that?" I asked as we walked.

Big Motl explained that a klinnehz cleaned clothes. You took a pair of creased pants, stuck them into a machine built like a flat oven, shut the lid, pulled a lever—and out came the pants as good as new.

"And what's your dzhahb?" Big Motl asked.

"Dehlivehrink noospeypehz," I said. "We bring them to our kahstemehz before skul. And after skul we voik in the biznis. We have a kawneh stend and make a living."

"Hey!" said Big Motl. "You speak pretty good English. How much do you two biznismen make?"

"About a dahleh a week," I say. "Sometimes a dahleh-and-a-kvawdeh."

"Dats awl?" boasts Big Motl. "I make three dahlehz a week. So what's this dzhentlminz neym?"

I said it was Mendl. Motl laughed and said, "Yuck!" "So what should it be?" I asked. Motl thought and said that Mendl should call himself

Meik. That sounded a lot better. "What do you go by?" I asked. "Meks," says Motl. "Since I'm a Motl too," I say, "I guess I should also be Meks." "Yaw Meks awredi," he says. When he left us he said: "Si yuh suhn, Meks! Si yuh, Meik!"

We agreed to meet on Sunday and go to the moofink pikshehz. We swapped addresses and went our separate ways.

♦♦♦

After Sunday dinneh Meik and I went to the moofink pikshehz to see Tshahli Tsheplin. Elye and Pinye came too. Tshahli Tsheplin was all Pinye could talk about: what a stah he was, and how much money he made, and how he was even a Jew. But Pinye and Elye never agree. Tshahli Tsheplin, Elye said, was not such a big deal. "I suppose you think anyone can make a thousand dahlehz a week," Pinye said. "How do you know what Tshahli Tsheplin makes?" asked Elye. "Have you counted his money?" Pinye said he read it in the peypehz. "And how do you know he's a Jew?" asked Elye. That, Pinye said, was in the peypehz too. "And how do the peypehz know?" Elye asked. "I suppose they were at his circumcision." "The peypehz," Pinye said, "know everything. How else would we know that Tshahli Tsheplin's a deaf mute, and can't read or write, and has a drunk for a father, and was a circus clown?" "Suppose it's all a big fat lie?" asked Elye, cool as a cucumber. That got Pinye sore. "For a Jew yourself," he said, "you're one big pain in the neck." Pinye's right. Elye may be my brother, but he sure is a pain.

♦♦♦

We had just arrived at the tikkit vindeh when we heard someone say:

"Hah duh yuh doo, Meks? Hah duh yuh doo, Meik?"

It was Big Motl. I mean Big Meks.

"Don't buy any tikkits," Big Meks said. "I'm trittink today."

He slipped half a dahleh through the vindeh and asked the tikkit girl for three tikkits in the belkehni.

"Who's this character?" Elye wanted to know.

I told him. Elye looked Big Meks up and down and asked why he didn't introduce himself. "I suppose you're too much of an American to speak Jewish," he said.

Big Meks didn't answer. But from the entrance came a voice that said:

"Joik!"

We all turned to look. There was no one there. Pinye and Elye scanned the lahbi. They looked at the ceiling and stared at each other. Who could it be? Big Meks took me and Mendl by the hand and the three of us went ahpstaihz. On the way he told us it was ventriloquism. He even did it for us again. Mendl and I laughed so hard that we were rolling in the aisles even before Tshahli Tsheplin's act began.

♦♦♦

I swear, you've never in your life seen a number like Big Meks! The greatest actor in the world is Tshahli Tsheplin and Meks does him down to the last detail. As soon as we left the theater he clapped on a little black mustache, turned out his feet, and started to waddle with his rear sticking out. You couldn't have told him and Tshahli apart. Mendl—I mean Meik—went so wild that he gave Big Meks a kiss. Everyone outside the theater pointed and said, "There goes the second Tshahli Tsheplin."

Even a grouch like Elye split his sides. Not for long, though. He stopped laughing pretty quick. How come? Because all of a sudden a voice said from a cellar:

"Joik!"

We all stared down into the cellar, trying to see who was there. Big Meks did too. Just then the voice called from overhead:

"Joik!"

Elye straightened up and stared at the rooftops. We all did. So did Big Meks. I tell you, it beat all! Only Meik and I knew where the voice was coming from. When we couldn't hold it in any longer, we burst out laughing.

Elye was sore as hell. If we hadn't been in the strit, he would have boxed our ears but good. But being smack in the middle of New York, he made do with a few juicy curses. When he had bawled Meik and me out, he pointed to Big Meks and said:

"Why don't you learn from your friend? He's your age and look how he behaves himself."

"Joik!" said a voice behind Elye.

Elye spun around. So did Pinye and the others. Big Meks looked startled. Meik and I stood there howling.

"In America," Pinye said, "even the sidewalks talk. I'd like to know who they're calling joik."

"Look in the mirror," Elye said.

Was he surprised when a muffled voice said from below the ground:

"You're dead wrong, Misteh Elye! The joik is you!"

That was Elye's last visit to the moofink pikshehz. He doesn't even want to hear about Tshahli Tsheplin any more.

THE BIZNIS GROWS

In America no one stands still. You have to get ahead and grow bigger and better. Since we didn't do enough biznis at our stend for seven people, we decided to move on to a staw. I've told you that in America you only have to look in the peypehz. There's nothing you won't find there.

A going staw isn't cheap. You pay more for the name than for the merchandise. Even our stend, which barely cleared ten dahlehz a week, was worth money because of its name. We sold it to a grinhawn. He didn't bother to check how much we made from it. It was enough for him to see seven people busy making a living. He was sure we had a good biznis.

We sold our stend with all its trimmings, the sawdeh fuhntin and the shawkays included. The one thing we kept for ourselves was Elye's recipes for sirips and seideh. All the money in the world couldn't get him to part with them. Let everyone make his own product, he said.

Take Elye's Passover wine. It already has a reputation, even though this is only his first try. All our friends and acquaintances in the Kasrilevke shul have told us they'll drink it next Passover. Pinye has edvehteized it all over New York. He's let everyone know that even the prehzident intends to serve it at his Seder in the Veit Howss.

Pinye is a fiend at edvehteizink. He says it's what America is all about. Every manufacturer edvehteizes his product. Every workingman edvehteizes his work. The whole world may know I make a drink that tastes like vinegar, but if I say it's sweet as sugar it will sell. You don't think what I do is worth a dahleh? I say it's worth a million—and now pay up! That's America. It's a free country.

♦ ♦ ♦

Having run an edvehteizink kempeyn for Elye's Passover wine all over the Loaweh Ist Seid, Pinye went to my brother and said:

"Look here, Elye. I've edvehteized your wine as the world's best. Don't let me down. Let's not have a wine like that drink you made in Russia. In America wine is wine, not barley beer!"

Elye was too offended to answer. He didn't have to because Brokheh did it for him. Did she let Pinye have it!

"You'd think America was a country of snobs and 'ristocrats who did nothing but drink wine and bathe in honey! Believe me, I wish I had a pehni for every quart of bread, kvass, and pickle brine that's drunk in this country every day! Why, I've seen with my own eyes an awreitnitshke on Grend Strit asking for a bucket of kvass and ten dozen sour apples. Believe me, they're better than all your ahrehndzhiz and grepfruhts that no one knows how to slice or eat . . . "

I'm only giving you the gist of what she said, because she's hard to stop once she gets going. Pinye knows that as well as I do. He put on his hat and walked off. That's the only way to deal with Brokheh. I do the same.

♦ ♦ ♦

Kendee–Seegah–Steshenree Staw
with Five Rumz. Gud Biznis,
Best Neighborhood.
A Bahgn! Singilmehn, Quick Sale.

That's what it said in the noospeypeh. When you're single and have no family to support, you don't haggle over the price. It looked like the biznis for us. In fact, it seemed tailor-made. We went to have a look.

The men went first. That's Pinye, Elye, Maik, and myself. Since we liked what we saw, the women went too—that's Brokheh, Taybl, and my mother. They didn't like what they saw at all. Each found something wrong with it. My mother thought it was too far from her synagogue. Of course there was a synagogue next door, but it wasn't the Kasrilevke shul.

"I suppose," Elye said, "that the Kasrilevke shul prays to a different God."

"It's the same God," said my mother. "It's just not the same Jews."

She's used to the Jews from Kasrilevke. She says they have their own way of praying. She can't imagine listening to any cantor but Hirsh-Ber.

That was my mother's objection. Brokheh had one of her own. What were we going to do with so many rumz? Who needed five of them?

Our neighbor Pesye had a suggestion. Why didn't we rent the rumz out? In America that's called taking in bawdehz. A bawdeh pays to live in your house and eat his meals with you.

"That's all we need!" Brokheh said. "A bunch of bawdehz at our table!"

"That's all we need!" Taybl repeated. "A bunch of bawdehz!"

"Maybe for once," Pinye said to her, "you'll say something original instead of parroting whatever Brokheh says!"

"It's easy to criticize!" said Brokheh, turning on Pinye.

"It's easy to criticize!" Taybl agreed.

"What will you do if Brokheh ever leaves you?" Pinye asked.

"What she does is her own business," Brokheh said.

Taybl said, "What I do is my own business."

"Foo!" Pinye spat and walked off.

♦♦♦

Don't think we were the only ones to have a look at that biznis. Our in-laws, friends, and acquaintances went too. The first to go was Yoyneh the bagel maker. After him went Riveleh. They went separately so as not to leave their knishes.

Moyshe the bookbinder was next, followed by Fat Pesye . . . baht ek-skyooz mee, eiv meyd ah misteyk. Fat Pesye went before Moyshe. He was followed by some friends from the Kasrilevke shul who know a thing or two about biznis.

The singilmehn wasn't nice to them. In fact, he drove them all away. He had never seen such a large family in his life, he said. My mother was so upset that she went back with Brokheh to talk to him. Brokheh gave him an earful. That made the singilmehn swear to God he'd changed his mind. He had wanted to sell his biznis, he said, in order to get married, but if a woman could have a mouth like Brokheh's, marriage was not a good idea. Better to stay a singilmehn and keep the biznis.

♦♦♦

That's just talk. The singilmehn wants to sell his biznis as badly as we want to buy it. We've almost sold our stend. I say almost because the grinhawn has already given us an advance. That's called a dehpahzit. We're beginning to feel sorry we took it because he hangs around our stend all day long. You can see he doesn't want to leave it.

He's a worse pest than my brother Elye. Elye is pure gold next to him. He gets on our nerves so badly that we've thrown his dehpahzit back at him. But he doesn't want to take it. He's fallen in love with our stend. He's sure we're making a mint from it.

"A grinhawn is always a grinhawn!"

That's Pinye's opinion.

♦♦♦

What exactly is a grinhawn? I wish you'd asked me something easier.

My friend Meik doesn't know either. It's a word everyone uses, so we do too. Just for fun I took some chalk and drew a picture on the sidewalk of the Jew who's buying our stand. I put a big green horn on his forehead. You should have heard everyone laugh! They all recognized our grinhawn.

The only person not to laugh was Elye. He didn't whack me. He just made me wet a rag and erase the grinhawn. Otherwise we'd have to pay a fine.

You pay fines here for everything. Try spitting in the strit and a pleesmin comes along and hauls you off to the steyshn. They make you pay five dahlehz there. It's a real strict place, America.

I suppose you think that because of that no one spits in the strit and New York is as clean as Antwerp. You're wrong. People spit and hawk up phlegm like all get-out. America is a free country. Maybe it's different on Fif Tevenyoo. I don't mean all of it. I mean the strits where the rich people live. A man spits when he's feeling bad. The rich have it good, so why spit?

♦♦♦ *Notes*

THE LETTERS OF MENAKHEM-MENDL AND SHEYNE-SHEYNDL

p. 7 Rosh Hashanah: The Jewish New Year, which occurs at the end of summer or in early autumn. It is customary on it to eat a fruit that one has not eaten all year and to say a special blessing over it, thanking God for the renewal of His bounty.

p. 11 Gambetta: In 1906, ten years after this chapter of *Menakhem-Mendl* first appeared, Sholem Aleichem published the opening section of a story about a Kasrilevke lawyer named Velvl Gambetta. As the author never finished the story, it never revealed how Velvl was given the name of the French lawyer and patriot Léon Gambetta (1838–1882). The Gambetta encountered by Menakhem-Mendl on the Odessa Exchange seems to be an earlier version of the same character.

p. 11 Bismarck: Otto von Bismarck (1815–1898), the Prussian prime minister who orchestrated the defeat of France, in the Franco-Prussian War of 1870–1871, and the unification of Germany.

p. 13 a drink that's sipped through a straw: Menakhem-Mendl has been drinking pernod, the French anise-and-licorice flavored liqueur.

p. 28 Brodsky: The Jewish brothers Lazar (1848–1904) and Lev Brodsky (1852–1923) were Kiev sugar magnates. Amalgamated into a single figure, they embody the mythical Russian Jewish tycoon in many of Sholem Aleichem's stories.

p. 34 *Geltmangel:* Literally, "money shortage."

p. 36 no one decides when to enter this world: Sheyne-Sheyndl is thinking of the dictum in the Mishnaic tractate of *Pirkei Avot* that says, "Regardless of thy will thou art conceived; and regardless of thy will thou art born; and regardless of thy will thou livest; and regardless of thy will thou diest."

p. 44 Miriam-Beyle has stopped wearing a wig: According to Orthodox Jewish law, a married woman is forbidden publicly to bare her hair, which she generally covers by a kerchief. Since a wig, however, is not considered her own hair, its use is also permitted and was widespread among eastern European Jews.

p. 45 *pilagshim:* "concubines," in Hebrew; *Kepsweiber* has the same meaning in German.

p. 47 he slips a ring on it: In Jewish law, a valid marriage has taken place when the groom puts a ring on a willing bride's finger while saying, "Behold, thou art sanctified to me by the law of Moses and Israel." This is what Berish has done.

p. 48 "What's mine is yours and what's yours is mine": A well-known passage in *Pirkei Avot* divides attitudes toward property into four classes: that of the righteous, who say, "What is yours is yours and what is mine is yours"; of the wicked, who say, "What is mine is mine and what is yours is mine"; and of two intermediate types, who say, "What is mine is mine and what is yours is yours" and "What is yours is mine and what is mine is yours."

p. 58 since Jews are barred from the villages: Even within the Pale of Settlement most rural villages were out-of-bounds to Jews, who generally lived in towns as a result.

p. 60 Tammuz: The Hebrew month corresponding to June–July.

p. 61 Dr. Herzl: Theodor Herzl (1860–1904), founder and leader of the Zionist movement.

p. 67 Dreyfus: The Dreyfus affair, a legal and political battle that occupied France and Europe for many years, began with the arrest in 1894 of the Jewish French army captain Alfred Dreyfus (1859–1935) on the charge of being a German spy. It formally ended in 1906 with Dreyfus' acquittal, following an inconclusive retrial in 1899 (at which his lawyer was shot by a right-wing nationalist) that affirmed his conviction while releasing him from his life imprisonment on Devil's Island, a French penal colony off the coast of Guiana. The French author Emile Zola (1840–1902) was a prominent supporter of Dreyfus, and his book *J'Accuse* (1897–98), which correctly blamed French anti-Semites for framing the Jewish officer, had a powerful effect on public opinion; the ferocity of right-wing attacks on him made Zola move for a while to England. Ferdinand Walsin Esterhazy (1847–1923) was the French major who gave German intelligence the secret documents that Dreyfus was accused of transmitting. Georges Picquart (1854–1914), a lieutenant-colonel in French intelligence, was instrumental in clearing Dreyfus.

p. 71 "Keep your eyes on the ground . . . ": Sheyne-Sheyndl is perhaps thinking of the Talmudic saying that a man should not look "at what is above [in heaven], what is below [in the underworld], what is ahead [at the end of days], or what is behind [at the time of creation]."

p. 76 Sukkes: The holiday of Sukkot or the Feast of Booths, which comes in early autumn after the High Holy Days.

p. 81 I will lift up mine eyes unto the hills: Psalms 121:1.

p. 90 *pozhaliste:* "please."

p. 91 *Naprimer:* "for example"; *Viditye:* "look here"; *Sobstevenno:* "personally"; *ponaprasno:* "not possible"; *Po krayne meri:* "at least"; *obrazaveto:* "educated person"; *fanatitcheski:* "[religiously] fanatic"; *obrazovanye:* "education"; *utshebe zavadyenye:* "academic studies"; *barishnye:* "young lady"; *znakome:* "acquainted"; *dazhe:* "even."

p. 98 kaddish: The mourner's prayer said daily by adult males during the first year after a close family member's death, and subsequently, once a year on the death's anniversary. It must be said in a prayer quorum of ten men, which is why Menakhem-Mendl has to look for a synagogue to say it in.

p. 100 *Otse dobre dilo:* "That's very good."

p. 101 *dabern:* "talk"; *niyor:* "paper"; *ksive:* "write." These are all Hebrew words that are not used in ordinary Yiddish and would not be intelligible to a Christian knowing some Yiddish.

p. 107 *Tate:* Yiddish for "father."

p. 108 Simkhes Toyreh: The holiday of Simchat Torah, or the Rejoicing of the Law, which comes at the end of the Feast of Booths.

p. 109 kiddush cups: The *kiddush* is the blessing over wine that commences Sabbath and holiday meals. In most traditional homes, a special silver cup is used for it.

p. 109 Mishnah: The six rabbinic books of commentary on the Bible that form the first part of the Talmud.

p. 110 hallah: A braided bread commonly eaten on Sabbaths and holidays.

p. 110 matso: The specially baked unleavened bread eaten on Passover.

p. 112 the night of Shavuos: The holiday of Shavuos, or Pentecost, comes in late spring and marks the giving of the Torah at Mount Sinai. It is customary on it for men to stay up all night studying. In Jewish folklore there is a belief that the heavens open up fleetingly in the course of this night and that any wish made at this exact moment will be granted.

p. 112 after the Torah reading: A portion of the Pentateuch is read in synagogue on Sabbaths, holidays, and certain days of the week. On Sabbaths and holidays it is followed by the Musaf service, in which most virtuoso cantorial singing is concentrated.

p. 113 dairy for Shavuos: Unlike other holiday meals, in which it is customary to eat meat, milk dishes are considered appropriate for Shavuos. According to Jewish law, meat and milk may never be mixed.

p. 114 the kaddish: See note to p. 98.

p. 116 *Yisgodol veyiskodosh shmey rabbo:* "May His great name be magnified and sanctified," the first words of the kaddish; *veyatzmokh purkeney:* "and may He bring about His redemption"; *le'eylo ule'eylo . . . :* "far above all songs and blessings."

p. 122 Rosh Hashanah: See note to p. 7.

p. 124 He said the blessing: In Judaism, every food must be eaten with its own special blessing. For fruit it is "Blessed be Thou, O Lord, king of the universe, who createth the fruit of the tree."

p. 131 *tallis koton:* The fringed undershirt worn by male Jews beneath their clothing, in obedience to the biblical injunction "And they shall make fringes on the corners of their cloaks."

p. 134 *kometz-alef-aw: Alef* is the first letter of the Hebrew alphabet, and *kometz,* pronounced "aw" in eastern Europe, is one of the vowel signs that can accompany it. The combination *kometz-alef-aw* was customarily the first consonant-vowel sequence learned by beginning readers.

p. 136 Rambam: The Hebrew name of the renowned medieval philosopher and jurist Maimonides.

p. 150 *daber:* "talk"; *akhi:* "[my] brother"; *yad:* "hand"; *yovon:* "Christian"; *ragloyim:* "legs"; *pleyte:* "getaway." These are Hebrew words that would not normally be understood by a Christian who knows some Yiddish.

p. 156 *selikhe:* A penitential prayer recited in the month before the High Holy Days.

p. 156 Haggadah: The slim book containing the rituals and prayers said at the festive Passover meal, or Seder.

p. 161 Haman: The villain of the bibical book of Esther.

p. 162 Plevne: The Bulgarian city of Pleven, the site of a major battle between the Ottoman Turks and Russian-assisted Bulgarian rebels in 1876.

p. 166 shofar: The ram's horn blown in synagogue on Rosh Hashanah.

p. 166 goy: Yiddish for a Gentile. Though sometimes pejorative, the word need not necessarily be so.

p. 176 verst: A Russian measure of distance equivalent to two-thirds of a mile.

p. 180 Alexander von Humboldt: A well-known German scientist and philosopher (1769–1865).

p. 180 Slonimski: Chaim Zelig Slonimski (1810–1904), Polish Jewish mathematician and educator.

p. 182 Eishishok, Otvotsk, Drazhne, Semyonevke: All small towns in Lithuania and Russia.

p. 182 Novoselitz, Brody: Towns on the border between Russia and the pre–World War I Austrian Empire.

p. 182 Ungeny: A town in Bessarabia, on the Russian-Rumanian border.

p. 186 *beheimeh:* Yiddish for "cow"; *sheigetz:* Yiddish for "young Christian" or "rascal." In Polish Galicia, under Austrian control until World War I, the Russian-Yiddish vowel "ey" was pronounced "ei." Part of the humor of this chapter is based on the fact that Motl and his family think the Jews of Brody are speaking German when they are simply speaking Yiddish with an unfamiliar accent.

p. 190 *khron* or *khran:* This is how Elye and Pinye imagine the Yiddish word *khreyn* would be pronounced by the Jews of Brody. (In fact, it was pronounced *khrayn.*)

p. 190 *a har: Haar* in German means "hair"; *har* in Yiddish means "gentleman," which is *Herr* in German; *aher* in Yiddish means "this way" or "over here"; and *hier* in German means "here."

p. 191 *havdalah:* The prayer, said over a lit candle on Saturday night, that separates the Sabbath from the week.

p. 192 Lemberg: Today the Ukrainian city of Lviv, about fifty miles southwest of Brody.

p. 195 *vozglyad:* "look at"; *polozhenye:* "situation"; *totshke zrenye:* "point of view"; *voyenske povyonost:* "military duty"; *samastoyatelnost:* "freedom"; *styesnitelni:* "backward"; *progres:* "progress"; *vozdukh:* "atmosphere"; *vovterikh:* "secondly"; *yevreiski vopros:* "Jewish question."

p. 196 *tomu podovne:* "so on and so forth."

p. 196 Buckle: Henry Thomas Buckle (1821–1862), English historian.

p. 197 Cracow: The largest city of Polish Galicia, about 150 miles west of Lemberg.

p. 198 Proshepanye: A humorous Russian Jewish word for Polish, in which *prosze pani* means "Please, madame."

p. 207 the Alliance: L'Alliance Israélite, a Paris-based Jewish organization that sponsored relief and educational programs throughout the Jewish world.

p. 212 Mezhbezh: The Ukrainian village of Miedzyboz.

p. 215 tefillin: Phylacteries, the leather prayer thongs that a Jew slips over his head and winds around his arm for the morning prayer. Starting with bar-mitzvah age, a boy is expected to wear these when he prays.

p. 220 *meine Frau:* "Madame."

p. 231 Disraeli: Benjamin Disraeli (1804–1881), Jewish-born British prime minister and novelist.

p. 231 Vaytshepl: The London neighborhood of Whitechapel.

p. 232 Berdichev: A city in Ukraine with a large Jewish population, often humorously cited as the epitome of the Jewish shtetl.

p. 233 bar mitzvah: Over thirteen years of age, the time at which a Jewish boy becomes responsible for observing all the commandments and may be counted as part of a prayer quorum.

p. 234 *Skolke vifl?:* Both words mean "How much," the first in Russian, the second in Yiddish.

p. 242 Yom Kippur: The Day of Atonement, a twenty-four-hour fast from sundown to sundown.

p. 243 Kol Nidrei: The opening prayer of the Yom Kippur service, known for its great solemnity and the deep emotions it arouses.

p. 248 *Meh onu umeh khayeynu:* "What are we and what are our lives," a Hebrew phrase from the High Holy Day prayer book. *Moshul kekheres hanishbor:* "worth no more than a broken pot," another such phrase.

p. 252 Haman: See note to p. 161.

p. 257 *Buona sera:* "good evening"; *Mia cara:* "my dear"; *Prego, signore:* "At your service, sir."

p. 258 Mazel tov: "Congratulations."

p. 260 like Spain when it expelled us: The Jews were expelled from Spain in 1492.

p. 267 siddur: prayer book; yarmulka: skullcap; mezuzah: a metal or wooden amulet containing biblical passages written on parchment and fastened by Jews to their doorjambs.

p. 270 sukkeh: The small outdoor structure erected for the Feast of Booths, usually having decorated wooden walls and a roof of green branches. Orthodox Jews eat all their meals in it during the eight-day holiday.

p. 289 shul: Yiddish for synagogue.

p. 310 *Abi ir veyst az bei mir:* "As long as you know that by me."

ABOUT WHITE GOAT PRESS

White Goat Press, the Yiddish Book Center's imprint, is committed to bringing newly translated work to the widest readership possible in English. We publish work in all genres—novels, short stories, drama, poetry, memoirs, essays, reportage, plays, and popular fiction, including romance and detective stories.

WHITE GOAT PRESS

WHITEGOATPRESS.ORG
The Yiddish Book Center's Imprint